Kay St[illegible] orkshire. She sp[illegible] g life as a librari[illegible] eral short stories and a [illegible] ing *West Riding* and *North Riding*, both set in the Yorkshire she knows so well.

Also by Kay Stephens

West Riding
North Riding
Pennine Vintage
The Soaring Fells

Stones of Calder Dale

Kay Stephens

KNIGHT

First published in Great Britain in 1993
by HEADLINE BOOK PUBLISHING PLC

First published in paperback in 1994
by HEADLINE BOOK PUBLISHING

This edition published 1998 by Knight
an imprint of Brockhampton Press

10 9 8 7 6 5 4 3 2 1

ISBN 1 86019 6667

Typeset by Avon Dataset Ltd, Bidford-on-Avon

Printed and bound in Great Britain by
Mackays of Chatham PLC, Chatham, Kent

Brockhampton Press
20 Bloomsbury Street
London WC1B 3QA

ACKNOWLEDGEMENT

For advice and information while researching the background of this book I am very grateful to Mrs Irma Bull of the Royal Institute of British Architects. I am also greatly indebted to Mr A. E. Bartholomew who supplied further details from his involvement with the education and examination of architectural students during the period covered by *Stones of Calder Dale*.

Chapter 1

Helen Clegg smiled, all the excitement of the drive down from Yorkshire surpassed by a new elation. Nobody would stop her now. Everything was possible if you wanted it enough to work as hard as you could. Wasn't she standing here, gazing across the Avon at the proof? The Shakespeare Memorial Theatre, opened just a month ago on 23 April. *And it was designed by a woman.*

Beside her Marian sighed, sounding exasperated. 'How much longer? We've stood here for hours, while you've done nowt but gawp.'

Helen grinned. 'Sorry. I was getting carried away. But it's been nothing like an hour, not much more than twenty minutes.'

Her sister laughed. 'Happen you're right, only my legs are growing numb with hanging around. And what's it all for? You haven't a snowball in hell's chance of ever becoming an architect.'

'She did,' Helen persisted, nodding towards the theatre, 'Elizabeth Scott.'

'I daresay, but you're still not being realistic. You've got a decent job, Helen, you want to hang on to it. Especially living up north like we do. I haven't forgotten being out of work a couple of years back in nineteen-thirty. There were two million of us unemployed.'

'I know.' She felt guilty about wanting more than other folk. 'But that doesn't stop me longing to do the job I've always fancied.'

'You've allus been full of fancies! They're not for folk like us, lass, can't you see? We should be content if we've brass to enjoy life with, and maybe enough to set up eventually in a nice little home.'

But seeing how she'd made her sister's grey eyes turn misty, Marian smiled and gave her an affectionate squeeze. 'Don't take on so, love. Tell you what – if you promise never to let on at home, I'll leave you on your own for a bit to study the place.'

'Would you? I'd love to do a few sketches.'

'Aye, go on then. See you back at the hotel.' Marian looked at her watch. She was meeting Denis in ten minutes. He was an Assistant Stage Manager at the theatre, could only spare her half an hour or so before she and Helen were due to go in for their evening meal. 'Just don't speak to anybody, think on,' she warned over her shoulder as she turned away.

Briefly, Helen gazed wryly after her nineteen-year-old sister, who was trying to look all grown up while barely restraining the urge to run. From the way Marian talked, nobody would think she was the one dashing off for a covert meeting. Not that any of this made much sense; Helen herself was only fifteen, yet she'd been brought along on this visit to Stratford upon Avon because their parents didn't believe Marian should come here alone.

Maybe they had a bit of an idea that their Marian might be up to something. They hadn't said owt, but they must be aware by now that her blonde hair and blue eyes, to say nothing of her long shapely legs, got all the young chaps interested.

Determined to make the most of this opportunity to concentrate, Helen felt in her pocket for the pencil and pad she always carried, leaned against one of the trees that guarded the riverbank, and began to draw. She wished she was totally enthusiastic about the design of this place, it looked too ordinary to her. But that feeling didn't stop her being thrilled that a woman had completed the design, any more than it could possibly curtail her own deep-seated ambition.

Commencing her sketch with its riverside terrace, Helen sensed that the theatre might be growing on her. With a matinee in progress, and actors glimpsed by the long windows of what evidently were dressing rooms, it was coming to life. And, as she had read since its opening, it was after all a functional structure, designed for presenting Shakespeare's plays to best effect. Until tonight when she was to judge the interior for herself, she would try and curb her desire for a more attractive building, truly in keeping with Stratford itself.

She had fallen in love with the town already: its picturesque timbered houses and inns, the streets better suited to horse-drawn vehicles than cars like the Austin Seven which Marian handled with startling dexterity. And the small hotel in Warwick Road where she herself was treated like an adult, and her sister aired all the graces which seemed to flow so readily from her slight figure. Maybe this instant affection for Stratford had encouraged her wish for a more classical setting for Shakespeare. There was her preference for good Yorkshire sandstone as well – almost every place built in brick like this began with a disadvantage in Helen's eyes!

After half an hour she had roughed in the outline of the theatre, and quite a lot of detail around the terrace overhanging the river. She'd need more time for getting all the windows in proportion. That could wait till tomorrow. She looked forward to coming back here. She'd be surprised if Marian hadn't arranged to see Denis again.

Smiling to herself, she stuffed her sketch pad into her pocket and paused for a second to watch a pair of swans take flight and land again on the Avon. How lovely the river here was with its meadows and gardens and Holy Trinity Church; so different from the Calder back home, pressing between the mills it had drawn to its banks.

Heading for Clopton Bridge and the walk towards Warwick Road, Helen began marvelling again at their Marian's audacity – the cool way she'd brazenly announced she felt she needed a break, and that she was thinking of Stratford. 'You know how I've always liked a good play.'

If either Mum or Dad had suspected there was more to it than that, they hadn't said. And it wasn't like either of them to keep silent if they were bothered about what was going on. But then they'd never been told how Marian had met Denis when she was trying to get hold of a fancy dress costume and had come up with the brilliant idea of approaching the company at the Grand Theatre in Halifax. Naturally, they'd heard nothing either of Denis's insistence on attending the party with her. Helen knew the whole story off by heart, and how keen on him Marian had become, how upset she'd been when he got this better job backstage here. Stratford had seemed so far away.

Still, she herself wasn't sorry their parents had stipulated that she should accompany her sister. As they had pointed out, if the girls shared a room, it wouldn't cost so much more. Relieved that her plan hadn't been quashed, Marian had volunteered to pay her sister's rail fare – but hadn't explained they weren't actually travelling by train. Denis had left his car behind in Halifax for repairs. Marian had promised to drive it down to Stratford.

'Isn't it grand that you can afford to pay for her, love?' their mother had exclaimed while they were making plans. They'd had to scrimp to finance their elder daughter's training in shorthand and typing, but that period out of work had been short and she was earning good money now in a solicitor's office.

All Marian wanted was a job that brought in enough to give her a bit of independence. She liked a good time and, now that she'd met Denis, needed to be able to see him as often as she could.

Helen sympathised with that, even if her sister's earlier obsession with partying had seemed proper daft.

It was Marian, though, who frequently expressed doubts about *Helen*'s sanity. 'All that studying, when you could be out enjoying yourself! You must be wrong in your head.'

But Helen had always meant to do well at school. Dad had been determined that both girls would better themselves. He himself had never risen above chief maintenance man at the toffee works, and wasn't going to have his daughters in factory jobs.

Helen had a good head for figures and had been taken on in the accounts office of a local carpet mill. Delighted simply to have her in a job where she didn't get her hands mucky, Dad had been unable to grasp the fact that she wasn't contented. When she'd attempted yet again to explain her ambition he'd tried to laugh her out of it.

'Nay, love, it's time you put such ideas out of your head. Architecture's no sort of a job for a lass – you'd be getting wed and having bairns long afore you'd got anywhere near qualifying.'

Her father hadn't been the only one to ridicule her hopes. Mum was always too kind to do more than smile to herself whenever architecture was mentioned, but that smile revealed every ounce of her doubts.

Going up the steps into the hotel, Helen was wondering if this meeting with Denis would accelerate Marian's hopes of getting married. That *would* be a surprise for everybody at home. Not that Marian had ever seemed unlikely to marry early; with her slender figure and eyes that challenged you to laugh life in the face, she entranced folk.

And I certainly don't! Helen thought ruefully, running up to their room. She was tall and big-boned like Dad, and if she even glanced longingly at a cream bun the inches piled on in all the wrong places. Tonight, she was going to need time to work on her mid-brown hair and on her face which always seemed merely serviceable. She wanted to look different. Denis had got her and Marian tickets for the stalls.

The play was *The Merchant of Venice* and Helen had resisted the temptation to read it through before coming away. She wanted each scene to be new to her, just like everything here.

Any reservations she might have had about the exterior of the Memorial Theatre were forgotten as she and Marian went in through one of its tall glass doors. The foyer seemed full already. People with all kinds of accents were exclaiming and enthusing and greeting each other. Folk were pressing together, some edging through the crowd or waving to friends. Women were wearing gorgeous dresses, daringly low-backed and cut to flare out as they neared the ground, but many so tight around the hips that Helen wondered however they'd manage to sit. A lot of the men wore evening dress which transformed even those with the most ordinary of features.

After thanking the young man who'd checked their

tickets and indicated the direction of their seats, Marian began gabbling on again about Denis and how important his backstage job was. Helen could no longer concentrate on what she was saying. In any case, she'd heard it already all through their meal.

Suddenly, she was standing quite still in the aisle, oblivious to amused looks from people obliged to detour around her. When Marian turned and hurried back to give her sleeve a tug, she came to with a lurch. She'd been stunned by it all – how well designed everything was, and how tasteful. She stared slowly all about her, up towards the balconies and the boxes then finally at the stage.

'Eh, isn't that grand!' she gasped. 'Why did I have any reservations about the outside? This couldn't be better.'

As soon as they were seated, Marian opened the programme, found Denis's name in tiny print, nudged Helen's arm.

She tried to enthuse with her sister, listened again to how marvellous he was, reminded herself that but for Denis's move to Stratford she wouldn't be here. She owed him and Marian a bit of attention.

But her other senses were diverted. Her ears alone occupied, she drew in a deep breath, savouring the atmosphere of anticipation in the buzz of conversation as people took their seats, and savouring as well the smell of new carpeting and upholstery. Running a hand along the seat back in front of her, she turned to her sister.

'What do you reckon, was this woven in t'West Riding?'

Marian groaned. 'I haven't the faintest idea. You're not here to dissect every little detail. And if you don't look at the programme you'll not know the first thing about what is going on.'

Helen read through the cast list. 'I've heard of Fabia Drake, the one that's Portia. Don't know any of the others.'

'Not Randle Ayrton? Denis says he's very much the big star.'

She shook her head. But once the play began it barely mattered to Helen that she was unfamiliar with the actors – she was enraptured.

'Gosh,' she said during the interval, 'I never knew Shakespeare could be so exciting. And isn't Randle Ayrton good? He makes you understand how Shylock feels, even when you're meant to hate him.'

It was Portia, though, especially in the trial scene, who ultimately won her admiration.

'She would, of course,' said Marian, suddenly serious when Helen confided in her after all the final curtain calls. 'She's a strong, determined woman. Just your sort.'

Helen gave a little, nervous laugh. But they were lingering while other people filed towards the doors. On her insistence, they were going right to the back of the auditorium to view it all from there.

'I'd give anything to build somewhere as good as this.'

'Oh – build it yourself as well, would you?' Marian mocked.

'You know what I mean. *Design* somewhere.' But Elizabeth Scott had begun with a big advantage. Both Gilbert and Giles Scott were relatives. Helen herself had only determination. Could that be enough?

She remained motionless, breathing in the scent of new wood, and a trace of recently dried paint which mingled with the still strong odour of new upholstery and carpeting. It was quite different from where they'd been sitting; there, she'd also been conscious of the smell of the painted set which wafted to them on the draught each time those magnificent heavy curtains opened.

How must it feel if you were the person behind all this – if your plans had been the foundation of such a tremendous scheme? More than ever, Helen knew that architecture was the only thing that inspired her. As soon as she got back to Halifax, she'd tackle Dad again.

Daniel Clegg was strict – some of Helen's friends thought him dictatorial – but he wasn't unkind. She had intended using the car journey back to Yorkshire for working out what to say to him. But it hadn't turned out like that at all. Denis had agreed to drive them home like this on Sunday, then set off back to Stratford straight away. But Marian argued that *she* would drive to Halifax. He'd taught her, hadn't he, so that she could take over?

Unfortunately, Marian behind the wheel when Denis was there was quite different from the girl who'd so impressed her younger sister while they travelled down to Warwickshire. Her driving today consisted of screeching around corners and generally compelling the little car to struggle for maximum speed on roads that seemed to have acquired far more bends since the outward journey.

'Steady on, darling,' Denis protested regularly. He was an easy-going man, as a rule, whose hazel eyes and straight dark hair combined with a rugby forward's build to make him appear powerful.

But Marian was at her dizziest, giggling at his alarm. When they finally drew up a street away from their grey stone terraced house, Helen felt as though she'd been through her grandmother's mangle.

She was no less sure, though, that the time had come to try one last time for the career she wanted. Once they had finished tea, and their parents had listened to Marian's edited account of the holiday, Helen asked their father if she could have a word with him. Her sister and mother were staring with curiosity they didn't bother to disguise. Because of having only the one living room and a small kitchen, there wasn't much scope for talking in private.

'It's about being an architect, I'm afraid,' Helen began. 'Yes – again. Seeing the Shakespeare Memorial Theatre has made me sure I'll always regret it if I can't even give studying a chance.'

'Nay, love – I thought you'd decided to be sensible, that you were putting them ideas behind you.' Her father hardly knew how to continue. He'd been flabbergasted when he first learned of Helen's notion. Where had she got it from? It must have been somebody at school; it had never been thought of here.

His own parents were simple folk: his father had been a blanket weaver, his mother in service. Wanting both his girls to do well, he had visualised nothing more ambitious than office work for them. He hadn't been brought up to believe ordinary people should want to get that far above themselves.

'Eh, lass,' he said at last. 'I'm proud of how well you've done at school, you know that. Let that be enough. That, and being set on to do figure work. Don't be allus moithering for more.' He'd been reared as a non-conformist. Perhaps believing simplicity was a virtue made it hard for him to appreciate the value of ambition. He became uneasy, suspecting he might be to blame for first instilling ideas of Helen's bettering herself – which suddenly were getting right out of hand.

'If I find out about all the studying I'd have to do, and if there's scholarships that I could go in for, would you consider it? Would you, Dad – please?'

But her father was only shaking his head, troubled by this abnormal ambition which threatened to disrupt all their lives.

'I don't want to talk about it any more, do you hear? We're ordinary folk, love. We've nowt behind us to finance studies that'd go on for donkey's years.'

For a time after the visit to Stratford Helen tried to will herself to accept life in the office at the carpet works. She hated her parents thinking her ungrateful for the start they had given her. And she didn't like the feeling that she made Dad uncomfortable because he was unable to provide the education she desired.

Marian hadn't helped when she announced her intention of marrying in the near future. Helen wouldn't forget the Sunday tea when her sister had brought that out into the open.

'I'm thinking of going to Stratford again before so long,' she'd said carefully as she cut the fat away from her slice of boiled ham.

Their mother had frowned. Kathleen Clegg hadn't had a holiday for over six years, since the General Strike in 1926 made surviving harder than ever, especially here up north.

'Nay, lass, you've nobbut just got back from your last trip.'

'How can you afford it?' their father asked. 'And what makes you so keen on the place?'

'It's a young chap, I'll bet,' his wife observed, before her elder daughter could speak.

'Whatever makes you think that?' Marian began.

Kathleen interrupted smartly. 'You were that elated afore you went, *and* when you got back. But that soon wore off. And for long enough now you haven't been going out as much as you used to. What happened to that friend of yours, somebody here in Halifax that were teaching you to drive a motor car?'

Smiling, Marian gave a little shrug. 'I ought to have known you'd put two and two together, shouldn't I? I didn't tell you at first because – well, I didn't like you getting concerned when it mightn't come to anything.'

'And will it – come to owt, I mean?' their father demanded, thinking already that he should have had some warning if he was going to be landed with providing a do for his daughter's wedding.

Marian's smile widened, her blue eyes glowed. 'Aye, Dad – so long as you're not bound to object. Denis rang me up on Friday . . .'

'Rang you up?' Kathleen asked. Who did their Marian know who had a telephone?

'Aye, at work. It's him that's got a job in Stratford these days, you see. And he's missing me a lot. He wants us to get married.'

'Now just a minute, lass,' Daniel interrupted, aware now that this daughter of his hadn't been quite straightforward about her motives for the original visit to Stratford.

He didn't like the sound of their Marian plotting to go off to meet this chap, and liked even less the holes he detected in her tale when questioned about how much time she'd spent alone with him. Helen was dragged into it because of their parents' initial supposition that she and Marian had spent all their time together. And because the sisters had always automatically supported each other, Helen was the one reprimanded for conniving with Marian.

'I'd never have let you go,' Kathleen had declared then, 'I'd not have had an easy minute if I'd thought the pair of you weren't together the whole time.'

It had taken days for Daniel Clegg to come round to agreeing to see Denis when he came up to the West Riding. 'If you do get wed, though – and I only say *if*

– you'll have to make a few sacrifices yourself, Marian. I'll give you a reception somehow, that's only right. But I can't run to providing your frock an' all. You'll have to wait till you've saved enough for that.'

Being told to bear that in mind hadn't dampened Marian's eagerness; she was that keen to marry Denis, she'd go to the altar in one of the theatrical costumes he could borrow, if that was the only way. But that was a feeling she couldn't mention at home; she had hedged when questioned about Denis's work. She had written to him emphasising that he must stress how secure his job was when he came to speak to her father.

Helen didn't know how her sister had the nerve to keep so much from their parents, and privately admitted that she thought Marian had been daft not to put them in the picture completely once the matter was aired. Neither Mum nor Dad would like learning the whole truth later on. There'd only be more trouble while Denis was here. Meanwhile, her own problems worsened. With a wedding on their hands, and one less wage coming in after, there'd certainly be no hope of Helen's throwing up her job to start studying. She hadn't a cat in hell's chance of going in for architecture.

On Monday morning Helen was sitting at her desk, reading while she waited to begin work. She always got into the office early; today more than ever. She'd had to get away. Marian was as daft as a brush, giggling and singing up and down the house because she'd got her own way. From what Helen could gather, Denis had been given a hard time of it but he had got Father to agree to their marrying. Ever since she'd been told, Marian had gone potty. She'd even danced their father around the room – something Helen had never seen before, Daniel Clegg wasn't accustomed to letting himself go like that.

'I'm glad you're suited, Marian,' Mum had remarked, her expression dour. 'I hope you'll look back on this happily in a year or two. It's not a rest-cure, you know, marriage. You'll soon find that keeping good meals on the table and a decent roof over your heads isn't quite the fun you expect it to be. And don't forget you're giving up a good job to move down yonder. Is there much short-time round Stratford?'

The weekend's events were forgotten now, though, while Helen examined photographs of Broadcasting House which had recently been opened in London. It did look grand, especially with Eric Gill's figures of Prospero and Ariel. She'd read about the building ages ago when the plans were first approved and construction was beginning.

That was what had started her off longing to design buildings. Miss March, who taught art and had always encouraged Helen's natural flair, had been studying copies of drawings of Broadcasting House. Seeing her pupil's interest, she'd told her to come along after school and they'd examine them together. Miss March's father had been an architect so she was more interested than most in such designs. The journal in which they had appeared had carried other articles about new buildings. Helen had been so fascinated that Miss March had let her keep it. Dog-eared now from much re-reading, it still emerged regularly from her drawer in the dressing-table she shared with Marian. Or had done until the new situation at home made her hopes even more improbable.

These photographs of Broadcasting House which had appeared in the Sunday papers were renewing her longing to create something equally important, making her aware of the years stretching ahead and how she would grow to resent her tasks in the carpet works' office.

'Why so glum, Miss Clegg? You've hardly had time for the place to get aired, I trust you're not fed up here already?'

The voice was their Senior Accounts Clerk's, and he wasn't normally so sharp with her. But then Helen wasn't frowning as a rule, and nor did she often look so despondent.

He wasn't an unkind man, and he'd already recognised Helen's talent for putting her back into hard work. 'What's up then?' he inquired.

'Nothing,' she said hastily, concealing what she was studying. It would never do to let on here that she wasn't wholehearted about her job. There'd be plenty of lasses thankful to take over from her.

But he had glimpsed one of the photographs. 'Broadcasting House, isn't it?' he said, wondering what seemed so fascinating about that to a girl of her age.

'Yes, it is actually,' Helen admitted, her face flushing.

'Interested in architecture, are you?'

'Well – yes. Not that there's much chance of it ever coming to owt.'

He looked pensive. 'You never know. You've a smart head for figures – that's something which would stand you in good stead.'

Helen hadn't really considered before that her ability with arithmetic would be useful if she were able to follow her chosen career. She'd found geometry easy to understand as well. Somehow, awareness of this made the whole prospect seem less impossible again. And that article in the paper had reminded her about Miss March. She'd be a fool if she didn't at least go and ask her advice.

* * *

Fenny March lived in a massive house on Albert Promenade which on that Saturday afternoon seemed to glow golden in the June sunlight.

'We can sit outdoors if you like?' Fenny suggested.

Helen happily agreed. Screened by laburnum and lilacs from the road, the terrace was raised above the rest of the front garden. The view across and over the Promenade was magnificent: distant mauve-tinged hills, their slopes densely wooded, and a sky far more blue than you usually saw above Yorkshire. This distance from the edge of the escarpment, the industrial valleys didn't show.

'I've always liked the Rocks,' Helen confided, and sensed her former teacher smiling at her. 'That's what we allus called it when we were little. Of course, I suppose it was more the rocks themselves that attracted us in those days, rather than the view from the top here.'

'There's a cave as well, isn't there, not very far down?'

'You knew it an' all! Just above the top path that meanders through the woods.'

'I used to play there a lot, while this house was being built.'

'Did – did your father design it then?'

'He did indeed. Must be forty years since now. I'll have to ask him the date when I see him tomorrow.'

'You mean he's still alive?'

Fenella March laughed. 'Why do school mistresses always seem too old to have parents?'

'I never said, I mean – I wouldn't . . .'

'I know that, Helen. Come on, don't go all embarrassed on me. You're here to talk, aren't you? Seriously, I suspect. And that's what we shall do, just as soon as I've poured this tea. It must have brewed by now.'

Glancing sideways towards the house, Helen was studying its large windows, the arched doorway, the pleasing slant of the slate roof. And the glorious stone itself. She examined the matching slabs of the terrace where they were sitting, the myriad shades from palest cream to burnt orange with minute crystals that sparkled beneath the sun. There were darker layers also, black even and dark blue, incredible contrasts to the overall gold.

'You love sandstone, don't you?'

She laughed. 'It always looks far nicer than brick! I was going to tell you. I've been to Stratford, saw the new theatre.'

'Designed by a woman.'

Helen met Fenny March's eyes, grey like her own, though paler. Eyes that always seemed understanding.

'I was coming to that. But about Stratford – I was a bit disappointed that the theatre looked so . . . well, plain on the outside. I might have liked it better if it hadn't been brick. But I loved the interior – it thrilled me. Our Marian thought I were proper daft.'

'You went there with Marian? How is she?'

'Very well, thank you. Can't talk about owt but getting married.'

'So that's on the cards, eh? Somebody local?'

'No. It's caused a bit of a rumpus at home. Denis works in the theatre, backstage. That's how the trip to Stratford came about. Marian met him when he was working here in Halifax, at the Grand.'

Miss March's eyebrows, threaded with grey like her hair, were steadily soaring.

Helen grinned. 'That's right – the idea isn't too popular at home. Dad gave his consent, but I think he knew that if he didn't Marian was quite likely to run off to Denis any road.'

'She always did tend to be somewhat unconventional.'

'Unruly – wasn't that what most of the staff at school called her?'

Again they laughed, but affectionately.

'And you, Helen – always just the opposite. That is why you're here today, to talk about your future?'

'I feel awful about it. I wish Mum and Dad could understand. It isn't that I'm ungrateful for my job. I do know how lucky I were to be taken on as soon as I left school.'

'But the carpet factory office isn't what you want?'

'I never told you, did I? Everybody but you – the Head, our form mistress that last year – said how well I'd done. They knew, of course, the circumstances at home. That the most Dad could ever manage would be to give me the sort of course our Marian had taken. And I'd turned that down. I'd no wish to end up a secretary.'

'So tell me now – when it's too late to offend those who were so delighted about the position you secured – what is it your heart's so set on?'

'I think you've guessed, haven't you? Architecture. Can't seem to put it out of my head.'

Fenny March grew very thoughtful. Helen imagined the teacher's anxiety on her behalf: the length of training, the years while she would be earning little or nothing.

'The studying'd take too long, wouldn't it? Mum and Dad only just make ends meet as it is. And now with our Marian's wedding to pay for – then there'll be one wage less after she's gone.'

'All a bit daunting, eh, love? Don't think I can't appreciate all the difficulties. Do you know what I believe, though?'

Dispiritedly, Helen shook her head. 'Go on.'

'There's generally good cause why a longing – an ambition – remains rooted in the soul against reason, or so it seems. Certainly against practicalities and opposition. Maybe you're not meant to foresake all that you want to do. Happen that's what hope exists for.'

'But it's five or six years, isn't it, the training?'

'All of that. Could be more if you only study part time.'

'And I couldn't live on fresh air meanwhile, could I?'

Miss March shook her head. The pale eyes seemed to look beyond Helen, way into the past. 'I had an ailing mother. Father was often away from home, visiting sites.'

'So you'd have become an architect if you could have?'

'I haven't regretted teaching.'

'*But* . . .'

'Quite.' She paused. 'I don't believe you should resign yourself, surrender all hope. Not quite yet. There might be something we can do.'

Chapter 2

Helen had never seen so many biscuits. Thousands of them passing on the conveyor belt, still soft, hot from the oven, and smelling – always smelling. This sweet, cloying smell had met her as she walked up the road from the tram on that first evening four years ago, and had clung with her ever since. Some days she hardly noticed it; other folk did, of course, on her clothes and in her hair. Alex was always complaining. Despite how meticulous she was about having a strip wash as soon as she got home, and keeping her hair short so that it dried quickly. Thank goodness some people still wore their hair bobbed.

It was worth it, though, was enabling her to survive. She had completed over four years of studying at Leeds College of Art. There was nothing now to stop her becoming an architect. Eventually.

And but for that talk with Miss March, none of this would have happened. Helen would never forget how good Fenny March had been, going the very next day to the nursing home where her father was, telling him all about her former pupil's ambitions. There had been meetings after that, sitting in the over-warm room in that lovely house in Harrogate, listening to the old man's grumbles about the staff there and the other residents. Listening, and waiting – until he came to the point and began discussing architecture. Then once he'd begun he had been transformed, with vigour in the lined face, colour in faded blue eyes, strength in shoulders wearied by too many years of living. And, on the very first day that Helen had met him, there'd been his satisfied smile as he put the proposal to her.

'Tell you what I'm going to do, lass – and it's as much for Fenny here as it is for you, so you mustn't ever get cocky about it. I'm going to create a scholarship so's you can study. No, hang on a minute, don't go thanking me till you hear all the conditions.' He had paused there, enjoying the tension almost as much as he was enjoying the ability to give again, at his age. 'I'm naming it the Fenella March Bursary. Yes, Fenny, my mind's made up – you didn't think, did you, that I'd forget what you sacrificed?

'And now, young lass, we come to what's expected of you. You'll have enough to see you through college, that's all arranged. But once you begin earning, you'll put some of it back. All of it, if you can without stinting yourself. It'll be there again then – ready for the next one that deserves a bit of a hand.'

Helen had immediately invested one shilling and sixpence in obtaining a form to apply for architectural probationership, affirming to herself that there could be no turning back.

The scholarship didn't cover all her living expenses, of course, and nor had it been intended to. Mr March was a firm believer in the fact that folk most appreciated something for which they'd had to work. That was certainly the word for the biscuit factory job, especially these days while they were producing presentation tins to mark George VI's Coronation. With the abdication at the end of 1936, they'd had to abandon all the tins bearing King Edward VIII's picture. But this occupation didn't make heavy demands on her already over-taxed brain, and it definitely didn't require the kind of concentration which had been necessary in the carpet mill office.

Strangely, Helen had been rather sad to leave her first job, the place where she'd come to appreciate putting in a full day's graft and being paid for it.

And she had hated explaining at home that though Mr March's generosity was enabling her to begin at college, despite this evening work, she couldn't contribute so much to the family budget.

Dad had surprised her with his equable acceptance of what was happening. They were sitting at the chenille-covered table in the living room which was dominated by a Victorian sideboard which Kathleen Clegg regretted inheriting because, being mahogany, it showed every mote of dust. Helen had always loved the piece, especially its mirrors and intricate carving, and she enjoyed polishing its twisted columns.

'We'll manage somehow, love, remember that,' her father had said. 'Your mum and me both want what's best for you. And if we couldn't give it to you, we're glad somebody else has the means. We mightn't be enthusing as much as you'd like about what you're doing, but that's only because we're older, can foresee more of the problems. It's such a long time, Helen, such a large slice of your life to be taken up wi' learning.'

'We're just afraid, you see,' Kathleen had added, grasping her husband's arm in a gesture that showed their unity. 'Afraid as how you might be sorry later on that you've had to study for so long, and so hard. And happen afraid an' all that you might miss out on having a life of your own because you'll be that intent on putting all you've got into your work.'

She had hugged them both, loving them all the more after learning that their reservations about her career were based only on concern for her.

Shifting all her weight on to one foot, she raised the other, trying to flex her toes. The shoes she wore to the factory were old because no matter how regularly the floor was cleaned there was always some residue of biscuit waste. Standing so long in one place, just watching that all the freshly baked biscuits were flawless, really took it out of your feet and ankles; especially when it also seemed to make your feet spread until you could do with a size larger shoe. And because the task was so monotonous there wasn't much to take your mind off your complaints.

Helen had liked her first job in the factory rather better. That had been on the packing line where there had been other women and girls to talk with, the chance to have a laugh. And it hadn't been nearly so hot. The trouble was all the supervisors and charge-hands knew that she was only staying here while her training in architecture continued, and so weren't above giving her the worst jobs. The only good thing about this one was the opportunity to think over all that she'd been learning in recent weeks. She could also look forward to anything special which was coming up.

Next year a few of the more advanced students in her grade were going across to the Continent. Travelling to see some of the famous buildings from past eras, they would actually go as far as Italy. Helen hadn't believed she'd be able to afford the trip, but old Mr March had insisted that it was something she must not miss. He had described magnificent ancient buildings in Rome and elsewhere, and some that weren't quite so old. There was an abbey church at Einsiedeln which he still recalled very clearly. She had known then that she would have to go somehow, and had begun making the necessary economies.

Instead of getting the tram all the way to the factory each evening, she was walking a good mile of the distance. That saved only a few pence each week, but it would mount up. And she'd started taking bread and dripping from home to eat at lunch time at college. By only spending on cups of tea there, she was already accumulating a tidy sum. The exercise might counteract the fatty diet, and it would take more than this stringent economy to spoil her life at college.

Helen had loved it there wholeheartedly since the first day which she still recalled so clearly. Some of the students had seemed rather nervous as they went up the steps and through the heavy doors. She was just so thankful for the opportunity to study there that she strode eagerly towards the board displaying class lists.

Seeing 'Helen Clegg' just three names down gave her such a thrill that she was all but running as she found her way along the corridors. Four or five students had arrived ahead of her and were grouped around their tutor's desk. She had met Mr Wilkinson at her interview, and although his blue eyes could appear cold and daunting, they also took on an occasional crinkle of amusement.

Mr Wilkinson was smiling when she entered, and called to her: 'Ah – Miss Clegg. Over here, if you please. Do you know any of the others?'

She hadn't done, and the only name she recalled immediately afterwards was Alexander Stone's. As Tod Wilkinson explained, Alex was the son of Joseph Stone, one of the most respected architects in the Halifax area. Helen had discovered that day that she was the only female architectural student in their year; within a week she was suspecting that this was the cause of Alex's special interest in her.

From the start he had ensured that they sat close together in class. By the end of the month he'd offered to run her back and forth to college. That was when Helen had been obliged to explain about her evening job. To her surprise, Alex had applauded her determination.

'Gosh, but you make me think I've had it too easy!'

For years his father had been introducing Alexander into the family practice, taking him to new sites and then returning with him at various stages of construction. And, of course, there was the prestige of the name. Nobody in Halifax remained unaware of Joseph Stone – an alderman of the borough, from a family which had produced several councillors. During this Coronation Year, he was Mayor of Halifax.

'Pity I'm nowhere near qualified yet,' Alex had confided to Helen yesterday lunch time. 'Father's employing a chap to cover for him this year, otherwise the business would suffer from his absences for attending functions.'

She had expected that Alex would be eager to be in on the reception at the Town Hall for King George and Queen Elizabeth's visit. But the other day he had laughed at the suggestion.

'You don't know me at all if you can say that! Father's in his element when he's climbing socially – 'fraid I'm not, old thing.'

'But the King and Queen . . .'

He shook his head with its rich golden waves of hair all the more emphatically. 'I'd not cross the street to look at them. The monarchy ought to be abolished. Why hang on to them? They're no better than us. You saw how Edward went to pieces over that woman . . .'

Helen grinned. 'Mrs Simpson's attractive enough. Thought you'd be all for her.'

'Hardly. Not when she had him sacrificing his job. And it is just a job, Head of State. To my way of thinking, they'd do better to have a politician in ultimate charge, somebody who's had a grounding in ruling the country.'

'Surely the royal family has?' Helen ventured.

His grey-green eyes narrowed. 'Some, maybe.'

'Well, I think we shall soon find that the new King and Queen are champion leaders.'

Alex wouldn't have that, and when they turned to analysing which of the current politicians he would support it soon was clear that Alex was a bit of a Bolshevist. Helen was quite fascinated. She'd never come across anybody who wasn't very much a Royalist. This discovery led to further arguments between them which only ended in yet another agreement to disagree.

Their opinions seemed to differ on most things, as they had ever since the beginning of that first term when, as soon as Helen felt at home, she'd started saying what she thought. Their first clash had concerned Alexander's personal life – which wasn't really anything to do with her, but she'd been that incensed she'd had to comment.

Walking into class early one morning, Helen had caught him laughing with Harold Tilsley, another student, evidently about his previous night's outing.

'So, Harold, I said to her: "If you don't like it, love, you can walk home. It's only another couple of miles." Naturally, she suddenly grew more amenable.'

Harold laughed. 'You'd have thought she'd have given her eye teeth to ride around in your father's Rolls-Royce, anyway.'

'Ah, but it wasn't eye teeth I was intent on extracting from her, was it?'

'And did she – you know – cooperate entirely?'

'Not quite, worse luck. Still, half the fun's in the pursuit, isn't it, old chap? And even in my own little Morris I don't have much trouble finding . . .'

' . . . a willing victim?' Helen interrupted, her face flaring with anger. She felt degraded on behalf of all females who seemingly were expected to consider Alex Stone's attentions a privilege. 'Do you know what? The way you behave is as common as muck! And I thought you were supposed to be better off nor most of us. Has it never occurred to you that the lasses you hope will cheapen themselves for you mightn't have had all your advantages? That they'll be flattered just to go out with you, though Lord knows why. And all you can think of is ruining 'em for settling down with a decent fellow.'

The only thing that placated her was that it wasn't Alex but Harold who laughed. 'Is that right, Alex? Are you so expert you ruin their hopes of finding another fellow who's as good at it as you are?'

More than a little shocked, for her non-conformist father never permitted even a vague allusion to anything connected with sex, Helen had refused to say another word to either of them.

By the following day when she still answered in monosyllables whenever Alex addressed her, he was growing more perturbed than she would ever have imagined. That evening he was waiting outside on the college steps.

'I'll give you a lift home from Leeds,' he offered. 'And you have my word I don't class you in the same category as my girlfriends.'

'That's as may be,' She retorted. 'And thanks, but it makes no difference any road. I have a job to go to.'

'A job?'

'Aye – some of us have to earn a living.' That was when she'd explained about the biscuit factory and had been thankful that she didn't have to bring him into line for ridiculing that as well.

In fact, when he proved to be so understanding

about what she was doing, she'd felt quite sorry she didn't hold with the way he carried on with other members of her sex. He was a bit of a funny mixture. Maybe all men were – she'd not had the experience to be sure. And certainly, from what she'd seen of their Marian's Denis, *he* wasn't the one who'd put himself out in their household. Still, Marian was happy enough now they were married and starting a family.

'Aren't you ever going to settle down?' she asked Alexander in the car on the way to the factory. As she'd understood it, shortage of money was all that normally kept people apart. 'Or do you plan on continuing to use every lass that falls for you?'

He didn't like that. 'It's only girls who're out for a good time, you know. Ones who are of a like mind to myself, believing there's time enough in the future for being serious.'

She wondered where love came into it, but that wasn't something she'd ever ask Alexander Stone. He seemed so full of himself that it'd be just like him to think she was getting keen on him. Later, though, outside the biscuit works, he'd nearly made her late, he was so intent on explaining how he felt about *her*.

'Don't write me off entirely, Helen, please? I want to make it clear that you've already earned far more respect from me than any of that lot I go out with. You're going be a brilliant architect, I can sense that by now, and I've got to hand it to you for tackling evening work to help pay your way. Whatever happens, you'll always have my admiration.'

Soft talk, she'd thought, running across the setts to clock in. But, strangely, in all these intervening years, Alex's attitude towards her had actually reinforced what he'd said that evening.

They got a lot of enjoyment out of their classes, and

this was greatly enhanced for Helen by their common-room arguments about architectural styles. Over the years, it had become accepted in their crowd that Alex was in favour of ultra-modern, while Helen always spoke up for traditional, even Gothic lines.

Their first disagreement had concerned Bull Green House which had been opened during 1932. Whilst Helen accepted that it was a great improvement on the rough ground surrounded by hoardings which once had occupied the site between Bull Close Lane and King Cross Street in Halifax, she would have preferred a more elaborate building.

'Nay, but it's meant to be functional,' Harold Tilsley had argued. 'You don't want something like Manor Heath.'

'Oh, I don't know,' Helen had begun. She'd always loved Manor Heath, an elaborate mansion built for John Crossley, the son of the famous carpet manufacturer.

Before she could say any more, Alexander was asserting his view. 'Bull Green House isn't nearly modern enough. Halifax ought to be looking at what's being constructed elsewhere.'

'Such as?' Helen inquired, waiting for him to cite the Shakespeare Memorial Theatre as an example. She wouldn't mind telling him that she'd seen it, and what her impressions were of the exterior.

But Alex was thinking of places even further afield. 'There's the *Daily Express* building, for one. And the Hoover factory in west London – that was designed by a New York firm.'

None of the others had first-hand knowledge of either so his argument had fallen rather flat, but Helen had noticed ever since that Alex relished any discussion which made him appear more up to date than the rest.

Strangely, though, their very different ideas on architecture hadn't prevented friendship developing between them, any more than their totally dissimilar backgrounds had created a barrier. This had been proved on the day that the entire class was invited to The Stone House, the home which Alexander's father had designed for himself on the hillside overlooking Brearley, along the Calder Valley.

Reared in a back-to-back house just off Queen's Road, Helen had struggled for years against her initial envy of school friends who lived in through houses. Even though Kathleen Clegg's addiction to housework was no less than any Yorkshire housewife's, and the living-room furniture always gleamed from her daily dusting, Helen had felt uncomfortable in the past about bringing new friends home. They couldn't help but notice the carpet worn threadbare under the table which had been moved to conceal the thinnest places, and the old-fashioned fireplace that Helen was obliged to black-lead every Saturday because Kathleen wouldn't have a daughter of hers growing up unskilled in housewifery.

Worst of all, though, was having to explain to folk that the lavatory was out in the yard. Time and again, both she and Marian had begged their father to have a way through constructed so that going right outside was unnecessary. Daniel Clegg had been just as persistent in his assertion that he'd do nothing of the kind.

'*If* I had the brass for that,' he'd told them the last time the matter was raised, 'I'd be spending it on summat we could appreciate all the time, not on a necessity out of sight. I'd see your mother had an electric oven, and have this range taken out of the house.' Helen had started noticing recently how the living room was always referred to as 'the house', a fact which she supposed had roots in the past, though it seemed illogical to her. Maybe it went back to a time when people and their stock shared the one building, and the family quarters could then rightly be termed 'the house'?

Visiting Miss March's home along Albert Promenade had, at first, been an awesome experience. Helen had felt quite inhibited and constantly watched what she said, but that was only until Fenny March's ability to comprehend a girl's mind had put her at ease. Knowing something of the background of her past and present pupils, Fenny had skilfully bridged the gulf between them by concentrating on things that were familiar. Her father had scorned over-stuffed furniture, for instance, and his old Windsor armchair proved to be similar to one in Helen's home. The kitchen range had been a larger version of the one in the Cleggs' living room and, best of all, the set of balloon-backed dining chairs was similar to those inherited from Helen's grandmother. Having established that they had several items in common, Fenny had then succeeded in drawing Helen out on the subject of her pastimes.

Overshadowed as they were by her love of architecture, her other pursuits were few, but both Daniel and Kathleen Clegg were avid users of the public library and had passed on to Helen a great love of reading.

'You'll never lack an interest so long as you read,' Fenny had assured her, beaming, and they had settled to chatting about their favourite authors.

I wish I believed this visit would be half as easy, Helen had been thinking on the day she set out with her fellow students for The Stone House. From their homes between here and Leeds, they had converged on the centre of Halifax where they were catching the tram to Brearley. That must have been over a year ago now, she reflected. The trams had been replaced by buses along the Calder Valley during 1936.

She could hardly credit now that it was so long since she'd got to know Alex's father. He had so impressed her that the day was still fresh in her mind.

It had been hot, and she and her fellow students had clattered upstairs on the tram, scarcely aware of its juddering and swaying, so interested were they in Mr Wilkinson's account of The Stone House. Evidently, Joseph had drawn up the plans while he was only a student himself. Adjusting details, amending elevations, but always keeping the building substantially the same, he had preserved the drawings until he was successful enough to afford to have the house constructed by the best builders in the West Riding.

'If anything demonstrates the power of hanging on to a dream, that house does,' Tod Wilkinson enthused, his eyes gleaming.

Somehow, even the more rebellious among them remained a little awed, and it was in this mood of quiet anticipation that they descended from the tram at Brearley. Alex was waiting for them, and they surged across the road and began the climb up a narrow lane. Pausing occasionally for stragglers who stopped to admire the view across to the other steep hillside, Alex chatted with their tutor and those of his fellows who had breath remaining from the uphill climb.

Suddenly, his home was in sight from a bend in the lane where a drive took off at an angle between tall wrought-iron gates.

'Come on, Helen, let's have your arm,' Alex said then, drawing her with him to the head of the group. 'I've been telling Father about you, he's mightily impressed.'

She was still wondering whatever she might have done to impress someone of the stature of Joseph

Stone when they arrived at the steps leading up to the studded oak door.

A manservant admitted them, and sent a pair of darkly dressed maids to usher them into the reception room where their host awaited them.

Joseph Stone was taller than his son, though his shoulders stooped from all the years at a drawing board. His hair was as luxuriant as Alexander's and equally wavy, but greying to a pleasant shade midway between gold and silver.

'Welcome, all,' he exclaimed, his smile encompassing the entire group as they flowed about the room. But his eyes swiftly focused on Helen. She noticed his slight nod which appeared to be of approval.

'So you're the lass who's staggered this son of mine by proving to have an uncommon grasp of architecture?'

She felt the flush surging upwards from her neck, and the other students gawping, for all the world as though they'd never before noticed she was of a different sex.

Mr Stone deserved an answer, though, and she exerted considerable will-power to make her voice light and conversational.

'You're very kind,' she said. 'I hope you won't be disappointed. I'm rather afraid Alex may have over-exaggerated in the build-up he's given me!'

'Miss Clegg is always too modest,' Mr Wilkinson remarked, coming to shake Joseph Stone by the hand.

It seemed that the two were already acquainted and had arranged between them this tour of the house. Helen was glad to have attention diverted from herself as they were invited to examine the room in which they were standing.

'You'll see the windows are large,' Joseph Stone began, 'that was one of the first things I decided on.

Plenty of light in the place, and full benefit from the view.'

They followed him to look out towards the far side of the valley, three or four of them clustering at each of the five tall windows.

Helen felt Alex gazing at her, awaiting her reaction. Beyond the road and the River Calder soared grassland and wood – so many different greens she'd never finish counting them. 'By, but that beats rows of grimy terraces!'

He wasn't grinning back at her. Emotions seemed to war on his face. Surprise was surrendering to something closely resembling tenderness.

His father had heard too. She could sense him looking at her over the heads of her fellow students. His expression wasn't so easy to read, yet she sensed the warmth of understanding.

Helen turned from the view and blinked her eyes to try and refocus her concentration. Joseph Stone was indicating the large marble fireplace and the alcoves to either side.

'A shameless copy of Adam styling,' he confessed, smiling. 'I knew I'd not afford the genuine article, even if I could locate one and have it transported here. So I made sketches – visiting well-known houses in much the same way as you do yourselves. Providing that it's not at the expense of expressing your own individuality, I see no harm in acknowledging that there are certain masters worth emulating.'

'So you see, Father's a bit of a fraud,' Alex murmured into Helen's ear.

His remark was noticed. His father shrugged, but then as an afterthought turned on Alex. 'Right, boy, let's see how much better you are! Take over the description – you've heard it oft' enough.'

Beside her, Alex had flinched at 'boy' but Helen

soon realised that there was nothing immature about his response to the challenge.

'Thanks, Father,' he said smoothly, leaving the group to stand in the centre of the room.

'The alcoves, which you see accommodate some of the family glassware and china, were constructed to draw the eye down from the height of the room, and create a more intimate atmosphere around the fireplace.'

Helen could picture a log fire in the massive grate, and folk sitting on the two brocade sofas facing each other across a long low table.

'As I said, the ceiling's high. Its vaulting is of wood though modelled on a cathedral's stonework. Some might call it ostentatious.'

Joseph chuckled. 'And old fashioned, eh, Alex?'

'Some might.'

The rest of the class were grinning, relaxing already, a few of them wishing, like Helen, for a father whose architecture might aid their own. But Alex was continuing, directing them to inspect the columns ranged in a line parallel with the windows.

'Though these appear to support the vaulting, their main purpose is to provide a dividing point in the room. Father's gatherings aren't always of large numbers; by setting sofas, side tables, and other furniture between the pillars, guests are confined to the smaller area. Works quite well, too – feels much cosier than when we use the entire space.'

Watching their host's face, Helen detected a smile which seemed to reveal that he'd been unaware of his son's approval of the concept.

'Anything more in this room, Father?' Alex inquired.

'Not unless you wish to elaborate on the doors or the surrounding embellishments?'

'What can I say? Doors of mahogany, as you can see. And they are set in stone which has been carved to echo the decoration around each window.'

The entrance hall was next to be inspected and Joseph resumed the description. 'I'll admit to ostentation here – and again to being influenced by other men's ideas.' He paused, letting them gaze at the staircase curving to left and right from the centre rear, with balusters which had to be less fragile than they appeared.

'The Royal Hotel in Scarborough, wasn't that where you gleaned the notion?' said Alex.

'To your disgust!' Smiling unconcernedly, Joseph Stone addressed them all. 'I hope you've learned by now that an understanding of architecture doesn't necessarily involve appreciation of all its facets. Indeed, healthy disagreement breeds new attitudes, fresh concepts. Eh, Helen?'

'Somebody's been talking,' she exclaimed, feeling suddenly as though only she and Alex were here with his father.

'Those two will never agree,' somebody observed.

'I hope not either,' Harold Tilsley put in. 'We'd have a dull old time if it weren't for those two arguing for their different tastes.'

'Good, good,' Alex's father approved.

'You don't say that while I'm disagreeing with you,' Alex remarked.

That was met with laughter. 'I should think not, indeed. You'll mind your place here, son. Keeping you down has done you no harm so far.'

Helen was thinking that Joseph Stone's idea of keeping folk down seemed extreme lenience in comparison with her own father's. She'd never considered either she or Marian were particularly repressed, but they wouldn't have felt they could speak up like this to

Dad in front of a lot of visitors. And discussions at home, even in private, didn't allow for serious questioning of parental opinion or taste.

The rest of the tour of The Stone House had proved equally enjoyable, and just as much of an eye-opener. It was no wonder that all the way back in the tram the rest of the class were envying Alex his father as much as his home.

Even now, all this time afterwards, Helen had a clear picture of Joseph Stone, could readily recall his voice. And while she stared at the conveyor belt with its interminable rows of biscuits, she thought back again to that lovely house on the hill, its elegant gables, the portico at the front entrance, and all those windows enhanced by intricate stonework.

If she wasn't so much of a realist she'd dream of one day building a similar home for herself. I wonder why Alex is so keen on severe modern stuff? she reflected, as she had so often after seeing The Stone House. Was it purely reaction to his father's affection for something different?

Somehow, the certainty that Joseph Stone had approved of her meant a lot. Helen awakened in the night sometimes and felt warmer for suspecting he also might be glad they appreciated similar traditions. And much good will it do me, she told herself, when the cold draught from the empty iron fireplace in her room brought her back to reality.

I mustn't ever become discontented because I don't live among folk like that, she reminded herself quite regularly. When I've done training somebody somewhere will employ me in their practice. Until then, I'll be gathering experience and I'll enjoy it all, especially when there's things coming up like that trip to Europe.

Since seeing Alex in his home environment Helen had grown to realise how likeable he could be. She couldn't help admiring the authority with which he spoke. But there was more to it than that. He was so attractive that she couldn't feel anything but pleased when he took her arm, or even when his arguments about architecture were directed at her. She could hardly wait for the day when they would all set out together for the Continent.

Chapter 3

'I'm beginning to suspect you're not really interested in architecture at all,' Helen had said first thing that morning. They were in Lucerne now, where they had arrived late the previous night. The rest of them had been up early to begin the tour arranged for their interest. Alex had come down to breakfast just as they were gathering in the foyer around their English-speaking guide.

'Make my apologies, there's a love,' he whispered to Helen. 'Say I'm ill or something. I can't bear another day of inspecting fusty old buildings that look as dead as the folk who created them.'

Alexander was disappointing Helen a great deal. Being unbearable, in fact. She wasn't the only one who'd sharpened their tongue on him. Even Harold Tilsley had ceased to laugh at his behaviour. No one had expected Alex to enthuse about the historic buildings of Rome or Florence, but he had made such a show of being bored while they were exclaiming over the magnificence all around. And in Pisa he had outright distressed their guide by leaving the rest of the party who were fascinated, wandering around the Baptistry, the Cathedral which was begun way back in 1063, and of course the leaning tower. Alex had claimed the early March weather, even in Italy, was too cold for him.

Although she had passed on his excuses today, Helen was livid. But at least he wasn't ruining the day for the other nine students in their group. She forgot him entirely while they viewed the courtyard of the Ritter House, marvelling that its triple-storeyed arcading was constructed in the sixteenth century. And now they'd moved on to cross by the covered wooden bridge, Helen felt she could remain here all day, inspecting all the paintings which illustrated the history of Lucerne.

'The tower here once was a belfry,' their guide explained, then grimaced. 'It also contained a torture chamber.'

Looking out from the fourteenth-century bridge, first to one side and then the other, Helen sighed with sheer pleasure. Who'd have imagined she'd ever see a place that was so beautiful? It couldn't be more different from the industrial West Riding. She'd have such a lot to describe to Mum and Dad when she got home. Across the water were red-roofed buildings, every one of them clean and bright because there wasn't all that dreadful mill smoke. Nearer at hand the antics of the waterfowl made her smile, briefly reminding her of Stratford swans.

Some of the others paused beside her, asking where Alexander was, and surprising her because it seemed that over the years they'd grown to accept that a special relationship bonded the pair of them.

And did it? she wondered, after recounting his casual dismissal of the outing. Today she'd no wish to be associated with his arrogant offhandedness, but normally . . . ? She supposed she'd always been glad to have one person in their class who could be relied on to be friendly to her. At the beginning there had been a few occasions when some of the other young men had appeared dubious about having a girl among them.

These days, they took her for granted. But was there more than a certain closeness between herself and Alex following that visit to his home?

'Alex is a real old grouch, all of a sudden,' Harold Tilsley remarked. 'You're better without him.'

'Aren't we all?' she laughed. 'Come on – let's walk to the end of the bridge, then we'd best be off to wherever our guide wants our next stop to be.' It was their last day in Lucerne and she wanted to see as much as she could.

They arrived back at their hotel as some of the other guests were coming downstairs for dinner. Alex was standing in the reception area, clearly watching for their party.

He strode straight towards Helen. 'Sorry, old love, I've been a bit of a boor. But you know me and all these old ornate places. They're too rooted in the past for me.'

'They're not all ornate. You should have seen the old bridge.'

'I did, on my own, this afternoon.'

'Good. Everything's all right then.'

'It isn't though, is it? Not between us.'

'It's no worse than it's been sometimes in the past. You have your opinions, I stick to mine. We'll neither of us change in that.'

'I'd like to make it up to you, though. We could stay on here, let the others go back home without us.'

Helen's eyebrows arched. 'Nay, Alex just a minute. I know too much about you, remember? I'll not fall for that one.'

'Have you never believed me? Not ever, right from the start? You're the one girl I respect, Helen. There'd be no funny business. We'd still have single rooms, and keep to them.'

When her hesitation continued he took her arm.

'We could hire a car, see something of the scenery round about. That *is* something we could enjoy together.'

Hiring a car, however, generated further disagreements. After waving off their fellow students amid a chorus of the remarks they'd anticipated about why they were remaining in Lucerne, they got into the Volkswagen and looked at each other.

'Where to then?' Alexander inquired. He genuinely wanted to patch things up with Helen. Even he himself wasn't entirely sure why he'd felt so miserable throughout this trip. It certainly hadn't been at all as he'd imagined. Maybe he hadn't anticipated how obtrusive the others would seem. And the low temperatures hadn't helped – he'd pictured them strolling beneath the warm Italian sun, there was nothing romantic about battling to stand up against icy winds. Here in the mountains it was worse still, with occasional scatterings of snow. At this minute ice was frosting the car windows.

'Just drive,' Helen suggested. 'It's all new to us, isn't it?' She was, in fact, feeling uncomfortable now about her swift decision to stay on here with Alex. But she had wanted to find out what it was that had troubled him so much that he'd behaved badly. He wasn't really lacking in basic courtesy; if he was trying to sort out some problem she could only help by getting him on his own. Seeing the others depart, though, had left her with a strange foreboding.

Alex took the road hugging the shore of the lake and they stopped eventually to have lunch in a restaurant overlooking the water. As they ate a traditional fondue he began to realise how relieved he was that the two of them were alone. Helen might not be the prettiest young woman he'd known – she was taller and rather heavier than the girls he usually took out – but she had an intelligent face which glowed with enthusiasm. Her grey eyes were extraordinarily appealing. One straightforward glance was enough to stir him.

Alexander enjoyed being stirred. He'd always relished having a female in their class; had been glad he'd ensured they sat near to each other. These days, especially during this trip, he'd discovered that he resented her attention being diverted away from him. And what was wrong with that? He had promised he meant her no harm. All he wished was to spend a bit of time concentrating on something more personal than architecture.

'How about going back to the hotel this afternoon?' he suggested. 'We could sit for ages talking over tea – they do serve tea – then have a really relaxing evening.'

'What about the car? I thought you'd hired it so we could get around here . . .'

'There's tomorrow, and the next day. Where do you want to go, anyway? You don't know anywhere.'

'There's the abbey at Einsiedeln.' She'd seen on the map that it wasn't all that far away, and had been wondering ever since they crossed the Channel how she might manage to get there.

'You're off again about old buildings, aren't you? Drat it!'

'It *is* why I came to Europe. I thought it was the same for you.'

'If you must know, I pictured the two of us exploring places together. Thought it'd be fun.'

'And so it has been. I've loved every minute.'

Alex saw how true that was, watched her beautiful eyes glinting with joy. Again he felt dejected, aware that he'd contributed nothing to her enjoyment. And that was his own fault. By withdrawing because he'd resented having the others around, he'd missed the opportunity to share her pleasure. Worst of all, though, was learning that she had been content without him.

'We'll go somewhere tomorrow – where shall it be?' he asked, trying again to recover the easy relationship with her on which he'd hoped at last to establish something more intimate.

'I've made my suggestion,' Helen reminded him quietly.

'But Einsiedeln's so baroque. Its interior is far too ornate. You know that's not my style. Anywhere but there, love, anywhere at all.'

'You choose then. It's the only place I can think of.'

It had begun snowing by the time their meal was over, and Alex hadn't come up with any alternative for the afternoon and evening, or for the next day. Wearily, Helen agreed to return to their hotel.

The evening wasn't a success. She was so full of all the amazing buildings she'd seen in Florence and in Rome, she couldn't keep them out of the conversation. And Alex's expression repeatedly revealed his displeasure.

'Do you really dislike architecture?' she inquired gently, ready to sympathise if Joseph Stone had insisted Alex should follow this career.

'Not in the least, but I don't believe in living in the past. The things I build will show future generations something of now – of this age, Helen, not just echoes of the past.'

'But the past has lasted, and can teach us so much.'

'Which we adapt and improve on.'

'Granted.'

'The things I design are totally modern, built around my ideas. *Mine*.'

'You say that as if you're designing already. We've none of us started yet.'

‘That’s where you’re wrong,’ he said, surprising her into staring at him across the table. ‘You knew I’d spent some time in Father’s practice, surely?’

‘Yes, but . . .’

Alexander was smiling at last. ‘I made him give me a chance. A year or two since now. It was during the summer when we’d no classes. I persuaded Father to allow me just one design of my own. I really worked at it, love, put all I’d got into it.’

‘And?’

‘I pulled it off! Even he could find no more than one or two minor flaws. I couldn’t believe it myself. He only altered a few lines on one elevation.’

‘What sort of building is it for?’

‘Nothing very grand – a farmhouse. But a very good farmhouse – Yeoman’s Grange. I’ll take you there when we get home. It’s only a little way farther up the Calder Valley from us, on the hillside just beyond Mytholmroyd.’

‘It’s been completed already?’

‘Last year. July.’

‘But you never said. Not to Mr Wilkinson, nor to any of us.’

‘Wilkinson wouldn’t have approved, you know he thinks we’ve got to progress at his rate. He wouldn’t like me getting ahead of the class.’

‘But the rest of us?’

‘And have it coming out in front of him? Somebody in a class the size of ours would have let it slip.’

‘I don’t think it would have mattered. Still, I’m pleased for you. A bit envious an’ all. Must be marvellous to see your plans come to life.’

‘It is pretty special.’

Even though she was delighted that Alex had confided in her, Helen didn’t believe that he should close his mind to so much that had been devised by past masters of their profession. And nor had he the right to dismiss her opinions – was that just because she was a woman? She was too keen to remain silent about her feelings, too young to know not to persist.

'Just be fair – see for yourself,' she finished, as they walked slowly towards the stairs. 'Come with me to Einsiedeln, and come with an open mind. I'm so certain there'll be something you can like.'

Alex was no less sure that she was wrong. By daylight next morning when they met over an early breakfast he was, if anything, more adamant.

'You go if you wish, Helen. Take the car and go there. It won't do a thing for you.'

She hesitated, drawn by the possibility of seeing the abbey, and knowing that she'd be unlikely to come this way again. What was it their Marian had always said? 'This isn't just a practice for life, you know. If there's summat you want, it mightn't be offered again.'

'Well, when my brother-in-law taught me to drive, he said it'd open up opportunities. I suppose this is one I'm not going to miss.'

Helen had been scared more than once during the journey. She'd soon found there was a vast difference between driving on familiar roads in Yorkshire and here in the Alps, especially when sudden flurries of snow increased the danger of her not noticing all the icy patches. But the instant that she saw Einsiedeln in the distance every scrap of unease drained from her.

Standing out from the monastery buildings as well as from the little town itself, the twin towers seemed to urge her towards them. Farther along the narrow road, Helen glanced between conifers and noticed how white the abbey gleamed, contrasting with the green pastures beyond, the blue of Lake Sihl and of the sky. Only the snow-covered mountains had a similar brilliance.

Einsiedeln was even better close to. After parking opposite the front of the abbey, Helen gazed towards the elegant façade. But she was too exited to remain where she was, and moments later was approaching the heavy door.

Her first sight of the interior was so staggering that she stood for several seconds just inside the entrance. The sun, low in the sky, beamed in through the windows, silhouetting the Chapel of Grace which stood isolated in its black marble, but glowing from within when she approached the chapel's open gates. The glow, far brighter than any sun, was golden, seeming to hang in clouds and numerous light rays, and surround a black-faced Madonna and Child. Both were robed in red silk embroidered with gold. Below their feet an altar frontal echoed the colours.

When Helen finally began to move away from the chapel her eyes were so dazzled that the panels in gold relief decorating its dark exterior looked dull, and she felt drawn to continue staring towards that source of light above the altar.

Gradually, though, she was becoming aware of the rest of the area where this chapel within a church was housed – of splendid arches and columns of white embellished with gold and touches of red. In a daze, she backed away from the chapel to begin examining the building which soared above and about it. She had never seen such magnificence. Very slowly, she walked around, pausing by every arch, glancing upwards towards each window.

The sun seemed to have disappeared yet still the abbey shone, its carvings and its statues growing out of intricate gilded ornamentation. And then, just when she had progressed in a half-circle so that glancing back she saw the rear of the Chapel of Grace, Helen looked straight ahead of her. The amazing beauty which she'd seen already was only a portion of the whole.

Beyond this splendour were further sections, even more gloriously decorated, with painted cupolas. The mural she could see from here was of the Last Supper. In the far distance beyond the magnificent nave and delicately wrought gates was the choir.

It was inside the choir, whilst admiring the ornate abbot's throne, that Helen began to feel overcome. She'd expected masses of decoration, no baroque building would be lacking in that, but nothing had prepared her for so much within the one edifice.

Suddenly aware that she needed to get away from it all, if only for a short while, she began hurrying back through the different areas of the abbey towards the door.

Fumbling in her confusion, she struggled to turn the handle and all but stumbled as she went through to the open air.

She steadied herself against the wall, was compelled to lean for a moment against the icy chill of its stone. A bitter wind keened across this broad plateau amid the Alps, knocking out of her what little breath still remained, making recovery even more difficult.

A few snowflakes fluttered over her face, landed on closed eyelids, making her conscious that she'd shut her eyes as she attempted to come to terms with all that she had seen. How ever could Alexander belittle so much loveliness, and the craftsmanship which, over the years, had contributed to its creation?

'Excuse me, are you all right?'

She opened her eyes to find a young man studying her with concern. Snow gathered on his dark hair while he waited to see that she was all right.

'Yes, I – yes, thanks.' She managed a smile, and saw his rather thin lips curving in relief.

'You were . . . overwhelmed?' Sherry brown eyes smiled understandingly. His face was surprisingly gentle though his clothes – black trousers and sweater – hinted at a certain austerity of character.

Helen's laugh was rueful. 'Thank goodness you didn't want me to explain. I'd never have found the words!'

The man glanced about as though looking for somebody. 'You came here alone?'

Again she laughed, this time more freely. 'It's 1938, remember. Women have learnt to drive cars. We're even allowed out unescorted!' But then she realised that her joking response might have been misconstrued.

'Sorry, I didn't mean to be rude, but you looked so astonished that I'd come on my own today.'

'You're not on holiday out here alone then?'

Helen shook her head. 'Not really on holiday either. I'm studying architecture. A group of us have been to Italy. We're staying in Lucerne now.'

'Are you driving back there straight away?'

'I suppose so.'

'You're up to driving, are you?'

If it had been Alex implying otherwise, she'd have soon put him right, but this fellow was genuinely worried that she might not have recovered sufficiently from the impact of the abbey.

'You're too observant. I'll be all right in a few minutes.'

'And even better after a coffee or something.' He glanced away from where they were standing. 'There's a cafe.'

When Helen nodded, thanking him, he smiled once more. Before striding off, he grinned and fastened the top button of her tweed coat for her, turned up its fur collar. Neither Alex nor any of the other students ever paid her such small attentions.

'You're being very kind,' she said, and repeated the words minutes later when a steaming cup of chocolate was placed before her. 'And I still feel a bit of a fool. I was . . . well, the only word's gobsmacked! It was such a shock, you see. Alex had refused to come with me. As a matter of fact, he spends most of his time condemning ornate buildings like this. Driving over to see the abbey, I was beginning to wonder if I was wrong – if I shouldn't like it.' She paused. 'Oh, isn't "like" an inadequate word? I was so overcome, in awe of it all.'

'I know the feeling.'

And *she* knew at once that these weren't empty words. They smiled again at each other.

'It's funny, you know,' Helen continued, 'Alexander and I have been pals since the day we started art college, yet we never agree on architectural styles. And he is rather forceful.'

'Then you should be too, surely? Your opinions are just as valid as his, or anyone else's.'

'I'm not so certain about that. Alex should know what he is talking about, his father's Joseph Stone, the architect. I'm afraid I'm the old-fashioned one in the class. And that's not good, not when I should be thinking by now about the sort of job I'll have eventually.'

'How much more training's ahead of you?'

'A lot, though the worst's behind me. But even if I pass my finals at the first attempt there's still the practical side, with a firm of architects.'

'And what will you tell this Alex about today? The abbey?'

'That it moved me.' Suddenly, she was forced to confront the full significance of the experience. 'That I wanted to be a part of it, longed to have a share in creating something so lovely.' Her voice lowered. 'And that I wished, for the first time in many a year, that I was sure I believed in what it stands for.'

'And you're certain that you don't?'

'I've had plenty of time to weigh it up. Church, an' all that. My father's a strict non-conformist. He tried for ages to get me to go with him.'

The sherry-coloured eyes sought her own again, briefly, before he glanced away to the spoon with which he was tracing intricate designs on the table cloth. 'We are talking of belief, you know, not proof. Faith, not the certain knowledge of an established fact.'

'But . . .' Helen began, then sighed. She'd never yearned before to belong amid so much that witnessed to reverence.

'Have you never considered that willingness to keep an open mind might be enough? For a start, at least.'

'No, I haven't. You either believe or you don't. And no amount of wishing for the comfort of belief . . .'

'Comfort?' he interrupted, and snorted. His eyes glinted with some private wry amusement, and were very searching.

He made Helen feel awkward. She glanced at her watch.

'I'd better be on my way. Thank you very much for the hot chocolate – sorry, I don't remember your name.'

'Chris. Christopher Maitland. You ought to return to the abbey, you know, give it another chance. The first impact is pretty startling. You're too disadvantaged to take in all that's there. Even the material side.'

'I know. I might do that, if there's time. Depends what else Alex wishes to see before we leave for home. That's the thing about architecture – wherever you go, there's so much that's interesting.'

Christopher smiled, rising with her, finding money for the bill without taking his gaze from her face. 'I'm sure. You're fortunate that your occupation is something so . . . tangible. It must prove very rewarding.'

Helen grinned. 'You'll have gathered by now that I'm rather obsessed. Like now. So carried away that I haven't even asked about your work.'

'I'm a student,' he said hastily.

While they were saying goodbye, Helen was struggling not to show her surprise. She was twenty-one now, he looked two or three years older . . . and still studying?

As she carefully followed the road over the mountains to Lucerne she felt as if the breathless awe she had experienced in the abbey had returned, and sensed it had somehow become intensified by her meeting with Christopher Maitland.

Alex wasn't in the hotel when she arrived back that evening, but while she was changing for dinner she glanced out of the window and saw him crossing the road towards the entrance. He was arm-in-arm with a flaxen-haired girl who was laughing up at him.

Berenice was at their table when Helen went down to the dining room. Smiling, Alex introduced them. 'Berry is here for a couple of days,' he explained, 'before going on to Zurich where her parents live.'

She was a pleasant enough girl, half-English, and talked excitedly throughout their meal. Afterwards, Helen couldn't recall what had been said, certainly little of any consequence, although she soon grasped the fact that Berry and Alex had spent most of the day together, and intended doing so tomorrow.

Nodding her approval, Helen smiled. 'If it's not terribly inconvenient, I wonder if you'd drop me off somewhere near Einsiedeln? There was so much to see

I only absorbed half of it today.'

'Use the car again, I don't need it,' Alex said airily.

It seemed Berry had a car of her own. Helen wasn't surprised that Alex had taken up with someone so evidently well heeled. Very much his sort, she supposed. But she was neither perturbed nor curious about the kind of relationship which might be developing between the pair. All she wanted at present was the freedom to follow old Mr March's advice and take a really thorough look at the abbey.

This time, entering the church, Helen felt a difference. Still awe-inspiring, still overwhelming, it now seemed more significantly a place of worship. She was conscious immediately of her nostrils prickling with the aroma of incense, of the rays of the pale sun focused on the dark marble of the chapel housing the Black Madonna, and of the urge to go and kneel near the chapel gates.

Unaccustomed to kneeling, she simply stood there, gazing at all the gold surrounding the image. All at once, she felt very alone, shut out maybe by her years of disbelief yet aching to be at one with something which she knew might be found here.

Silently, a darkly clad figure came to kneel beside her. Helen did not need to look to identify him, but smiled affectionately when she eventually gazed down at his bowed dark head.

Christopher grinned as he got to his feet. 'I saw the car, guessed where you would be,' he whispered.

Helen smiled back, pleased to see him again, wondering now if it was as much in the hope of this encounter as to see the abbey that she'd returned.

His hand rested lightly on her shoulder as they began walking around.

'Some of this was designed by Caspar Mosbrugger,

wasn't it?' Helen remarked.

Christopher nodded. 'And the Asam brothers were responsible for many of the frescoes. But this is only one of the many consecrated buildings to appear on this site. Way back in nine hundred and thirty-four, a monk came from Strasbourg, and that was the beginning of the monastic community here.'

'Does anything remain of the original buildings?' Helen asked, following him into the nave.

He shrugged. 'Haven't yet found that out,' he admitted. 'But I do know that a succession of fires destroyed parts of the earlier monasteries and the abbey.'

Because he was able to enlighten her about life within the order here as well as some of the history of the buildings, Helen remained fascinated. It wasn't for some while that she even considered anything beyond their glorious surroundings.

When they finally went out into the cold mountain air, Christopher smiled down at her again. Without asking he led the way across to the familiar cafe.

She felt quite easy with Christopher now. He might have been an older brother who was taking trouble to ensure that she enjoyed her visit. And she was itching to know more about him.

'Yesterday, we talked about me,' she began, smiling over the rim of her cup. 'Today I insist you have your turn. You say you're a student. What are you reading?'

He didn't reply immediately. He was looking into her eyes, thinking what an exquisite pearl colour they were. Yet it wasn't her loveliness that enchanted him so much as her manner. She could be direct, yet there was more sensitivity there than in many who made straightforwardness their virtue. She appealed to him far more strongly than any other woman he had met.

Not that he was an expert. Quite the opposite.

'For a degree at present,' he eventually answered carefully. 'Master of Arts, nothing special.'

'Which university?'

'Leeds.'

'That's where I'm studying – the College of Art.' She wanted to add that they could meet up, but knew she'd never suggest that. Women might have steadily taken more of a hand in determining their own lives since the day they'd ensured their right to vote, but there were still many areas where the man should lead. Her years among a class of male students had encouraged a feeling of equality, but she'd been indoctrinated in certain beliefs – and they most certainly didn't allow for any forwardness in young women.

Talking as they had on the previous day, they scarcely noticed how time was passing except when hunger compelled them to order soup and rolls, followed by Apfel Kuchen.

It was Chris who at last glanced at his watch. 'When do you have to be back at your hotel?'

'That can't be the time!' Helen exclaimed, but a glance towards the darkening sky confirmed how late it was. Then her smile returned. 'But I can't regret one moment of today. Thank you, Christopher.'

By the time they had settled the bill and emerged it was completely dark. There had been a light snowfall, beneath which the ground was icy. Beyond the abbey and its environs there was no sign of even one light shining from the town.

'Fog, filling all the valleys,' Christopher observed, frowning. 'Helen, I don't want you driving in this.'

'I'll be all right. I've got to get back.'

'Then I'll drive you there.'

'You can't. Aren't you staying in Einsiedeln?' She

had felt certain that he was located somewhere in the town here.

'Doesn't matter. I could always stop overnight in Lucerne.' Anything was better than thinking of her tackling that drive alone in this treacherous weather.

Helen agreed – with considerable relief. She hated fog and, not having her own car, was unused to driving in conditions as bad as these.

They had travelled barely a couple of miles – very slowly, for the icy road surface made them even more vulnerable to running off the road – when Christopher drew up on to the grass verge.

'I'm sorry,' he said, switching off the engine. 'Can't see a thing. I can't risk both our lives by continuing.'

'It's all my fault,' said Helen swiftly. 'I was irresponsible, not even thinking about the time. I was too interested in our conversation.'

His smile was momentary, and disappeared all too quickly.

'What'll we do?' she asked.

'Wait. Hope it'll clear.'

It was Christopher who eventually found the path to one of the mountain huts constructed as a refuge for skiers. Rather than lifting, the fog had intensified. Helen had shivered twice and he'd insisted on leaving the car. When they located the hut, though, she was puzzled by the grim air lurking behind his relief.

'It'll be infinitely warmer than the car,' he told her, yet still she noticed how tense he seemed.

He was right about the interior of the hut. She smiled appreciatively when he closed the door behind them. There was a torch beside the doorframe and he beamed it around their tiny quarters, revealing not only an oil lamp but a primitive heating stove. He lit them both while she took folded blankets from a well-insulated chest.

'Come and warm your hands,' he suggested, kneeling beside the stove.

Helen joined him at once.

Close beside him her perfume was drawn out by the heat, a fragrance that alerted all his senses. Chris knew he ought to move away, creating space between them. But Helen leaned her head against him in a gesture as innocent and as affectionate as a kitten's.

'If I had to be marooned here, I'm glad it's with you,' she admitted. She so enjoyed his company, relished the absence of the contention that always came with Alex's presence. And then there was the way Alex was with women. Look how readily he'd picked up with Berry! Despite his assurances, she'd not have felt easy alone with him here.

'Helen, don't . . .'

'But it's the truth. I thought you liked me being direct?'

Christopher didn't respond. How ironic to find himself isolated here with the one girl who could make him forget everything he was committed to.

'Chris – forgive me for asking, but are you married?'

He shook his head, and swallowed. 'No.'

She stirred slightly. Her hair brushed his cheek. Sighing, he rose and crossed briskly towards the blankets. He felt her watching him and could only guess her thoughts. Before he'd controlled the emotions making him move from the stove, she was beside him again. Unfolding the blanket, he discovered that was precisely what it was – huge, but only one.

'I suppose the idea is that you keep each other warm,' Helen said lightly. 'Come on.'

'You take the blanket. I'm all right.'

'Rubbish! You'll be frozen.' She paused, looking

into his eyes in the thin light from the lamp. 'What's wrong?'

He shook his head.

'We're fully clothed, for Heaven's sake!' Helen exclaimed. 'And not just a couple of fools.'

Still Christopher did not speak. Even last night, after seeing her only the once, he'd been too disturbed to sleep for wanting her. The longing had flared again today with renewed urgency. It might be endured from the other side of a cafe table. Here, it threatened to overwhelm him.

Helen was smiling. 'I'm going to take a risk,' she said forthrightly, 'and admit that I was hoping we might see each other again, once we get back to Yorkshire. I know we've only just met, but we seem to share so much.'

'Helen, please . . .'

She looked straight into his eyes. Christopher could not doubt the affection in her gaze, nor that it bordered on the emotion he was feeling for her. He tried to move away again, and felt his will weakening. Just this once, he thought. Just once . . .

Her kiss was impulsive, so unexpected that it took him by surprise.

'You see,' she said huskily, 'I'm drawn to you as well, Chris. It's not something to regret, my dear.'

'You don't know what you're saying.'

Again she kissed him, stopping his words with lips that prevented his from remaining aloof. Inwardly he groaned, yet could not let her go. He was kissing her feverishly, urging her lips to part for him. Her arms slid around him, anchoring him against her. He felt her fingers press his back.

Desire leapt within him in a million pinpoints of light and warmth.

Helen sighed against his lips, surrendering all

memories of the years when studies and work had left no time for love. For so long now she had struggled to learn, turning herself into the self-sufficient individual she was never meant to be. Here with Chris she had already discovered so much that could colour her life. She longed to discover more.

Abruptly, he broke away from her. His hands went to hers, wrenched them away.

'No, my dear.'

But his voice was soft and tremulous. And it confirmed to Helen all that she'd suspected. Now she knew he felt as she did, she couldn't accept that he meant this should not continue.

'It isn't just sex, is it?' she said. 'I'll agree it's very swift, but does that have to mean it's wrong? I'd not let anything happen – *you know*. I wasn't brought up to do owt like that without getting married, but . . .'

'Helen, my dear, I'm sorry. We shouldn't even continue seeing each other. I told you I'm studying – it's for the priesthood.'

'A priest?' she gasped. Eventually, after considering, she smiled. 'Happen I should have guessed. You'll be pretty good.'

They talked after that, about their very different careers and about Einsiedeln, no longer acknowledging anything that had passed between them. After a time they slept fitfully, backs to one another and drawing some comfort from the solitary blanket.

Although the fog had vanished, Chris insisted on driving her into Lucerne next morning. When he drew up outside the hotel he offered his hand.

'Goodbye then,' he said, and released her fingers. Briefly, he caressed her cheek. 'Take care of yourself, Helen.' His voice was ragged. Hurriedly he got out of the car, slammed the door and strode away without glancing back. She watched him hail a taxi, and then it drove away too quickly.

Inside the taxi Chris sat rigid, his hands thrust into his pockets. He was shivering violently in shock, biting on his lips as he tried to will control into a body which seemed drained.

He closed his eyes. 'God help us,' he prayed urgently.

Chapter 4

'Where the hell have you been?' Alexander jerked open the car door. 'I've never been more worried in all my life.'

Still shattered by the finality of the goodbye she'd said to Christopher, Helen stared at him, bewildered.

'I don't see why. You were with Berenice. Why bother about me?'

'You stopped out all night. And Berry's parents rang yesterday, insisted she went home. Why the blazes didn't you let me know where you were?'

'I couldn't, Alex. The fog came down, I spent the night stranded in a sort of refuge for skiers.'

'We'd better cut the explanations, get on our way. I've packed for you, paid the bills. We can sort out finances later.'

Watching him dash back into the hotel, Helen realised that the luggage placed just inside the glass doors was theirs. That Alex had been waiting there for her.

'Just a minute,' she began indignantly when he'd flung their cases into the car. 'I didn't hear you asking if I was ready for going home yet. If you think you're taking me back as some sort of punishment . . .'

'I don't, and I'm not,' he snapped, getting into the driving seat. 'We're quitting Europe as fast as we can because we've got to. Hitler marched into Vienna yesterday evening. We're not staying this close to the Austrian border, nor to Germany.'

'Hitler did what?' she asked incredulously.

'Marched his armies into Vienna. And was well received, by the sound of it. Not surprising, considering he was born in Austria.'

'Oh, Lord! Right then – I agree, we've got to get home. Thanks for packing my stuff, Alex. Sure you found everything?'

He started up the engine. 'I double-checked. Had time and to spare – I couldn't sleep so was up around four.'

'I am sorry you were so alarmed. But there really was no need.'

'Good. Then we'll forget the whole business.'

I'll never do that, thought Helen as Alex eased out into the traffic. There's no possibility that I shall ever forget Einsiedeln, and certainly not the man I met there. For the first time in years the prospect of learning more about architecture, even of qualifying, seemed less than exciting. She believed she would recover the urge to work, but nothing would be the same.

'It won't be the same, you know,' Alexander began, startling her by appearing to tune in to her thoughts. But then he continued: 'If we end up with a major conflict on our hands, building will cease. Or the sort that interests us will. There'll be government constructions but precious little else.'

'It mightn't come to war,' she said, wishing with all her heart that there was some means of influencing the future. If only she'd known all this yesterday in the abbey, she could have . . .

'We can only pray that the powers concerned have more sense.'

Pray? thought Helen, wondering how much he

really meant of what he'd said – and how she'd known him so long yet it was still so shallowly.

'There's nothing folk like us can actually *do*,' Alex added, 'not to affect their decisions.'

Grimly, Helen recognised how true she felt that was. Yesterday – ah, well, *yesterday* she'd been close to accepting there might be a means of harnessing some higher intervention.

'The future's being taken out of our hands. That's how I feel, any road,' said Alex dourly.

Helen was no more willing than he to accept the threat of war, yet she could not visualise any way of ensuring that they hang on to peace. Moments ago the prospect of returning to further her career had seemed less appealing; now she supposed that being allowed to do just that was the best she could hope for.

It wasn't yet an hour since she and Christopher had parted, but reality had come between them, as insurmountable as concrete walls. Away from him, she had her emotions sufficiently under control to recognise how many-faceted their brief relationship had become. Maybe if it had remained purely a matter of being attracted to each other, it would have troubled them less.

A priest. This man she'd grown too fond of was a priest. How could she have let that happen? Ordinarily, she wouldn't have been drawn to anyone connected with religion. But then – ordinarily she'd have found an abbey to be no more than an interesting structure.

'No time to look at any of the towns we pass through, I'm afraid,' Alex told her, and she was glad. Her senses were too raw for that. Pleasure would feel as bad as pain while this great gap yawned in her life.

'You're not saying much,' Alex remarked at last. 'Not scared are you, by Hitler's tactics? Britain won't enter the conflict yet awhile.'

'I'm not scared of that, no. I'm just tired out. I didn't sleep much either.'

She stayed quiet throughout their journey across France. Only when they were aboard the ship heading towards Dover did she begin to realise she must exert herself and take up her life again.

The interlude in Einsiedeln must become no more than that – an interval as beautiful as the abbey itself. And even if it was love that had brought Christopher and herself together, it was love of a special kind – blissful, thrilling to the senses and imbued with tenderness. But the truth of their situation was much harsher. There could be no future for them together in the real world.

The first few weeks back in Yorkshire were grim. Knowing that Chris would have returned to studying in Leeds didn't help Helen to settle to her own work. Some days, feeling that he was so near made dismissing the thought of him impossible. She went about the city, across the Headrow, along Briggate or Bond Street, in and out of Lewis's and Schofield's, often seeing in the distance a darkly dressed man with black wavy hair. And always being obliged to quieten her disappointed, racing heart because the man proved to be a stranger.

Even in class, mention of some religious building or other would resurrect mind pictures of the abbey, and of his face, his smile.

Helen hadn't reckoned with this inner yearning which reawakened so readily and remained to torment. And she certainly hadn't expected to discover she possessed a curious strain of morality which appeared to protest repeatedly, if silently, because of his calling. I didn't know, she often reminded herself. Until it was too late, I'd never once suspected there'd be a reason like that for not seeing him ever again.

But after a time, even the hours spent in the biscuit factory ceased to be surrendered quite so frequently to thoughts of Christopher. The threat of war had faded a little at home; in thanks for that, she willed herself to concentrate more intensely on her studies.

Alex reverted to his normal self, holding forth on the latest new buildings, deriding her affection for older styles. Their class went over to Halifax to study its eighteenth-century Piece Hall, and Alex started by asserting they were all barmy to bother looking at that. But during the course of their visit he began to reverse his opinion. The rooms, constructed in three tiers, were well planned for giving previous centuries of cloth merchants space and a bit of privacy for negotiating deals. And although the entire construction was colonnaded, it wasn't over-ornate.

'Maybe it was quite functional, for the time,' he conceded. And had them all grinning. 'What's wrong now?' he demanded, and several of their fellow students laughed. 'You lot look at me as if I'm the only one that's at all progressive.'

'Happen you are, Alex,' Helen suggested, though she was well aware that Harold Tilsley, for one, had been showing around photographs of the De La Warr Pavilion in Bexhill-on-Sea, and extolling it as the epitome of modernity.

They had all been obliged to hear Harold out on how it was the first new Continental public building in the modern style, concrete-clad but built of lightweight steel. That day, he had very evidently risen in Alexander Stone's estimation. Today, Helen noticed Harold was giving Alex a funny look, as if wondering if he could be believed.

She decided to have a bit of fun. Ever since visiting

Europe she'd felt more confident in her own judgement. Leaving the Piece Hall and beginning to walk uphill into the shopping streets, she paused and pointed over to their right.

'I daresay you'll have come round to realising that's very good an' all, Alex, won't you?' she exclaimed, pointing towards the Town Hall.

He all but spluttered with indignation. 'Never! Never, in this world. Talk about Victorian . . .'

'But it was designed by Barry – that's prestigious enough for owt – and I'll bet your dad would emphasise how *functional* it is!'

Glancing through the group towards her, Alex spotted the amusement in her grey eyes and groaned. 'All right, you've had me on. But you'll be laughing the other side of your face soon enough, when you begin looking for work and get turned down for being so out-moded.'

The other students were enjoying the exchange which was, after all, one of the many to brighten their hard slog. Helen, however, although continuing to smile, was privately uneasy. Hadn't she herself wondered from time to time if there would be a place for an architect who leaned so much towards styles out of the past?

'Do you think I'm old fashioned?' she asked her sister that evening.

Still holding the spoonful of egg which she'd been trying to persuade her small son to eat, Marian turned to her. 'Well, if you aren't, I don't know who is!'

'Thank you very much.'

Her sister smiled over her shoulder then returned to tidying the rim of egg yolk from around Mark's face. 'You shouldn't ask such daft questions. You leave yourself wide open. I hope you have more sense while you're at college.'

'But that's what it's all about really. There's always been Alex and me at opposite ends. He's allus been in favour of Art Deco and all that, and I suppose I'm just stuffy.'

Their father interrupted at that. 'Well, I don't pretend to know much about it, but there's some grand buildings gone up during the past ten years, and not all of them modern-looking. I'm thinking of the Viceroy's House in New Delhi – proper grand that was. I still have the picture that I cut out of t'paper.'

'Aye, but that was Edwin Lutyens, you see. I'm not reckoning I'll ever be as good as him.' She was pleased as well as surprised, nevertheless, that her father had been so interested in any building.

'Does it matter then?' Marian asked, as she moved Mark's high-chair and sat down at the table. 'Being old-fashioned, I mean?'

Helen's grin was rueful. 'Eh, I don't know. I'm afraid it might, if I don't fit in with other architects in the practice.'

'I can imagine that might lead to difficulties,' Marian said, nodding as she straightened her chair so her sister could take the next one to it.

'I'll just have to wait and see, I suppose. Any road, I'm already having to adapt some of my ideas in order to fit in with our student projects.'

'You'll find just the place, I'm sure,' Kathleen asserted, coming through from the kitchen with a tureen of tripe and onions. 'And it's only what you deserve.' She was that proud of the way their Helen had stuck to this course. Nobody on either side of the family had ever tackled anything that involved half as much studying.

Seeing the tripe, Marian wrinkled her nose, glanced sideways at Helen, and then remembered. Mum and Dad were being very good, keeping them and the two children for nothing until Denis started his new job. She'd made up her mind it was only fair not to let one word of complaint disturb things.

Marian had learned a lot during nearly six years of marriage. And if her love of fun had had to be suppressed sometimes, there wasn't much else that had gone by the board. She and Denis still got on well together, and even her mother could find nowt wrong with young Mark and Linda. They had had to be good for much of their short lives; Marian and Denis had often been in rented accommodation, sometimes with actors from the company as neighbours who had needed quiet at home while they were learning lines.

It seemed a long time now since they'd set up house so optimistically in Stratford. Although his job there had lasted until just the other week, their circumstances had changed. First Linda had come along, and then Mark, and there'd been no chance of Marian herself going out to work while she had them to look after. They'd been obliged to give up their first home, and that was when they'd started living in flats, most of them in houses owned by the theatre. The car had been sold. Denis now travelled around by motorbike which Marian hated.

They had moved back to Halifax so she could be near her mother who would help with Linda and Mark, freeing her to look for a job. Once Denis started as Assistant Stage Manager at the Grand Theatre in Leeds they would begin saving again for a place of their own.

Marian smiled to herself, watching the way her father was encouraging Linda to come to the table. Now she'd started school, she always wanted a pencil in her hand, or a slate pencil. Helen had bought her a wooden-framed slate, and it certainly made sense being able to clean the drawings off so that Linda could start all over again.

'I reckon she's taking after you, you know, Helen. It's allus houses she's doing.'

'Isn't it the same with all children? They're easy to draw.'

'It'd be nice, though, wouldn't it? You'd be able to teach her all she needs to know.'

Helen laughed. 'I doubt that. By the time I get to the end of my training, I'll have forgotten what I learnt at the beginning.'

'But I thought you'd have to remember it all, love?' Kathleen protested seriously. She tried to grasp everything it involved, but subjects like 'theory of construction', 'specifications' and 'professional practice' were beyond her.

'That is the general idea, Mum,' Helen replied patiently. 'It's only me going on about it taking forever.'

'We did warn . . .' Kathleen began.

Her husband cut in, smiling. 'You're taking our Helen too serious again,' he exclaimed. 'You only have to look at her to know she loves the work.'

'Our Helen's a serious young woman,' Marian announced, over the top of their father's voice.

All the adults plus young Mark laughed.

'What did you say that's funny, Mummy?' Linda inquired. She hated not understanding what was going on.

Marian gave her a hug. 'Eh, love, it was summat and nowt. I was only being daft.'

'You tell me off for that.'

'I do, an' all. And I'm afraid that's something that's going to happen for a long while yet. Not fair, is it?'

The child shook her blonde curly head, and her grandfather stroked the silky-textured hair. 'Never mind, Linda love – we have our bit of fun, any road, don't we?'

Greatly attached to each other, Daniel Clegg and his granddaughter spent hours playing dominoes or snakes and ladders. And the toffees he brought home from work contributed enormously to his popularity.

'What time will Denis be in?' Kathleen asked. She had finished serving out portions of tripe and onions and returned the lid to the tureen ready to put it back in the oven.

'Can't be sure, Mum, sorry.' Marian felt embarrassed already. Denis knew his in-laws liked to eat as soon as her father had washed after work. Her husband had been out all day in Leeds. One of his pals was the Stage Manager at the theatre and that was how Denis had heard about the job. And not having started there yet wasn't keeping him away. She knew how it would be, an' all – a few pints in the local every time they weren't needed backstage.

If they weren't so short of brass she wouldn't mind his drinking. He always knew when to stop, and it did put him in a good mood and usually made him quite amorous. That was one thing that hadn't changed – he was a lovely man, especially in bed. Marian had been worried for a long time after Mark's birth because they would never get on their feet if they risked having another. But then she'd been to one of the clinics opened by Dr Marie Stopes. She wouldn't dare mention that visit in her mother's hearing but it had put her own mind at rest.

Their Helen *was* old fashioned an' all, Marian reflected, remembering the day she'd told her sister how you didn't have to have children if you didn't want any more. Helen had been appalled. Even when Marian had explained that she'd only wanted her to benefit from what she'd discovered, Helen had still looked at her as though she was doing something really wicked.

'How can you see a couple of lovely children like your two, and wish to prevent any more being born!' she'd exclaimed.

'Just you wait,' Marian had retorted. 'Your turn'll come. And happen sooner than you think, after you've had all these years scrimping and saving. You'll have nowt behind you if you get married. You'll be too scun up to have a load of children round you.'

It was a pity their Helen was taking so long to qualify, Marian thought. She'd be a grand little mother, more practical in lots of ways than she herself was.

Helen's career called for a great deal of practicality these days. The students were often expected to visit sites – assessing their suitability, measuring up, and planning drainage and all the other essential services which must be incorporated in every building project.

She relished these outings which made the future seem nearer, and loved surprising her fellow students. The first time had been one murky November day while they were down by the River Aire in Leeds where an old warehouse had burned down. Developers were planning a mill there, but when Helen and the others arrived to inspect the site the original place wasn't quite demolished. Half a dozen rats shot out and some of her companions went ashen with shock. They seemed quite put out because she hadn't flinched. And she often proved herself their equal in physical tasks. She was glad now that she had a strong frame, had nearly forgotten the days when she'd envied her sister's fragility.

And Alex didn't seem to think there was much wrong with her. Ever since the trip to Europe he'd appeared less eager to go out with every attractive girl he could find. He made such a point of hanging around Helen when they were visiting construction sites that the other students were forever ribbing them. What the others didn't know was that she was often invited to Alexander's home now.

The first time she returned there, she had been wondering why it was that Joseph Stone had pressed his son to ask her to join them that Saturday. Rather anxiously, she had got out of Alex's car in which she'd been driven to Brearley. They had stopped on the way at her own home, so that she could clean up and change after spending the morning under instruction at a site where foundations were being dug.

At home, her parents were just starting their midday dinner, but they had welcomed Alex warmly enough when he was introduced to them.

'I'll just pop mine back in t'oven while I pour you a cup of tea, lad,' Kathleen Clegg had exclaimed, seeming far less perturbed than Helen had expected. 'I'm glad we're getting to know one of Helen's friends at last.'

'Aye,' Daniel had added, as Helen went into the kitchen to wash. 'And since you're a Stone, I suppose you'll be one of the family that's architects already?'

'That's right, sir. My father's Joseph Stone.'

It was after Helen had changed and reappeared at the foot of the stairs, though, that she really learned how well they were getting on together. Having reached their second course, Kathleen and her husband were inviting Alex to try a portion of sponge pudding.

'Go on, lad,' said Daniel. 'Helen's mum makes the lightest pudding in t'West Riding. It won't spoil your dinner at home.'

Handing him a plate, Kathleen was beaming. 'You

needn't let on to your own mother that you've already had a bit of summat to eat.'

'Actually, Mrs Clegg, we only have a housekeeper. I'm afraid my mother's been dead for many a year.'

'Eh, you poor love! Well, just you think on – if you ever want a bit of extra comfort, you know where to come.'

'You have lovely people,' Alex had told Helen warmly as they sped along Burnley Road.

But she had been less than happy about the impression she was likely to make on Alex's father when there were no other students to fill the conversational gaps.

She had reckoned without Joseph Stone's determination to learn more about her. During the period since her initial visit he had gradually probed until discovering from his son that Helen's course at the college had been facilitated by the bursary from old Mr March.

'I'm glad to learn you know Seth March,' he began as soon as he had given her a glass of sherry.

'You know him as well, do you, Mr Stone?' she exclaimed, her grey eyes shining delightedly.

'March taught me a lot, I'll have you know. When I was articled he was one of the bosses. Couldn't have had a better chap in charge, either. Firm, he was, but rightly so. Made us work damned hard but was generous with his knowledge. And with his brass as well – he footed the bill for a trip abroad for me and another lad. Took us to see some fine buildings. Berne was one place we visited, and the Abbey at Einsiedeln . . .'

Alex groaned.

His father gave him a look. 'Did you get to see Einsiedeln? You never said.'

While Alex shook his head, Helen smiled. 'I went there, though.'

'I didn't think it'd be his cup of tea. You liked it, I'll bet?'

'I said at the time that "liked" doesn't really express it.'

'I agree, my dear, heartily.'

After that kind of a beginning, Helen couldn't spend the afternoon feeling awkward with Joseph Stone. During the meal he continued drawing her out concerning the places she had visited in Europe. 'Waste of time asking him,' he declared, inclining his head towards Alex, 'he won't elaborate on anything he saw out there.'

'You know the reason, Father.'

Joseph gestured dismissively with a large, neatly manicured hand. 'You'll learn, given time, all this modern stuff you fancy isn't necessarily always best.'

During subsequent visits to The Stone House Helen had discovered that she wasn't the only one who grew tired of Alexander's perpetual support of contemporary styling. One evening Joseph reminded him he was becoming a bore, and pointedly began questioning Helen about her other interests. He thoroughly approved of her love of reading, and surprised her by having a taste for recent fiction. They found a common affection for J.B. Priestley, and discussion of his books soon led to comparing notes on the plays he'd written.

This brought Alex back into the conversation, and both men were interested to learn of her brother-in-law's job at Leeds Grand Theatre.

'You never told me he worked backstage,' said Alex.

'Mustn't have cropped up,' Helen replied, although she thought she had mentioned the fact some time during the past few years. It occurred to her then that, much as she liked Alexander, he didn't always take a lot of interest in other folk.

One Sunday during that summer of 1938 she was invited to his home for dinner. She'd had to check on the time she'd be expected to arrive – knowing how very much more grand the Stones' lifestyle was than her own family's, she had thought they would dine in the evening.

The meal, however, was at one o'clock and, although accompanied by a good claret – sheer luxury to her – it was essentially the kind of meal her mother would have prepared. After chatting with Alex and his father while they finished coffee, Helen was asked if she had any plans for the afternoon.

'Well, no, not really.'

Joseph beamed. 'Then I'd like to take you both over to Todmorden. There's a site I want you to see.'

Because none of them was dressed for trudging over rough earth from which chunks of sandstone still protruded, they remained in the car when they arrived there. But Joseph ensured that neither Helen nor his son missed anything.

'They're just starting to level the site, as you can see. It's a factory we've planned here – you, Alex, will be glad to know it's on modern lines. There's enough many-storeyed eyesores in these parts, with their uninspiringly featureless walls. This one's going to be different. Lighter, constructed in steel, then concrete-faced. And the windows will have a bit of character as well as serving their purpose. It's time we got away from rows of them, all looking alike.

'We're going to use the features of the land itself, as well,' he continued, pointing out the curve of the hillside as it embraced the area being cleared. 'The wall facing that way won't be straight but will follow the line of the hill. That's where the offices will be, with plenty of glass to prevent their being overshadowed. I'd wondered at first about putting offices at the front of the building, it's where they're usually placed, and there's a view over yonder towards the stream that's just out of sight from where we are.'

Joseph grinned. 'It was the boss who put a stop to that, claiming there'd be no work done if I made the outlook too pleasant. As it is, I'll give them some space between the offices and the hillside. And that'll no doubt come in useful for parking. It won't be long before everybody in business will get around by car.'

On their way back to Brearley, Helen noticed Alex smiling to himself. He nudged her arm. 'Look up there – quick. That's Yeoman's Grange, the house I designed, the one I told you about.'

Helen heard his father's laugh, but she was more interested in trying to lean near enough to the car window to see the house properly. They were too close to the hill for her to gain more than a brief impression of a large, well-proportioned building whose clean new stone was gleaming in the sunlight.

'Go on,' said Joseph genially. 'You've indulged me by letting me show you my latest scheme. I reckon we can indulge Alexander this once.'

He turned off to the left up a lane so narrow that Helen feared for the Rolls-Royce's gleaming bodywork while they swung around bends between the drystone walls. 'Oh, do mind your lovely car!'

Joseph Stone laughed. 'You like it then? Bought this in 1929.'

'It's gorgeous. I love the blue sides. They contrast so well with all that black. Does this model have a name?'

'It's a Phantom, my dear – Cabriolet de Ville.'

But now they were there, looking down on the farmhouse, able to appreciate its economical lines and flat roof, unusual for the West Riding.

'I said he was daft letting them go ahead with their ideas for a roof like that,' Joseph told her. 'But the folk who live there insisted, and they have a point. Whilst they have one bit of a garden, the rest is given over to the farm animals. They'd never manage to keep a larger area to themselves.'

'There's a grandmother lives with them, and she's not so fond of cows coming that close they almost get into the house,' Alex explained, 'And they've got several youngsters in their teens. I gather they use the roof a lot, for sitting out with the old girl in summer. It isn't so noticeable from here, but that's an edging wall for safety.'

Helen was nodding. 'I like it, Alex, I really like it.'

He pretended to be overcome. 'God, I never thought I'd live to see the day!'

She grinned. 'And the view is terrific – they certainly had to ensure that didn't go to waste.'

It was that evening when Joseph Stone first put the suggestion to her. They had pressed her to stay for tea and were sitting afterwards in a small drawing room, watching the sun dropping towards the far hill, darkening the full-leafed trees until their fresh greens turned the shade of cypresses.

'Have you thought yet where you'll work once you're qualified, Helen? I'd like you to consider the possibility of coming to Stone's.'

She was staggered, so astonished that she could hardly frame a coherent sentence.

'Oh. Mr Stone, I never in all my wildest imaginings . . . I mean – well, you'll be taking Alex full time naturally, and . . .'

'Think about it,' Joseph interrupted with a smile. 'A decision like that needs a lot of consideration.'

'Oh, but – I mean I'm not in the least reluctant,

you mustn't think that for one moment.'

'She's simply "gobsmacked" – that's one of your favourite words, isn't it, Helen?' Alex put in.

She laughed awkwardly. 'It's just about the only word for what I'm feeling, aye!'

And so no decisions were made, but Helen was delighted and immensely heartened to learn that Joseph Stone wanted her to work with him. She was less certain how his son viewed that prospect. And she was beginning to realise that she'd sacrifice quite a lot rather than disturb Alex.

As autumn came to the West Riding, however, in strong winds that tore the leaves from trees and buffeted folk walking its steep streets, Helen noticed that Alexander appeared undismayed by his father's offering her a position with the family firm. In fact, he seemed friendlier than ever, frequently taking her out to some eating house that was beyond her own pocket, or to the newly constructed cinema in Broad Street.

They had argued the first time, just as usual, over merits and demerits in the cinema's styling. But then they had laughed at themselves, and hugged each other in the sudden recognition that their friendship had weathered worse conflicts.

Helen and Alex returned to Todmorden on a Saturday afternoon in October. The site to which Joseph Stone had taken them was unrecognisable now, the offices all but completed and the adjoining factory level with the first-storey windows.

Joseph himself was growing over-familiar with the place, and had no desire to spend leisure hours there, but both Helen and his son enjoyed going along to inspect progress. They were sufficiently near the end of their training to be able to realise how they would feel when visiting the site of one of their own buildings.

'Do you want to stop for tea in Hebden Bridge?' Alex asked, reluctant to have Helen leave him. Although admitting it to no one, he was growing dissatisfied with generally seeing her only in company. And yet with her he needed more encouragement than he ever received before he would suggest they spend more time together. She was so different from the girls he'd known that even after all this time he wasn't really sure why she wasn't more responsive. She wasn't seeing any other chap, yet still she seemed to be holding back.

Helen was glad to have tea out with him. She'd never liked autumn – it always made her aware that the end of another year was approaching, making her think of all the things she hadn't yet achieved. This year, she still couldn't get Christopher Maitland out of her head, and seemed unable to return to the way she'd once been, content with her own company.

Before heading towards the cafe, they turned up their collars against the cold and strolled over bridges and through the narrow streets, trying to picture Hebden Bridge as it had been in the days when the weaving of cloth first moved from cottages into some of these forbidding mills and became an industry. Many of the factories and rows of terraced houses had changed hardly at all during the intervening years, but the local people had.

Watching some of the women in their shorter skirts and permed hair, Helen smiled to herself. How their grandmothers would have stared.

While they were having tea Alex asked how much she knew about this part of the Calder Valley. 'There's a lot gone on here. Have you ever heard of Nutclough Fustian Manufacturing Company, for instance?'

When she said she hadn't, he was happy to enlighten her. He admired workers with initiative. 'They got together round about 1870 – a band of fustian cutters. You know what fustian is, of course?'

'Some kind of cloth, isn't it?'

He nodded. 'Cord – corduroy. There's a great deal made round here. Anyway, they formed a highly successful producer-cooperative, one of the best in Britain. Not only that, they believed in education for adults. One of the weavers of fustian became involved in founding the Workers' Education Association.'

They talked so long that when they finally emerged from the cafe it had grown dark and all the gas-lamps were lit. Alex grinned.

'I suppose we'd better be getting back. Are you going to spend the evening with us?'

'Eh, I'd love to, thanks, but I ought to be on my way home. They'll be wondering wherever I've got to.'

'You can phone them, can't you?'

Helen gave him a look. 'Do you really think we run to having a telephone!'

'Sorry, I . . .'

Helen giggled. 'Don't go all uncomfortable about it. I'm not.'

Alex had driven half a mile or so, however, when they had to draw in to the kerb to make way for a clanging fire engine. A further mile along the road, they saw two more appliances tearing along from the direction of Halifax. Watching them turn off up the hillside, Helen noticed Alex had slowed the car again, and was staring, appalled.

'Oh, God – oh, no!' he exclaimed, before following the fire engines up the steep lane.

'Oh, Alex, it isn't . . .'

The farm which they had stopped to admire during their previous journey out here was ablaze. With only one eye on the walls lining the lane, Alex drove on, most of his attention riveted on the glow from the flames.

They were halted by a police officer before they could take off down to Yeoman's Grange itself. Four fire engines were filling the yard, a fifth was stationed in the nearest field. Alex wound down the car window.

'What about the family – have they got out?'

The policeman nodded. 'Aye, sir, thank goodness. The blaze was spotted by one of the farmer's lads coming home for his tea. He dashed in and made them all leave afore it got a proper hold, like.'

'Where had this lot started then?'

'Don't ask me. It'll be the fire brigade as has to fathom that. Though, to me, it looked like it had begun in the barn. That were well alight when I got here.'

'But that's yards away from the house.'

'I know, and I'm only surmising. It's not for me to hazard even a guess as to how it spread.'

'Where've the family gone then? To a neighbour's?'

'First of all, to leave the animals there. Then they'll go on to a brother of the old lady's, I think. Do you know them then, sir?'

Alexander nodded, swallowing. He choked on the smoke as the officer moved away to speak to one of the firemen.

'Dear, dear, what a tragedy,' said Helen, unable to think of anything to say that could make Alex feel any better. 'Let's get home.' She could see how distressed he was. 'There's nothing you can do, love.'

'How can I just drive off?' he demanded. 'How the heck can I?'

He got out of the car, leaving the door ajar as he ran towards the fire officer. He'd never have an easy minute if he didn't find out how the blaze had started.

The policeman was asking if all the farm animals had been rescued.

'Most of 'em, aye,' the brigade chief replied. 'They lost one of their cows and they're not sure they've got all the hens safe, but the rest's accounted for.'

'Where are they then?' Alex inquired, coughing as he tried to peer through the smoke and the flames silhouetting what remained of the buildings.

'I gather that the poultry were outside when it began, and they fluttered and scrabbled their way over into yon field. The cattle were rounded up. They were being led to t'farm next door when we got here. The milking parlour were t'other side of the barn. It'll not be fit for use, even if it's still standing tomorrow.'

'Did it begin in the barn?' asked Alex.

Both men gave him a dubious look. 'You don't belong to this place, do you?' the policeman said.

'No, but I designed the farmhouse.'

'I see.' The fire officer sighed. 'And it's not been finished more than a few months either. Well, sir, can't do no harm to tell you we believe it began in the barn, though what caused it to flare up is less certain.'

'But how on earth did it spread across to the house?'

'That we do know – the young chap who was on his way home saw it happening. He were right up yonder, on his way down through the fields, when he spotted the barn was ablaze and heard all the pandemonium the cattle and poultry were making. And then he saw that one cow, the poor bugger that set light to the house. Like a torch the beast was. Came tearing across the yard from the barn, its hide on fire. It panicked, made for the open house door. It was floundering, struggling to get in over t'step, when this lad caught up.'

'And the entrance hall had wooden panels,' said

Alex, aghast. 'They were that pleased with their panelling.'

The fire officer shook his head regretfully. 'Aye, it caught straight away by all accounts, from a bit of a curtain that the missus here allus kept across the door.'

'I remember that curtain. I thought it spoiled the whole effect, but she would have it. Said it kept flies out while she had the door open and prevented draughts in winter.' Alex was coughing repeatedly now and was compelled to turn his head away from the worst of the whirling smoke. He became aware of the heat, searing his face and hands even from this distance.

'We'll just have to be thankful there was no loss of life – human life, I mean,' said the policeman.

'But I don't understand – how could the family fail to hear all the commotion?' Alex asked.

'According to the son that got them out, they were all at the far side of the house, having a meal after they'd finished milking, and they had the wireless on.'

Watching him walk dispiritedly back towards the car, Helen yearned to put her arms around Alex. When he eventually sank on to the seat beside her, she saw in the light from the dashboard that his face was blackened with soot. The grime was streaked in channels below his eyes, and she sensed that it wasn't only the stinging smoke which was causing his tears.

'Do you want me to drive?' she asked, glad when he nodded and there was something she could do for him.

Except for coughing and blowing his nose, he remained silent until she had driven along as far as Brearley and taken the lane leading up to The Stone House.

'Stop here, will you?' he said in a voice that rasped when they approached the entrance to the drive.

'What is it, love?' Helen asked gently as she parked

the car and set the handbrake.

The car reeked of burning and Alex kept coughing. She'd have thought that all he'd want by now would be to go indoors.

'Just give me a minute, Helen.'

She saw that he was weeping still, making no attempt to check his distress.

'Eh, Alex love, come here.'

She drew him to her, held him while he cried out all the despair that had enveloped him while he stood there watching the first place he'd ever designed destroying itself.

Chapter 5

The night that fire ruined Yeoman's Grange was etched on to Helen's memory. Long after she and Alex eventually went into his home and began describing the horror of it all to Joseph Stone, they were still profoundly shaken.

She was disturbed most of all by how changed Alex was after witnessing the blaze – but maybe it was truer to say that he'd never before permitted anyone to see him moved. Certainly his father seemed staggered that Alex had taken it so to heart. It was the first time Helen had seen Joseph being gentle with his son.

After giving him a glass of Scotch, he stood behind his chair with a hand on each of Alexander's shoulders. 'You've had to endure something which I'm thankful to say I've never had to suffer. You'll not dismiss in a hurry such violent destruction of a building you designed, your first one and all.'

'I'll be all right once I get over the shock.'

But Alex had been quite unlike his usual self, and when Helen was leaving for home he drew her to him as if he couldn't bear her to go away. He kissed her on the lips, something else that was new, then looked her straight in the eyes. 'You've been marvellous to me today,' he said. 'I shan't forget.'

For weeks afterwards he remained subdued. It hadn't helped when the cause of the fire was officially given as spontaneous combustion of damp straw.

If the barn hadn't been in use for segregating the sick cow which panicked and spread the blaze, the farmhouse might have survived.

Even becoming involved in discussions with the builder who was to reconstruct Yeoman's Grange did little to brighten Alexander's spirits. And since he seemed to wish to spend any free time with Helen, she too began to suffer from an irrational dread of other things proving impermanent.

She thought afterwards that it was perhaps this that made him so understanding on the day he was confronted with another person's loss. It was a Saturday, Helen and her fellow students were meeting that afternoon to study Shibden Hall. She decided to spend the morning telling old Mr March how thrilled she had been by the abbey at Einsiedeln. For ages after returning to Yorkshire her emotions had been too sore for her to wish to relive memories of Christopher and her visit there. More recently, believing that she'd been neglecting the old man, she'd felt awkward about seeing him.

Today, however, she resolved to put that right and telephoned Fenny's home to make arrangements. There was no answer and she was astounded when the operator said the phone had been disconnected. Wondering what on earth was going on, Helen set out, walking briskly as far as the Marches' house on Albert Promenade.

But the place was locked up, no one came when she rang the doorbell repeatedly, and somehow it all looked totally deserted.

Helen was glancing back towards the house after closing the gate behind her when a woman called to her from the next-door garden.

'Are you looking for Miss March, love?'

'Yes. Do you know where she's gone, please? It's not like her to set out on a Saturday except to see her father. And it's early yet for that, I was going to go with her.'

'Eh, dear – you haven't heard then?'

'Heard what?' asked Helen, alarmed. Surely she wasn't about to learn that the old man was ill, or worse still had died?

'You'd better come in for a minute.'

Inside the elegant sitting room Fenny March's neighbour waited until Helen was seated. 'It's going to be a nasty shock, I'm afraid. Did you know Miss March had a sister lived in Austria?'

'No I'm afraid not, but . . .'

'Fenella was worried about her, naturally. She was married to somebody in the university there, I believe. And with them being Jewish . . .'

'I didn't know Miss March was.'

'No? Well, I don't think she was a practising Jew, not for a long time. Anyway, that's why she went out there – to bring her sister back with her.' She paused, swallowed, looked at Helen as though weighing whether she could take the truth.

'Go on – please.'

'If she'd got there sooner, it might have done some good. From what she'd been telling me, lots of folk have managed to get friends and relatives over to England or even to America.'

'But what happened to Miss March?'

'Eh, love – I'm right sorry to have to tell you this. I know you've visited her for years. I've seen you in the garden and so on. I'm afraid she was killed.'

'Oh, God! Oh, no . . .'

'I'll never forget that date, just over a fortnight since. On t'tenth of November there were firebomb attacks on all the synagogues in Vienna.'

'And her sister – was she killed as well?'

'We don't believe she was, though any news you get is unreliable. So far as I know, Fenny March had gone with this sister to her synagogue. I expect they wanted a bit of strength from somewhere to prepare them for the journey. I think word of Fenella's death only reached her father because of her having a British passport.'

'Poor old Mr March. He must be devastated.'

'Aye, he is very cut up about it. Me and my husband went to see him as soon as we heard.'

'He's still in the nursing home, I suppose?'

'Oh, yes.'

'I must get over there straight away.'

Crossley and Porter School clock was striking eleven as Helen thanked the woman and left. She realised that if she was relying on buses to get her to Harrogate and back she wouldn't be in time to join the other students that afternoon. Nor would she be up to going on anywhere. Feeling in her handbag for change, she headed for the nearest telephone kiosk.

'Can I speak to Alex, please, Mr Stone?' she said urgently. 'It's Helen.'

'What's up?' he inquired anxiously as soon as he came on the line. 'Dad said you sounded upset.'

'I am, very. Oh God, Alex, something dreadful's happened. You know the Marches – Fenny who taught me art, and her father who created the scholarship for me?'

'I remember, yes.'

'Well, it's Fenny. She's – she's dead.'

'That's sudden.'

'She's been killed, in Austria – Vienna, I think. I didn't know but they're Jews apparently, and . . . there was a lot of destruction. All the synagogues.'

'I heard about it on the wireless earlier this month. But how?'

Helen told him the rest. Before she'd finished speaking he was offering to drive her over to Harrogate. 'Doesn't matter about Shibden Hall, we can go there any old time.' He told her to go home and wait for him there. He'd be with her in less than half an hour.

Mr March looked rather better than Helen had expected, and his eyes lit up when he saw who was visiting him.

'By, but I'm glad to see you, young Helen. I wondered if I'd ever set eyes on you again.'

'I know I've been neglecting you, and I'm sorry. I'm sorrier still, more upset than I can ever say, to hear about your Fenny.'

'Aye, aye, thank you.' He swallowed, shook his head wearily. 'It's a bad do. When you get to my time of life you don't expect to outlive your offspring.'

'Is there – is there any word of your other daughter?'

'No, love, no. I don't suppose there will be, not while there's so much trouble out there. I'm afraid the best I can hope is that she's been interned – that way, she might survive.' He sighed and cleared his throat. 'All we can do is carry on somehow. I'm glad you've come. It's you young folk we must concentrate on now.'

Looking up, Mr March became aware for the first time of Alexander. But before Helen could introduce them, he was smiling.

'By, but I can guess who you are – specially with Helen thinking of nothing but architecture. You'll be Joseph Stone's lad. There's no mistaking your features.'

Talking of their common interest and filling in

Mr March on how Joseph Stone's practice had progressed seemed to ease some of the sadness. Only when they rose to leave did the old man's expression become grave again. He turned towards Helen.

'Just think on, that's all I ask of you, *think on*. Like I said at the beginning – it's the Fenella March Bursary. As we told you, she had to give up hopes of becoming an architect. Through you and them that benefit after, she won't be forgotten.'

Helen wept most of the way back to Halifax in the car, venting all the emotion held in check whilst visiting Mr March.

The November drizzle drove between the hills. As they crossed North Bridge, she felt a gentle hand on her arm. 'Where to, love? Shall I take you to your family or back to our place?'

She didn't know what she wanted to do, only that she didn't really wish to be with anybody. She shrank from talking about the cause of her distress even to her parents. No one had been in while she was waiting for Alex. Her mother had been busy with Saturday shopping and Dad at his customary football match.

Making the decision for her, Alex headed for his own home. He'd already told his father what had happened. There'd be no need for explanations.

Neither of them had eaten since breakfast. After the briefest of conversations, Joseph Stone left the two of them together in the big panelled dining room. Helen had no appetite, but when Alex attacked the cold beef and salad provided by Mrs Hartley their housekeeper, she made an effort to eat something.

'It's really knocked the stuffing out of me,' she confided afterwards as they sat over a pot of tea.

'That's only to be expected, love, it was such a shock,' said Alex. 'I'm just glad you let me know. You certainly shouldn't have gone over to Harrogate on your own to see Mr March.'

'Thanks for being there. That was all that made it bearable.'

Alexander's company became the thing that most helped Helen to accept the loss of Fenny March, which had made her feel she'd had to grow up very suddenly. Her attachment to her former teacher had been neither fiercely dependent nor nurtured by frequent meetings, but Miss March had been there and Helen still needed at least one person to understand how she felt about her work.

The stress of their final year was upon them, making patience thin at times, but she and Alex were old enough friends now for there to be less chance of any serious friction. If they argued, they bore no grudges, and even when exhausted by revision and exams they still could laugh, mostly at themselves.

Helen was delighted when Joseph Stone repeated his suggestion that she should consider joining his practice. 'You and Alex couldn't be more different in your approach to architecture, but that's all to the good. You'd temper his wilder excesses and he might urge you forward into this twentieth century!'

She smiled and told him that there was nowhere else she'd rather work. And then privately, during her first week there, Joseph Stone said the one thing which set the seal on her sense of achievement.

'I'll never let on to Alexander, Helen, so this'll only be said the once, but you've more natural flair than he'll ever possess. I'm fortunate you've consented to come to us.'

She gladly gave up the evening job at the biscuit factory, and was surprised when the other young women clubbed together for a leaving party and a present. Because she was so absorbed in her architectural studies she had never made any real friendships there; these tokens reassured her that they hadn't thought her entirely stand-offish. And the gift, a set of pens and pencils, delighted her.

When she showed them to Alex in the office, he appeared perturbed.

'What's up?' she asked. 'I thought it was a lovely present. They'll come in ever so useful.'

'I know,' he said. 'I know.' He squeezed her shoulders, and sighed. 'I suppose I've come to forget that you've had to budget for every thing you've ever needed. This has made me realise that I'd have loved to have provided these for you.'

'That's nice, but does it matter? I've got 'em now.'

Alex remained serious. 'You don't see, do you? I've always had so much, it's time I was making up to you for what you've sacrificed.'

She felt touched by this unfamiliar side of him, and began wondering if she'd been blind to what Alex might be feeling for her.

They were too busy, however, for her to dwell on such thoughts.

Joseph Stone was a typical Yorkshireman who believed in obtaining value for money. He had never employed more staff than he required, and almost before they had settled in behind their draftsman's desks, both she and Alex were expected to take their full share of the work.

They were sent out from the office, initially with Frank Barclay, Joseph's right-hand man. They worked long hours: surveying new sites, checking each other's measurements because neither of them would risk errors, and then incurring Frank's displeasure for being slow. They also accompanied him to Council offices while local bye-laws regarding construction were checked, and spent hours discovering where essential services such as drainage were situated.

They inspected partially built factories and houses, chatting with all sorts of building workers until they both felt they had a thorough understanding of far more than the theory of construction which they had studied. Joseph Stone occasionally tossed them a casual word of praise; more often, he merely told them what they next ought to master.

Alexander frequently grumbled about the pace his father expected from them. Helen was simply thrilled to be actually working at last, and thankful to be able to give her mother a decent amount of board money and begin putting something back into the bursary.

At home life was congenial. Both parents were proud as well as relieved that she had only this final practical year to complete. The threat of a world war seemed to have abated, and they were also less worried by now about Marian's situation. The last few years when Kathleen's willingness to care for her grandchildren enabled Marian to work had paid off. Denis had been promoted from Assistant to Stage Manager at Leeds Grand Theatre, and this together with Marian's earnings had ensured them the deposit on a house near Roundhay Park.

Although she spent a lot of time in Alexander's home, he was still an infrequent visitor in Helen's. Inwardly, she knew that this was largely due to her reluctance to invite him there. No matter how well her talent for design developed, she remained rather inhibited by her background and how different it was from his. She wasn't going to let herself become any keener on him unless she had more assurance about Alex's feelings towards her, but he wasn't a man to reveal what they were and gave the impression that he was in no hurry to change a lifestyle that relied on material comfort. Another difference in attitudes.

Helen had never thought that when he did finally surrender his freedom it would be to settle with somebody as ordinary as herself. It was more likely to be for a girl similar to that Berenice, the one he'd clicked with in Lucerne.

She would be sorry if it came to that; she hadn't doubted since the night of the fire that she was fond of Alex. And while she was still so upset by Fenny March's death his concern often warmed her. Even if their affectionate relationship never developed beyond the occasional hug, or perhaps an arm coming about her when something disturbed her, he was always around and she couldn't help being glad that was so. She often noticed how attractive he was, with those lovely grey-green eyes.

It was a wonder that he hadn't prevented her thinking so much about Christopher Maitland since that short encounter in Switzerland. She still frequently needed to remind herself that Chris was only one out of lots of men whom she might meet – that she ought to relegate him to the back part of her mind.

Helen was remembering him on the day in March 1939 when she and Alex set out on the first job they were tackling unsupervised. Driving through an area of Leeds which wasn't familiar from attending the College of Art, she noticed a Hall of Residence connected with the University. It made her ache to see Christopher again.

But Alex was talking, in an ebullient mood now that they were being allowed to exercise a little initiative. He wouldn't let her lapse into reverie. Life was too interesting. They were making for Knaresborough where land acquired by a Halifax businessman was to be used for building a house which seemed to Helen almost a mansion.

Under Joseph Stone's briefing, she and Alex had drawn rough plans and elevations which, after a few alterations, had proved acceptable to their client. Before preparing more detailed plans, they were now going to survey the land, measuring and checking levels. They also had appointments with council officials to formalise arrangements.

Drawing up plans with Alex had been an uneasy process. They still argued over so many aspects of design. Helen had visualised a house something like Shelf Hall, a distinguished mansion of considerable elegance for their part of the West Riding. As she'd anticipated, Alex favoured a far less complex structure with none of the adornments which enhanced the Hall's exterior, and certainly with nothing resembling its portico.

Helen had been delighted, though, when their initial drawings were submitted. The prospective owner had suggested having rather more ornamentation, and the final designs were developing some of the characteristics which she'd originally intended.

Today, however, they were happy together, embarking on their task and looking forward to being entrusted with the groundwork, and to making contact with the builders who had been appointed.

'We'll take some time off as well,' Alex promised suddenly. 'I've squared it with Father.'

'Are you sure about that?' Helen asked, not quite able to forget the time abroad when Alex had been anything but conscientious about his purpose in going there.

'Of course. We're working now, aren't we? That's different altogether from when we were just students. I shan't let him down – and I'll make sure you don't.'

'Steady on,' she reminded him. 'We're supposed to be equals. You're not here to keep an eye on me.'

He laughed. 'Thought that might make you sit up! But you do ask for it, you know. There's many a time when you behave as if you're the only one endowed with a sense of responsibility.'

'Am I that bad?'

Alex smiled sideways at her. 'Actually, you're much better than I give you credit for – in lots of ways. You've been a good pal to me, more than once. And you're the only woman I can say that about!'

Helen studied his face as he concentrated on the traffic and on avoiding the tramlines that bisected the setts of the roadway. She *did* like him. His hair appeared darker here in the car and had a tiny hint of copper in among the golden waves. His eyelashes were long enough to make her or any woman envious, and his mouth had firmed up these past few years, adding a pleasing air of determination to the smile which so often could be winning.

'What is it?' he asked lightly. 'Are you making up for the months when we haven't had time to look at each other?'

She chuckled. 'Happen so. Must admit it's not often I do.'

'I'm well aware of that.' And now the seriousness in his voice surprised her. 'Whereas I could describe you in so many different ways, Helen. Your absorption, and all the emotions you show when you're beside me at the pictures. The way your hair slides over your cheek when you're at your drawing board. The way your eyes glow when you're happy. No one I know has more expressive eyes.'

Helen was so surprised she couldn't think how to reply before Alexander continued.

'Then there's your strength. So often when we're on site I'm astonished by the way you baulk at nothing. And since that awful fire at Yeoman's Grange, well –

you've become special to me.'

By speaking of that night, showing how close he considered they had grown, Alex was sweeping away a lot of her misgivings. Helen felt quite moved. She'd never been so sure that she mattered to him.

Helen had been to Knaresborough before, of course, but never this early in the year. With few visitors in the town, and many of its residents evidently keeping out of the keen north wind, their view of the river seemed very different. The houses clustered about and beneath its bridge looked cosier and more compact as though the chill enforced their close proximity.

'I do love Knaresborough,' she exclaimed, and began hoping there would be an opportunity to wander around the castle. 'It's not a bit like any other town I know.'

'There's certainly no other in these parts with a cave resembling Mother Shipton's.'

'When I was quite little Mum and Dad brought us here, and our Marian got me ever so scared. She really convinced me that Mother Shipton still lived there. "She'll turn you into stone," she said, and nobody could get out of me why I wouldn't stop blubbing.'

'Something tells me I wouldn't take to your Marian.'

'Oh, but you would. All the chaps always have done. Still do, in fact, even though she's been married for years. Marian has a way with her. She's got the most gorgeous blue eyes and blonde hair. That and being so slim make her look fragile. Isn't that what you all go for?'

'For a passing fling maybe, not necessarily for anything lasting.'

Alex was parking the car outside their hotel. As the engine died he turned to her. He was smiling, and not at all in the manner that so often was calculated to ensure he got his own way. Helen realised yet again how happy she was to be with him.

They spent the afternoon on site, checking dimensions and aspects, and confirming the precise area which the house itself would occupy. The owner had chosen wisely. There would be a view of hills to the rear and, beyond its own garden, the house would overlook the steep slope down towards the River Nidd.

'Wouldn't mind living here myself,' said Alex. 'What about you?'

'It's certainly very lovely, though we'd be a bit of a way from work!' She wondered if he fancied a house as grand as this would be.

'Could always open up another branch of Stone's, here or in Harrogate . . .'

Although they weren't very serious, these remarks made Helen think. Did Alexander wish perhaps that their relationship could develop into something deeper?

How much she herself would want that she wasn't entirely sure. He'd been just a pal for such a very long time. She hadn't had romantic ideas about him. Yes, things were changing, but was she ready for settling down? For admitting that hanging on in the hope that she'd someday meet another man who would affect her in the way that Chris had done was unrealistic?

Their work finished for the day, they returned to the hotel to wash and change, then got back into the little Morris. Alex wanted them to spend the evening in Harrogate, and had booked a table in an elegant hotel overlooking the Stray where they lingered over dinner.

Helen was thankful she'd brought her best frock, and that it had long sleeves. This early in spring the evenings anywhere in Yorkshire were cold. Of deep blue artificial silk, it was nicely draped, and she'd always felt it made her look slimmer.

Alex was very smart in a dark suit and tie, worn with an extremely white shirt. His hair was freshly washed, gleaming under the lights of the hotel dining room. He seemed much happier than he had for ages, entertaining her with recollections of things that had happened in their long period of training. Although most of what he said was light-hearted, much of it was illuminating. He was far more observant than she had credited. And a great deal of his interest had focused on herself.

'I didn't know,' and 'You never said at the time,' she remarked repeatedly, until Alex began laughing.

'You needn't have labelled me a total boor,' he teased.

Helen smiled back at him. 'I never have.'

'Your selective memory has discarded the early days then,' he contradicted. 'When you reprimanded me for my attitude to women.'

'Oh, that! No more than you deserved.'

'I agree.' His eyes looked more green than grey tonight, and were glinting. 'I only hope you consider I might have improved with age.' Surprising her, he reached across the table to cover her hand with his.

'Helen,' he continued, totally serious now, 'I couldn't admire you more – and that's quite some admission from someone like me who doesn't go in for pretty speeches.'

Silently, she agreed. And she wasn't at all sure how to respond. This unfamiliar Alex made her feel quite differently towards him, but along with this new excitement he seemed to be generating a touch of alarm in her, inner suspicions that she might not be entirely safe.

They strolled after their meal – beneath the street lamps and glancing about them to the elegant spa buildings and the now darkened gardens for which Harrogate was famed. The night air was cool and when Alex placed an arm around her Helen began feeling reassured as well as warmer, and as if any sense of threat she had detected had been imaginary.

Driving the short distance back to Knaresborough he was preoccupied, speaking only once or twice and then just to make sure that she was warm enough now. After he had drawn up near the hotel entrance, he turned to her and smiled.

'I've loved this evening, Helen. The whole of today, in fact. Can't help wishing it needn't end just yet. We're not the same, are we, away from home? It's as if we've rid ourselves of everything routine and mundane.'

She smiled. 'I know. And I've enjoyed every minute, thank you. The meal tonight was so nice, and the way we talked.'

He kissed her then, more fiercely than ever he had before, his mouth possessing hers insistently as though he couldn't bear to be parted from her. 'Let's go indoors.' His voice was husky.

Hand-in-hand they crossed the foyer and sauntered up the wide staircase. When Alex paused beside the door of his room, he pulled her hand towards him, held it against his chest. The cloth of his coat was cold from the night air outdoors.

'Let's talk for a while longer, eh?'

She smiled again as she nodded. What an idiot she'd been ever to wonder if he could be interested in her. They shared so much – such a lot that Helen wanted to use every minute finding out other ways in which they complemented each other.

His room seemed slightly cramped, smaller than the one she'd been given. Helen noticed that its furnishing was completed with a large armchair and a glass-topped occasional table.

Alex took her coat and hung it on the door before removing his own and unfastening his jacket. He was smiling when he turned back to her. 'Soon have you feeling warmer, love.'

He paused beside the gas fire, finding a match to ignite it and then adjusting the flame. The only other light in the room was from a single Art Deco lamp at the bedside.

Watching Alex as he walked towards her, Helen grew aware that she felt slightly dizzy, and strangely conscious of a longing to have her hand in his again. Had she stopped needing to prove her self-sufficiency?

'Come here,' Alex said gently, taking her hand as she had hoped and drawing her with him towards the chair.

Sitting, he pulled her down on to his lap. She heard him sigh and his head came towards hers. His lips traced the line of her jaw, lingered below one ear, and travelled to her throat.

'I've waited so long for this,' he admitted, kissing her mouth.

Briefly, she wondered why he *had* waited. Patience was hardly a quality she'd have associated with Alex Stone. But then this couldn't have happened earlier. As well as being distracted by overwork, she had been too inhibited to respond. Maybe for both of them there had been a need to surrender old ideas?

Whatever their reasons for delaying, there could be no doubting the excitement they felt now. With each kiss it mounted, sending tremors coursing through Helen. Only once before in her life had she experienced such delicious attraction. This time there was nothing to keep them apart. She didn't have to stop and think. Alex was as free from ties as she herself was.

'I do so love you, Helen.' He sounded astonished – as astonished as she was that such feelings were overtaking them. 'You're such a vital part of my life. I hope you know that?'

She kissed him eagerly, willing her whole being to convey the love they were discovering. Alex began stirring against her, thrilling her with the strength of his passion. Through the silky textured dress, he was caressing her breast, making her wonder if she was at last turning into a beautiful woman.

That was what had been so special about today. Every moment seemed to emphasise this new phase in their relationship. By his admission this morning about noticing her over the years, Alex had introduced her to the joy of being admired.

Maybe Marian was right, thought Helen, and I *had* neglected to make time for this aspect of growing up. I've never had anything to be vain about, but it is lovely to be made to believe that I can thrill and be thrilled, just like every other girl. That I don't necessarily have to continue sacrificing everything else in order to succeed in my career.

Suddenly, her entire future looked brilliant. They could work well together when they tried, and Alex knew her so thoroughly that he would always understand the strength of her feelings about her job. And now there was this growing attraction, the headiness of discovering that he needed her. She felt as if glowing coals were burning deep inside her, as reassuring as they were exciting, because she was loved.

His tongue parted her lips and tested the sharpness of her teeth. Their kisses grew feverish, demanding, exhilarating.

'I need you so much, love,' said Alex urgently, the hand circling her breast creating tumult inside her. His touch on her lips grew gentle now. He seemed pensive. 'You've been the other half of myself for so long, making me forget every other girl.'

Helen was not far from tears when she recalled how she had feared he might think her too ordinary. Everything seemed blissfully simple. They had grown so close without realising, so close that they needed only each other. She slid a hand beneath his shirt.

The touch of her fingers on his back awakened in Alex a fiercer yearning, willed him to trace the line of her ribcage, her hipbone, and then down over her firm stomach. Feeling her response was heightening all his feelings, urging him to unite them. But she had promised nothing – in words had given no encouragement. And Helen was the last person he would take if there remained one ounce of doubt about her agreement. 'Don't you believe we belong together after all this time?' he pressed her.

Helen thought of couples belonging together – of Marian and Denis weathering hardship to form a family. And she thought of herself and Alexander, and of their future which now appeared solid, assured. Hadn't they earned some happiness after concentrating on all that studying? Didn't they deserve some enjoyment? Of each other – perhaps of having a family?

'Happen so, Alex love, happen we do.'

His mouth instantly returned to hers. Helen thought how pleased her parents would be that Alex wanted her. But thinking was growing impossible. His lips and these caressing hands lured from her a longing that raged as every nerve ending came alive beneath his touch.

His kisses traversed her throat, and then lower to her breast's curve beneath the edge of her dress.

'Take this off, eh?' he suggested, smiling. 'It's getting creased.'

Helen hesitated, but Alex was working on the row of tiny buttons at the back. He urged her to stand, slid off her frock so swiftly that her only embarrassment was for the cheap petticoat she wore. He pulled her back to him at once, love in his eyes now, in his words and in his touch.

'You're so lovely, Helen,' he exclaimed, his mouth yet again covering hers while his hands drew her hips towards him.

She had never expected to feel eager like this. Hadn't dreamed that his delight in her would make her wish this nearness might last until the morning.

A small sound startled them both. The sigh of the gas fire going out. Some time afterwards Alex noticed that Helen's bare arms had grown cold.

'You're getting quite chilled, my love. Time we shifted from here.'

The thought of going to her own room while she felt so overwhelmed by longing was unbearable. She shook her head. 'I'm all right, Alex.'

'Don't be silly. I'm going to take care of you.'

He pushed her gently from his knee, rose and gathered her to him.

Stilling a sigh, Helen held him away, turned to pick up her frock.

'Not yet.' Smiling, Alex was removing his jacket, shaking his head. He slid his fingers down her arm to grasp her wrist.

'This is right for us,' he asserted as they moved towards the bed. 'We know and love each other, don't we? We've both waited that long, we're hardly rushing headlong with somebody we don't know.'

Helen couldn't argue about that. She was ready for love, more ready than she had known. And there was no one else for her, no one who wasn't forbidden. Alex needed her. Accepted her as she was. She couldn't live the rest of life on regrets.

'I want you so much it hurts,' he said, his eyes darkening as they entreated her. 'And you'd be being cruel to yourself to refuse – you know that, love, don't you?'

Wordlessly, Helen acknowledged how true that was, that this craving was a kind of pain. She couldn't endure it for ever. 'I know,' she murmured at last.

His lips returned swiftly to her mouth. The hand about her wrist tightened. She stirred in answer to his urgency.

Conscious of nothing but this amazing need, she scarcely noticed she was slipping beneath the covers. Briefly, Alex paused to discard his clothing. He drew her towards him swiftly, across the chilly sheet to his warmth. With his arms about her she felt the last traces of her old anxiety evaporate like frost on the moors encountering morning sun.

'You see,' Alex whispered into her neck, 'how good you make me feel.'

Helen had wondered once why Marian wanted to make love if it wasn't so she'd have babies. Now she marvelled at her own failure to understand. But tonight was as much to make Alex happy as for herself.

He was taking charge, easing away her underclothes. And then his fingers were bliss, focusing all her yearning until she gasped out his name. Slowly at first, he entered her, and his loving began to accelerate. The seconds of pain were brief, she gave herself freely to savouring with him the life pulsing between them. Holding each other completely, they gave and took and gave yet again.

Afterwards, when they had dozed, she awakened to see Alex smiling.

'You're wonderful, Helen,' he said. 'Thank goodness you're mine.'

Chapter 6

Helen felt as if her emotions were the yo-yo that she had watched her niece trying to master the week before. Alex had again made love to her on their second night in Knaresborough, and she had revelled in the exhilaration. Sharing herself with him induced such feelings of belonging and being accepted exactly as she was. It had seemed as if Alexander's importance in her life had developed over the years precisely for this purpose. Now, though, they were driving back into Halifax and the familiar buildings and no less familiar mist of mill smoke had jolted her back to a realisation of all the facts.

She sensed already that as soon as Alex left her and drove out towards The Stone House she would acknowledge that deep down, beyond this excitement, she was perturbed. And sure enough, when he drew up at the end of her street and spoke, her heart began plummeting.

'We must do that again sometime,' he said with a grin. But the kiss he gave her felt almost off-hand.

Walking along the street and through the yard to the front door, she started wondering if he ever intended their relationship to progress in the way she had supposed. Had all he'd said about loving her been merely the result of passion?

'How did it go?' her father inquired eagerly. 'Did

you manage to get that site surveyed?' He had taken enough interest in Helen's training to learn a few of the terms, and was glad that she seemed to appreciate being able to talk over the work involved.

'Yes, thanks,' she answered quickly, then turned to greet her mother who was coming out of the kitchen.

'You look tired, love,' Kathleen exclaimed. 'I expect you didn't sleep so well in a strange bed, eh?' When her daughter didn't respond she persisted. 'Everything's all right, isn't it?'

'Yes, of course. I'll just take my things upstairs.'

Helen closed the door of her own room thankfully, put down her suitcase and sank on to the bed. She flinched, she was very sore from the ferocity of their lovemaking; but worse than the pain by far was this sudden uncertainty. She had pictured Alex insisting that he must come in with her and speak with her parents. She had imagined him so eager to announce their decision to marry that he'd be unable to delay for even a few hours. Instead of that, what was it he'd said? No more than that they ought to repeat going away together *sometime*.

Her mother called from the bottom of the stairs that they had waited tea for her, and was she ready?

Helen felt anything but ready for sitting at the table and behaving with any sort of calm while they taxed her with the inevitable questions about the trip to Knaresborough. All at once anxiety about her future was overshadowed by more immediate worries. How was she to behave in anything resembling her normal manner?

The meal was such an ordeal that she fully expected one or other of her parents to ask what had happened to change her so completely, but they appeared to have reached their own conclusions. When the evening was finally over and she rose to go up to bed, her mother smiled.

'You seem altogether different for being away for a bit. I think it's done you good – you seem much more self-contained.'

Thank goodness you can't know, Helen thought as she kissed them both goodnight. Thank goodness you don't suspect the truth that I'm containing!

Only the following morning, however, she was shaken into realising that the whole story could emerge. Preoccupied with wondering how on earth Alex would behave when she saw him in the office, she was getting washed at the kitchen sink when Kathleen turned aside from the toast she'd been making.

'Whatever's that mark on your neck?' she asked, and came closer. 'Is it that Alex Stone who's been giving you love-bites?'

'Where?' Helen looked in the mirror.

'You'll not see it, it's round the side here. It was him, I take it?'

'Yes. Actually, Mum – we're in love,' she announced rashly, praying that Alexander's declarations were genuine. 'I daresay he'll be wanting to talk to you both before long, about us getting married.'

'I see. Well, we'll have to find out what your dad thinks about that. Not that we could put a stop to it, not with you being over twenty-one.'

Helen's anxiety found a fresh dimension. 'Would you, Mum – try to prevent us marrying?'

'I can't say it's an idea I'm in favour of, not by any stretch of imagination. He's nice enough, just – not our sort. I don't want you stuck with somebody who'd always make you feel at a disadvantage . . .'

'Nay, don't say that! Alex isn't like that at all – we've both had the same training, haven't we? We're equals, him and me.'

'Oh, aye? And I suppose I just *imagine* that he lives in that big house out yonder, that his father's been an alderman for years, and has been the mayor. That they own the firm which only employs you.'

'And which won't be employing me much longer, if I don't get a move on. I'm afraid we'll have to discuss this another time,' said Helen, relieved to have a reason for getting away.

'Happen it's as well. Let me think about it all. There's only one good thing about this, as far as I can see – you were brought up proper so we've no cause for worrying that you'll let the situation get out of hand. You know what I mean. You want to be more careful, though, love. If you've got him that worked up that he's leaving marks like that on your neck, you're not being fair expecting him to hold back every time.'

Helen's journey on the bus to work was miserable. Concern as to how Alex might react on seeing her again in their everyday environment had been submerged by an enormous weight of guilt. She couldn't be relieved because her mother assumed so automatically that she had kept Alex's desire in check. On the contrary, she felt as if she'd have been glad to have the truth in the open. That would, at least, have reduced the complexity of her own emotions. And it might even have made her parents more ready to accept that she and Alex would marry.

Whatever am I thinking? she asked herself silently. She couldn't really be even considering such a disgrace preferable to this confusion?

Alex and his father, together with Frank Barclay, were at their drawing boards. The offices of Joseph Stone and Associates, situated near the church high on the hillside at Luddenden Foot, were full of light flowing in through large windows designed to facilitate close work. All three men responded to Helen's good morning, and Alex winked in her direction.

'You had a good trip, I gather?' Joseph Stone observed, beaming. 'I'm delighted with you both. From what I hear, most of the essential services to the site are in hand. And as to the actual survey – well, the quick glance I've already taken at your notes seems to confirm that all's in order.'

Later that day he also indicated that he would send them out together again. 'Just one more time. After that, I'm going to have you work independently of each other for a while. It's the only way I'll assess with any accuracy what your capabilities are.'

After they had finished in the office that evening, Alexander waited for Helen and walked down the hill with her to the bus stop.

'Marvellous, isn't it, that the old man will send us off again on a job? Something to look forward to. And in the meantime we must see more of each other, of course. There'll be evenings out, and weekends. You could stay with us, couldn't you? The house is plenty big enough for us to lose ourselves away from everybody.'

'That depends . . .'

'Depends? On what, for heaven's sake?'

Helen glanced along the road towards Mytholmroyd. She didn't want to say this and then just leave it because the bus was coming.

'Well, love – you know . . . what we intend in the future. I thought – well, while we were away I believed you meant that you were thinking about us getting married.'

The dulling of his grey-green eyes was only momentary, there was hardly any hesitation before he gave her shoulders a squeeze. 'Well, naturally, that's what I want. But these things take time, don't they?

You're not so unreasonable, I'm sure, that you'd say we have to wait now until that's all sorted out?'

What made matters worse was Helen's own suspicion that she would be unable to compel Alex to wait. She was too much of a realist to deny to herself that she had enjoyed making love. If her body hadn't been reminding her throughout the long day that he was near, her silly heart would have been prompting her to notice him. I've fallen for him and no mistake, she acknowledged during the bus ride home. She just wished that she could feel one hundred per cent certain that her falling had not been into a trap.

The discussion she'd been anticipating began as soon as she and her mother had cleared away after their evening meal. Instead of sitting in his favourite armchair, Daniel Clegg was at the table, shifting around a Woolworth's notebook and pencil on the brown chenille cover.

'From what your mother says, it's time we had a talk. I gather that wedding bells might be in the air, if we can agree to it.'

'Now, Daniel,' his wife interrupted, finishing drying her hands on her apron before drawing out a chair. 'Remember what we said – we're not going to cause any ructions . . .'

'That's as may be. But our Helen's got to hear what I have to say.'

'Go on, Father,' Helen prompted. She was willing herself not to flinch, nor to give any sign of her growing misgivings about what had happened in Knaresborough.

'We're not daft,' he continued. 'And, much as you might think that unlikely, we were young ourselves once. We understand as how you and this Stone chap have been thrown together for years while you've been studying . . .'

'Yes, but along with a lot of other students, Dad. You've got to remember that, and that now we've – chosen each other.'

'Chosen?' He snorted dubiously. 'Or is it that it's turned out very convenient for him that you're allus around now you're working for them? Isn't it only to be expected that he'd try summat on?'

'You make that sound as if I'd no will of my own about this – it isn't all one-sided, not by a long chalk.'

'Fancy him, do you?' He regarded her curiously, making Helen suspect that it was only today that her father had realised she possessed the feelings of a normal woman. 'Aye, well, he's a fine-looking young man, I'll grant you that.'

'But handsome is as handsome does,' her mother put in.

'No need for that, Kathleen. We're not trying to make out the chap has behaved badly towards our Helen. Not as yet.' He paused, seeking words. 'You see, love, it's for your own good . . .'

Helen swallowed down a groan.

Daniel cleared his throat. 'Your mother and me think you'd be best deciding to wait. It's not asking a lot – we're not saying you mustn't end up with him. Only that you must bide your time. And we think you'd be well advised to stop at home on the next occasion when he's planning one of his trips.'

Helen felt her colour rising. 'It wasn't Alexander's idea this time. And actually his father's already arranging for us to go off to . . .'

'Then he can unarrange it,' Daniel snapped, rage suddenly gripping him. 'I'm not having a daughter of mine gallivanting off like that on her own with a single young fellow.'

'But this is business, Father, a job of work.'

'Nay, there were more to it than that afore, from

what your mother says. And I won't have it. I won't, do you hear?'

Kathleen interrupted. 'Now, Daniel, there's no need to go on so. Our Helen's a good lass, you know that. She'll never give in to owt.'

'She won't, that is certain. Because she'll not be tempted again, I'll see to that.'

'You're getting it all wrong, Dad. Alex is thinking of us being married one day.'

'That's as may be – and it doesn't affect my opinion. He's not right for you, Helen. You'd better school yourself to accept that. Whatever I thought of him afore, I can't take to a chap who's used his position to make a set at my daughter.'

'Alex hasn't a position to use, even if he would, Father. He doesn't own Stone's, it's Joseph who does. Alex and I are equals.'

'Whatever gave you that idea?' Daniel asked. 'Nay, lass, I thought you were brighter nor that. He's a man, isn't he? And the boss's son. There'll never be any sort of equality between you.'

'That's the only thing that worries us, love,' Kathleen said gently. 'But it's a big worry. He's bound to treat you differently from a young woman whose family had a similar standing.'

'You're worrying unnecessarily,' she told them. 'It's me that Alex wants.' Hadn't she been thrilled because that was so?

It was the wrong thing entirely. '*Wants?*' her father shouted, springing to his feet and simultaneously slamming both hands flat on the table. 'Aye, I reckon that just about sums it up – and that's why I'll have no more of this talk. His sort have allus thought they were entitled to take everything they wanted. Time somebody learned 'em different!'

'I'm sorry, love,' said Kathleen after they had both

watched him stomp to the foot of the stairs then listened while his boots creaked on every step and along the landing.

'Happen he'll come round. Maybe if you could have a word with him . . .' Helen began.

'I'm sorry,' her mother repeated. 'But your dad was really speaking for us both, even if I wouldn't have put it quite so strongly. Folk like the Stones don't settle down with people like us, love. Can't you just forget that couple of days you were away? We know Alex is nice-looking, but he's not the only one.'

Her parents' opposition to any relationship between herself and Alexander immediately focused all Helen's feelings towards him. After a restless night, she set out for work the following morning, more certain than ever that he was the man she wanted to marry.

Her mum and dad just didn't understand, she thought, watching raindrops running down the bus window. They ought to be able to see that because she and Alex had grown together during all these years there were no barriers of the kind they visualised. And hadn't he said, right from their first term in college, that he didn't think of her in the same way as the lasses he used to mess around with?

His behaviour as soon as she arrived at the office seemed to confirm his affection for her. The walk from the bus was across a bridge, then up the steepest slope she'd encountered anywhere. Pouring with rain, as it was today, there was no way of avoiding a drenching. Nobody, however young they were, could have hurried up that hill.

As soon as she opened the inner door of the office, Alex came to take her dripping raincoat.

'Eh, love!' he exclaimed. 'Haven't you got an umbrella?'

'I have an' all. I've just left it in the stand by the entrance. But it was blowing that hard across from t'other side of the valley nothing would have kept the rain off.'

'Well, come and sit down. I'll make you a cup of tea. Sally's not in yet, gone to the dentist.' Sally was the firm's secretary.

Before putting the kettle on, however, Alex drew Helen towards him.

'Steady on,' she said. 'Not here, love.'

He chuckled. 'Dad and Frank Barclay won't be in, they've got a meeting. Called all of a sudden, with the builders of the new factory.'

'Trouble?'

'Nothing that Stone's can't handle – something to do with the distance they are from the mains services. I gather the builders are creating because they hadn't allowed sufficient for laying everything on.'

'And is that our fault?'

Alex shook his head. 'Hardly. It was plain enough on the plans. But we shouldn't be worrying about that. This is the first time we've had the place to ourselves.'

'And what if Sally walks in?'

'Her appointment isn't till half-past nine, in Halifax.'

Before Helen could say any more his mouth was covering hers, and he was holding her to him, so close that his suit buttons were prodding at her breast.

'I've been thinking about what you were saying,' he told her as he eventually moved his head away. 'And getting married is the only way. My feelings for you are so strong, love. I just seem unable to think about anything else.' After once being with Helen, his freedom appeared a small sacrifice to be made in exchange for having her always.

'You'll have to convince my father first, I'm afraid.'

'All fathers are alike about their daughters, aren't they?' he said dismissively, and kissed her again. 'Nobody's good enough for them. Anyway, you're not that young that you require his permission.'

'I'd prefer not to marry against his wishes.'

'Of course, love. Naturally.' He leaned a little away from her to smile into her eyes. 'So long as I can convince *you*, that's what bothers me most. Especially at this moment.'

His arm still about her, he took her through with him into his father's inner office.

Helen frowned. 'I don't think we should, Alex. What if a client comes?'

'They never do, do they? Not without an appointment.' Those who had their own transport were obliged to take a circuitous route all along the hillside; those who came on foot had to suffer the climb which Helen daily endured. Neither was undertaken when there might well be a wasted journey.

Going behind the impressive desk, Alex seated himself in the no less imposing leather chair. 'Suits me, don't you think? But nothing like as much as you suit me . . .'

He drew her down on to his lap, one hand travelling to her breast while the other went to the back of her head, tilting it so that their lips met. His tongue parted her teeth, tracing them, sending her giddy with longing.

'Touch me,' he groaned. 'Hold me, Helen, hold me.'

'Nay, Alex, not in the office. We're here to work.'

'All right then. Just a few more kisses . . .'

His mouth returned greedily to hers, alerting all her senses again, compelling her to stir as he was stirring.

'I suppose you're right,' he admitted eventually. 'This only makes it more frustrating. I just can't live without you, Helen.'

She smiled, brushed her lips affectionately over his cheek, and was swept yet again into a fervour of urgent kisses. He had loosened the fastening of her blouse, and she felt his fingers insistently tracing first her breast and then her nipple. Deep within her the tremors of yearning increased, impelling her to kiss him back, to explore his teeth with the point of her tongue.

'We've got to stop,' he gasped. 'Or I'll have to take you in here, on the floor. Just promise you'll see me tonight, love, somewhere alone.'

'You're not going to come and speak to my parents then?' Helen needed to have everything sorted, couldn't make love with Alex repeatedly without knowing they would one day marry.

'Are you making that a condition?'

'No, love. Not really.'

'But you were brought up to marry first. I know. So was I.' He sighed, then turned it into a smile. 'I'll come and see them tonight. Get them to agree, somehow. But then I shall want you to arrange to come and stay at the house sometime soon. Very soon.'

Working that day was extremely difficult. The desire Alex aroused didn't simply go away because he returned to sitting at his drawing board while Helen worked at her own. And even when their secretary came in after her dental visit there was little to break the tense silence surrounding them. Sally had needed an extraction and was scarcely in a state for making conversation.

By the time they were leaving the office at five-thirty, Helen felt dazed by the force of her feelings.

'I'll run you home,' Alex suggested. 'Speak to them straight away.'

'If you don't mind, I'd rather you let me tackle them on my own first. That way they might be in a more receptive frame of mind when you arrive.'

Helen had been over-optimistic. When Alexander knocked on the door, she admitted him to a room that felt positively chilled by parental reluctance. Sure enough, Daniel Clegg only managed a bluff 'Evening' in answer to his greeting. But then Alex turned to Kathleen.

'I gather Helen has been telling you both how much I hope you'll agree to our marrying?'

'That's right, love,' she responded, automatically offering him a seat near the fire.

'I can understand your reservations,' he continued genially. 'You've not had the opportunity to get to know me yet, and you naturally wish to be assured that I'll make Helen a fitting husband. She has a warm and loving personality – much like your own, Mrs Clegg.'

Helen saw that her father was scrutinising Alex, trying to see beneath the charm and the flattery.

But Alex persisted in addressing her mother. 'In a way, you know, you're responsible for bringing all this about. On the first occasion I met you I was struck very forcibly by what a wonderful homemaker you are.'

Kathleen sat more upright in her chair, smiling as she smoothed the flowered pinafore she rarely discarded.

'Having grown up in a home deprived of a mother, I'm bound to notice such things. You made me long for a place to which I could always return and find a heart-warming welcome. And I needed to look no further than Helen to know that she's inherited all the skills which would provide just that.'

'There – did you hear, Daniel?' Kathleen enthused.

He wasn't in the least impressed. 'I heard all right. I was just wondering when I might get a word in.'

'My apologies, Mr Clegg. My unbounded love for Helen does tend to run away with . . .'

'And that's just it, isn't it?' her father observed. 'You young folk seem to think it's in order to let feelings run away with you.'

'I did say *love*,' Alex reminded him, his tone respectfully quiet.

'I'm not going to argue the toss over words. It's feelings I'm concerned about, and how they get the upper hand. Don't think I don't know.'

Glancing at him, Helen wondered if a man who could look as dour as her father was looking at present could ever have warmed enough to experience love.

'I have feelings an' all, you know. Feelings about the daughters I've raised. I've seen how our Marian has had to struggle while they were getting on their feet. Not that it seems to have harmed her. What concerns me about our Helen here is that her struggles might be of a very different nature.'

'She'll always be well provided for, you have my word.'

'Ah, yes. That's what I'm coming to. Believe it or not, I've been beholden to nobody all my life, and that's how my two lasses were brought up. And now you come along, with your nice manners and your expensive clothes, and this "love" you keep harping on about. But money'll never buy the kind of loyalty that ought to exist between husband and wife. And nor does it prove you'll allus put what's best for Helen afore owt else.' He paused, challenging Alex with darkening hazel eyes. 'That's about it. I'm not saying you shouldn't get wed. Just that you should wait – to make sure you're the man our Helen thinks you are.

It'll soon pass. I thought a couple of years, that's all.'

'Oh, Dad,' Helen sighed.

'Have you considered, Daniel, that by asking them to do this, you might force them to take matters into their own hands?' Kathleen asked her husband agitatedly.

'Helen has more sense nor that.'

'Might I say something further?' Alex began. In answer to a curt nod, he went on: 'There's the possibility of war to be considered also. Isn't this a time when we all need more security, not less? Something of substance to which we can hold on . . .'

'He's right, you know,' Kathleen said, and was stilled to silence by a frown from her husband. His eventual sigh sounded exasperated.

'You'll do as you like, I suppose, in the end,' he said finally. 'I'm not daft enough to put my foot down and have you both exclude us from your lives. Just don't expect me to be pleased if you decide to rush things.'

For Helen, her father's grudging acceptance that she would marry Alexander was a real dampener. But Alex himself was too elated to let her remain subdued for long. And he kept her to the promise that she would go out with him that evening. She certainly wasn't sorry to do that. Her father's attitude was hardly encouraging her to remain at home.

Alex had parked at the end of the street, and she was astonished to see Joseph Stone's Rolls-Royce in place of the Morris.

Alex grinned when he saw her expression. 'Well, I told Father what my mission was, and he endorsed my opinion that I needed to give my chances a boost by appearing in this.'

Helen had grown perturbed. 'Don't either of you understand at all the sort of folk we are? If your father had heard Dad tonight, he'd have been in no doubt that this would finish everything before ever it began!' And how could Alex set so much store by evidence of wealth?

But he merely hugged her to him and laughed. 'Stop worrying, love. Once we're married, everything will sort itself out.' And he meant that to be far sooner than any two years. 'Your dad will come round,' he assured her. 'Give him a while to get used to the idea.'

And, meanwhile, he wouldn't permit her to concentrate on anything beyond the two of them. Without consulting her, he drove out of Halifax, down past the Calder and Hebble and out towards West Vale and Greetland. He didn't stop until they were far beyond civilisation, where only birds roamed the skies above the darkening moors.

'I don't think so, Alex,' she protested when he suggested moving into the back of the car. She hadn't forgotten all his tales about the girls he'd taken out in this Rolls-Royce Phantom.

There was no possibility, though, that she would hold back when his arm went around her and he began kissing her – just as if nobody in the whole world but Helen Clegg could ever have meant a thing to him.

'I love you so much,' he said, glad the words came readily now, for he was indeed becoming increasingly pleased with the prospect of their eventual marriage. Helen was clever enough to be a wife who'd do him credit, with her qualifications and latent homemaking ability. And what could be finer than never being denied her glorious sensuality?

He had pulled her close against him and was tracing her ear with a thumb, while his other hand began its descent from her breast. Her hair was cool against his cheek, and sweet-scented. These days she wore it longer, falling towards her shoulders in waves that glinted with red-gold highlights. Now she was offering kiss for kiss, no less eager than he to explore this wonderful new pleasure, inciting him to obey the hammering in his veins. He was wondering how he'd resist, how in the world he would hold out as he privately had vowed he must, when she shifted uncomfortably, trying to ease the cramp induced by being trapped against the car door.

'It really would be more comfortable in the back,' he reminded her. 'Only for a cuddle, if you like. Let's be practical – these cars aren't designed to give the driver all the luxury, are they?'

He settled her into one corner of the rear seat, then stretched out against her, smothering her face and neck with delicate kisses. Her arms soon came around him, drawing him closer still.

'What sort of an engagement ring will you choose?' he inquired into the soft hollow of her throat. 'I'll take you to buy one on Saturday.'

'I haven't thought yet,' Helen answered breathily, suddenly dazed by the pace and excitement of it all.

'We'll have fun looking. That's what I want for you, you know, love – *fun*. You've had to work so hard and so long.'

'And haven't you?'

'Getting to know you is my reward.'

His lips were devouring hers again, filling her with the ache to be his once more, to ease this need that seemed to swallow every thought but those about Alex. She could hardly think beyond his lips – his lips and his fingers which had found the secret places he had schooled to receive him.

'You said not here, and I won't insist,' he murmured huskily, while desire hardened him.

How could she be cruel to them both? thought Helen. How deny him?

He deserved some consideration for his refusal to let

her father prevent their getting wed. *And they were going to marry . . .*

The confines of the car and the luxurious scent of its upholstery seemed to heighten her sensuality. The proximity of this attractive man whom she'd grown to love as well as to like was compelling her to heed her impulses. She was only faintly surprised by her own eagerness when she began unfastening his buttons.

For several delicious minutes Alex held himself against her, and then there was no longer any possibility of their holding back. He loved her with careful skill, gently at first and then ever more urgently, matching his desire to hers until their joy soared with the skylark which rose from the nearby heather.

'We'll marry soon, my love,' he said, glad they hadn't received a bald 'no' from her parents. 'When we're in our own home there'll be nobody happier.'

Their home was the one thing that caused reservations in Helen, purely because the house was owned by Alexander's father. Liking Joseph Stone as she had from the first, and being delighted that he was pleased about their plans, still didn't prevent her wishing he had left them to find their own place. A small though detached property, it was built on the same parcel of land as Stone's offices. Alex himself was so thankful that a home had been found so readily that he was prepared to live with its Victorian styling. 'Aren't we lucky, love?' he exclaimed to her after they had been given the key for a preliminary inspection.

Unable to bring herself to mention to him that she didn't like the idea of his father providing their home, Helen had fallen back on admiring the generous proportions of its rooms and the high ceilings. If only it had been a house which they themselves had been able to purchase, she would have devoted herself wholeheartedly to living here. Even while it was still influenced by the previous inhabitant's taste for drab decor, she could visualise lighter walls and beautiful curtaining at those lovely big sash windows. But how she wished she didn't have this dreadful feeling that she was being *bought* by the Stone family.

In time, her practical nature made her accept that neither she nor Alex could have afforded even the deposit on a house, and as their wedding day approached she began looking forward to having her own home.

They had talked her father round to the idea of their marrying in July, which allowed little time for making her wedding dress, something that Helen decided was essential when she first began looking around at gowns in the more stylish shops. She was glad to be occupied, initially with designs and then with making up the gown on her mother's ancient treadle machine.

Kathleen was elated to be asked to help with fittings, and had to be chased out of her daughter's room for Helen really wanted the dress to be her own work. As she sewed she often found her mind racing, and not always forwards to the day when it would be worn. Although she felt sure that she loved Alex, this was a time for adjusting to reality as it was. And for surrendering past dreams.

Only just over a year ago she had been in Switzerland, and in that glorious abbey had met Christopher Maitland. Until quite recently she had succeeded in convincing herself that meeting Chris had been an experience touched with romance, though scarcely connected with the real world. She had come to believe that refusing to dream of how life might have been with him was all that was required. Now, however, imagination plagued her anew with fantasies while memory furnished mind pictures of his thick dark hair and the sherry brown eyes which had smiled into her own. Silly little things, like the concern shown in his buttoning her coat against the cold, arrived out of nowhere to lodge in her head, tantalising her with yearning.

Each night when Helen laid aside her sewing she put away her memories too, reminding herself that when the gown was completed she must relinquish thoughts of Christopher, for good. She was firm in her resolve about putting all she'd got into this marriage. She wouldn't contemplate going to Alex accompanied by any remnant of what she had felt for Chris.

They were marrying in St Paul's church and their reception was to be held in the nearby Queens Hall. Joseph had offered them The Stone House for the occasion, and Helen had found a tactful refusal difficult. Somehow, though, she had managed to remain on good terms with her future father-in-law whilst conveying her own father's determination that he would provide the reception.

A meeting between the two families had taken place, on Kathleen's insistence in the Cleggs' home, and Helen had been relieved as well as delighted when Joseph Stone had appeared at ease there. Her father had pleased her by offering sherry – not something which normally appeared there – and if his own abstention was noticed it certainly didn't depress the atmosphere.

'A most convivial evening,' was Joseph Stone's verdict as he and Alex rose to leave. 'I hope that it means we shall continue to meet like this after the young people's plans have come to fruition.'

Although doubting that was likely, Helen had been glad, especially when the get-together seemed to have tempered her father's disapproval of the marriage. She was compelled to admit that he was showing good grace now that there could be no turning back, and Alex appeared to have dismissed the earlier opposition he'd received from Daniel. Kathleen helped, of course. Her concern for the lad who'd grown up without a mother was revealed nearly every time that Alexander arrived in their home. If she wasn't offering him some titbit from her recent batch of baking, she would be spotting a button that hung by a thread and obliging with a hasty repair.

'I did tell your mum that we have a housekeeper, didn't I?' he asked Helen one evening. 'We're not exactly neglected over there, are we?'

Helen laughed. 'She loves fussing over you, don't spoil things for her. It saves you mentioning owt that needs doing when you're at home.'

He grinned. 'If your mother did but know it, Mrs Hartley has been complaining for years that neither Dad nor I have any system for bringing such jobs to her attention.'

'You'd better make the most of all this – once we're wed you'll find out how little I notice holey socks and missing buttons.'

Although said lightly enough, the phrase brought a frown to his pleasant features which perturbed Helen.

'What's up now?' she inquired. 'It was only a bit of a joke.'

'I know, love, I know.' He was smiling again.

Later when he was alone Alex returned to considering what his future bride had said. And he began to acknowledge that his idea of their life together mightn't entirely coincide with hers. He had visualised the sensual side, of course, and how good it would be to have a home where they were free to live as they chose, without any of the restraints he'd experienced in his father's household. What he hadn't acknowledged fully perhaps was Helen's obsession with her work – which he knew, in fact, to be stronger than his own. And suddenly he had foreseen that she could be less than enthusiastic about the domestic scene, and certainly would have little time for what he saw as housewifely tasks.

I wonder, he thought, am I tying myself to someone who'll put me second to her own ambition?

Chapter 7

Alexander had no such reservations on 15 July when Helen walked down the aisle of St Paul's church towards him. Her dress of brilliant white seemed to make her hair appear darker as it gleamed through the delicate net of her veil, and her face glowed with such radiance that she looked quite beautiful. Thank goodness he'd persuaded her to wear white, he thought, unable to contemplate her being dressed any differently. There had been an entire evening's discussion, though, the other week, while she experienced all that ridiculous guilt because she'd already given herself to him.

For the life of him, he hadn't been able to see how Helen could suppose she ought to advertise the fact that she was no longer a virgin. He definitely felt no remorse, but nor did he wish to have his father – much less *hers* – inquiring the reason why she hadn't dressed traditionally.

Gazing at her fondly as she drew near to his side, Alex experienced a feeling of relief for today's especial happiness. Only last week Helen had assured him that she'd received the monthly evidence that he'd been as careful as he'd hoped. Strangely, he realised now, it was as much for his future mother-in-law as for anyone that he was glad there'd be no awkwardness.

Helen herself, these days, possessed so much

assurance that he felt positive she wouldn't have quailed for long had the true details of their relationship emerged. Kathleen Clegg, however, was an altogether different woman: thoroughly good and well intentioned, but possessed by a naivety which he found touching.

Now that Helen was beside him Alex collected his thoughts, preparing to face the vicar who had instructed them in the service until he, at least, felt confident about the responses.

As the ceremony progressed Alex was surprised for Helen appeared not only assertive as she made her vows, but when she glanced his way he read in her vibrant grey eyes such intense joy that he dismissed every doubt about her attitude towards this marriage.

He felt quite overwhelmed by his good fortune, hardly a familiar emotion. Whatever they set out to achieve in the future, Helen would not only be a desirable partner but a confident one. He felt his father's gaze on them, and sensed across the yards separating them the total approval which Joseph had not always accorded him.

By the time they had returned from the vestry after signing the register, Helen felt like singing. Alex's dad had claimed a kiss, smiling down at her and remarking in a voice that was surprisingly unsteady with emotion that she looked very lovely. Her own father had been quiet since that morning when she'd appeared dressed like this in their tiny living room and, though she suspected he wouldn't say, she knew that he too had been astonished by the transformation in her.

Mum had given her a hug in the vestry, beaming at her from beneath tear-sparkled lashes. 'Your frock's fair lovely, bless you – and you are an' all. I'm that proud today.'

Even Marian had tended to be a bit emotional,

kissing her on both cheeks as she adjusted the veil for her before they processed back into the church. 'I'm that glad for you, Helen. It weren't right the way you had to sacrifice so much *life* until you qualified,' she said earnestly, before turning away to restrain Mark and Linda who were becoming over-excited about attending the bride.

Alex had invited Harold Tilsley to be his best man, which increased the entertainment factor of what, otherwise, might have become a somewhat serious reception. Even the solemn little speech that Daniel Clegg delivered with nervous sincerity was concluded by a comment from Harold which had them all laughing. And the bridegroom's words were interrupted so frequently that, despite her amusement, Helen began wondering if her new husband might lose patience. A dapper young man with suave dark hair, Harold relished having an audience. The only time that he became at all uneasy was when Joseph Stone insisted on adding a special finale.

'Dear friends,' Joseph began, 'for all my relatives, I'm glad to say, are also friends to me – dear friends, this is quite the happiest day I can remember, since poor Cynthia was taken from me. As most of you know, when Alexander and Helen were near to completing their training, I became aware that I wanted her in my firm. I couldn't have dreamed then that I might be so fortunate as to be welcoming her into my family in the way that I am today.

'Helen, I do welcome you, most warmly, as you become a Stone. You must always consider me an ally if that should be what you need – and certainly someone on whom you can lean. You will, I hope, believe that Alex will always keep you so happy you'll require nothing more of anyone. But please remember this – it is for you *both* that I am here. You have a good father, I know, also a wonderful mother. But here's a second father now – "in-law" and, I hope, for life.'

Helen left her place beside Alex to go and kiss his father and everyone applauded before taking their cue from her and beginning to move around and mingle. She was glad to see that Joseph Stone was taking her parents with him to meet members of the family. What a lovely man he was!

Alex came to her side, encircling her waist with one arm. 'You look marvellous, Mrs Stone,' he murmured into her ear. 'Come away with me now, this instant.'

She laughed. She was enjoying their day so much that it didn't seem very long before they were getting into the maroon Standard Flying Nine which was Joseph Stone's wedding gift.

Helen had already been hurried by car to her old home to change into the silver grey silk-textured dress and coat she'd chosen for going away. Kathleen had helped her get ready, and Helen had been feeling very emotional as the car took them back to the reception. 'You're a lovely mother, have I ever told you?' she'd said, her grey eyes glistening while she grasped Kathleen's hand.

Her mother had only smiled and squeezed her fingers, but neither of them could speak until, after swallowing hard, they'd regained their composure and opened the door of the room where their guests were assembled.

Alex was waiting near the door, only half his attention on his father who seemed to be having a solemn talk with him. Seeing Helen, he shook his father's hand and waited, his impatience thinly veiled, until Helen had hugged Joseph and her own parents.

'Can't wait to get you on my own,' he confessed as he started up the gleaming new Standard. 'It was a day to remember, but I found it a bit of a strain.'

'Not you!' Helen contradicted, smiling.

But Alex had spoken the truth. He had felt more at ease in church while he needed to concentrate on what was happening, but had been less happy afterwards while they seemed just to be on show. And having everybody telling him how lucky he was to have Helen for his bride had induced an unaccustomed inadequacy, making him wonder if he would measure up.

They were spending the first two nights in the Devonshire Arms at Bolton Abbey before travelling farther up Wharfedale. By the time they reached the hotel they both felt glad they had chosen somewhere fairly close to home.

'Getting married's an exhausting business,' Helen remarked, kicking off her grey kid shoes and removing her coat and the dashing little hat which she'd worn tilted provocatively over one eye.

'I know,' Alex agreed. He grinned engagingly. 'The bed looks tempting if you're in need of a rest.'

Although she smiled back, Helen was wishing that this was all new to them, that they'd never before slept in each other's arms. She'd have loved to have had the excitement today of discovering one another, which maybe would have roused her from this sudden tiredness.

They undressed and slipped into bed. Alex seemed eager to make love to her, and she wouldn't disappoint him, but the sleep which followed seemed to be what she herself most wanted.

The next day was better. They both wakened early to passionate kisses which quickly led to feverish consummation of their love. After lingering over breakfast they strolled beside the abbey, and then walked along the wooded banks of the Wharfe.

That night they dined in the hotel and sat over drinks until their need for each other eventually took them up to their room.

'I'm glad we came here,' said Alex the day they moved on. 'We'll never find a more beautiful spot to concentrate on being together.'

Their honeymoon had been a short spell of stepping back from everyday life. Returning a week later to their new home, they both realised that war was fast approaching. Listening to the wireless, they had thrust upon them the fact that while they had been away two thousand Nazi guards had been sent to Danzig.

By the end of July Britain was threatening to go to the assistance of the Polish people there if force should become necessary to support them against German infiltration. And it wasn't only here that concern was growing; an Anglo-French delegation had travelled to Moscow for discussion of a three-power defence pact.

In common with most men in business, Joseph Stone was extremely uneasy, sharp with everyone because of his preoccupation with every scrap of news from across the Channel. He'd known for well over a year that the peace was fragile but had willed himself to believe it could hold. Times should have been so good for Stone's, with his son now qualified and Helen adding her flair as well.

Alex was proving to have sound business sense, a complement to his reliability as a designer which boded well for the future. If only the firm was permitted to concentrate on work.

By 9 August, however, the King was inspecting an auxiliary fleet comprising over 130 ships. Less than a fortnight later Britain was reaffirming her promise to assist Poland amid constant stories of German activity on the border with Upper Silesia. Before the end of the month children were being evacuated from Paris and London. And treasures from principal museums, art galleries and Westminster Abbey were being removed to places of safety. On the last day of August reservists of both the army and RAF were being called up, while mobilisation of the Royal Navy was beginning.

'War's inevitable, isn't it?' Helen said with a sigh that evening, alarmed by the prospect of all building work ceasing, and men being compelled to enlist in the forces. How would she bear it if Alex was sent away while they were still adjusting to each other? Playing at living together. Although they seemed to get on, this life of theirs didn't yet seem real. There was so much more that she'd hoped to do towards establishing a sound marriage.

'Yes, there'll be no turning back now.'

She gave him a look. 'You don't sound all that sorry.'

'I'd miss you, of course, if I was forced to join up.'

'You'd miss our work as well, surely? Stone's . . .'

He shrugged. Today he was less than sure on that score. Already depressed by the curtailing of so many of their schemes, he had lunched alone with his father in order to discuss contingency arrangements pending the outbreak of hostilities. And Joseph Stone had said something which had slapped him in the eye.

'Helen's had the same training as yourself, remember, Alexander. If you're conscripted, we'll cope between us.'

Alex hadn't liked that. 'And, after all, there'll be precious little civilian building going on,' he'd observed quickly.

'Even if there were more,' his father had continued, 'I don't question her ability to cope. She has a natural instinct.'

'Are you saying I haven't?'

'Since you press the point, I reckon you'll always excel at making a good deal, keeping us afloat. Your comprehension of architecture is quite adequate, don't get me wrong . . .'

'Quite adequate' had stuck in Alex's throat. Despite his feelings for Helen he couldn't help wishing she was employed anywhere but in their family firm. It would take more than this constant physical need of her to make him regret the prospect of some breathing space.

Alex was still trying to decide which of the armed forces he would prefer when he received a confidential communication. As soon as war was declared men were being sought who possessed the knowledge that would help construct aircraft hangars, off-shore and coastal defences, command posts. He volunteered immediately, rather than risking call-up which might intervene to take him into something less congenial.

Helen felt torn when he told her. A part of her was thankful that he would be involved in an aspect of the war which carried less threat of real danger. On the other hand was his imminent departure, and that seemed well-nigh impossible to accept.

On his last night at home he took her fiercely as if compelling her with his body to acknowledge his strength, his superiority even.

Towards dawn, she turned to him again, seeking a gentler, loving reassurance. But Alex was sated still, and more than that, aware that permitting too much tenderness might sap his will to leave.

'It's only London I'm going to, initially, love. I'll be home for weekends, I dare say.'

Before he returned, though, there were nights to endure in the little house on the hill which hadn't yet lost its air of unfamiliarity. Her father-in-law had suggested at once that she might move into The Stone House. Helen had thanked him and declined. She couldn't say as much to him, but if she went anywhere it would be to her own parents, not that she intended resorting to that either.

Both Kathleen and Daniel regretted her making that decision, they'd have welcomed her company. They, too, were having their lives disrupted. Daniel's engineering skill had ensured that he was one of the first men locally to be sent to work on munitions. And Kathleen was faced with the prospect of taking more responsibility for Marian's children.

'Denis is volunteering for a special unit,' Marian had announced one Sunday. 'It's for keeping the troops entertained – ENSA. He's going to adore being involved in that.'

'And what about you, love?' her mother asked, some additional sense warning her already that young Mark and Linda would soon be seeing very little of either parent.

'I can drive, can't I? They'll need lots of drivers. I'm trying to get taken on for handling an ambulance.'

'Round here, do you mean?' Daniel asked, frowning.

'Probably, not sure yet. But you could cope, Mum, couldn't you, with the children.'

The arrangement seemed far from ideal, but Kathleen wasn't the sort to protest without giving it a try. Both Mark and Linda were used to her, after all. Linda had started school, would have lessons to occupy her. And besides, it was a lot worse for children down south who were being sent to strangers.

Helen's working life was totally changed. All civilian construction had ceased, to be followed by a period of visiting sites and checking that the builders concerned were ensuring they were left in such a state that they wouldn't deteriorate too drastically while work was halted. An abnormal stillness settled on the office. Frank Barclay had joined the navy. Joseph himself had been turned down as unfit for the First World War on account of some problem with his heart. He was pretty certain to remain where he was this time.

He was also much older than Helen had suspected. At fifty-five he was unlikely to have been conscripted had he been fit. And suddenly he seemed to age, whiling away time, keeping the firm ticking over, but with all purpose drained from him.

'Do you think they'll happen want you doing something similar to Alex?' Helen had asked one day, hating to see him so inactive.

Dismally, Joseph had shaken his head. 'Their reply wasn't encouraging when I offered my services. Maybe they think I'm past it.'

Alex arrived home one weekend, delighting Helen as well as bringing relief from her anxiety. He wasn't given to writing letters, and in all the weeks he'd been away had only managed an occasional short note to her. He had telephoned her in the office, but had told her so little that his calls had merely left her aching with the frustration of learning nothing about his new life.

'So tell me all about it,' she began now that he was home.

They had flung themselves into bed half an hour after his arrival, and now were glowing in the aftermath of their lovemaking. Helen felt she was relaxing for the first time since he'd gone away.

'Not much I can tell, I'm afraid, love. Top secret, most of it.'

'You can tell *me*, surely? What're you designing? where are you working – in London itself?'

Even that couldn't be revealed. She was dreadfully

disappointed, and strangely hurt, so hurt that she felt choked. It was over seven years since she had first had a part in Alexander's life. Now they were married and he was excluding her as he never had in the past.

Things seemed no better on the next occasion that he returned to the West Riding, and by this time her life at Stone's had grown so uninteresting that Helen felt she was being stifled.

'You don't really need me here, do you?' she said to her father-in-law on the day that Alex had gone off again.

Joseph smiled. 'You'll always have a place in Stone's, Helen my dear, you know that.'

'And nowt to do until the duration?'

'Terribly boring, isn't it?' he admitted. 'Bad enough for an old fellow like me. It's particularly hard for people like yourself who've only just become qualified.'

'What would you do if I found something more useful, just while the war was on, of course?'

'Stay here, much the same as I'm doing now. But I've got something else on – I'm becoming involved in the Local Defence Volunteers. Matter of fact, I'm making parts of The Stone House available to them.'

'That's good.'

'Gives me something to think about.'

'A bit of purpose, aye. Well then, happen you won't object to my idea. I had enough of factories when I worked evenings at that biscuit place, I want to avoid that if I can. What I thought was – well, they're crying out for women to help with growing food.'

'The Land Army, you mean? Good thinking, Helen.'

'With a bit of luck, I mightn't get sent too far away from home,' she began. She felt a certain responsibility towards quite a few people, including old Mr March, who must be visited as well as her family. 'I could keep an eye on my mum and dad – you know she's looking after our Marian's two? And I could still pop over to see you.'

Joseph was so obviously pleased that she was thinking of him that she was reminded all over again what a *genuine* man he was, and not a bit of side to him.

The farm where Helen began her introduction to the Women's Land Army certainly was nearer to home than she had dared to hope. Just the far side of Huddersfield, quite close to Holmfirth, it spread acre upon acre across bleak but beautiful hills. Because of the altitude, and exposure to the winds which drove in from all directions, it was a cold spot in that spring of 1940. She shuddered to think what it would be like in winter.

She was greeted on that first day by a broad, harassed-looking woman who came tramping out into the farmyard, shooing ahead of her a couple of hens which evidently had wandered indoors.

'Mrs Templer?' Helen inquired, and announced her own name. 'I'm one of your land-girls.'

'*Miss* Templer,' she was corrected fiercely. The hand which was offered was the size of a man's, and felt stronger. 'Thank goodness one on you's arrived. I'm on my own here, you know. Have been since my brother was taken.'

'Oh, dear,' said Helen sympathetically. 'Was his illness sudden like?'

Miss Templer laughed. 'Not dead, lass – taken to work in Sheffield. The war effort, of course. Ordnance factory.'

'Oh, I see.'

'It were his own fault. Farming's a reserved occupation, but no – he had to go and do summat different. Men! Any road, we'll show 'em, soon as I get more like you.'

'Are you expecting others soon?' Helen inquired as she was led through a hall reeking of cabbage towards some steep stairs.

'I were expecting somebody day afore yesterday, but no one turned up. There's no organisation, you know, all at sixes and sevens. I could do better myself.'

Helen was to discover that this last remark was applied to most tasks which affected any part of Miss Templer's life. For the present, she was allowed no time to consider what had been said. The third door along the landing was flung wide, revealing six camp beds with a mere foot of space between them, one drab brown wardrobe and a small chest of drawers.

'Nothing fancy, I'm afraid. I daresay you'll be too tired to notice, any road. Unless you're used to farm work?'

'Not really.'

'None of 'em will be. You'll learn. Dump your stuff for now, will you? I were just thinking of rounding up ready for milking.'

Her hostess had clomped along the landing and down to the foot of the stairs by the time Helen had emerged from the bedroom and closed the door behind her. When she eventually reached the outer door, a bellow greeted her from the far side of a drystone wall.

'Over here. Is that t'fastest you can move?'

The pasture was tussocky, very wet, and spattered with the inevitable cow dung. The first time Helen slithered in an evil-smelling patch brought the smile back to Miss Templer's face. 'You'll get plenty of that, lass.'

A high-pitched whistle summoned the farm dog, a black and white animal, part collie, part indeterminate, which bounded past Helen, lashing her with its dusty tail. The cattle were scattered over the field, munching contentedly but beginning to show interest as the dog went from one to the next, snuffling around their heels and emitting an occasional tiny bark.

'Ranger's better nor any cow-hand for bringing 'em in . . . just you watch.'

Helen was impressed. One by one the brown and white beasts turned towards the centre of the field and ambled on, the dog nudging them into line and onwards to the gate.

'You'll not have done any milking, I suppose?'

'Afraid not, Mrs – Miss Templer.'

'You'd better watch this time then. You can have a go tomorrow.'

It was the only thing over which Helen was allowed any lenience. After milking, the sheep had to be fed.

'The ground were frozen solid all winter, and now they've cropped it bare. Fodder's in the barn over yonder. And you can see where they're grazing, just under the brow of the hill. You'll need to look sharp or it'll be dark afore you've fed 'em. Oh – and keep your eyes open, will you? There's none due for lambing till next week, but if there's any dropping them now, you must think on to call me.'

Helen's arms had never ached so much in the whole of her life and her back felt as if it simply wouldn't straighten again. Who'd have thought that spreading feed for a few sheep would be such hard work! The slope of the hill hadn't helped, either. She was breathless by the time she'd finished, and scratched by the numerous beds of thistles.

'You're married, I see,' Miss Templer remarked, during supper, nodding towards Helen's left hand. 'Joined up, has he, your husband?'

'No – actually he's involved in designing war

defences, that kind of thing.'

'Oh, brainy, is he? Good job there's others like us, isn't it, lass? Not too proud to do a bit of hard graft. Pity about you being wed,' she added.

When the other Land Army girls arrived next morning, Helen noticed Miss Templer taking great interest in whether or not they were married. She began wondering if the woman's disapproval of men was extended to include anyone who had a male in her life.

One day shortly afterwards a telephone call from the ministry advised them that they were to be joined by three fellows who had proved unfit for factory work or the services.

'Never mind, we'll give them all the boring jobs and them that's furthest from t'farm,' Miss Templer assured the girls with relish.

When the men arrived, Helen soon found she was glad of the bit of spice which their presence brought. Mealtimes were very lively, with plenty of banter from the men, who all seemed to be around forty. Each of them was married, happy to pass around family photographs, and glad of any opportunity to dash off home to Sheffield. The heavy industry there made the city a target for enemy aircraft, and they needed regular reassurance that all was well.

One of the men, Kenneth Potter, rather reminded her of Alex. He had similar golden hair, and was of roughly the same build. Kenneth was asthmatic, and was quite badly affected by many of the grains they were obliged to handle, and by some of the local plants. He remained cheerful, nevertheless, and grateful when Helen and the other girls relieved him of some of the tasks among things that made him react badly.

'I'm determined to do my bit,' he told Helen one

day while she distributed fodder. 'And, much as it mightn't look that way, I'm a lot better here nor I were in yon factory.'

They teamed up as much as possible after that, as often as they could without Miss Templer becoming aware of it, exchanging jobs so that Kenneth tackled some of the digging and planting while Helen dealt with anything that hindered his breathing.

To her relief, Miss Templer seemed unaware that any changes were made to her allocation of work. 'She never appears particularly bothered what I'm doing so long as I never let up,' Helen confided to one of the other girls when they happened to be the only two in their cramped room one June evening.

Jessie, a pretty dark-haired lass who never looked strong enough for manual work, gave her a funny look. 'Well, she wouldn't, would she? Templer's only interested in girls who are single. The rest of us are just hands that get the work done somehow.'

'How do you mean?' asked Helen, bewildered.

Jessie's astonishingly loud laugh startled her. 'Nay, Helen – don't tell me you haven't spotted what's going on? You've been here longer than any of us.'

'Going on?'

'Where do you think Iris gets to when she slopes off while we're out in t'fields? And like t'other night when her bed wasn't slept in . . .'

'Wasn't she off with some chap? I thought happen she'd gone over to Kirkburton or Holmfirth or somewhere.'

'Not she! It's not fellows that her and Templer need. Surely you noticed how the old girl was eyeing up the talent when we all got here? She tried it on with Mavis, I believe, but she weren't having any. Mavis is keen on a chap in the navy, and certainly wouldn't look at another woman.'

'And you're saying that some lasses – that Iris . . .?' Helen was incredulous.

Again, Jessie's loud laughter echoed round the room. She glanced towards the door, checking it was closed. 'Do you mean to tell me this is t'first you've heard of owt like this? Didn't you mix with a lot of lasses in your job back home?'

'I studied architecture, that's the work I've been doing. With mainly males all around.'

'Lucky you! I see now why you've not met anybody with lesbian tendencies afore.'

'I'm beginning to think I should be thankful for that. What do they get out of it, though? I mean – whatever do they do?'

Jessie seemed to find this hilarious. 'That I can't tell you, love. But it seems to keep 'em happy. Just you watch. Even old Templer softens up when Iris is about. And Iris is always making up to her.'

For some weeks after learning this Helen was very observant whenever Miss Templer and Iris were both around at the same time. And although she still found the idea of two women having some sort of sexual relationship rather incredible, she couldn't deny that they did behave like a pair of lovers.

She felt terribly naive for having had no previous knowledge that such relationships could exist, and wondered for a few days if the other lasses might think she was a bit simple. If ever they laughed without her being aware of the cause she would ask herself if they could be making fun of her.

Suddenly, though, without warning, Alex returned to Yorkshire and gave her something more serious to think about. The first she knew of his visit was when he came striding along the lane that skirted the field where she was busy. She had been forking hay all day and had paused to wipe sweat from her face, laughing up at Kenneth who was driving the cart. After the weeks of hard work toughening up her muscles, she enjoyed tossing hay, and Ken appreciated sitting where he was, far enough from the horse to protect his allergies, and at a relatively safe distance from the crop.

'Do you reckon I'm getting conditioned to this, any road?' he asked her.

'Could be, I suppose.'

'I certainly haven't had a bad wheezing do for a while.'

'That's good, love,' she replied, then turned from him to grin towards one of the other fellows who was propelling a massive bale in their direction.

'You'll have muscles like a prize fighter, shifting all that hay, Helen,' he called.

She laughed. 'Aye, won't that be champion?'

'And will it be champion having a face parched by the sun, and hands that're calloused?' asked a serious voice from the other side of the drystone wall.

'Alex!' Helen exclaimed. 'Eh – this is a lovely surprise!'

'Is it?' he inquired, the grey-green eyes unsmiling.

'Well, of course. Look, there's the gate over yonder. Come on through. Meet Kenneth and . . .'

'I'll stay where I am, thanks. Not dressed for trudging among that lot.' From his expression he was less suited for meeting the men working alongside her than for tramping through hay.

Helen went to join him in the lane, gave him a hug, and thrust down her disappointment when he didn't kiss her. Happen he found having the others looking on inhibiting.

'You'd like Kenneth,' she said, 'the other two an' all. They're all three of them about as used to farm work as the rest of us! But we all muck in . . .'

'Evidently.' Alex had taken one of her hands and was inspecting it closely, noting the blackened and splintered nails, the blisters and overall roughness. Sighing, he planted a kiss on her cracked knuckles, then grasped the hand between both of his. 'We must talk,' he said. 'Soon. Can you wangle a night off? It is our anniversary, after all.'

Helen swallowed. 'I'll try, love. I ought to be able to square it with Miss Templer. I haven't been taking time off, we've been that busy.' So busy that she hadn't given their anniversary a thought. How could she have overlooked it? No wonder Alex seemed so disgruntled.

When he refused to go up to the farm to wait for her, she explained that there was a little tea room half a mile away. 'They lay on a decent cuppa. Come back for me at half-past five, I'll have a word with old Templer before then.'

Having got the night off, and the following day as well, Helen should have been feeling elated when she joined Alex that evening. Somehow, though, their earlier encounter had induced a sense of foreboding.

'I needn't be back till last thing tomorrow night,' she announced, getting into the Standard while he held the door for her. 'Where are we going?'

'Home, naturally. You do recall that we have a home, I suppose?'

'Oh, Alex, don't be like that. There's no need.'

'No? When I arrive back there and find how neglected it feels?'

'You know I'm working over here.'

'It's not the other side of the earth. If I can make it from London, you could exert a bit of effort.'

'There was nothing wrong there, was there? Sally promised she'd keep an eye on the place for us.'

'Sally's not with the firm any longer – joined the ATS or something. She handed the key back to Father. You didn't believe he'd feel obliged to keep going to the house, lighting fires and so on? And Mrs Hartley's not getting any younger. She has enough on these days keeping house for Father, and no other help there now.'

'I didn't expect either of them to do owt. But somebody could have let me know. I'd have made time to pop over then.' She couldn't help wishing she was working further from home so that this would never have arisen. 'Let's not argue, eh, love? I'll do what I can while we're there.'

Alex seemed not to be listening. He started up the car and drew out into the lane before speaking. 'Father's not at all well.'

'Eh, I am sorry. We'll go and see him then. What's wrong? Is it his heart?'

'Nothing like that. Nothing you can define. He just – isn't himself. Half the time he doesn't even seem to listen to what you're saying. And he asked me when I arrived if I could tell him what his sister's name was. Said it had slipped his mind. Not at all like him, you must agree.'

'Well, this war is an upset to everybody. Happen if we go and cheer him up a bit . . .'

'We'll see,' said Alex glumly. He'd managed to obtain a decent bottle of wine, and had asked Mrs Hartley to buy them a couple of chops or something. All he wanted was Helen and himself in their own home, celebrating this special day of theirs which she gave every sign of ignoring.

All the way back towards Halifax and out in the direction of Luddenden Foot Helen was willing herself not to suggest they should go elsewhere. Strange though it was, she was dreading returning to their home, terribly scared by the thought that she'd be unable to tear herself away afterwards.

'Do you want to just pop along and see your father first?' she asked before they turned left off the main road.

'He'll be having dinner. Leave it till tomorrow.'

As soon as they unlocked the door and went inside, Helen realised that she'd been wrong to feel reluctant about coming here. This was where they belonged, where they must rediscover one another. And Alex had done his best to make their living room welcoming. There were flowers on the table, and he'd set it – however crookedly – with her best drawn-threadwork tablecloth and their one good set of china.

'Eh, love, you've made it look right grand!' she exclaimed, and hugged him.

His kisses were feverish over her lips, but he didn't part them, and nor did he press close in the way he had of urging her to equal his passion. Helen wondered whatever was going wrong.

Whoever Mrs Hartley had bribed to supply the chops, she'd done a good job. They tasted delicious, accompanied by vegetables which Helen had been pressed to accept by Miss Templer.

Pleasantly mellowed by the unaccustomed wine, Helen washed the dishes afterwards while Alex leaned into the doorframe, watching. She'd have appreciated a hand with the drying up, but reminded herself that Alex hadn't been brought up to understand that such chores existed, much less that he should assist with them. If she continued expecting too much of him, she was in for a lot of disappointments. And he had provided the basis of a lovely meal. She just wished she wasn't almost asleep on her feet . . .

They talked for a while afterwards, mostly about the war which had halted their careers even though, in this part of Yorkshire, folk had yet to face any real danger. Only a few days previously the Luftwaffe had attacked British convoys in the Channel, and Alex was afraid this indicated it wouldn't be long before there was fierce bombardment of the mainland.

'How safe are you, love?' Helen asked anxiously.

He reassured her quickly. 'Very safe – don't forget the government needs chaps like us to design features essential to their strategy.'

It sounded extremely important. If she didn't enjoy her own farmwork so much she would be envying him. But suddenly when he spoke again she felt agitation rise within her.

'I wish I could say I approved of what you are doing,' he began. 'I'm afraid I can't. I hated seeing you labouring in the fields, and look what it's doing to you. Your hair's all dried up.'

'That's the sun. Once the summer's over it'll get back to normal.'

'It's taken the colour out of it as well. And your hands are dreadful, Helen.'

She laughed. 'That's summat and nowt. I'll try and get some Glymiel jelly. That's supposed to make 'em smooth again.'

Alex didn't laugh with her. There was more than the effect upon his wife's appearance to trouble him, but he wouldn't mention the other factor that made him loathe what she was doing. Seeing her smiling up at the chap who was handling the hay cart, and grinning at the other fellow, had cut right through him. He couldn't blame the two of them for responding. Helen had a smashing figure, these days; no doubt the exercise had pared away every ounce of surplus fat. And this one thing that hadn't been ruined by that damned job was making her more attractive to men like those two. He felt like giving her what for, though, because she had seemed to be egging them on.

'Shall we get to bed?' Helen suggested, and felt relieved when Alex agreed. She missed him while he was away, she was certain about that, but when he was home they seemed to be on edge with each other.

How good it was to have fine cotton sheets, she thought, slipping into bed, and a proper mattress instead of that camp bed. It was utter bliss to escape from the chatter of the other five lasses, and to have no smokers in the room. She could smell honeysuckle and night-scented stocks wafting in through the open window. And it was so quiet here, with no crashing around from the attic above where other farm workers had to shift the stirrup-pump and precautionary buckets of sand in order to reach their beds.

Maybe if she had a good night's sleep while she was at home she'd feel better able to withstand Alexander's disapproval, which kept upsetting her so much that the lump in her throat seemed permanent.

Helen was nearly asleep when she felt Alex get in beside her. She tried to respond when he started kissing and caressing her, but she was too exhausted to hold out against her own weariness. She was hardly conscious when he began making love to her.

Chapter 8

Alexander seemed unforgiving at breakfast. Only afterwards when Helen insisted that they should go back upstairs did he begin to smile again. She couldn't blame him. Falling asleep like that when he'd come all this way was something no man would consider a compliment! But still he kept condemning her farm job.

'I know you were tired out, but this work's ruining everything, Helen. Surely there's some other way you could help the war effort?'

'I like what I'm doing. Though not the way it's annoying you. Come on, love – don't let's spoil our bit of time together arguing.'

This lovemaking more than made up for the previous night's. Alex's mood improved and he suggested later that they should call on her mother. 'I suppose your father'll be at work.'

'I expect so. Wait a minute, though – he could be in. I'm sure they're working shifts. Don't forget there's your dad, an' all. I want to see him.'

'That's only a few strides away, isn't it? He'll be in the office, won't he? It's a Tuesday, not the weekend.'

Joseph Stone greeted them both with his old enthusiasm, and hugged Helen so hard that her ribs felt bruised.

'You're looking well, love,' he told her, delighting

her so much that she had to curb the impulse to give Alex a triumphant glance.

'Must be the fresh air,' she said lightly. 'And I daresay all that exercise does no harm. But how are you?'

'Bored,' he admitted ruefully. 'There's precious little to occupy me here at work. I'm only content when I'm doing something for the LDVs – or Home Guard, as we're going to be called. It's no secret that's the new name that Winston Churchill is giving us. We've got some grand fellows there, you know. Just because some of them are getting on a bit or have a disability that keeps them out of the forces, doesn't mean that they can't fulfil a useful function.'

He began asking her about the Land Army and showed all the interest which had been lacking in his son's attitude. But then, thought Helen, he's not personally involved in the way that Alex is – he won't take it to heart because my hair's a mess, and my hands are rough.

Her own parents were both in the house, although Daniel was just pulling on his overalls ready for going on shift at two o'clock.

'I hate this shift work,' her mother told them after a round of hugs and kisses. 'We have to have our meals at peculiar times, and your dad can't seem to sleep the same, specially when he's on nights.'

'I don't suppose having Mark and Linda during the day will help when you're trying to get to sleep, eh, Dad?'

Her father stifled a sigh. 'I wouldn't say that. They're not naughty, either on 'em. And Linda's at school during t'day, of course.'

'Where's Mark today then, Mum?' asked Helen.

'Marian's got the day off. Worked a solid fortnight, she has, on them ambulances.'

'Round here? I didn't think there'd have been the need. There's not been owt much in the way of air-raids.'

'Eh, no. But she's over in Sheffield these days. They were crying out for ambulance drivers.'

'I see. So you've got the little ones most of the time then?'

'Aye. Not that I mind. They're getting to be right good company. And I'm glad of that, the hours your dad's working. But never mind us, we're all right really. What about you two?'

When Alexander said very little, Kathleen began prompting him. 'Are they looking after you proper down south? It is there that you've gone, isn't it? They're not like us, are they? Don't seem so thorough somehow. All top show, eh?'

'I've no complaints, Mother,' he responded swiftly.

Helen had never heard him address her mum like that before. Things could be so good, if he'd only stay so agreeable. He was talking right enough now, telling Kathleen the Tower of London moat had been dug up to make allotments. She just wished he'd stop going on about her Land Army work; knowing how strongly he disapproved would make her miserable when she returned to the farm.

In fact, Helen felt no more than the odd twinge of homesickness once she arrived back there. Naturally she'd been sorry to say goodbye to Alex when he set off for London, but she was relieved of the tension of wondering what he'd say next in condemnation of this place.

She couldn't deny that she'd been disappointed that he had been so critical, but she was determined it wasn't going to spoil what she was doing. Helping to feed the nation and to prevent merchant ships making so many trips across dangerous seas was bound to do nothing but good. And perhaps by the next time he came home she would have thought up a way to make him happier about it all.

She had more notice of his next visit to Yorkshire, had used one of her days off to go over and brighten up the house, and had reflected hard during the intervening weeks, coming up with a plan that ought to get them through the couple of days more cheerfully. They weren't going to dwell on the way things were now, nor on how it had been in the past when they weren't suffering the frustration of having their careers suspended. She wouldn't let this war ruin their marriage. They were going to discuss the future, imagine how grand it would be when they were in their own home permanently, and working to build up Stone's again. How they would design such splendid buildings!

They had enjoyed the pie she had made for dinner, even though the meagre amount of meat had been eked out with plenty of potatoes; and the baked custard she'd made using dried egg and household milk powder hadn't tasted bad at all. They'd had a treat afterwards – Miss Templer had given her a bottle of the plum port which she'd made out of damsons and some of their precious sugar. Alex had grimaced when he compared it with real port, but it had made a nice change, and seemed to give Helen a bit more spirit.

While she was feeling bright she began her attempt at encouraging him to look forward to the future. 'We'll really appreciate it, won't we, love, when we can get back to our own work again? It'll be such fun designing together.'

'Except that we don't agree on that any more than we do on most things, do we? Or are you prepared to acknowledge now that it is time that we architects came up to date in what we're offering?'

Why should I be the one to change? wondered Helen. Why is it *my* ideas that always are wrong? Suddenly deflated, she could arouse no enthusiasm for the future, and certainly none for the prospect of surrendering all her notions to her husband's. She told herself that the war was to blame for this inability to look forward together to the peace that was bound to come; the lives they were living now were so abnormal that they couldn't be expected to plan ahead.

Somehow, though, each time that she and Alex managed to be together, her doubts about their affinity were increased. Nothing she said seemed to be right. And he upset her deeply with his efforts to get her to try some other kind of war work.

As she learned more about farming, Helen was growing steadily more enthusiastic about what she was doing. Since she couldn't get on with her career, she'd put her heart into this job. She made friends among the other girls, and if some of them moved on to different areas, Jessie remained at Miss Templer's. The three men stayed there. During some of the coldest months Kenneth's asthma confined him to bed, and Miss Templer threatened to have him replaced by someone in better health, but that didn't come to anything. And eventually, in the autumn of 1942, when Italian prisoners of war were allocated to local farms, their team was increased by Vittore Fabri.

Vittore was a striking young man, with his black hair and eyes that were scarcely any lighter; although he wasn't quite as tall as Helen herself, he was extremely strong. It wasn't for any physical reason, however, that Helen first was drawn to him. Indeed, after their initial introduction, she hardly noticed Vittore until a day or two later.

It was Kenneth who called her across one morning while they were finishing off the milking. 'What do you think, Helen – this chap's an architect an' all.'

'You're not, are you?' she exclaimed. 'Well, I never!'

Vittore's usually solemn expression warmed into a massive smile. 'But yes, I am. And most surprised, I do assure you, to learn that architecture is your work also.'

Helen grinned as she glanced up from the pail she was lifting. 'Oh, aye? I hope your surprise isn't because I'm a female in your line of business?'

He shrugged ruefully. 'A little perhaps. But mostly, I must emphasise, because you are the first fellow architect whom I have met since I left my home in Florence to join our navy.'

'And you come from Florence – by, but that's a grand city!' Helen was so excited that she hardly noticed the milk splashing out of the pail she was handling carelessly.

'Steady on, lass,' said Ken, glancing down at the milk seeping into the ground.

Helen grimaced. 'Don't let on about that to Miss Templer, will you? But I'm that thrilled to know what you do, Vittore. You and me will have to have a long talk.'

They soon began the first of many lengthy, revealing conversations. Digging potatoes and other vegetables, tending stock on the windswept hillside or collecting eggs, they revelled in discussing the similarities and the differences in their backgrounds.

'Your training was much like my husband's,' Helen remarked on learning that Vittore's late father was an architect. 'I did it the hard way – although I was very lucky to be helped by a bursary.' She grew silent, remembering Fenny March, and wishing her twenty-five shillings weekly wages (though it was more than the minimum) allowed her to put back some of the money which had enabled her to study. And wishing as well that she could snatch more than the very occasional couple of hours for going to see Mr March.

'Perhaps, though, *you* appreciate more the training which has resulted in your ability to practise architecture?'

'Do you know, Vittore, I think you're right. There was a lot that Alex took for granted. So much so that I believe some aspects of our work bored him.'

'And you were never bored?'

'I didn't have much time to be. We'd hardly got started after all the years of training when the war came. What about you?'

'Through being in my father's firm, I had considerable practical experience. Also, I am older than you, I think. The day I was captured in the Mediterranean it was my thirtieth birthday.'

'How awful for you. What happened – do you want to talk about it? Or not to anybody on our side maybe?'

Vittore grinned. 'Since coming here I have not been made to feel conscious of there being "sides".'

'Or not until you get back to camp every night, eh? Well, then . . .'

'We were manning a cruiser which, along with two destroyers, was sunk by British forces. Initially, I was more thankful to be pulled out of the sea than perturbed to be taken prisoner.'

'I seem to remember hearing summat about the incident on the wireless. When did you say it was?'

'In June – the sixteenth.'

Helen nodded. 'I bet that was what we called the "Battle of the Convoys". They gave it out on the nine o'clock news.'

Trudging one day over the scrubby hillside as they brought the sheep down to a lower pasture, Helen remarked on Vittore's English. 'It's that good, I keep forgetting you're foreign!'

Laughing, he thanked her. 'You are the second person to say that. When I arrived over here I worked on making buildings safe after they had been bombed. Hadgraft – the boss – seemed quite impressed because we could converse. He wanted to know why my English was so correct.'

'And why is it? You must have studied a long time?'

'Certainly, I did. At university. And it began mainly because of architecture. I am a great fan of Edwin Lutyens, discovering more about his work was easier in English.'

'But surely reading foreign books is difficult, though?'

'A challenge at first, perhaps. After a time I became so fascinated that I persevered until I was even thinking in your language.'

When Vittore never mentioned either his wife or any family, Helen was eventually driven by curiosity to ask if he was single.

'No, I am married, but my wife . . . she did not live with me any longer, even before I went to sea. I do not talk about this. In Italy, you understand, is big disgrace. My family are Roman Catholic, very devout.'

'I see.'

'The Catholic faith has much to answer for, I think. Holding people together when they no longer love.'

And keeping them apart when they love too well and unsuitably, thought Helen fiercely. Suddenly, she was overwhelmed again by the emotions which Christopher Maitland had evoked. Beginning to think of him, she was seized by a need to know where Chris was, to be reassured that he wasn't endangered by this wretched war.

'What is wrong?' Vittore inquired gently. 'You are distressed.'

Helen sighed. 'It's something I thought I'd got over long since.' For no reason that she understood, she began telling him about the meeting with Chris, and how his vocation had prevented their relationship developing. 'I've never told anyone else about him,' she added.

Vittore was smiling wistfully. 'Then I thank you for confiding in me. You should not regret your meeting with this priest in training, you know – it cannot be easy for them to resign themselves to living without the warmth of close relationships. Who knows? Perhaps meeting you has given him a more comprehensive understanding of human feelings.'

'I wish I could believe that. All it's done for me is provide comparisons that I should never be making.'

His dark eyes were frowning suddenly. 'But your marriage, surely, is happy?'

'It will be,' Helen asserted fervently. 'When this lot's over and we can be together again, then it'll be a right good partnership.' She had got to believe that – had got to use all her determination to make her life with Alex work.

For the present, there was very little that she could do to hold their marriage together. She wrote frequently to Alex, but he replied only rarely, and his visits home had become rarer still. There were times when some little reminder brought her up sharp, making her wonder if they would ever be a proper family. A few days ago she had caught herself staring at one of the 'Lend to Defend' posters designed to encourage investment in National Savings Certificates. She had realised all of a sudden that *she* wanted a fair-haired lad who might be gazing into the future like the one depicted with a Meccano set.

Even though there were fewer air-raids here in the north, wartime was biting. One of the other land-girls had got married the other week and Helen had felt deeply sorry for her. The best the confectioner could provide as a wedding cake was a rented one constructed of cardboard with 'icing' made out of chalk. Helen was glad she'd been able to help out by lending her own wedding outfit. The poor lass had been upset that day, as well. The news at breakfast time was of a bad raid on Canterbury which was her home town.

Instead of going to her new husband's parents for their one-night honeymoon, the youngsters had set off by train to find out how her own folk had stood up to the bombing in Canterbury. The only good thing had been seeing her family. She'd been disappointed earlier that her parents' work prevented their travelling to Yorkshire for the wedding.

'They were so glad to see me,' she told Helen afterwards, 'we sat up talking most of the night. My new hubby wasn't half cross!'

Overhearing, Vittore cast his expressive dark gaze towards the sky above their heads which was heavy with rain clouds. 'I can sympathise. I hope that you were very nice to him to compensate!'

From the shade of the young bride's cheeks, it seemed that she had been. Vittore laughed and turned to Helen. 'Now I know that it is true what they say – you English do not share our hot blood.'

'You reckon?' she asked, thinking of her own husband. 'I daresay it's more true that we're a bit of a mixture. Some of us have our moments . . .'

He grinned back at her and winked.

It was only then that she realised that her remark

could have been interpreted as flirtatious – something which she certainly hadn't intended. She was thankful that they were jolted out of the light-hearted discussion by sounds of great frivolity from the kitchen.

The first large drops of the gathering storm drove them to abandon the potatoes they were picking. They were due for a tea break and dashed in through the kitchen door.

The laughter they'd heard was Miss Templer and Iris, in fits over the latter's attempt at helping with the cooking. They were making a Somerset recipe, Rook Pie, and a fiddly job it was proving. After soaking overnight, the rooks had to be skinned.

Miss Templer was still wiping tears from her round face. 'I thought I were cack-handed in t'kitchen,' she exclaimed, 'but Iris, bless 'er, beats me.'

'But they're such titchy things to skin. And I didn't know you could only use meat off their breasts and legs.'

'Go on, you're doing champion,' Miss Templer encouraged her. 'You've picked out all them nasty bitter pieces of meat that you shouldn't ought to use. It'll be right enough now. And the topping you've made for it'll be fair scrumptious.'

'I hope so,' said Iris. 'It's just a pity you lot came in while it's at this stage.'

Miss Templer laughed again, but not unkindly. 'Don't take on, Iris love, it's same whatever we serve these days. You know what the Ministry of Food advise – don't tell folk what the dish is made from, until they've eaten it.'

The Rook Pie wasn't a tremendous success, but it did provide another substantial hot meal, essential this high on the bleak hills, and Miss Templer defended Iris from the others' ribbing.

Looking around the farmhouse table that evening, Helen realised all over again what a happy bunch they were, much like a big family of widely differing individuals. Somehow, though, it was always with Vittore that she felt the strongest affinity now. They'd spent so many hours talking about Florentine architecture while they tackled milking, harvesting and other strenuous tasks, that Helen felt it was only recently that she'd visited Italy.

She wouldn't have admitted anything of the kind to one of her companions, but privately she was growing aware that she looked for Vittore's arrival from the detention camp each morning. She also felt his absence when he returned there at nightfall. Even while summer was kinder to them, the farm was isolated.

They occasionally made their own amusement. Ken suggested that Miss Templer might be able to obtain permission for Vittore to stay later at the farm one evening. They had decided to hold a harvest supper. They weren't short of vegetables, and could hoard their meat rations for the occasion. Miss Templer had bottled masses of rhubarb, and custard made with powdered milk would combine well with it. Ken and the other two chaps had arranged for their wives to come over for the night, and the newly married girl was bringing her husband.

Vittore was so grateful to be allowed to attend that he had given a large chunk of his wages to provide beer which, despite its wartime wateriness, would be acceptable to all.

As an antidote to their sheer hard slog, gathering in the farm parlour which had been opened up especially soon proved to be a tonic. The three wives who'd arrived at teatime from Sheffield had all brought home-made cakes to add to the feast. Most of all, though, they had come with spirits high at the prospect of a night with their loved ones. Helen began wishing that Alex might have been present, then almost at once recognised that he wouldn't really have fitted in here. A lump rose in her throat as she wondered where she'd failed with him.

Strangely, Vittore mentioned her husband's absence. 'I suppose you would give anything if he could be with us tonight?'

'It'd be good to see him, aye. He's not been home for a while. I've got to admit, though, that I was just thinking he might not feel all that comfortable here.'

'And why is that? Surely, everyone is most agreeable.'

'They are an' all.' Even Miss Templer was mellowing as her relationship with Iris progressed.

When she didn't elaborate, Helen felt Vittore looking at her, concern shadowing his dark eyes. He knows there's summat not quite right between me and Alex, she thought, and was less perturbed than she'd anticipated to have him understand that difficulties existed.

The night wasn't meant for introspection, however, and as soon as all the food had been devoured Iris turned to Miss Templer.

'Why don't we have a bit of dancing? Just for fun. We can clear the table out of here, bring in the gramophone . . .'

They began with country dancing, Miss Templer showed she was particularly adept at demonstrating routines long-forgotten by most of them. They were followed by the Waltz Cotillion and The Lancers, both suggested by Ken's wife. Although frequently protesting that he couldn't follow any of these dances, Vittore was hauled on to the floor and pushed and pulled through the steps, partnered in the main by Helen.

Taking a breather at last, they walked towards a couple of chairs, laughing still with exhilaration. All at once, however, he grew serious, compelling her to look him in the eyes. She was astonished to see unshed tears below the dark irises.

'I am so happy tonight,' he told her quietly. 'Impossible though that may sound when I am a prisoner in England. And you are the one who makes my stay in your country a pleasure not a punishment.'

'Nay, get away with you. It's not just me,' she began.

Vittore continued nevertheless. 'Your attitude to me has always been so generous. You have never treated me like an enemy, simply as another human being whose life is disrupted by war.'

Helen was strangely moved by his admission, and anything but sorry when Jessie had found a record of dance music and Vittore drew her to her feet again. She was glad everybody else seemed to have got up for this one, she wouldn't have wished to make the pair of them conspicuous, but it did feel good to have his arms holding her close, to have his breath stirring tendrils of hair about her neck. That dance led to another, but just as Helen was admitting privately that she couldn't enjoy herself more the sirens began their dismal wailing.

'It would have to happen tonight!' somebody exclaimed, while one of the wives from Sheffield said they must have drawn the bombers away from the city. 'Can't we have one night off without this lot?'

Almost immediately the electricity was cut off, leaving them with only the light from the fire that was already dying to ashes in the grate.

'Come on, into t'kitchen, I'll find us some candles,' Miss Templer's voice commanded. 'Then we'd best see if we need to take cover in the cellar.' Only rarely here were they troubled with air-raids so serious that they need go underground for protection.

Vittore's grasp grew tighter over Helen's hand. 'One moment, please.'

They let the others go and remained as they were, standing where the dance had been interrupted. 'Helen?' he inquired, gazing steadily at her in the firelight.

Slowly, she nodded. Equally slowly, Vittore's head came closer until his mouth was brushing hers. Gentle as the touch of a moth's wing, his lips savoured her own. 'Helen,' he murmured gravely. 'You are so strong, you give me endurance to survive. And so warm that even the summer heat of my own country seems tepid . . .'

'Bit of a romantic, aren't you?' she said, smiling against his cheek.

His lips returned to her mouth and the arm about her drew her nearer. And now his kisses were more passionate, pressing urgently yet still without parting her lips.

'If we were free,' he said huskily. 'I free to live life as I wished, and you free to consider all the promises I would make to you . . .'

'Only we're not,' she responded, trying to lighten her tone, though she recognised deep in the private places of her soul that not being free induced heavy feelings of regret. 'And we're also a couple of sensible beings who won't go wishing for something they can't have.'

Although he nodded his agreement, Vittore continued to hold her and his mouth again claimed hers, though still he did not part her lips. There was no overt sensuality in his embrace, yet they were standing very close and Helen became fully aware of his arousal. Answering tremors of excitement developed deep inside her, urging the release which she'd been denied for too long. Not clinging to him required every scrap of will-power that she could muster.

'We should join the others, I think,' Vittore murmured huskily, and took her hand as they went out and along the darkened passageway.

His fingers were stirring over her own, caressing in mute expression of emotions which must be submerged.

For days afterwards Helen remained acutely aware of Vittore, sensing his approach before she glimpsed him, coming alive to his nearness in the farm kitchen or wherever they worked together.

But she also grew aware that she knew very little of the real Vittore. She could only form a picture from what he had told her about his work, about his home life. *His* version of the way things were. Here in England, he might be a prisoner but he was free of responsibilities, able to concentrate on projecting his friendly disposition, on making himself liked. She was aware that she was seeing Vittore in a very particular and not entirely natural situation.

Alex eventually came home once more and they spent a cheerful couple of days, relishing being in their house together, and spreading their good humour among her family until, on their last afternoon, they visited Alexander's father.

In spite of his enthusiasm for the Home Guard, Joseph seemed to be ageing fast. When she'd seen him previously, Helen had felt reassured that he appeared far better than she had feared from Alex's description; today, he gave the impression of being exhausted and not quite orientated. The minute he asked what day it was, she felt Alex stiffening beside her in alarm, but his next question made them even more perturbed.

'There was a chap worked with me – he joined one

of the services, but I'll be hanged if I can remember which. I can't quite recall his name, Alex . . .'

'Frank Barclay,' was the terse answer.

After he'd replied Alex drew in a sighing breath. Helen wasn't surprised he was shaken. How could Joseph have failed to remember someone who'd worked with him so long, and so closely? 'I don't like leaving him on his own any more,' Alex admitted on their way back home. 'I think it might be an idea if you accepted his suggestion of living at The Stone House. For the duration at any rate.'

Helen was shattered. She had never known that Alex had been aware of that suggestion's being made, but what disturbed her most was his supposition that she could simply give up her war work just like that.

'I know it's upsetting,' she began, nearly in tears herself, 'I don't like seeing him that way any more than you do. But he does have Mrs Hartley. She's a very responsible sort, and devoted to him.'

'Family would be better.'

Helen resisted the impulse to suggest that *he* might spend more time there. And even continuing with this government job, Alex could write letters, give his father enough attention to ensure that he wasn't quite so cut off from the stimulation of familiar, caring company. Instead, she found herself promising to come over more frequently.

The offer wasn't sufficient for Alexander, but she ignored his baleful look and willed him not to persist in demanding that she give up her job completely. She doubted whether she'd have been permitted to stop working on the land anyway, but certainly resented his voicing that particular suggestion.

Later that night, on the last bus back to the farm, Helen felt crushed by her husband's picture of what her life ought to be. Had he no understanding at all, expecting her to resign herself to keeping an eye on his father and doing nothing else while millions of folk were slaving their guts out to bring this wretched war to an end? Did he think there was anything to do in the business, these days, when it couldn't even keep Joseph occupied?

Vittore could hardly miss her agitation next morning. They were milking, a task which normally was enlivened by discussions about architecture. Today, Helen hardly spoke at all to him.

'Have I said something to irritate you?' he inquired, passing her as he moved on to the next cow.

'Course not,' she assured him. 'Take no notice. It's only me getting on my high horse again over summat and nowt.'

'Do you wish to tell me?'

She sighed, leaned her head into the beast's side, and replied without glancing away from the warm milk beginning to stream into the pail. 'Aye, go on. But you'll only think I'm proper daft. Alexander's father isn't too well – we're not sure what's wrong, or even if anything really is . . . only he often seems a bit confused – distant, like, from the rest of us. Any road, Alex thinks I ought to give this up and go and look after the old chap. I wouldn't mind, but he's got a perfectly good housekeeper.'

'And your husband has been unwilling all along for you to work here.'

'He'd do under and over to try and stop me, if he thought it'd do the trick,' said Helen, wondering how much else Vittore understood about her and Alex.

'I do not suppose there is much chance that you would be allowed to leave the Land Army in those circumstances,' Vittore reassured her. 'I think perhaps you need not worry too greatly.'

Maybe not, thought Helen, but remained perturbed

that Alex could even expect it of her.

During his next visit to Yorkshire they were both greatly relieved to find Joseph in better spirits, with no sign of memory loss. He told them eagerly that he was working as an advisor, helping some of the builders recalled from the forces to reconstruct war-damaged property.

'Some of the chaps are good workers but don't possess sufficient knowledge on the theory of construction. That's where I come in.'

Vittore smiled when she explained this to him on her return to the farm. 'Is very good, I think,' he said, nodding. 'I feel sure there will be much rebuilding in my own country also when the war finally ceases.'

'I hope there aren't too many famous buildings ruined.'

Vittore seemed not to know. Although newspapers and broadcasts carried word of all the campaigns, such details didn't always emerge. And in any case, he seemed these days to have conditioned himself to not dwelling on the situation in Italy until the war ended.

On Christmas Eve in that grim December of 1942 Helen was reminded how truly he had involved himself in life over here. It was a Thursday and they were all preparing for having not only Christmas Day but the Saturday and Sunday in their homes. All, that is, except Vittore.

Helen's heart was wrung when she found him, depressed, sitting on an upturned pail in the cowshed. The rest of them were rushing through their chores before sitting down to the special meal Miss Templer was concocting as a start to the festivities.

'Eh, love,' Helen exclaimed, 'I bet you're wishing it were possible for you to get home for Christmas . . .'

Vittore shook his head, surprising her. 'On the contrary. I just wish, selfishly, that none of you was going away. This place has become home to me these past months.' He went on to explain that he had volunteered to work during the Christmas break. 'But with none of you others here, I shall feel sad.'

Helen suddenly longed to get permission to invite him home with her, but realised just as suddenly that such a gesture would be confronted by her husband's disapproval. Alex would understand her sympathy for the Italian even less than he understood her farm work.

'It'll soon pass,' she assured Vittore, which won a grin from him.

'You must think me like a small boy who needs to be coaxed through a difficulty,' he said ruefully.

She shook her head, but only afterwards did she fully comprehend that she thought of Vittore as anything but a small boy.

The meal had been enjoyable, with plenty of banter to lift their minds above the food which, although plentiful, was only a token of what a farm Christmas dinner should be. The men had each bought a small gift for one of the girls, and Helen wondered how much wangling had gone on when Vittore was the one chosen to give something to her.

He was the last to make a presentation, and did so as the party was breaking up and people were getting ready to depart for their homes.

'You need not open it yet,' he told her awkwardly, handing over the quite large package.

'Of course I've got to,' Helen insisted. 'I can't wait.'

The box she unwrapped had a hinged lid, carefully constructed so that she could look inside without disturbing the contents. As soon as she opened the lid, she gasped in sheer pleasure.

'Oh, it's a model – of the cathedral in Florence!'

'Only made with matchsticks. It was all I had available.'

'Well, it's a credit to you, Vittore, really lovely.'

She kissed him then, full on the lips, and felt his arms come around her.

'I would give you everything,' he said seriously, 'if only that were possible.'

Chapter 9

Helen felt quite furtive placing Vittore's gift in one of her cupboards as soon as she arrived home for Christmas, but there was no sense in antagonising Alex, which she knew she would if she explained who the donor was. They would have struggle enough to make this a happy time, with so many restrictions governing the food they were allowed, to say nothing of the penalties they invited if they dared to display festive lights. She wasn't going to risk anything that could destroy the season for her husband and herself.

Alex came in, exhausted, a couple of hours after Helen and just about managed to remain awake for the supper that she had made.

'I hope you're not wanting to get up early,' he remarked as they went up to bed.

'No, love. Eight or so will do nicely.'

'*Eight*? What on earth for?'

'I told you – my mum's expecting us all for dinner. Our Marian and the kids'll be there already. And now she's asked your father an' all, he's offered to pick us up on the way.'

'That's news to me.'

'Didn't you get my last letter, I posted it over a week since?'

Alex sighed. 'Maybe I did. It must have slipped my mind about Dad going there as well.'

Helen restrained the look which she felt like giving him. He was tired out, after all. But she'd been very pleasantly surprised that her mother was inviting Joseph Stone. She couldn't imagine anybody overlooking something as good as that.

'I don't suppose he'll mind hanging on a bit if we're not quite ready,' she said. 'I can show him some of the presents we've got.' It occurred to her then that the one thing he might enthuse over most was the only item she couldn't bring out here. *Was* it Alex who was difficult, she wondered, or would any man resent another chap giving his wife something at Christmas?

Just thinking about that delightful model of the cathedral made her long to look at it again. She was glad when Alex decided to have a bath, leaving her free to go to the cupboard. She couldn't help feeling touched. Vittore, bless him, had spent many an hour making this, and especially for her.

During Christmas Day Helen noticed how frequently she remembered the model, and with what delight. If she was honest with herself, she knew it had pleased her far more than the set of utility Celanese underwear for which Alex had sacrificed some of his clothing coupons. But being aware of this made her equally conscious of how readily Vittore impressed her. Far more than was good, she was sure. She would have to make a real effort not to think so much about him.

Despite shortages, or even partly because of them, that Christmas in Halifax was a lot of fun. Kathleen Clegg had them laughing over the few prunes, the five dates and the handful of sultanas which had been supplemented by finely chopped vegetables for the cake. And its topping tasted quite like marzipan, so long as you didn't know it was basically haricot beans with the addition of ground rice, almond essence, and a bit of precious sugar and margarine.

Marian's children seemed to love playing with their new toys, and didn't understand why anybody felt sorry for them. They had a renovated fort and dolls' house (both gleaned from jumble sales) and toys made out of cotton reels, matchboxes and other discarded objects. Neither Linda nor Mark was lacking in imagination. Extending it to convert makeshift items into whatever they fancied appeared only to increase the pleasure.

'We shall make it up to them, of course, once this lot's over,' Marian asserted several times, and hoped that Denis would make up to her for his long periods abroad.

Her husband's involvement with ENSA seemed to Marian to keep him away for even longer spells than if he'd been serving in one of the armed forces. He no sooner finished one tour than he was dispatched on another, and hardly ever given time for leave at home between them. She missed him quite fiercely. If it wasn't for her ambulance driving she would go crackers with yearning. Then there was the anxiety as well. She didn't half envy their Helen for having Alex still in England.

Denis was in North Africa now, from what she could gather, not that she was told very much. They were allowed to write more about the kind of shows they were putting on, and he was very happy about that. He was taking part in a lot of their sketches and doing a bit of singing which he enjoyed even more than the backstage work. And, naturally, as the sets they had for an entertainment out there were anything but complex, the stage management side wouldn't occupy him fully. Marian rather hoped he'd keep to appearing on stage after the war. She fancied having a husband who was an actor.

The children were playing nicely together today, first with Mark's things, then with Linda's. Marian was very thankful. They weren't always like this, not for her. They'd got that used to being with their grandmother that they usually played up when she herself was around. She would have hated that in front of Alex's father. Come to that, she'd not have been best pleased to have them letting her down with their Helen in the house.

She didn't know what it was about her sister – happen it was just this everlasting awareness that Helen had passed all those exams, had had so much education. Marian only knew that her sister made her keep wondering what she thought of them.

'You're looking a bit peaky, Marian,' Helen said now, smiling sympathetically. 'Have you been called out a lot at nights lately?'

Marian smiled back although she hadn't liked the implication that she was looking a wreck. 'Well, I've been on night duty this past week. But only so's I could get tonight off. I swapped turns with one of the other lasses. She wants New Year because her fiancé might be coming home.' She didn't go on to explain that she often took over nights from the other girls. It never seemed as bad being on her own in bed during the day.

Watching Alex sitting on the settee, an arm casually across Helen's shoulders, Marian felt her eyes filling. If only she could just see Denis, even for an hour, to know that he was all right.

Hurriedly, she stood up. 'Got to go down the steps,' she said and all but ran towards the outer door.

'I wanted to go to the lav,' Linda complained, surprised that her mother hadn't made the normal inquiry into her needs.

'Never mind, love,' Kathleen said, 'you can go out after.'

'Is Marian all right?' asked Helen. 'She looks quite poorly.'

'She misses him a lot, you know,' their father put in. Daniel Clegg didn't always say very much, but he was well aware of his family's emotions. 'They were married that young, you see. Marian never had much experience of standing on her own feet. And there's the responsibility,' he added softly, gazing fondly at Linda and Mark.

'Still, she's lucky to have such grand youngsters,' said Alex. 'It's what we all need. Somebody to plan for, to make you look to the future.'

Beyond her own instant panic, Helen noticed Alex's father raising an eyebrow at that, realised his astonishment was as great as her own. His gradual smile, though, revealed that he warmed to the prospect far more than she had herself.

Joseph nodded as his smile reached his eyes. 'Yes, well – there's one here who'll be delighted once there's a little Stone to continue our name. Maybe you'll think on that, you two!'

Helen tried to smile back at him, and didn't quite manage it. 'I hope you mean once the duration's here. I don't think somehow that it'd be such a good thing in wartime . . .'

Joseph inclined his head genially. '*Whenever*, my dear, whenever. I know these are difficult times – and I know also that you are as concerned as Alex here about keeping the family going.'

Alex wasn't saying anything. He's shot his bolt, thought Helen, and she was wary of being cornered into promising the old man a grandchild in the near future. She'd have to be careful, though, if Alex was thinking along those lines.

It wasn't that she never wanted children, she simply didn't want them yet. Especially while there were so many ways in which she felt she hardly knew Alex. Somehow, she would have to have a quiet word with their Marian. She knew how babies could be avoided.

There was an opportunity to talk privately while they were washing up. And, for once, Marian was entirely in agreement. 'You're right, love, not wanting to risk a bairn while the country's in this state.'

'So how do I go about it?'

'Well – t'easiest way is to get your Alex to wear summat.'

'Wear?' began Helen, not fully comprehending.

'You know, a rubber sheath.'

'I'm afraid he'd never do that.'

'It'll be up to you then. You want to go to the clinic. They'll fit you up with a sort of cap to go inside you, and there's a sponge an' all.'

Helen groaned. It sounded a terrible palaver, but maybe it would be worth it to ease her mind.

Marian grinned at her. 'It's not so nice going to the clinic the first time, but you get used to it, and to thinking on at home to get prepared.'

Confronted so suddenly with how real the risk of conceiving was, Helen hadn't considered that the nearest Marie Stopes clinic might not be open during her short Christmas break. When she finally screwed up her courage and went along then found the door locked, she glanced about hoping nobody she knew had seen her there, and walked away again. She couldn't pretend that she wasn't a bit relieved, although now she would worry each time that Alex made love to her.

Two days after returning to the farm Helen received evidence that she hadn't started a baby. For once, she endured feeling rough quite cheerfully. Since the moment that Alex had expressed his longing for a child, she had grown steadily more perturbed about beginning a family.

The war had been an unwelcome interruption, halting her career long before she'd begun to get her teeth into it. She and Alex had spent that long learning what it was about, but they'd been prevented from practising much real architecture. Even though she enjoyed her work on the farm, she looked on it as just a stop-gap, a means of doing something useful, but only until she could go back to her proper job. Did Alex honestly think she would be happy denying herself the opportunity to design all those buildings that seemed to be queuing up in her mind's eye, as impatiently as a lot of housewives outside a fish-monger's?

'You are looking very serious today, Helen, what is wrong?'

It was Vittore. He'd taken over from Ken behind the horse and plough laboriously working the frosted earth. Helen was in the next furrow, following on, taking out the larger stones they were turning up, a task that could only be done by hand. There were hundreds of stones as well – this was a field that hadn't been used for years, if ever. According to Miss Templer, it hadn't been considered worth cultivating for as long as she could remember.

Helen smiled back at Vittore. 'Nothing much, really, I were just thinking how grand it would be to get back to designing.'

'And for me also. During Christmas while you were all away, I sat in the camp working out what I would most like to plan.'

'You'll have to show me the designs, love.'

He merely shook his head. 'You have not understood – they are in my mind only. We are not permitted supplies of paper except when we write home.'

His words made her realise that by comparison her own difficulties were negligible. They also gave her an idea. Even during the winter they were often obliged to take packed lunches out into the fields. She ensured now that she also took a pencil and paper. It was awful stuff, like blotting paper – the result of salvaging – but Vittore valued it as greatly as the high grade paper produced pre-war.

'Are you sure you do not wish this yourself?' he asked on that first day.

'No, go on – so long as you let me watch. Do a bit of a sketch of the sort of buildings you'll design when you get back to Italy.'

Even well wrapped in coats and scarves, and sitting in the angle of a drystone wall to protect them from a keen wind which carried an occasional flurry of snow, they were chilled to the marrow. Somehow, though, they forgot all that while Vittore drew the outline of a splendid house which he dreamed of building on one of the hills surrounding Florence. There were echoes of the Palazzo Vecchio, though without being nearly so high, and with large ground-floor windows which acknowledged modern needs yet didn't detract from typical Florentine styling.

'I wish I could combine some of our older traditions with contemporary requirements,' Helen exclaimed. 'There seems to have been that much ultra-fashionable stuff that folk have dismissed anything built before about 1930 as not worth considering.'

Vittore grinned sideways at her, pausing as he completed a splendid doorway. 'It may be that you will – you could be the person who will eventually show other British architects that it does not have to be *either* old-fashioned or ultra-modern. That there is a place somewhere between the two. That way you create buildings that live happily alongside those from different eras.'

Helen was nodding. 'I'd like to think that was summat I could do. Happen it's a bit fanciful, though . . .'

Their designing sessions continued, however, and although ribbed by the others they both found not only enjoyment but fresh hope during the snatched minutes with pencil and paper. Beside him in a field, the sharp corners of the wall's uneven stones pressing into her back, Helen often gazed out across the range of snow-topped hills which seemed so high and open that they might have been the summit of the world. Despite the winter bleakness, she loved this part of Yorkshire for the sense of freedom it gave her, seeming to generate the belief that she might look forward to a better future.

Those interludes also brought Helen even closer to Vittore, widening their relationship, and yet at the same time narrowing her awareness of other lives beyond the farm. It was with a shock that she read in a rare letter from Alex that he would be with her for the last weekend in February. An even greater shock was her own private recognition that she would far rather remain here than go home to be with him.

Shattered by these emotions, she volunteered to take fodder to the sheep on the far slope of the hill. She needed to get away, especially from Vittore. She must school herself to remember that all the loyalty she had pledged was to Alex. But surrendering the stimulus of these past few weeks was more than she could face. Long after she had doled out the last of the kale and the water, Helen remained on the scrubby hillside, battling with the feelings which rebelled inside her.

It was all but dark. She started when a voice reached her above the sound of the wind sighing in nearby telephone wires.

'Helen . . .'

Vittore was on his way back to the prison camp. Thinking of him returning to that bleak place, and of herself steeling her will to set out the next day to meet Alex cheerfully, she gulped.

'Helen,' he repeated, running over the rough tussocky ground to reach her.

She had thought it was virtually dark. There was still just enough light to silhouette the crags against the sky. And to reveal to him the tears spilling from her eyes.

Wordlessly, Vittore raised a hand, touched the moisture on her cheek. 'Why, *cara?*'

Helen shook her head. 'Take no notice. It's just me being proper daft.'

He drew her against him. She felt the strength of arms which seemed to lock out the despair of their world.

'I hate this bloody war,' she said fiercely. 'What it's doing to you – and what it's doing to me, an' all, I suppose. Having everything disrupted. Never being able even to plan going back to our real work.' And, she added silently, for making me forget what I loved about my husband.

'You are to take a break, though, no? Tomorrow, is it – you will be in your own home?

'Aye. And happen that's what's wrong, because it doesn't feel like home. Nowhere does.' She paused. 'Where do I belong, Vittore?'

He yearned to say 'here', and convince her of his willingness to make *her* his home, his future. But he would say nothing of the kind. His own tattered marriage wasn't reason enough to draw her away from her husband. It would have taken a tougher man than himself, though, to resist the appeal in these grey eyes gleaming with tears.

His kiss startled her but Helen didn't move one inch away. Her arms went around him and her lips returned to his mouth. There was no other way to express this immense longing.

Emotion surging through him, Vittore kissed her and went on kissing. His tongue parted her lips. God, but he had waited so long, aching to demonstrate the depth of his affection for her. And it was affection – something rarer by far than the desire which he had resigned himself to deny.

'Helen,' he gasped, and willed back anything further. Love was too vital a word for uttering and later dismissing. And dismiss it he must; she wasn't the sort of woman he would encourage into an illicit association. He fought to control his imagination before it presented him with pictures of the future they might have together.

'You're a good pal, Vittore,' she said lightly. 'I feel a lot better already.'

But there was nothing light about the way she returned his kiss. His hold on her tightened. Through the layers of thick winter clothing she felt bruised by his lean body. She heard the groan he stifled in his throat.

The prompting of their bodies could not be mistaken, any more than the depth and intensity of their kisses. About them on the hill keened the wind, stronger now, wailing in the telephone wires, rattling bare-branched trees, as wild as their attraction.

Iced by the elements, her cheeks and forehead felt exposed, the sharpest ever contrast with this heat raging within her.

Abruptly, Vittore released her, turned away and

ran, stumbling and staggering down the steepest part of the hillside. Helen listened for his footsteps on the gravel of the path, heard them out until they were swallowed by the wind.

Shakily, she started off towards the farm. Her legs weak, head woozy with longing, she hardly knew how to keep her feet. Thank heaven Vittore had stopped when he did. She'd been on the verge of losing awareness of where they were heading. And surrendering to this enormous need would have finished all that they meant to each other. Wanting him was such a small part of it all.

The sleet began driving across from the distant hills when she was still a quarter of a mile from the farm buildings. Wetter and far colder than rain, more gruelling than snow, Helen felt it was a just comment on her recklessness.

Travelling back towards Halifax in the bus next day, Helen began to recognise how seriously she had neglected to consider her marriage.

Even after she and Vittore had wrenched themselves apart, her only immediate thankfulness had been that they hadn't damaged the friendship between them. If she hadn't quite failed to remember that she was married, she had ceased to put her marriage first.

Alexander was at home before her, with a kettle boiling for tea to heat the chill out of her bones, and a warming invitation. 'Dad wants us there for lunch, Mrs Hartley is relishing doing something special.'

Helen smiled, picturing Mrs Hartley's thin form bustling round, her sparse white hair drawn back in its neat bun. 'Bless them both.'

Alex gave her an eager hug. 'I dropped in on Dad first thing. I got an overnight train.'

'What was the journey like, love?'

He grinned. 'Best forgotten. There were a lot of wounded on board, and other service chaps. I was forced to stay in the corridor, as per usual. There was too much stopping and starting, of course, because of raids. And that dim lighting gave me a thundering head.'

'Have you taken anything for it?'

'Didn't need to. I walked it off, from the station to The Stone House. Had an early breakfast with Father and his Home Guard cronies. What about you? You're looking done in.'

Helen made herself smile. The guilt she felt for her abandoned behaviour with Vittore was *her* problem. It mustn't be permitted to encroach on the happiness she should be creating for Alex.

Strangely, their time together did turn out to be happy; never once did they argue or voice misgivings about the future or anything else. And the news from Tripoli was good. Rommel was retreating as the Allies managed to turn around yet another offensive.

During that afternoon they visited Helen's mother and spent some time getting to know Marian's children all over again, noticing how they had grown up during those few weeks since Christmas.

'I know,' Kathleen agreed. 'I think it's summat to do with them being with your dad and me so much. It's many a year since we brought up you and our Marian, isn't it? I tend to forget and talk to this pair as if they were older than seven and eight.'

'That's not doing them any harm, any road, Mum,' said Alex, and gave her an affectionate squeeze.

Kathleen herself, though, was looking wan and exhausted. Helen insisted on helping make tea in the kitchen. 'Is it looking after the kiddies that's getting you down?' she asked.

'Nay, love, it's not them. They're not much trouble.'

Helen noticed then the extra plate waiting by the sink. 'Are you keeping an eye on old Mrs Tomlinson again?'

'Only a bit, and that's no hardship. She's nobbut next-door.'

'But she has family, surely?'

'They have their work to go to. They're tired out when they get home at night.'

Tired? Wasn't her mother beyond tiredness? But she'd always been like this, helping whenever neighbours were in need. Popping in and out if somebody was too old or ill to manage on their own.

Alex was in the doorway, listening. 'It's grand of you to look after those who live around you, Mum. Just don't go overdoing things, mind.'

Alexander's loving concern for her mother made Helen even more aware of her thankfulness that she hadn't harmed her own relationship with him. Whatever happened from now on, she was conscious of the danger, must steel herself against all her feelings for Vittore.

He himself was the one who made this easier. Without saying one word about the way they had embraced out on the hill, he somehow conveyed that it would never be repeated. A subtle change in his manner allowed them to remain as friendly as in the past, yet left no doubt that the attraction they had both experienced would be disregarded.

They still continued to discuss architectural ideas, sitting over bits of paper while they ate lunch out in the fields or meadows or less frequently in the farmhouse kitchen. Both agreed that appalling though this war was, the destruction it wrought might afterwards generate a whole new wave of building.

Later that year several events abroad drew Vittore closer in spirit to everyone at the farm than ever he had felt towards the German cause which his country had supported. First of all, in July, came the US bombardment of Rome, when the Allied pilots concerned went in with strict warnings to avoid historic buildings and the Vatican.

'Do you hear that?' he asked as they all sat listening to the wireless while taking a break for tea. 'There is civilised behaviour, a fine example. When I learn something like that I wonder how ever my countrymen failed to see the difference between your Allies and the Nazis.'

He had even more cause later in the year to reiterate heartfelt thanks that it had been the British who had captured him. The announcement by General Eisenhower of Italy's surrender in that September of 1943 was followed by dreadful German atrocities.

'They have been looting in Rome,' Vittore announced horrified. 'Stealing valuable manuscripts, priceless works of art, old masters.'

That was only the beginning. A week or two afterwards, Vittore came to Helen as she was busy with the evening milking.

'You will never guess what is happening in Italy now,' he began, unable to check the tears spilling down his cheeks. 'Naples is suffering a reign of terror. The retreating German troops are taking revenge. The worst was that they planted land mines beneath a room into which they drove a hundred civilians. Then the mines were detonated.'

Hospitals were being ransacked and their food stocks ruined, water supplies were deliberately contaminated.

Italian soldiers were being herded into sealed trains and transported to Germany to be used as slave labour. The day this news reached Yorkshire, Vittore astonished Miss Templer by hugging her. 'I am just so glad to be here,' he kept repeating. 'I do not wish to leave all you good people, ever.'

By the end of October the Allied armies were 'like a bug on one leg', in Winston Churchill's words, as they tried to fight their way up the boot of Italy. By this time no one at the farm could bear to miss a news broadcast. They followed every detail of the troops' movements over marshy terrain towards Monte Casino, the monastery which the Nazis had rendered almost impregnable.

Although 1944 began with British and American forces landing at Anzio, making everyone share with Vittore the hope that the war in Italy soon could end, battle continued relentlessly on other fronts. The siege of Leningrad had been broken, but the launching of a massive assault on the Pacific came at the end of February, reminding them (if they had managed to forget) that more than one enemy was being confronted.

Wearied to death with years of anxiety, shortages on the home front and sheer hard work, they all seemed to grow progressively dispirited. More and more frequently Helen became depressed by the length of time that her career had been suspended. She began to take less interest in the designs that Vittore still enjoyed producing. She wouldn't dream of saying as much to him, but she very much feared that it might be many a year before anyone, anywhere, could start erecting buildings of the size and scope that thrilled them both.

There were highspots, like the day early in June when Rome was finally liberated by the Allies. Nobody at the farm was left out of the celebration that Vittore insisted on organising. And within days news of the D-Day landings had them rejoicing again. By the end of the month German forces were being driven out of Normandy, yet still Helen failed to remain optimistic for any length of time. All around on the Yorkshire hillsides harvesting and trees heavy with foliage proclaimed the heart-lifting spirit of summer, while she felt she had waited so long already that her own ambitions would never approach their zenith.

During July, when the Government announced that between three and four million houses would be constructed in the first decade after hostilities ceased, her emotions remained just as mixed as ever. Good though this planning for peacetime was, it appeared to leave little scope for the kind of work in which she yearned to be engaged.

She and Alex discussed these Government plans during his next visit to Yorkshire.

They were sitting up to the table, still surrounded by dirty dishes and the remains of the economy-style trifle which hadn't been anything like so tempting as the recipe had made it sound. She had never felt more exhausted, but admitting that to this husband of hers would only have invited another outburst against the work she was doing.

Alex himself was in fine fettle. He considered that much of the hardest work of *his* war had eased. He could afford time to look to a future when re-establishing Stone's as a lucrative practice would be their only worry.

'We'll cash in on everything that's happening, don't you fret,' he assured Helen now. 'So – building will initially be concentrated on supplying homes. We'll just have to prove our worth at that.'

'Aye, it'll be something, I know. Not very exciting, though – not when you think of all the things we dreamed of designing.'

'They'll be good houses, love, the best. They're determined on that, you know.'

'Who are – the Government?'

He nodded, smiling. 'Of course. They'll be the ones with the brass, and to issue restrictions. But they've promised new homes will be bigger – three-bedroomed, and with larger windows. Once we've shown how up-to-date we can be with them, we shall be better positioned for proving ourselves on more complex assignments.'

Helen had restrained the look she might have given him when he was going on about being up-to-date. He was the same Alex. But she hadn't lost the hope that *she* might eventually be the one who would prove that it was possible to blend new buildings and modern facilities with the older styles existing in their vicinity. She loved her part of the West Riding, and couldn't bear the thought of it changing too drastically.

On one thing they were agreed: pulling Stone's back into shape as a going concern would be up to the pair of them. Sadly, the last few years of war had accelerated Joseph Stone's decline. Although he was quite often lucid enough when they were around, Mrs Hartley increasingly related evidence that his once-keen mind was, to say the least, unreliable.

'I doubt if Father will work again,' Alex confided now. 'Or only as a sleeping partner. We shan't be able to depend on him any longer.'

'Isn't old age sad?' said Helen. And was reminded by her husband that his father at sixty wasn't really all that old.

'I blame the war. So does his doctor. If Father had been permitted to carry on working as he had in the past, he'd never have lost touch with reality in the way that he's doing now.'

Helen could have wept. She'd grown to love Joseph

Stone as much as she'd always respected him. Whenever she'd managed to set aside difficulties wrought by the war and look beyond the duration to the future, she had pictured him there. She'd always wanted to show Joseph Stone that he'd been justified in having enough faith in her to take her into the firm. That she'd do him proud whatever she tackled.

When Alexander went back down south Helen, for the first time in longer than she cared to admit, began to panic that he might not return safely to her.

'It's proper daft,' she confessed to her mother who had asked whatever was wrong when Helen called in to say goodbye on her way back to the farm. 'He was there all through the blitz, and although, naturally, I was concerned, I didn't get all worked up about it.'

'You're worn out now, aren't you? We all are,' Kathleen said, and gave her a hug. 'They allus say the night's darkest afore the dawn – and we're hoping that this lot won't last much longer, aren't we?'

Her father, who had walked along the street with her as he came home from his shift at the factory, turned from washing his hands at the kitchen sink and gave her a tired grin. 'Your Alex is a survivor, you take my word for it – it'll take more nor Hitler to finish him! You're just a bit upset, like, seeing him off again. And we're all sick to death of war work, stands to reason everything gets us down.'

In the bus, though, Helen realised that it wasn't only weariness making her react like this to her husband's return to London with all its flying bombs. She was unnerved about everything, and especially by what he had said about his father's inability to cope with work in the future. Much as she reminded herself that she and Alex had grown up long since, and should possess the ability to restore Stone's to a thriving business, she couldn't stifle her misgivings. How would she get on if she was receiving no support from the old man whenever her ideas and Alexander's conflicted?

It wasn't for her sake alone, though, that she wanted Joseph Stone there: she longed to see him glad that the three of them had survived to breathe new life into the firm.

Chapter 10

Halifax looked damp and grey and miserable, as West Riding industrial towns excelled in looking during November when rain collected soot from the mill smoke, bespattering its townsfolk and muddying pavements. Helen's spirits felt hardly any better. Alex had asked her to go and see his father. He himself couldn't get away, and he didn't want the old man to be on his own today.

Yesterday, the Home Guard had been stood down. To lots of people its being disbanded was another sign that the war wouldn't last much longer. To a man like Joseph Stone, who had made it the interest that kept him going throughout the war, it was yet another sign that he was finished.

Helen had decided he mustn't be allowed to think that way. She was going to march into The Stone House and impress on her father-in-law that he was still needed in the business. She wasn't going to listen to any protests, nor to any suggestions that she and Alex would cope without him. When they re-opened after the duration, he would be there. Working.

Passing between the double row of shops as the bus was travelling through King Cross, Helen realised with something of a shock that they were only weeks away from Christmas. I hope to goodness this is the last one of wartime austerity, she thought, remembering how even these modest shops used to put on such a good display at this time of year. She had a lot of memories of saving up her spending money to buy presents or to treat herself when she was little. And of more recent years when the Co-op bazaar, its counters crammed with bargains, so often yielded just what you were seeking. Thinking further back, the things that she recalled were stranger – the shudder she always experienced when Mum took her into the tripe shop. Then there was the peculiar excitement induced (in the Co-op again) by the swish along overhead wires of those neat cylinders devised for conveying change from the cashier. She pictured the tiny Post Office which she could never recollect without tasting the tangy ironwork of its grille which must have been sampled in days long ago when her little tongue had to explore everything.

Her best memories of all, though, were of nearby Spring Edge and Savile Park – 'the moor' to local people. Had she even been there once in many a year? At one time she'd have been staggered that she could keep away from her favourite place. Yet trying to contact Fenny March was the last occasion that she remembered crossing the moor.

Helen was still thinking about Miss March when the bus approached Brearley. A part of her regretted being distracted from her intention of planning more of what she would say to Joseph but the other half felt curiously renewed by memories of her former art mistress. But for Fenny and the old man she'd never have trained, certainly wouldn't have met Alexander Stone or his father. She'd been fortunate. She would do all she could now to ensure Joseph's happiness.

Mrs Hartley opened the door and came close to hugging her as she ushered her into the chill of the hall.

'I'm that glad to see you!' she exclaimed, a wide

smile replacing an anxious frown. 'The master's been really down this morning. You're just the tonic he wants.'

As soon as she was taken through to the sitting room Helen saw how greatly in need of cheering Joseph was. Hunched into a chair, he was making no pretence of reading the book that was open on his knee. Even when Helen appeared before him, he took several seconds to recover his customary courtesy and rise.

He smiled then, however, and his eyes showed a glimmer of light. 'Helen, my dear – this is a nice surprise.'

She kissed his lined cheek, felt the prickle of unshaven whiskers. He wasn't himself.

But Joseph was brightening by the minute. He turned to Mrs Hartley. 'Have I had a cup of tea since breakfast?' Before she could reply he continued anyway. 'We'll have a pot now, any road.' He glanced towards Helen. 'Or do you prefer coffee? It might be only Camp, that chicory stuff?'

'Tea would be lovely, thanks.'

Discussion of his health lasted until the tray was brought in, and revealed nothing beyond his desire to conceal the way things really were. Maybe still caring what she thought was a good sign. Giving the tea in the pot a brisk stirring, Helen launched in on him.

'We're in a bit of a spot, Father – Alex and I. Fact is, we've decided it's high time we were looking to the future and getting the business operational again. The war's bound to end next year some time, and there's going to be a lot of folk crying out for builders – and that means architects besides.'

From beneath bushy white eyebrows, he was regarding her warily.

'Neither of us can get away for long enough to be any use,' Helen pressed on firmly. 'That's where you come in. We don't even know what stocks we have of working materials, never mind how long it's going to take supplies to come through once they're being produced again.'

'You mean after . . .?' Joseph asked slowly.

'Once the war's over, aye. We want to be prepared, you see – need somebody who knows what they're about. Somebody who has the sense to see what we've run short of, and knows the suppliers who must be contacted.'

Her father-in-law was nodding. 'Firms who get their orders in now will stand more of a chance when production turns back to items required in peacetime.'

'We wondered if you could happen start sounding them out? Learn when we can expect supplies to begin trickling through. And then there's the jobs that were left unfinished when war broke out. There'll be sites to visit – we shall need to know what condition they're in now, especially if they've been used for other purposes. *And* what's happened to every company of builders that were working to our plans. Happen you worked with some on reconstructing?'

'That's going to take months . . .'

'Why do you think I've come to see you now, Father?' Helen said with a grin, handing a cup and saucer across. 'There's nobody else can set us ahead in this way. And I expect it'll be hectic once the Government begins rebuilding programmes. Every architect that's been forced to suspend work till the duration will be trying to muscle in on whatever's going. This way, Stone's won't be held up – we'll be there in front of all t'others.'

'By, but you're a grand lass, Helen!'

'These aren't just my ideas, you know. Alex wanted me to come and talk to you.'

'Oh, aye?'

He looked sceptical but not displeased. And Helen was aware as ever of how highly Joseph Stone esteemed her ability.

Suddenly, he startled her with a chuckle. 'I always thought that our Alexander was the one with more of a leaning towards the business side. I see now that you've as good a grasp of that as he has. And, as I've always said, you've that bit extra in your designing flair.'

She smiled back at him. 'It's to be hoped I still have – that I've lost nowt these past five years. You can't tell me that there isn't going to be a great deal of competition. No matter how many buildings have to be replaced up and down the country.'

'A lot of that will be down south, though,' he reminded her gravely. 'I've been thinking about that, and don't mind admitting I've been daunted by it. I'm past competing by dashing off to London.'

'Happen you are, and happen you're letting these years of being held up get on top of you. But it's here in Yorkshire we shall be needing somebody to anchor the whole business. You know as well as anybody, you can't run an efficient firm without sound management.'

'I could begin straight away – see what sort of shape the office is in. We might have to replace furniture and maybe some of the equipment when it's been shut up this long. I daresay after the war they'll be selling off a lot of army surplus . . .'

'What are your thoughts on staffing? Is Frank Barclay coming back into the business?'

'Afraid I don't know, my dear, rather lost touch. Suppose I could drop him a line tonight. He'd been given a shore job, last I heard – Portsmouth. He had a bad time of it on the Russian convoys.'

'Oh, aye – I think there was a bit about him in the

Halifax Courier. We shall need clerical staff an' all. What do you feel about having more than one secretary? If Alex or I have to go on long trips, we'll want somebody to cope with the paper work.'

'The girl we had afore – what was her name? I forget. She won't be coming back. Don't recall how I heard, but she had a couple of youngsters and one of them is disabled.'

'Poor lass, what a handful!'

'Her chap was lost as well, shot down over the Channel.'

They talked for a while longer, bringing up everything they could think of which might need sorting out before they could even begin running Stone's effectively again. By the time Helen left him her father-in-law was sufficiently alert for her to believe that her visit had been well worthwhile.

And Helen herself felt infinitely better. Just discussing the time when they would open up the practice again had made the end of the war seem nearer, and more inevitable. There were only two things that bothered her now: how would she ensure that she and Alex settled down happily together, and how endure saying goodbye to Vittore?

The break with the Italian architect came quite suddenly, during the following March and even before hostilities ended. The department responsible for prisoner-of-war camps had organised inspections with a view to winding them down, and the place where Vittore had spent the past few years was declared unfit for habitation.

He arrived for work one Monday, drawn-faced and dejected. Helen was the first to hear that he was being moved, and therefore would no longer be employed at the farm.

'I shall hate it, I know,' he stated grimly. 'I have become so attached to you.'

She tried to avoid considering that his words related to her personally. Vittore, however, soon left her in no doubt. 'You are a lovely woman, Helen, I only wish that we had met years ago.'

She had been about to remind him that he wouldn't have long to wait before being repatriated to Italy; somehow, the words seemed inappropriate now. When Vittore went on to speak less than enthusiastically about working there when he returned, she began to wonder if his home life was even worse than she'd suspected.

'Happen you'll feel better once you're back there again, and starting to get the firm on its feet. I know it's cheered me up since that day I saw Alex's father about our practice.'

Vittore only shook his head. 'Did I not tell you – since my father died, my partner is the brother of my wife. And you know how she and I live separate lives. Her brother wanted me out before the war; from the few letters I have received, it seems he is yet more antagonistic towards me.'

'What will you do then, join another firm?'

'Eventually, perhaps.'

Helen's sympathy for Vittore deepened during those last few days before the camp closed and he was moved from the area. Although he rallied and made an effort to conceal his misery, she couldn't help feeling depressed on his behalf even while the others laughed and joked throughout the tea party Miss Templer put on for him.

Vittore made a short speech, thanking Miss Templer and the rest of them for making him so welcome in and around the farm.

'You have given to me a home,' he told them, tears

glistening in his dark eyes. 'I shall never forget this place, nor any of you.'

He repeated the words about never forgetting to Helen when she walked alone with him towards the path that led to the camp. And now tears were tracing his cheeks, and the sigh he gave prevented him from continuing to talk.

'Nay, love,' said Helen gently. 'You mustn't take on like this. We knew all along, didn't we, that working here wouldn't last? We both have our careers to look to.'

'There will never be a time in mine when each design does not remind me of my sweet English lady architect.'

He drew her to him, lips salty from his tears. 'I pray we shall meet again,' he said huskily, kissing her fiercely.

'Maybe we will,' Helen answered carefully, but wondered already how that could ever come about while she was working over here, and with her husband.

Vittore's response was another kiss, more fevered, eloquent of passion.

After finally parting, Helen heard him running from her, resurrecting memories of that other occasion when they had clung so closely to each other. Walking slowly back to the farmhouse, she felt uneasy again, experiencing a strange premonition that she would meet Vittore at some time in the future, and that the encounter might not be entirely easy.

Once Vittore had left it began to seem that they were all, however unconsciously, winding down. Food rationing was intensifying, but with a lessening of the threat to vessels bringing supplies from overseas, there was hope that the situation would improve. Way back in the previous November when the last major German warship, the *Tirpitz*, had been sunk it had begun to look as though things would return eventually to normal. So long as nothing was wasted, work on the farm might be allowed gradually to diminish.

Helen was the next person to return home, shortly after street parties, bonfires and massive crowds gathering in front of Halifax Town Hall marked the end of the war in Europe. Having Joseph Stone back in the office had paid dividends, ensuring that their firm was, indeed, in the forefront of those architects who would work on designing homes for the millions of needy. No one could deny that she would fulfil as useful a role there as ever she had on the land.

Saying farewell, Helen wept over the other land-girls, especially Jessie who had remained at the farm throughout, and even over Miss Templer. Ken and the other chaps were each given a prolonged hugging. Ken was healthier by far than he had seemed on arriving there; his asthma attacks were less frequent and not half so alarming. Maybe the country air had helped.

Not greatly attracted by the prospect of living on her own until Alex was released from his war work, Helen had been toying with the idea of staying with her parents.

Her visit to them on the day she returned to Halifax quickly put that notion right out of her head. Young Mark and Linda were still being cared for by Kathleen Clegg; Marian's job driving ambulances was as necessary as ever, ferrying around the wounded arriving in the north for care in already overcrowded hospitals. Helen soon saw, though, how wearied her mother was looking after caring for the two youngsters.

Helen must not present her with another person to care for. She knew full well that she herself would be working long hours for Stone's and would have little time to spare for contributing much in the way of help at home.

I shall make the best of a bad job, she told herself firmly. I shan't like being alone in that house, but I shan't even think about the neighbourliness here. And it is on the doorstep of the office . . .

Working again with Joseph Stone was a joy which amply compensated for solitude elsewhere. There seemed to be no evidence now of the confusion which had plagued him during the war. Helen began to believe that getting him working again was all that had been required.

Because Halifax and its immediate surroundings had got off lightly, with only one direct hit from a bomb, a great deal of the permitted rebuilding was further afield. For a time Helen felt reluctant to use the car which Joseph had given them on their wedding day. She was unused to driving and really thought of the neat little Standard as belonging to Alex. Within a few weeks, however, she had seen the sense of using the petrol allowed for business, and was driving off to consult with builders and inspect construction sites.

One or two of these were in and around Sheffield, and she was glad to arrange meetings with her sister. On the first occasion that she saw Marian again, Helen was staggered.

With such a long interval since their last encounter, she had warned herself privately that there might be changes. Nothing on this earth could have prepared her for the overweight individual who had replaced the slender blonde whose beauty had always overshadowed hers.

Trying not to stare incredulously, Helen hugged her sister before following her inside the cinema cafe where they had arranged to have lunch together.

'Before you begin telling me, I know,' said Marian ruefully, grinning across the table, and pushing back a few strands of the fair hair which was wound around an old stocking in the 'Victory roll' style, encouraged to enable women to manage without hairpins. 'It's the sitting down that does it. In the ambulance, and when I get back home at night too tired to shift out of my chair.' She had a rented room in Sheffield to which she would not invite anyone. She believed living like a slob was her own business.

As soon as they ordered and began their meal, Helen saw also that Marian had lost all fastidiousness regarding food; she was wolfing down her bangers and mash, and made short work of one sausage which Helen left uneaten.

'I love potatoes, don't you?' she said, beaming. 'And they're easy to cook when you've been out all day. Must admit I fill up on them many a time. There's not been much else, has there? And I've got a sweet tooth these days. A lot of the lads we carry are Yanks. They're pretty free with their chocolate.'

Helen wondered what Denis would think of his vastly altered wife, and commanded herself not to ask. For once, Marian seemed quite interested in what her sister was doing. When she began asking about Stone's, Helen was glad to bring her up to date.

'And are you liking planning new houses for folk?' Marian inquired.

'It's all right for now, though a lot of it's council stuff. They reckon they want four local authority houses built for each private home. And all the private sector's regulated by licences. I just hope there'll be an opportunity later on for getting on with the kind of designing I really want to do.'

'I expect there will be. There's lots of public buildings have been destroyed, to say nothing of them that would have been going up anyway, if the war had never happened.'

'Maybe so, but there's still these Government restrictions, you know – and will be for many a year, by the sound of things.'

'I see. And what does Alex think?'

'Oh, he's not home yet.'

'Really? But I thought – well, surely he was working on stuff for our defences. Hangars and coastal fortifications, wasn't he?'

'That sort of thing, aye. So far as I could tell. He wasn't supposed to talk about any of it. I imagine folk like him would be responsible for Bailey bridges an' all, and air-raid shelters.'

'Well, then – there's no call for them any longer, is there?'

'I know. But they seem to want to hang on to him for a while. Don't ask me why. He's got that used to not discussing his work, he doesn't tell me owt.'

'Never mind. You'll be all the more excited when he does come home for good.'

When Helen didn't respond, Marian gave her a searching look and reached across to grasp her arm. 'What's up, love? Everything is okay, isn't it, between you?'

Helen smiled. ''Course it is, so far as I know. It's just – well, we'd hardly got to know each other, had we, afore the war began? Since then, we're bound to have changed, both of us. And look how often our ideas collided head-on.'

'Happen he'll have mellowed a bit. Folk do, remember.'

Her sister snorted. 'Alex? Do you really think so? I reckon it's more likely he'll be even more fixed in his ideas. With all the years that have passed.' She couldn't help being thankful that Government stipulations would limit some of his concepts about architecture.

'It isn't only going to be up to Alex, though, is it? Your notions will be just as valid as his, surely?'

Helen caught herself gazing across the table at her sister, unable to speak, remembering an occasion all those years ago, in that other life which seemed now unrelated to her own, when a man training for the priesthood had reminded her of the value of her own thinking.

'And there's his dad, isn't there?' Marian continued. 'Isn't he the one who thinks you're the bee's knees?'

And *that* perhaps is more than half the trouble, Helen reflected, adding this to all the rest of her misgivings.

Within weeks of Alexander's final return to Yorkshire, some of Helen's doubts were proving justified. At home she felt awkward with him. It was so long since they'd been together there for more than the odd few nights that she might have been adapting to living with a stranger. And it didn't help when Alex so often appeared preoccupied that she began wondering if he'd ever again share his thoughts with her.

At work, sensing that her husband secretly resented her rejoining Stone's ahead of him, she kept trying to prove that this had given her no advantage. But his father's evident bias in her favour was undermining the relationship between them. Helen couldn't prevent Alex experiencing a certain resentment that she was bound to admit was only natural.

This surfaced in his criticism of her plans for half a dozen semi-detached houses. Very ordinary in appearance, their main asset the speed with which they might be constructed, there was scope for neither originality nor error. Alex, however, decided the elevations should be re-drawn.

'Any fool could have produced these,' he declared, dropping them on Helen's desk. 'Whoever's going to put up with places that are totally lacking in character?'

'Anybody that's been made homeless,' she answered swiftly.

'Oh, very smart. Pity your designs aren't equally sharp.'

'They're what's expected of us, love. You're as aware as I am of all the blessed instructions. They don't want owt fancy, they've got to build houses as fast as they can, haven't they?'

'Not necessarily by totally sacrificing taste. A kid like young Mark could have done a better drawing.'

Helen was relieved when Joseph came in before she could snap back at her husband. Because he had heard Alex's last sentence, though, he turned on him.

'That's uncalled for, Alexander. Helen's been doing a grand job ever since she came back here. Agreed, these designs are simplified – that's what everybody's after.'

His remarks didn't help. Alex swore under his breath, swallowed as if trying to contain his disgust, and faced his father. 'I don't care what the Government, Town and Country Planning, the local council or anyone else expects of us! We're the ones who will have to live with the crude buildings that are just being shoved up anyhow.'

'Folk need homes, it's that simple,' Joseph continued calmly, though Helen could see his patience was growing thin. 'I know round here we've been lucky and it isn't very obvious how severe the housing shortage is, but . . .'

'You don't need to talk to me about lack of housing. I spent most of the war amid all that bombing, didn't I?'

'Then you ought to understand we have to make this a priority. Once we tackle the problem of close on two million homes that have been either damaged or destroyed, we can look to all the niceties.'

'I still say we ought to do better than this,' Alex persisted, glowering at the plans which so offended him.

Helen couldn't pretend she wasn't put out. What was more she recognised that if she didn't make a stand now she'd have Alex criticising everything she ever did. She did, however, long to ease the antagonism that had flared between them.

That evening, when she was serving their meal, she smiled across at her husband who had hardly spoken since the disagreement.

'Happen we'd better make a pact not to fall out about work, love. It's not worth it, especially just now when our hands are tied by restrictions that govern every mortal thing we attempt.'

'Maybe you're right. I certainly didn't bargain with having this sort of conflict as soon as I got home.'

'And we won't let it happen again. After all, we know things are far from ideal. I'm just as eager as you, you know, to get my teeth into designing something big, something really original.'

'Yes.' Alex sighed. 'I daresay you are.' But he wouldn't have been half so perturbed if his own father didn't always side with Helen against him.

On the next occasion when this occurred, it was for rather different reasons. Amid all the replacement of housing that was being planned they were given the opportunity to design one really good scheme. A school in Manchester was to be rebuilt, and Joseph got wind of it before architect's drawings had been submitted.

'The school governors have specified that they want the new building to be in keeping with the present surroundings. I'm going over there tomorrow to have a look, but I gather that it's adjacent to a Victorian church which has survived intact. The nearby houses are Victorian and Edwardian and all. I want you, Helen, to come with me.'

She was torn. Delighted though she was finally to have this opportunity to work on the sort of thing for which she had first begun her training, she was only too aware that Alex felt slighted.

'It's not your style of building, I know,' she heard his father telling him. 'That's the only reason I've chosen Helen rather than you. You'll be far better getting on with something else, something more modern.'

Alex hadn't been appeased. Even the following weekend when he went with Helen to visit her parents, he was still disgruntled.

'Is something the matter, love?' Kathleen Clegg asked him while they were having tea. Her son-in-law wasn't normally so subdued.

'It's my fault, I'm afraid,' admitted Helen when Alex didn't answer. 'His dad's taken me to look at a site over Manchester way, and has given me the job of drawing up plans for a school.'

'By, but that's good, love,' her own father exclaimed quickly.

Helen wished that he hadn't. Alex was looking more downcast than ever. Her mother was glancing from one man to the other.

'How can you say that, Daniel?' she reproved her husband. 'Can't you tell that Alex is the one who ought to be given a job of that size?'

'It's only because of the style they're wanting,' Helen began explaining. 'They don't want anything too modern . . .'

'Do you have to make it sound as though I'm incapable of adapting to clients' wishes?' Alex demanded.

Helen pressed her lips together, determined to say no more. Whatever was said, the atmosphere only became steadily worse. Eh, love, she thought, gazing at her husband, can't you see it's because you've spent too long proving you're inflexible?

And even when some of the houses on which Alex was concentrating were allowing more scope for incorporating his ideas, he remained unhappy about the work Helen was doing. After her first visit to Manchester with his father, she returned there several times alone. On each occasion she was met with her husband's bad humour when she arrived home.

By the time her plans were drawn and approved, he was going around as though burdened by some massive problem. Nothing she did, either at home or in the office, seemed to make any difference. Things came to a head one Sunday evening as they got ready for bed.

Helen was planning an early start the following morning and had been checking the documents that she must take along. She had an on-site meeting with the construction company and the chairman of the school governors. The fact that Alex had a meeting also, to discuss details of a new development of council housing, cheered him not at all.

'Naturally, I'm disappointed,' he confessed. 'You would be as well if you were still waiting to begin on a decent job that would extend you a bit. Instead of all these footling little tasks that a trainee could manage with one hand tied behind him.'

'All right,' she said. 'And I do understand. Why don't we have a talk with your father before anything else worthwhile comes on the horizon?'

'If anybody talks to him, *I'll* be the one, thank you. I don't need somebody to speak up for me. And my patience is daily growing more exhausted. It seems as if all I ever do is wait – first it was wait for that God-damned war to end, now it's wait for this thing and then the other. There's nothing to look forward to any longer.'

Later that night, when they were in bed, Alex continued his catalogue of complaints. 'This is another thing I'm fed up of waiting for an' all. When folk were apart during the war, what was it they clung to most? Families. And where's ours, eh? You've put this off before, but I'm not going to hang on much longer, Helen. I want a child, preferably a son. And the sooner you accept that it's time you gave your mind to being a mother, the sooner we'll get back to a more agreeable way of life.'

It wasn't the most propitious, and certainly not the most romantic, way of coaxing her to make love. Helen wouldn't have denied him anything that night, but she couldn't obliterate certain feelings of resentment. Okay, so the war had kept them apart, had prevented their even really feeling married until now. But they were still young enough to be able to delay starting a family without either of them feeling deprived.

Alexander took her fiercely, making her recognise his determination to have her submit to his will. Helen caught herself hoping that they weren't conceiving a child in such disappointing circumstances. And immediately felt guilty. She shouldn't be hoping anything of the kind. Whatever was wrong between them these days? A few years ago they'd hardly been capable of resisting each other, and she'd been less worried then than she was now about bringing a bairn into the world.

It was this same problem again, she supposed. Having had to wait until now to really get cracking on her job. Even though she was better off than some folk. Architectural students who were returning from the forces were confronted with difficulties. There was a new requirement coming into force which could mean that they would have to spend an extra year acquiring work experience after the five-year course before they could even sit the Professional Practice and Practical Experience Examination.

Pondering the difficulties faced by present-day students, Helen was so preoccupied that she didn't realise that their lovemaking had ceased until Alexander's even breathing against her neck told her that he was asleep. She began feeling still more guilty, until it occurred to her that she was hardly to blame for his being totally absorbed in taking his pleasure without any regard for her own.

Whatever is happening to us? she wondered, appalled. During the rest of that wearisome night she lay thinking, summoning all her will-power until she eventually resolved that from tomorrow morning she would put more effort into making their marriage succeed. It was so often up to the wife to prevent a couple drifting apart.

She began by getting up early enough to prepare a decent breakfast, intending that they would eat it in comfort before she had to set off for Manchester. Alex, however, seemed to take forever washing and shaving and getting dressed. And then just as he finally sat down at the table, the telephone rang.

'I'll see who it is,' she said, rising from her chair.

'You get on with your breakfast, love.'

The caller was a woman. She sounded young and rather posh, Helen thought, and she was asking for Alexander.

'Just a minute, I'll get him for you. What's your name?'

'Candida. What's yours?' was the sharp reaction.

'Helen Stone, why?'

'I didn't know Alexander had a sister.'

'He hasn't – I'm his wife.'

Chapter 11

Helen missed her train for Manchester that morning, the first time ever that she'd set out late for an appointment. But she did catch the next train, even though she had only a vague grasp of what she was doing. It seemed to her that the already rocky state of her marriage to Alex was doomed to be reduced to tatters.

The cool manner with which he'd taken the receiver from her shaking hand had upset her as much as anything. He had made no pretence of being more than embarrassed by Candida's call, and nor had he troubled to disguise his end of the conversation that followed. By the time she heard the click as the receiver was replaced on its rest, Helen was in no doubt that his relationship with this Candida was, if nothing worse, very friendly.

'I had asked her never to call me here,' Alex began as he walked through from the hall.

Could he really believe wanting to keep her in the dark made it better? 'I'll bet you had!' Helen exclaimed. 'And how long has that been going on? All the time you were working away?'

'There isn't anything "going on" – we became friends, that was all, and only during the latter part of the war. Candida is a most efficient secretary. And, if you must know, enormous fun to be with.'

'While I'm just an old sober-sides?'

'Have I said that, have I? Be fair, Helen.' She read in his grey-green eyes the perpetual need to be liked.

'Fair? I like that! And is it fair – on either her or me – that you've concealed the fact that we are married? That I even exist!'

'You had friendships while you were away at the farm, you know you did. What about those chaps from Sheffield?'

Helen thought of Ken and the others. She thought of Vittore Fabri, and of how hard she had found denying her emotions for him. Oh, yes, she had formed friendships. 'Yes, I agree,' she told him quietly. 'But every man I met was made well aware of the fact that I am married. I wish I thought for a minute that you have been equally straightforward.'

She had hurried out of the house at that. If she had remained, she'd have been compelled to keep on at him until she found out all there was to know about this Candida woman. And she'd have been in no state by then for setting out for a business meeting.

All the way over to Manchester in the train Helen was gathering her wits, summoning her self-possession so that she would be up to coping.

She mustn't think about it, that was all; by thrusting Alex and that wretched woman to the back of her mind, she would somehow be able to get through the next few hours.

The entire day felt nightmarish. Fortunately, her early work on the scheme had been very thorough, and the quantity surveyor had been efficient; this meant that the construction company's boss had a full understanding of what was required. Hour by hour, she witnessed agreement being reached between the builders and their client. When they both complimented her on doing a good job, she tried to smile.

All she could really feel though was dread, because now she had to go home and sort some kind of sense out of the mess between Alex and herself.

There was still a light in the office after Helen had climbed the hill at Luddenden Foot. When the house was empty she knew that she'd have to go along there. If Alexander was staying on late in order to avoid a confrontation with her, that wouldn't work. There was no way that she was going to leave this wretched business unsettled any longer than she was obliged to.

She was thankful to discover that Alex was alone there, and wasn't sorry that he had the grace to look shamefaced when she opened the door and went in.

'How did it go?' he asked, but she read in the shifting of his eyes how wary he was with her.

'Very well, thanks. Fortunately, I'd done most of my work, and didn't have to contribute too much today to ensure that it all went ahead smoothly.' If he says how sorry he is, she thought, and if he gives his word that nothing really wrong happened with that woman, I'll forgive him. It had begun in wartime, after all. Lots of folk were being flung together . . .

'It was only because of the war,' Alex said as if her thoughts had cued him. 'It didn't mean all that much. We were just . . .'

'. . . flung together?' she finished for him, falling back on the words already in her mind. But suddenly she *knew* that he had been unfaithful. And this woman had come back into his life, into their life. She felt her eyes narrowing. 'You had sex with her then, you don't deny that?'

'I'm not in love with her or anything. I've never even imagined I was.'

Helen straightened her shoulders, willed herself to be calm and firm. How could she go on living with him if whenever he was out of her sight she'd wonder who he was with and what he was doing? 'That's her hard lines, and yours. Because we're finished. You'd better beggar off to her now. If you couldn't keep our vows after that short time, there's not much hope for the future.'

'You don't know what you're saying, Helen. I've never cared for her, not like . . .'

'And while you're going, make sure you pack all your stuff. There's all your dirty underpants in the basket and four days' shirts.'

'Helen, you're not listening!'

'I heard enough this morning, enough to last a lifetime. You've as good as admitted you've been unfaithful, and *not* loving that woman makes it worse, not better.'

Too late, she heard the door behind her close. Alexander's face turned ashen as Joseph came in.

'What's all this?' he asked severely.

'Your son'll tell you. I'm going,' Helen began, swinging round ready to leave.

But her father-in-law caught her by the arm.

'Alexander?' he prompted.

'This is just between me and Helen,' said Alex hastily.

'I think not,' his father contradicted. 'Helen knows, and so do you, that I've always told her she can rely on me. Now there seems to be trouble between you. I want to see it sorted.'

His son said nothing. Helen again made as though to leave, and felt Joseph's fingers tighten, preventing her.

'So there's another woman – that it, Alexander?'

'I'm trying to explain, she doesn't mean a thing to me.'

'But you slept with her, I can't believe you didn't. And what do you suppose that means to Helen, here?

Why the hell didn't you give that a bit of thought before you lost your head? Nay, lad – I didn't bring you up to treat folk that badly!'

Helen could feel the old man shaking with rage. She was terrified he might have a seizure. He had problems with his heart, hadn't he – severe enough to keep him out of the forces?

'Let it go, Dad,' she said quietly. 'It's like Alex said, it's up to him and me to sort this.' Or not, she added to herself, certain that she was too shaken to continue living with this husband of hers.

'I'm damned if I'll let it go,' Joseph persisted.

'But it was only with being away from home,' Alex put in. 'You've got to understand . . .'

'Wrong,' his father contradicted. 'We don't *have* to understand anything, and Helen isn't even obliged to try to. You've done the most dreadful thing you could to her. No one would blame her for wanting you out of her life.'

Alex was growing increasingly alarmed. He saw himself being deprived of his work as well as his home, and all for one escapade! He'd have to grovel if that was the only way, promise anything so long as he wasn't kicked out of here as well as from the house. Thank God he literally didn't care enough about Candida to want to meet her again.

'I'll never see another woman as long as I live – and I'll make sure this one knows we shall never meet again. I'll be a model husband from now on.'

Happen so, thought Helen, but the fact remains that I shall never have an easy minute now. It seemed particularly ironic that after struggling for so long against her feelings for Vittore, she had been let down by Alex who hadn't hesitated to sleep with this Candida.

Nothing was resolved that day. She and Alexander

went off home together, but she could hardly bring herself to talk to him, her mind was in such turmoil. In a way, she could understand how easy it was to fall for somebody else, but succumbing to temptation was altogether different. And there was the way that Alex kept insisting that he *hadn't* fallen for this woman. She wondered if she'd ever really known him.

For weeks they remained in the same house and spent most of every working day in the same office, but the tension between them did not ease. They hadn't slept together since that first night. Helen had brought her pillow and spare bedclothes downstairs to sleep on the settee. She wanted to get as far away from him as she could, and certainly didn't want him to touch her.

'Don't be like this, Helen,' Alexander had pleaded.

'I can't help it. I know I shan't sleep with you near me.'

In the end he had taken the settee, and used it every night since.

On the next occasion when she visited her parents Helen intended going alone. She was desperate to talk to them. When she was getting ready, however, Alexander announced that he would accompany her.

'It's bad enough upsetting you. I don't want your mother finding out and thinking badly of me as well.'

Within five minutes of walking into the house, though, they learned that Kathleen and Daniel were aware of the situation.

'We've had a visitor,' Kathleen announced, while Helen was wondering why her parents looked as uncomfortable as she was feeling. 'Your father came here t'other night, Alexander. Told us there'd been a bit bother.'

'What on earth did he do that for?' Alex began.

His father-in-law answered him. 'He said as how he

didn't want owt going wrong between us families. And happen if we knew there'd be summat we could do.'

'*Is* there?' Kathleen asked, concernedly. 'We only want to help.'

'You'll help most by keeping out of something that just affects Helen and me,' said Alex. 'And I don't mean that unkindly – I appreciate your caring, only involving so many folk is making the whole business more important that it was.'

'More important?' Daniel demanded. 'What's more important than our daughter's happiness, that's what I want to know?'

Helen decided it was time she had her say. 'Dad – Mum, I know you mean all this for the best, but Alex is right about this. It is up to us to make up our minds whether we're going to stay together.'

'Eh, love – don't say it's come to that!' her mother exclaimed. 'You wouldn't separate?'

Helen didn't reply. The distress in Kathleen's grey eyes was bad enough now. She was determined not to make it worse.

'That's up to Helen,' said Alex eventually, with a sigh that seemed to emphasise his dread that their relationship was ending.

It wasn't until a further six weeks had passed that any conclusion was reached. And then it was for Joseph Stone's sake, rather than his son's, that Helen made a decision.

The old man had aged visibly during these weeks, and even in the office appeared to be quite disorientated. Helen had caught Alex watching him anxiously, but they never discussed anything but business these days.

One day, however, Alex was out meeting the local housing chief, and when their secretary had left for home Joseph detained Helen as she was tidying her desk.

'Have you a minute, love, for a bit of a chat?'

'Of course,' she said. 'What is it?'

'I wanted to talk to you about our Alex. All this trouble is playing havoc with me. I don't seem able to think straight. Somehow, folk's names keep going clean out of my head and . . .'

Helen smiled. 'That happens to all of us, at times.'

'Not every day, and for most of the day! And I keep forgetting what day it is, come to that – what month even. The other night, I wakened up in a right sweat. Couldn't remember for sure whether the war was over or not.'

'You know what, don't you? You want to put us two right out of your mind, forget what happened. It wasn't anything you could help, and if we can't sort it out . . .'

'It's you I'm concerned for most, Helen love,' her father-in-law interrupted. 'Alexander is the one who did wrong, he deserves what he gets. But I hate seeing you so miserable. There's the firm, as well, naturally. I'd always been that thankful that there was the pair of you to run it. I don't think I could bear it if it were to go downhill because of all this bother.'

'You want us to stay together, to patch things up?'

'Nothing would delight me more, love. I know it's more than Alex deserves, but he's not all bad.'

'I know that, Father. He's got a lot of you in him. I'd be sorry an' all to see Stone's go down. I can still recall how thrilled I was that first day you asked me to think about coming into the firm. And I suppose I can't have been all that sure I wanted us to split up when all this time has passed and I haven't done owt about it.'

She had a long talk with Alex that night. 'You've

made me feel terribly insecure in our marriage,' she said finally. 'I don't know if I can put that behind me, but I am prepared to have another try at making a go of it.'

Alex rushed to hug her.

'You'll have to be patient with me,' she told him, holding him a little away from her. 'It's going to take a while to get over this. Things like sharing a bedroom and that. I shan't be able to forget – well, you know.'

In the end, it was through Joseph Stone again that this final barrier was overturned. She and Alex had been called to The Stone House by Mrs Hartley. It was a weekend and for days they had been concerned because the old man was growing increasingly confused and unable to concentrate. Helen had caught him out when he was supposedly studying a letter from one of their clients. He had appeared to read every word, turning over from one page to the next as necessary. When they began discussing the details that it contained, however, she quickly found that he hadn't taken in anything. And now, a day or two later, he had evidently lapsed again into an agitated state where he could not be convinced that Britain wasn't still at war.

'I can't get through to him, I'm afraid,' Mrs Hartley said when she admitted them. 'And he won't let me call the doctor.'

Joseph greeted them cheerfully enough, but his ramblings did not cease, even when they had been sitting talking with him for an hour or more. Alex went to ring the doctor then sat with his father again while Helen tried to learn all she could from Mrs Hartley.

'He doesn't seem to take stuff in any more,' the housekeeper confided, alarmed. 'He reckons he's reading the paper, but I'll be hanged if he is. You talk to him five minutes later on, and he knows nowt about anything that's in it. He's the same about letters, an' all, I'm afraid. I found that out when somebody kept writing and then called to see us. Summat to do with that new-fangled washing machine that the master would insist on buying.'

When the doctor had given Joseph a thorough examination, he asked to speak with Alexander. After he had driven away, Helen went to find her husband. He was sitting near one of the large windows in that huge reception room which, except for a faint light from the moon beyond the glass, was in total darkness.

'He brought me up,' he said in a choking voice. 'There was just the pair of us for that long. I can't bear this, Helen, I can't.'

She crossed swiftly and put her arms round him. 'I know, love. I do know. I wish there was something I could do . . .'

Even while she was speaking she understood that there was. She wasn't certain it could help Joseph Stone now, but it would help this man of hers. 'He's resting now, isn't he? Let's see if Mrs Hartley has a room ready for us.'

'I had a feeling you might decide to stop the night,' the housekeeper told them. 'I've aired the bed in Mr Alexander's old room.'

After they had gone upstairs, however, Alex still needed to talk. Sitting at the desk which stood between two long windows, he faced the wall for a few seconds, thinking, then swivelled round to see what he could read in Helen's expression.

She was gazing at him, concern darkening the lovely grey eyes, while the distress of the past few weeks was evident in the shadows beneath them.

'I feel as if I'm losing everything,' he admitted. 'First you, now my father.'

'You haven't lost me, not entirely,' she reminded him calmly. 'We could still make this into a good marriage, but that's going to require commitment on both sides.'

'I can see that. You'll need convincing that you can trust me.'

'Aye,' Helen responded grimly, well aware that it would be a long time before she would be able to do that.

'I was weak, I'll confess,' he said miserably. 'Foolish. If you've not been tempted yourself, you'll doubtless find that hard to understand.'

'I've never said I haven't,' Helen began, and was checked by her husband's immediate surprise which soon changed to what seemed to be comprehension. 'That chap on the farm, I suppose? The one with chest trouble.'

Almost, Helen shook her head. Just in time she thought better of enlightening him. Ever since the war ended she had thought of Vittore, frequently and affectionately. When Alex was being difficult, she had yearned to get away from here to Italy. She could continue her career out there. But she'd kept her feelings to herself this far: now that Alex and his dad needed her, she'd ensure that they remained interred.

'As I see it,' she said firmly, 'we have got to leave the past where it is. Up to the other week, we haven't had any real reason to think we shan't make a go of it. Now there's your father's health to consider. And the business. I've always been very fond of your dad – you know that. I hate seeing him like this. And if our patching things up can help him to improve, that's what we'll do. It'll ease his mind a lot. As for the business – well, there's only us that's fit to build

Stone's up again. We'd best give our minds to that, and stop fratching.'

'Bless you, Helen – you're marvellous.'

'Time'll tell,' she responded enigmatically, far from convinced that she could carry out her own suggestions. She only knew that she felt compelled to put all she'd got into trying.

As she got into bed Helen noticed how exhausted she felt, like an old dishcloth. And Alex looked worse. She believed he genuinely was distressed by the rift between them, on top of that this anxiety about his father appeared to be more than he could take. Instinctively, she drew him against her.

'You've always been so good to me,' he murmured into her hair. 'Ever since that fire at Yeoman's Grange.'

Tired though they were, neither of them slept readily that night. Helen wasn't surprised when Alex began making love to her. And she wasn't sorry either. After keeping him off for so long, she'd been dreading a return to their normal relations. Like this, there was less awkwardness. And afterwards they managed to get off to sleep.

Joseph Stone rallied a little under his doctor's care, and seemed to regain more of a grasp on what was happening around him. He started taking an interest at the office again, and appeared to be able to follow what was going on there. And if Helen and Alex acknowledged in private that the old man no longer fulfilled a useful role, they agreed that he must be allowed to believe he was indispensable to them. Certainly, they both were far happier about his state of mind.

The news which was to really act as the tonic Joseph needed was their announcement that Helen was at last expecting a child. Alexander also was utterly delighted. And if she herself was less than thrilled about the timing, she was prepared to accept that this was an essential part of the pact to make their marriage work.

Having put Alex in such a good humour, she was compelled to admit that their life together took on a happier aspect. For once in his life, he became deeply concerned for someone other than himself, and within his limitations couldn't do enough for her. The limitations were as Helen might have expected. Reared with a housekeeper and other staff to tend every need, Alex simply wasn't aware of the innumerable tasks involved in keeping a home running. He failed to see that their carpets needed hoovering, or that the stack of dishes would remain beside the sink until somebody washed them.

When Helen's tiredness made him comment and she pointed out that she was trying to keep going both at home and in the office, it was at Stone's that Alex quickly suggested they should acquire some help.

His wife shook her head. 'No, that's not what I meant. I shall keep going there as long as I can. It's what I enjoy doing, isn't it? I had to wait all through the war for this, didn't I?'

Alexander didn't argue with her. He was learning that he shouldn't cross Helen too regularly. He would have to wait. With the old man still installed in the office, introducing another qualified architect might make for difficulties. And Helen was good at her job, and more reliable than somebody new might prove.

'I'll get someone to help with housework,' she announced one evening while they were sitting after finishing their evening meal. 'That way, I'll be able to carry on at Stone's, and happen just set somebody on there to cover for a month or two when I have the baby.'

'A month or two?' That didn't suit. 'That's not what I had in mind at all. I don't want my wife working when we have a family. It isn't as if you had to for the money.' The firm would do better once building licensing eased. And they didn't live extravagantly.

She managed a smile. 'Well, we'll have to see,' she said. But was conscious already that she would see to it that she continued to work after she became a mother.

Her sister told her she must be wrong in her head the first time that was mentioned in her hearing. Marian had asked her over to Leeds one Saturday to look at the cot which she had used for both children. Alex had taken his father to watch the local cricket club, and Helen was pleased to have the opportunity to go somewhere without him. She had included a visit to Harrogate as well, to see old Mr March who seemed to be taking on a new lease of life. His second daughter had been restored to him after the war had ended and the inmates of prison camps had been repatriated. Her husband hadn't survived, but she herself was gradually recovering from internment, and had settled in a pleasant flat not far from her father's nursing home.

In good spirits after being able to tell Mr March how the bursary was swelling now that she was earning good money again, Helen only laughed at Marian's astonishment. 'I'm beginning to think I'm not the maternal type, any road, though it's a bit late for deciding that. But it was to be an architect that I studied all those years. I'm not going to abandon that just when it's getting interesting again. There's going to be fewer building restrictions afore long, you know. That's what I've been waiting for.'

'But it'll be nowt but work still, Helen. Don't you want to have things a bit easier?'

'What for?' She could think of nothing more boring than just looking after the house and a bairn. Whatever would she do with all the designs and the schemes that still came surging into her head, just as they always had done?

'You could come over here more often, like this. We could go round the shops together. Lewis's is still there, you know, and Schofield's.'

'Look, love, I'm glad you enjoy that sort of thing, but it isn't for me, really it isn't.'

'Linda and Mark are looking forward to you having a baby, they'll love a little cousin. We could take them all into Roundhay Park, and further afield. We can both drive, can't we?'

It was mention of Linda and Mark that set Helen thinking. 'It's a pity you live so far away. I'd be asking you if you'd baby-sit for me, regular like. I'd be glad to pay you . . .'

When Marian beamed at her, Helen couldn't immediately understand why. But her sister soon enlightened her.

'You just might find we aren't living quite so far apart before very long. I wasn't going to say owt yet, but we mightn't be stopping in Leeds. You remember how Denis did a lot of acting with ENSA during the war?'

'Yes. Well?'

'Don't breathe a word to Mum and Dad yet, you know what a thing they have about being secure, but Denis is hankering to act again, says he's that sick of backstage work he'll take a cut in wages if he can get the job he wants. Anyhow, he's auditioning next week – in Halifax. The repertory company lost their male lead and are after somebody now. Wouldn't that be great, getting taken on where he began as an A.S.M.!'

'Would it be a lot less money than he's getting as Stage Manager at Leeds Grand?'

'Don't know really, but he's afraid it would. It's not as important a theatre, is it? Wages in rep are notoriously low. But we're thinking of it as just a start. He could be fortunate and finish up in the West End. That's happened for more than one of the folk that he was with in ENSA.'

'And wouldn't you mind moving house again?'

Marian glanced around the lounge of the house which was comfortably, if not elaborately, furnished. 'Happen so – a bit. But this place hasn't felt quite the same since we came back when the war was over. I'd let it, you know, while I was in Sheffield and Denis away such a lot. The folk we had in kept it nice, but it hasn't felt like mine, if you know what I mean.'

Although determined not to set any great store by what her sister had told her, Helen couldn't help hoping that Denis would get the job which might ensure bringing them back to live near Halifax. The day that Marian telephoned with the news that this was what they were doing, it seemed almost as though their arrangements had co-ordinated to provide a means of securing her own way of continuing her career.

Before that could occur, however, the final months of her pregnancy must be endured. And without letting Alex see how greatly those summer months of 1946 were taxing her. Perhaps due to the proximity of the office to their home and consequent lack of exercise, or maybe simply her natural tendency, Helen had put on a great deal of weight. Even though she'd never considered West Riding summers particularly hot, in her condition this one felt extremely so, and endless. The baby was due in October and she was counting the weeks, not so much in anticipation as to have her burden eased.

To Alexander's relief, she had consented to work only part-time from July onwards and to cease coming into the office altogether four weeks before the birth was scheduled.

Helen hadn't breathed a word to anyone, but she and Marian had made a tentative arrangement that in the new year she would hand over care of the infant to her. She suspected that Alex would be appalled, but she would not let that deter her. Marian was good with kiddies, and liked not going out to work. Fortunately, on the occasions when they got together, Alex enjoyed the company of both Denis and Marian – he wouldn't have any reasons for objecting on the grounds of *who* would be caring for their child.

Towards the end of August Joseph Stone began declining again. Although he himself never admitted as much, both Helen and Alex concluded that he must realise that his active life was ending. Daily, he was driven as far as the office by the young woman who had been taken on to assist Mrs Hartley at The Stone House. And each day he tended to sit increasingly listlessly at his desk, making no pretence now of achieving any real work. Worst of all, he was becoming incontinent. Bad enough in the home, this created great difficulties in a professional office.

'We'll have to tell him to stay at home,' said Alex on the day when, for the second time, they'd had to summon the car to take his father back for dry clothing.

They were often obliged to find excuses for keeping clients out of the old man's office at times when he was in no state to meet anyone.

'Nay, love, we can't do that to him,' said Helen, her grey eyes filling. She had been recalling the fine man whom she had greatly admired and who had since commanded such a large slice of her affection.

Joseph had indeed recognised for himself that his working life had ceased. Although he might have appeared oblivious to the extent to which he was losing control of his bodily functions, he did experience quite lengthy lucid periods in which he was aware of the indignity such malfunction caused. He telephoned his son at home that evening.

'I shan't be coming in tomorrow,' he declared. 'Time I recognised that I'm getting to be nothing but a nuisance there. You and Helen will get on a lot better without me.'

On the next occasion when they visited the house, Joseph clearly was far more confused, rambling on about the war again, with no inkling that it had long since ceased. And Mrs Hartley was showing the effects of caring for him now. She herself was well on into her sixties and the additional washing, together with anxiety, was wearing her down.

Even the doctors admitted that there was little that they could do for the old man now. And he could linger on for years, thought Helen, while unable to bring herself to voice such a dread to her husband. But it was no sort of an existence for someone who had once been so fine a man. How would they all endure it if this continued indefinitely?

She and Alex were getting ready for bed one night in September. It was later than their usual time. Helen generally went up soon after nine-thirty these days, but tonight a fierce thunderstorm had torn its way back and forth along the valley since early evening. From the vantage point of their small house on the hill, they hadn't missed any of its alarming ferocity.

As she drew the bedroom curtains across lightning forked yet again and thunder rolled nearly overhead.

She didn't hear the telephone at first. Only as the rumbling faded did she become aware of its ringing. Alex was in the bathroom. Helen struggled back into her maternity smock, thankful that she hadn't taken off her skirt. Going downstairs, she glanced at her watch. It had gone eleven o'clock. This could only be an emergency.

Steeling herself, she lifted the receiver.

'It's Mr Stone, I'm afraid,' said Mrs Hartley agitatedly. 'I'm sorry to have to ring you, in your condition, but it's bad. I've called the doctor, he should be here any minute, but I thought you and Mr Alexander had better be told.'

'Of course, Mrs Hartley – how bad is it?'

'Well, I'm no expert, as you know, but I think he's had a sort of seizure.'

'We'll be there as soon as we can. You must stop worrying now, you've done everything you possibly could.'

Alex took the news badly when he came rushing down the stairs to join her. 'It's the end, I know it is!' he exclaimed, his face the shade of the mushrooms Helen had peeled for dinner that evening.

'We don't know that, love. We can only hope that it isn't, and just keep going to make sure we get there,' she added, wondering why words were so daft. You said what you felt you ought, yet all the while, deep inside, you were hoping the old man wouldn't drag on for ever like this. For his sake more than anybody's.

Rain drove at the windscreen all the way along the main road. 'Houses in Mytholmroyd'll be flooded if this doesn't ease up soon,' Helen remarked as lightning reflected back from water racing like rivers at the edge of the road.

'We don't have to go through there,' snapped Alex, and gave her a sideways glance that seemed to ask if she had lost her senses.

Helen didn't reply, but grew even more disturbed by recognising that he could spare no thought for anyone or anything that didn't affect his family.

The lane up to the house was awash as well, and smothered in the silt, sand and soil driven down the hillside by the force of the deluge. Despite their urgency, Alex was obliged to slow down as he negotiated every curve between the rough drystone walls.

The doctor's car was in the drive; Alex parked beside it rather than pausing to garage the Standard. Taking Helen's hand, he hastened through the downpour and began running up the steps.

Halfway to the door, Helen was obliged to free her hand and follow at her own pace. She had a stitch in her side already, and a pain was beginning to sear into her back.

The housekeeper had the door open and Alex was questioning her by the time Helen caught up.

'I'd just shown the doctor up there when you arrived, Mr Alexander. I daresay he'll be a while before he can tell us owt for certain.'

'And Dad – how did he seem? Is he conscious?'

Mrs Hartley was shaking her head. 'Eh, I wish I could tell you, I do that! But you know how he's been lately – never quite with you, in a manner of speaking. His eyes were open, though. Is that good?'

Before either of them could answer her, Helen felt something warm and wet cascading down her legs.

'Oh, no!' she exclaimed, shocked. 'I'm ever so sorry, it looks as if it's me now. I didn't even know I needed to go . . . I am sorry, Mrs Hartley, you've enough to do.'

But briefly the housekeeper's tired eyes lit up. 'Eh, love, don't take on. That's your waters, I'm sure!'

Chapter 12

Helen was still standing in the middle of the hall when the doctor emerged from one of the bedrooms and hurried down the beautiful curving staircase towards them. Although somebody had taken her coat, and someone else had produced a chair, she was too uncomfortable about the pool on the floor to think of sitting.

As Alex stepped forward to enquire after his father, Mrs Hartley, for once in her life venturing to assert herself, spoke first to the doctor.

'Is the master still holding on?' she asked swiftly, and when satisfied with a nodded reply, continued: 'Then could you take a look at this lady please – Mr Alexander's wife, you recall, Doctor? I think her bairn's on its way.'

The doctor took charge at once, checking which room was available and assisting Helen upstairs and along the landing. Somewhere on the way he turned to Alex who was following.

'You could go in and see your father. He doesn't appear to be conscious of what's going on around him, but there's still a good chance he might know you're here.'

Alex ran towards his father's door.

'I wanted to see him again,' Helen protested, but quite weakly. The pains had spread from her back already, and felt to be dragging so much they could turn her inside out.

'And so you shall,' the doctor reassured her. 'He'll last beyond this night, if I'm any judge. You'll be showing him this fine infant that's in such a sudden hurry.'

If this is being in a hurry, thought Helen hours later as dawn paled the sky over the far hillside, I'd hate to have one that took its time! The doctor had summoned the midwife, a broad Scots woman, and after checking again that he could do nothing further for Joseph, had gone home to his interrupted sleep. Mrs Hartley had been persuaded by Jane, the young woman they employed, to go to her bed and rest. With Alex as well as the midwife popping in and out, Helen had no opportunity for feeling neglected. In fact, assured now that the birth would proceed quite normally, she wasn't sorry when the midwife left her on her own. The suddenness with which her labour had begun meant that she needed some time for settling her mind. Together with anxiety about her father-in-law, concern about this premature labour was whirling out of control.

Thunder still hung around, startling her every time that she supposed it had cleared right away. And lightning kept forking the early morning sky. Between the meteorological shocks and those inside her, moments for thinking were scarce. Helen felt no more at peace by the time the midwife returned to her room.

A large woman, who reminded Helen forcefully of Miss Templer at the farm, she conveyed efficiency with an underlying kindliness.

'Are the pains coming more frequently at all?' she inquired. She had been asked by Alexander Stone to remain at the house until the baby was safely delivered. No matter how long that took. She knew she would be well rewarded. The family were private patients. No one living at The Stone House would be on any doctor's panel.

'Sorry, I keep losing track,' said Helen. 'It's this storm interrupting.' Wanly, she smiled. 'Caught myself just now counting the gaps between the lightning and thunder instead.'

'Aye, it's been a cruel night, the worst we've had for ages. We'll time you for a while now, see what Doctor thinks.'

'He's still here then? I thought he'd gone. How's Mr Stone?'

'The doctor left not long after midnight, but turned up again not half an hour ago. And Mr Stone's still holding his own.'

'That was what Alex said.' He had visited often during the night before returning to doze in his father's room. 'Happen if I'm still like this in an hour or two I could go in and see my father-in-law? He's always been good to me.'

Another fierce pain interrupted. The midwife stood beside the bed, her attention divided between her watch and Helen's face. The next pain came sharply on the heels of its predecessor. Helen was too wearied to contain a little cry.

The midwife beamed, nodding to herself. 'Not long now, Mrs Stone. I'm just going to check downstairs that they have everything to hand. Shan't be a second.'

Alone again, Helen couldn't credit that her time was almost here. Maybe because of having so little real warning, she found picturing herself a mother before this day was out highly improbable. But then the pains recurred, stronger and more urgent. Thinking became impossible.

The midwife opened the door and ran towards the bed. 'Right, lassie – just try to do everything I say . . .'

Helen had wanted to remember the birth, to lodge in her mind each vital moment that was introducing this child of theirs to a separate life. But she was hurting too much to do more than reach through this agonising haze and grasp instructions from the large capable woman who was helping them. By the time she felt the final thrusting and the moist slithery being emerging between her legs, she could only pant, and pray a bit, and hope.

'Is it all right?' she gasped when the cord was cut. 'What is it?'

'A grand wee lad,' she was told, and that instant heard his first cry. 'Hear that now, Mrs Stone – hasn't he got fine lungs? And he's not over small for a bairn that's afore the time.'

Still blood-streaked, he was held up for Helen to see. 'I'll just clean the wee man up a mite, then you shall hold him.'

He felt heavier in her arms than she had feared, warm through the bit of blanket used as an improvised shawl. Helen pressed dry lips against his forehead.

'He is all right, isn't he?' she checked, unable to believe that the child was here and well.

The midwife chuckled. 'Aye – you may rest assured, there's no bits missing.'

'Has my husband been told? Can he come in now?'

'In a minute, lassie. When we've got you all clean and tidy again.'

Alex walked slowly across to the bed. He'd never felt so awed in the whole of his life. Helen looked different, pale with exhaustion and lack of sleep, but radiant, her beautiful grey eyes reflecting the early morning light. And the baby? He hardly dared to look. A part of him longed to stare and stare at his son, the product of their loving; yet the other half, the side unfamiliar with anything to do with this women's work, childbirth, might compel him to turn and run. He might so easily do or say something that was wrong.

He kissed Helen tentatively, aware of her sudden fragility, and risked one glance at the bundle that was his son.

Helen smiled after he had asked how she was. 'Bring up a chair, Alex. Then you can hold him.'

He didn't – wouldn't ever – know how.

'Nay, love – come on,' Helen chuckled, then grimaced when even a tiny laugh hurt. 'Just stick your arms out over the bed.'

He cradled the child against him, gazed down at the reddish, rather wizened face, wondered what colour his eyes were. When he asked, Helen said blue. She added that they always were, but might change later.

'How's your dad?' she asked. 'Any different?'

Alex shook his head, his eyes filling. 'It's been a long night.'

Helen grinned ruefully. 'You can say that again. But about your father – what did the doctor say this morning?'

'Won't commit himself, but he's coming back after surgery. It can't be so good.'

'The doctor's gone off again already, has he?'

'Not yet. Wants to take a look at you first.'

'I do wish your dad would come round – if only just so he'd know about his grandson. He used to be that keen to be assured the family would continue.'

Alex sighed, and blinked. Somehow, he couldn't keep the tears from reaching his lashes.

'Take the baby into his room, anyway, love. Please.'

'I – can't.'

He was saved by the door opening and the doctor

walking in. 'Let's have a look at the boy.'

He took the infant from his father, tested the weight, and smiled. 'I couldn't believe his birth weight, considering he's premature. That'll stand him in good stead, you know. There's no cause to be alarmed by his early arrival.' He glanced at Alex. 'If you'd just leave me with your wife for a minute or two . . .'

'Alex was just going to take the baby to his father.'

'Oh, no – I don't think so,' he protested.

'An excellent idea. Where's the problem?'

'Frankly, Doctor, when you came in I was just wondering how I could even manage to stand up while I was holding him!'

'Watch this – and you'd better catch on fast. There'll be some fetching and carrying while your wife's confined to bed.' Beaming to himself, the doctor beckoned with one hand and, still holding the baby carefully in one arm, conducted Alexander along to his father's room.

Alone with the old man and the infant, Alex glanced warily from the bundle in his arms to the frail features on the pillow. God, what a time! Even now that Helen was through her ordeal, he felt torn apart by anxiety. He couldn't have wanted this baby more – and a *son* – but the responsibility made him feel as though he were supporting the weight of this entire house on his shoulders. As, in another sense, he supposed he was.

Scarcely knowing how or why, he moved towards the bed, his steps faltering as he reluctantly drew closer to the presence of death. Almost unawares, he started speaking.

'He's here, Father, the grandson you wanted so much. I wish I knew what I ought to say, on his behalf *and* mine. I wish he'd come into our lives long before this, while you could appreciate him. He might have –

have helped. You'd have had a new interest, a bit of incentive to – well . . .' His voice dwindled on a sigh.

'Dad, listen, it's a boy. Helen's given me a boy. Given us . . .' He swallowed. Leaning forward, he laid his son close to the grandather who would have loved him. Feeling beneath the covers he located the hand, thin and wrinkled, almost bloodless but not quite cold. Gently, he pressed it beneath his own then held it gently against the baby's forehead.

'Dad, can't you feel? He's here now.'

Alex felt the fingers under his own stir slightly, as if caressing the still damp, fair down covering the front of his son's scalp. His glance jerking to his father's face, he saw the eyelids flicker, struggle to open with enormous effort.

Thinly, a voice emerged from cracked lips. 'A boy?'

'That's right, Dad. Your grandson. You're going to get well again, see him grow up . . .'

A strange sound rasped in his father's throat, his breath seemed to catch – and then was no more.

Alex stood there motionless while between his own hand and the infant, other fingers grew cold.

'At least it's meant that our son was born here, darling.'

Alex was with his wife and baby in a first-floor sitting room which hadn't been used for years. Helen had insisted on being up and about today, said she was feeling fine. And he couldn't have been more thankful for this one sign of their returning to a kind of normality.

The funeral was arranged for tomorrow. It had been a gruelling few days. As the only son, he had always known he would be obliged to see to everything alone. Somehow, perhaps because of Helen being confined to bed at the time, he had felt particularly isolated with his grief. Not that Helen's distress had been any less profound than his own. She had wept on several occasions and he'd noticed how her lovely grey eyes grew misty each time his father was mentioned. Including Joseph in the names they were giving their son was her suggestion – he would be Neil Joseph Stone.

'It'll be better once tomorrow's behind us,' she said now, smiling across at him.

Alex nodded. 'I expect so,' he said quietly, though in truth he could not imagine emerging from beneath this great burden.

It wasn't just the loss of the only parent he could remember clearly. That would have been bad enough but there was this place as well, and his total responsibility for the business. He wasn't acquainted in any detail with what the upkeep of The Stone House must be, but he had a good grasp of financial matters, could make an educated guess at the sum required. The house was too big to be run without staff. That Mrs Hartley would remain was not in question but Jane, the young woman whose primary task had been driving his father around, was already serving the notice which he'd been obliged to give her.

'It's getting you down, love, isn't it?'

That was Helen again, compassionate as ever, ready to share. Yet he'd not inflict on her the new anxieties induced by his father's death. He just wished he'd had more of an inkling that there might be so little available capital. Joseph Stone had been known for his wealth. Alex could hardly credit that, along with this place and Stone's, he'd inherited a budget which must be rigidly controlled.

'It'll take time, Helen, that's all,' he answered her, trying to lighten his tone. 'Just as it'll take a while to get used to living here.'

The way she paled so swiftly told him that she hadn't yet considered that they would be moving in. She didn't say, though, and he was compelled to admire the way her chin went up and a smile reappeared determinedly on her lips.

'I've always loved this house, you know that,' she assured him.

But would she love living here? The Stone House was so unlike the place where she felt she belonged. She yearned for life in a street where neighbours were friends. Maybe when Neil started to grow and was running about the house it might begin to be a bit like home. Until then she was afraid she'd feel as if she and Alex had been set down in a minor palace. Where she couldn't be herself. Still, once their Marian was looking after Neil so that she could get back to work, they wouldn't be spending all that much time here. And she'd always be busy at weekends. Ever since she'd got married, her hours at home had been crammed with more tasks than she would fit into them.

'I telephoned Harold Tilsley while I was in the office,' Alex announced. He didn't add that that had been days ago, and he'd sensed he was right to have reservations about telling her. 'There's a good chance that he'll come into Stone's.'

Helen frowned. 'But even if he is looking for a change, surely he'd not go for something temporary?'

'I can't manage on my own. I need somebody qualified in the office whenever the job takes me out of it.'

'I know that, don't I, love? But what I'm saying is – it'll only be a few months before I'm back there.'

'Will it?'

Helen swallowed down her immediate reply. She had seen his expression. And he'd had a lot of stress this week, tomorrow was his dad's funeral, this wasn't the time for asserting her views regarding her future at Stone's.

'We'll have to see, eh, Alex? See what we think when we've got used to coping with this young fellow here.' And living the different existence which this house will impose on us.

'I shall take Harold, if he's willing to come to us.'

Helen let him have the last word. For the present.

There was nothing funereal about the day, which was scorching for September. The sun had burned through the glass of the cars carrying them from the house to the church. Helen, who had insisted that she was well enough to attend, struggled with lightheadedness as she stood at the edge of the grave. She'd never seen such a big funeral, had felt overwhelmed by the throng congregating behind them in the church. As well as fellow architects and representatives of the many builders and contractors who were business contacts, present-day councillors and others who had served while Joseph Stone was mayor were present.

Thankfully, she saw that Alex seemed strengthened by the size of the gathering, or perhaps was helped by having to bear up in front of all these people. This morning he had cried desolately, trying to explain how he felt now he had no close kindred. But suddenly she understood that he would survive more than this ordeal.

Back at the house, she excused herself. It was Neil's feeding time, and she was glad to take him from her mother who had come for the day, giving help in whatever way she could. To Helen's pleased surprise, her dad had taken a day off work, as well, wanting to share their sorrow. He was with the others now, looking awkward among so many businessmen with their expensive suits and wives darkly dressed but like fashion-plates. Helen had never loved him more.

'Did your dad have a private word with you both?' Kathleen asked now, kissing her grandson's drowsy face before handing him over.

'With me, yes. I'm afraid Alex was busy with somebody – it's been that sort of a day.'

'Aye, I suppose it has. Did everything go off all right?'

'So far as I could tell. Not being at my best, I was concentrating more on watching I stayed on my feet. It's that hot out!'

'But you are all right?'

''Course I am, thanks. Just a bit tired. I had to be there, Mum.'

'I know. And Alex'll allus remember that you were. Poor lad, he'll feel fair lost for a long while.'

'I've been thinking,' said Helen, unfastening her blouse and easing the baby into position. 'It's a right good thing this one here arrived when he did. Alex is that suited with him – when he has time to be – Neil will give him something else to think about.'

'Aye, love, he will that.'

'He believes his father knew, an' all. Did I tell you? Alex swears he understood. They were his last words: "A boy".'

'He'll know now for sure, any road. Joseph Stone won't neglect his grandson. He'll be watching him grow up. Him and Alexander's mother, they'll be together again now. Does your Alex ever say owt about his mother?'

Helen shook her head. 'Do you honestly believe all that, Mum – about when you die? About any of it, religion and that?'

'Of course. It's like your dad says, we're not alone, none of us. Not here, not when we pass on.'

'Must be a comfort.' All at once Helen recalled saying something of the kind years ago, to a man who long since would have become a priest. She wished she could talk to him now.

'I always look at it this way,' Kathleen persisted gently. 'I can only continue to trust, and there's lots of folk cleverer nor me who believe there's somebody there to put that trust in.'

Helen nodded pensively. Death and birth – they were times that set you thinking. And made you wish for powers greater than your own for coping with fresh responsibilities.

'If I don't get a word with your Alex afore we have to go,' said her mother, 'tell him that I shall expect you both to bring young Neil to us some Sunday before so long. Now think on – it's times like this when folk mustn't be allowed to forget that they aren't really on their own.'

During the ensuing weeks, Helen frequently wished that Alex could be persuaded to take up her mother's invitation. Although plainly besotted with their son, he appeared to have no time for anything outside Stone's. He was entirely caught up in so many matters that required serious thinking. Joseph Stone's will had been simple in content, leaving Alex the only beneficiary, but had also named him the sole executor. And regarding the practice he was obliged to go through every file his father had handled, ascertaining which jobs remained unfinished. All too quickly, he had learned that his father's ability to work coherently had ceased far earlier than they had supposed.

Even Helen could not argue when he took Harold Tilsley into the firm. She could only plan for the future, and resolve that she also would have a place there as soon as Neil was big enough to be entrusted to her sister.

Moving all their possessions into the big house had created another upheaval, but one which Helen herself had enjoyed. Even if she still hadn't fully accepted the place as her home, she could make the best of things. No one would deny that it was a far more beautiful house than she'd ever aspired to, and at least she hadn't too many regrets about leaving the one on the hillside at Luddenden Foot.

Whilst busy clearing out their old home and packing, she had taken the opportunity to call into the office. It was hardly the best idea she'd ever had. Alex and Harold were evidently engaged in a man-to-man discussion on reallocating the work load. Alex made it plain that he didn't welcome the interruption, cutting her short while she was catching up on Harold's career to date, and suggesting she should have a cup of tea with their secretary if she felt like chatting.

There'll have to be changes, Helen thought determinedly, hurrying back to continue tidying out their old home. And straight after Christmas wouldn't be too soon. Admittedly, she'd had a lot on her hands, with the move and helping Mrs Hartley reorganise the household, to say nothing of the time devoted to Neil. But their Marian was settled into her new house in Halifax and was itching to help care for the baby. And in some ways his being born early had been a bonus. He'd be that much older and better able to adjust to seeing less of his mother.

Emptying the last of her cupboards that day, Helen had come across the box containing the model of Florence Cathedral which Vittore Fabri had constructed so carefully for her. Smiling at first, she had examined the beautifully crafted structure again. But suddenly tears had welled in her eyes. How could she deny her career, the impulse to create magnificent buildings, *how* – when she'd scarcely scratched at the surface of a job where she yearned to make an impression?

Christmas really seemed to creep up on them that year, and it wasn't until Kathleen Clegg reproached her younger daughter for not visiting earlier, and mentioned Christmas Day specifically, that Helen truly realised how near it was.

'We'd love to come to you for Christmas dinner, and no – I'm not going to check with Alex first. We're not stopping on our own in that big house, regretting that his father isn't still with us. We're coming to you. And if Neil's too little to know what it's about, *we're* going to enjoy our Christmas.'

To Helen's delight, Alex seemed thankful to have arrangements made on his behalf. 'I'll admit I was dreading Christmas Day, and feeling guilty about it as well. Knowing we've such a lot to be thankful for with Neil, yet knowing also that he's not old enough to appreciate a tree and Father Christmas and so on.'

'You'll enjoy seeing our Marian and Denis an' all. And the kids, they've really taken to little Neil. They're fair grand with him.'

On the day, however, it soon proved that Alex couldn't remain in agreement with his sister-in-law. It all began quite well, with Marian who was there already welcoming them in, and Kathleen appearing in the kitchen doorway to greet them while still continuing stirring the bread sauce she was making.

Denis was helping Helen's father who was trying to contain the excitement of Linda and Mark as they examined and re-examined some of the toys they had been given. Seeing their arrival, however, Denis straightened his back and strode across to hug Helen and kiss the sleeping baby before turning to Alex.

The two shook hands and Helen noticed how Denis brought his other hand up to grasp her husband's firmly. 'Glad to see you again, Alex. How are you now? We were both sorry about your father.'

Thanking him, Alex smiled. 'Yes – well, he's at peace now. Didn't have too much of that towards the end of his life. At least he lived to see his grandson.'

As Denis returned to the children, Daniel Clegg rose and came towards Helen. He put his arms round her as he kissed her, and surprised her then by holding them out again for the baby.

'Let's have a look at our Neil. I haven't seen him, have I, since we were over at the big house?'

Helen had visited her mother as well as Marian several times during the last few weeks, but always during the day while her father was at work. She was a firm believer in getting the baby home to bed early.

'You can make up for it today, Dad. I shan't mind if you take him over.'

'But I was going to look after Neil,' young Linda protested.

'You as well, of course,' said Helen, bending down to hug her niece.

'Are we really going to look after him soon like Mummy says?' Linda whispered.

'I hope so,' Helen whispered back, her entire body stiffening as she waited, wondering if Alex had heard.

If he had, he gave no sign and Mark was demanding attention now, rushing to his Uncle Alex with a clockwork car that Father Christmas had brought. Watching her husband with the lad, Helen recognised in his smile that he was savouring a sudden realisation of how it would feel when it was his own son who was sharing interests with him.

Lord, but I'm lucky, she thought. I might have ended up with a chap who didn't want a family. And, much as she looked forward to returning to her career, she'd grown to love Neil so deeply that she already wondered how ever she had been happy without him.

Just before family dinner Helen fed him, sitting in the bedroom which she once had shared with Marian. Gazing about her while Neil sucked away contentedly, she noticed how faded the walls were now, their distemper dulled from peach to a murky white where the sun had streamed in through the south-facing window. The curtains too had paled in streaks, so that the once-bright gold brocade now seemed tawdry. Marian had paid for the stuff for those curtains out of money saved from her first few wage packets, way back in the days when she was the only one of the sisters earning.

Helen was glad that she and Marian got on so well together these days. They had grown closer in outlook and in their interests over the years. And she could hardly believe how well Alex had taken to her brother-in-law. She'd expected somebody with his background would have found little in common with Denis who, despite the practical side which had made him a good stage manager, now appeared to be rather letting acting go to his head.

The two men were talking animatedly when Helen returned downstairs. She smiled to herself when she heard Alex holding forth.

'It's nationalisation that will turn this country around, isn't it? Give a bit of solidarity to some of the main industries.'

'True,' Denis agreed. 'As soon as we got Labour in control, I knew things would start looking up.'

Helen began wondering how her husband reconciled some of the views he held with his upbringing in a home the size of The Stone House, and waited on by servants. And what about owning a firm like theirs? She'd always known he was a bit of a Bolshie, hadn't she? All that stuff about not approving of the royal family. But they had never discussed politics in all the years they'd been married. She could well believe he might not consider her opinion worth inviting.

Helen said nothing now, content to put Neil to sleep in his carrycot then join her mother and sister in the kitchen.

'Where's Dad gone?' she inquired, filling the bowl and starting on the washing up that had accumulated during the morning.

'He's taken our two for a walk,' Marian replied. 'Just as far as People's Park. Said he wanted to work up an appetite. I'm only glad it'll use up a bit of Linda and Mark's energy.'

'They love Christmas, don't they?' her mother put in. 'They were that excited when they got here.'

'Too excited,' said Marian, but with a smile. 'Still, this is the first Christmas since the war that there's been anything worthwhile in the shops.'

As soon as Marian's children returned with their grandfather they all gathered around the table. Daniel made a little speech, saying how pleased both he and Kathleen were to have all the family there together. 'I might not have appeared all that enthusiastic when either of you two young lasses wanted to get wed,' he admitted. 'But, by Jove, you're both making a good job of marriage.'

Alex found Helen's hand and squeezed and she saw Denis and Marian exchanging a loving glance. This Christmas is far better than ever I expected, she thought, sparing a moment's reflection for Joseph Stone while being thankful for her own folk. And most of all, of course, for Alex and baby Neil.

The discord began just as the meal was ending. Linda and Mark had already asked if they could leave the table, and the grown-ups were lingering over cups of tea.

'So how soon do you want me?' Marian asked Helen. 'I can manage all right, even before these two go back to school, if you like.'

Helen felt Alex stiffen beside her. She wished to goodness their Marian had spoken up while they were on their own. As it was, she would have to answer her. And before she'd even raised the subject again with Alex.

Grimly, she cleared her throat. 'We haven't got it all worked out yet, but probably the first week in the new year.'

'What's this?' Alex asked tersely.

'About me going back to work. I did mention it . . .'

'And I said I didn't approve.'

The raised voices disturbed Neil who began wailing. Please don't start, little love, thought Helen. Let me concentrate on this.

'There's no reason for you to come back into the firm, not now Harold Tilsley's joined us,' Alex asserted firmly.

Helen bit her lip. She wouldn't remind him of what she'd said about that, not in front of her family. She didn't want a full-scale quarrel.

Neil's cries had increased by several decibels. Marian, who was nearest to the cot, went to pick him up.

Helen hasn't even the decency to attend to him herself, thought Alex, inflamed by seeing another woman rushing to his son. And this was evidently the way Helen wished it to be. She wanted to surrender responsibility for their child to her sister.

Neil had stopped crying, and was attempting to grasp the beads Marian was wearing. Helen felt torn, a part of her thankful that her sister had quietened him so readily – she'd needed reassurance that he wouldn't suffer by this arrangement – but she was also disturbed. Did he ever respond so immediately when *she* picked him up?

'I'm not trying to neglect Neil. Anything but,' she told them quietly. 'But there are three of us to consider. Marian couldn't be better with him, just look at them now, and she is my only sister. It's not as if I'm trusting a stranger with him.'

Nobody spoke. Helen could feel her husband's antagonism, and the alarm of everyone else. But now this had been brought into the open she meant to make her point. Still quietly, she continued: 'If I have to resign myself to never working again, there'll be a whole area of my life where I'll feel unfulfilled. You all know what the war did to my career. I can't accept that all that hard work studying was just for that short while since 1945, and with so many restrictions preventing us getting to the sort of work we always dreamed of.'

If she had hoped that might get through to Alex, she soon understood that it had done no such thing. He still did not speak and nor did anyone else. It wasn't until her mother began collecting up the dirty dishes and they all moved away from the table that any kind of normal conversation recommenced. Fortunately, Linda and Mark were too young to remain inhibited by the atmosphere, but it was only due to their presence that the tension appeared gradually to ease.

Helen wasn't surprised when Alex suggested early in the evening that they ought to be getting Neil home to his cot. She was no longer even sorry that the gathering which had begun so promisingly was being cut short. Embarrassed as well as hurt by his opposition, she wanted to get him away from here in order to thrash out this problem.

'We'll see you tomorrow, any road, shan't we?' said

Marian, while they were putting on their coats. Earlier in the day, she and Denis had invited everyone to their new home for tea.

'I'm afraid not,' said Alex firmly before Helen could utter a word. 'We have something else arranged.'

In the car, Helen could wait no longer. She'd always been one for sorting out trouble before it could fester.

'You might have waited, instead of making me out to be a neglectful mother in front of everybody. You *know* I love Neil, that I'm potty about him. But that doesn't mean I want to spend my whole life stuck at home looking after him.'

'Evidently not. You make me wonder, Helen, if you even want to spend your life in The Stone House at all. You seem remarkably eager to get out of it as much as ever you can.'

'Since you've brought it up, I've never been all that keen on living there, but I decided after your dad died that so long as you were happy there, I'd give my mind to it.'

'Big of you!'

'Alex – don't let's be like this. All I want is an interest outside the home, the opportunity to continue as an architect. I'm not necessarily even suggesting that I work full time.'

Alex sighed. 'Why can't you be more like your own mother, eh? You saw today how content she is. She's a real homemaker, relishes cooking, caring for home and family . . .'

'And she's a different generation. They weren't brought up to have much in the way of expectations.'

'Why not try it my way, Helen? Give it a year or two, concentrating on Neil, and on making The Stone House into a real home. For too long now the place has been at the hands of a housekeeper, as well you know. Mrs Hartley couldn't be better at that – but she's not the wife, not the person who should stamp her personality on the home.'

'Or we could try it my way, love?' Helen argued. 'Now, while Neil's too little to mind about having his auntie looking after him.'

Chapter 13

Alexander had eventually agreed to her going back to work, but he wasn't a good loser. Helen soon became aware that the next few weeks would be tough. And almost immediately after she had returned to Stone's he indicated very clearly that her insistence on taking her place was making life difficult.

She was working from ten in the morning until four, with an extended lunch hour in order to dash home to feed Neil. Unless she was to waste a lot of time waiting around for buses, this meant using the car. That didn't always fit in with her husband's arrangements, and became a nuisance when he needed to be out visiting sites or conferring with builders.

'I think I'm going to buy myself a little car,' she announced one evening while they were having dinner. 'I shall soon save enough. There's nothing else I need out of the money I earn, is there?'

Alex gave her a look, one she was learning to recognise as the prelude to objections.

'It's not only buying one, is it? There's running costs, insurance . . .'

'Can't they go down as the firm's expenses? Your car does.' And he'd recently invested in a new Rolls-Royce, having sold both his father's treasured Phantom and the little Standard.

'We're not making that much profit,' he told her

grimly. 'Think about it, Helen. There's Harold's salary coming out as well as what we're both taking from the firm.'

'Well, we'll wait a bit then. Now I'm back at work there are more designs being produced. That's bound to bring in more contracts.'

'You'd better resign yourself to a long wait, love. It'll be some time before profits increase substantially.'

Helen noticed during the following few weeks that Alex seemed to be quite obsessed with profitability. She wished he wasn't like that – it made her aware of the differences between them. That she wasn't always on about money; had been brought up in the belief that so long as she'd enough to survive on she could be content. But then, she thought, hadn't Alex always fancied showing off a bit? There'd been the way he always used to enjoy swanning around in his father's posh car. Wasn't the car he'd just bought equally impressive?

There are things about him that I've never really taken to, she reflected, although in many ways they were happy together now. Once she had started working again, she had insisted that they make a pact not to argue about her doing so. They were giving it a try, that was all. If Neil showed the least sign of being unhappy with this method of organising life, she would give it up.

Helen blessed their Marian for being so obliging. The only time she didn't turn up was during the worst of all the deep snow that fell early in 1947. And then, of course, Helen also was prevented from travelling to work. Normally, Marian arrived at The Stone House by nine-thirty every weekday, bringing Mark and Linda when they weren't at school. During lunch they all had a lovely time, chatting while they fed Neil and played with him.

Now that he was growing more interested in what was going on, he was charming Alex every evening with the little ways in which he was progressing. They had developed a routine which seemed to suit the three of them. Each day when Helen took over from Marian, she tidied the nursery and carried Neil with her down to the large kitchen where Mrs Hartley was preparing their meal. By the time Alex came in, she was ready to give Neil his bath, an occasion they savoured together, enjoying his antics before taking him to the night nursery.

This room was the one which Alex had used before him, and he began telling Helen snippets that he recalled from the days when his mother was alive. She smiled tenderly over his memories, aching for the lad who'd scarcely known a mother's caring, and remembering now his grief when Joseph Stone was lost to them.

Helen's deepest regret was that Marian's readiness to look after Neil seemed to have turned Alex against her. He denied that it was so, but Helen sensed that he blamed her sister for making it too easy for her to return to work. Instead of the outings with Marian and Denis and their kiddies which Helen had visualised, she was limited to the short encounters entailed in handing over responsibility for Neil.

As the year progressed and he developed, learning to stand and then to walk, Alex appeared engrossed in his son whenever he was at home, and Helen was no less enraptured by him. He was becoming a winning youngster, with her grey eyes but his father's glorious golden hair. His smile was the echo of his father's and employed as frequently as Alex's had been years ago.

He now smiled less readily, except with the boy. Helen noticed his new gravity, especially around their office. She couldn't understand the cause. Business would increase as soon as the emergency measures introduced that August were eased again and private housing permitted. Despite restrictions, schools were being planned for areas which had received heavy bombing. Stone's had submitted designs for more than one, and had been accepted. And there was the ever-present need for council houses and flats. These might not be the kind of jobs they would have chosen, but they did provide work for architects. When taxed with his gloomy appearance, Alex always hedged, seeming reluctant still to discuss any problems with her.

Anxious, Helen mentioned this one day to Harold Tilsley when Alex was out conferring with council officials.

'Do you want the truth, Helen?' he asked, seriously for him.

'Well, of course. When have I expected folk to mince words?'

'He's never really accepted you coming back to work again.'

'But Neil is fine – he truly is, Harold. He loves being with his Auntie Marian.'

'It's not only that. There's the contention here. Alex still doesn't agree with your ideas on design, does he? And he never will.'

'He doesn't say anything . . .'

'I suppose he knows it will do no good. Your ideas and his will never coincide. And he can't help resenting it when your designs are in favour.'

'But that's only part of the time. And, any road, it's not like him not to say . . .'

'It's not like the old Alex, agreed.'

Helen began observing then, seeing that her husband was indeed keeping to himself so much of what he was feeling. And not only in the office.

Ever since Neil's birth Alex had made love to her

less frequently. At first, she had accepted that her own health and the trauma of losing his father could be contributing to the waning of his passion. With each month, though, Helen began to fear that there might be some other cause, and dreaded learning that he was still hankering after that woman he'd known during the war.

Unable to bring herself to mention this, she was compelled nevertheless to tackle this matter which threatened to spoil their marriage. She chose a Monday evening when they both seemed relaxed after Neil's nightly routine, and neither of them was as tired as they became towards the end of every week.

'Is there something bothering you, love?' she asked while they were having dinner.

'Not especially, why?'

'Things aren't the same between us, are they, Alex? Is it – is it that you feel we ought to wait before risking another baby? If that's it, I think like you – and I could do something about that. There are clinics . . .'

'No,' he said firmly, gazing coldly across the table.

Helen wasn't sure whether he meant she mustn't try to prevent another child, or simply that the cause was different. 'Do you mean that you wouldn't want me doing that, because you'd like more children?'

'I would have liked more, yes. Not immediately, of course, Neil deserves some time as the sole focus of your attention.' He paused, sighing. 'But that's the whole crux of the matter, I'm afraid. It's you, Helen. You're just not the person I thought you were. Agreed, Neil doesn't appear neglected, but nor is he receiving the devotion I'd expected you to show.'

Helen swallowed and laid aside her knife and fork.

'I do love our baby, Alex, I keep telling you – far more deeply than I could have imagined. He has a good life the way things are. Marian couldn't be kinder or more fun for him. He dotes on her.'

'And doesn't that fact tell you anything?'

'That I should be disturbed because it isn't only us that he feels this way about? Once or twice, I admit, I've wished some little thing he's done, or a loving gesture, had been for me instead of my sister. But he knows well enough that we're his parents, Alex. And how much he matters to us.'

Her husband merely shrugged.

'In any case,' Helen continued, 'I don't think it's a bad idea for kiddies to be used to other folk from an early age. There's nothing worse than little 'uns that cling to their mummies. Especially lads.'

When Alex still said nothing, she took a deep breath. 'Any road, I didn't think we were talking about Neil so much as us – what's going wrong between us.'

'And you expect me to divide my general dissatisfaction from what happens in our bedroom, do you? Really, Helen, you can't seriously believe that's possible?'

'Dissatisfaction?' she uttered miserably. Her life seemed to be collapsing about her.

'You began this discussion, remember? I was prepared to wait, hope things might get better. Oh, Helen – why aren't you more like your mother?'

'You've said that before, and I wish you wouldn't. I couldn't live her sort of a life,' she told him earnestly, tears welling in her throat.

'Lots of women do, quite contentedly.'

'Used to, you mean. These days, they're beginning to want to be valued for themselves, for the things they're interested in . . .'

'You imply that your mother, and others like her, are boring.'

'No, I don't. Only that their lives would bore me.'

'Okay, leave it for now, eh?' Alex was sensing that if this conversation continued he'd not guarantee that he wouldn't say something irrevocable. And he didn't want that, he really didn't. It was early days still for their marriage, it should be given a chance.

'But how can I leave it? You're not happy, I can tell. And I . . .'

'You ought to be happy, Helen. Right from the start, you've done only what you wished. First insisting on that Land Army job . . .'

'But you weren't even here then,' she protested.

'Then wanting to delay starting a family. And now that Neil's here, you're just as determined to go your way and set him aside so you can satisfy your ambitions.'

If he was hoping she would give in and come out of the firm, it was more than Helen was willing to do. She couldn't sacrifice all the hopes and plans she had carried burning inside her for so many years. But how could she stick to her determination *and* make her marriage more contented again?

'Happen you're right, love – we ought to leave this for now. Maybe with a bit of time we'll sort something out. We do still love each other.'

Alex said nothing in reply, and from that day Helen began to believe that he no longer did love her.

For months there was no obvious alteration in their relationship. They still worked alongside each other and, together with Harold Tilsley, were improving the business as much as possible given continuing shortages and restrictions. They still relished the hours they spent with Neil. They still slept in the same bed, though that made no difference to the absence of love-making between them.

Helen began suspecting that Alex might have met someone else. His no longer needing sex was so totally unlike him. Certainly, for ages now, he hadn't said he loved her. And did she love him? Love, yes, she realised, though she was less sure that she was *in* love with him. She was beginning to wonder if she'd ever been in love with Alex.

Memories of that all-too-brief encounter with Christopher returned, and others of her friendship with Vittore Fabri. With each man she had known a soaring of the heart which she'd never experienced with her husband. But then, their relationship was very different, had developed so gradually over the years. It had none of the excitement of love at first sight, nor the rapture of the sudden discovery of the one person who might be the other half of one's self.

The quarrel developed one weekend during the following summer, after a day when they had taken Neil to the seaside at Scarborough. Helen was feeling happier than for some time when they had tucked up the tired youngster in his bed, and were going downstairs for dinner.

'By the way,' said Alex, holding the door for her as she preceded him into the dining room, 'I shan't be at home this coming week. I've got wind of a new development just outside London, and I'm determined to find out all I can.'

'Oh. You never said anything to me.'

'Didn't think you'd want to be involved. The developers have specified that they want something very up-to-date.'

'I see. I wish you'd told me, though. About not being at home. And there'll be things you'll want with you. I'll have to pack . . .'

He shook his head. 'No need – it's all taken care

of. Mrs Hartley knows I'll be away. And she has my packing in hand.'

'You've told her without mentioning it to me?' Helen felt hurt, and suddenly threatened.

'She is our housekeeper, after all. The reason we still employ her is because you don't care at all for the domestic scene.'

'Don't say that, it isn't true,' Helen interrupted.

'I wish to God it weren't! I'd give anything for a wife who wanted to concentrate on making this a home.'

'I have tried,' she insisted. 'But this is such a massive place, it'd take more than me to make it homely.'

'If you don't like it here, you could always move.'

Helen was shattered, could hardly believe what she had heard. For what felt like minutes neither of them spoke. Eventually, trying to level her voice, she said, 'Is it that you've met somebody else?'

'No. And while we stay together I'm not likely to, am I?'

'But that's what you want, that's what you're hoping for?'

'If it weren't for Neil, I'd have had the guts to say long since that you and I have made a terrible mistake.'

Despite everything that had been said, Helen was sorry to see Alex drive off next morning. Hugging Neil to her, she watched the Rolls until it went out of sight round a bend in the lane. Going back indoors, she continued to hug the boy, until his wriggling made her aware that the poor little fellow was being squeezed until it hurt.

'Come into the bedroom and watch me getting ready,' she suggested. Normally, he enjoyed playing with her jars of cream and powder. She had never used a lot of make-up, but it made her feel more confident when she was meeting clients. Today, she was desperate to disguise the effects of her sleepless night.

Neil seemed uninterested in her dressing-table, choosing instead to kneel on the windowseat, looking out for his Auntie Marian. Helen grew more depressed as she read the eagerness in his grey eyes and in his restlessly bobbing golden head. She hadn't needed this reminder that there was some truth in Alexander's assumptions about their son's allegiance to Marian.

By the time her sister arrived Helen wasn't far from tears, and they were too close for her distress to remain undetected.

'What's up, old love?' Marian asked, putting an arm round her.

'It's Alex. We're having trouble. And now he's gone off.'

'You don't mean he's left?'

'He wouldn't, would he? This place is his – the family home. No, actually it's a business trip. But he said some awful things last night. As good as told me I could clear out.'

'We all say stuff we don't mean, 'specially when we're het up. Take no notice, love, he wouldn't mean them.'

'Not so sure about that.'

'Haven't you been getting on at all lately?'

'Not really, not for ages. He's sort of – distant. And we've hardly made love ever since Neil was born.'

'Happen too much occurred all at once – losing his dad and becoming a father himself. Then there's the responsibility of the business.'

'Which he doesn't want me to share.'

'That as well, eh? Poor you. Still, I'm sure you'll sort it out between you. For Neil's sake, if nothing else. He adores that boy, doesn't he?'

Helen wasn't reassured. Quite the opposite. Because thinking of her husband's devotion to his son produced an appalling supposition. If Alex really meant that she must go, he might insist that he was given custody of young Neil.

The longcase clock in the hall was striking nine-forty-five. She would have to leave for work. And now she realised she could hardly bear to be separated from her son for even a few hours. Hugging him before she handed over to Marian, Helen felt as if she would never let go. A sigh rising all the way from her heart, she left the house and began running down the hill to catch a bus.

Waiting at the stop, she reflected that she'd never got the car that she had wanted, and now she'd not mention that again. In fact, during this week she must weigh very seriously whether all this contention was worth it. Wouldn't she do far better to accede to her husband's wishes? Surrender her career in the hope that the sacrifice might restore their marriage and their home life?

Harold could see how perturbed Helen was as soon as she walked into the office.

'What's wrong?' he inquired. 'Letting it get you down because your Alex has gone off for the week?'

'Something like that,' she responded quickly, her hurt increasing with the knowledge that Harold had been aware of his plans. Everybody but her.

He dispatched Wendy, their secretary, to make a pot of tea. 'Want to talk?' he asked. 'I know Alex of old, don't I? Look what a boor he was when we all went to Europe that time.'

Helen swallowed back a sigh. 'It's okay, thanks. I'll be fine once I get down to some work.'

'It's no bad thing to have one of us here keen on

more classical styles of architecture, you know. It's where proportion is based. And two like me and Alexander going for contemporary stuff is enough.'

Helen forced a smile to her lips. 'This time it's nothing to do with the way we always clash on that.'

The cup of tea helped to steady her for concentrating on plans and elevations. By eleven o'clock she was beginning to adopt the calm resignation that would get her through this week. And if at the end of it she would face a heart to heart with her husband, that wasn't for several days. Maybe the period without him would give her a chance to see a way out of this situation.

Hearing distantly a woman's voice and a child's in the outer office with Wendy, Helen was puzzled. Neither she nor Harold had appointments that day. They both intended catching up on desk work.

'There's somebody to see you, Mrs Stone,' Wendy announced awkwardly. 'Your sister.'

'Neil,' Helen gasped in horror. 'Something's happened to Neil?'

'No, love,' said Marian, entering. 'He's here, and he's all right. Just look at him.'

Seeing the distraught expression in her sister's eyes, Helen grasped her arm. 'Marian, what is it? Is summat up with one of your two?'

Grimly, Marian shook her head, began propelling Helen towards a chair. 'You'd better sit down, love. Your secretary's going to keep an eye on Neil for a minute.'

'Is it Mum, Dad?'

Again, her sister shook her head, swallowed. 'I don't know how to begin to tell you this, love. I'm afraid there's been an accident, on the way down south. It's your Alex . . .'

'Oh, God! How – how bad is he? Where've they taken him?'

'You'll have to be very brave, Helen,' Marian gulped, her blue eyes full of tears.

'You mean – you can't mean he's dead?'

'Instantaneous, the police say it was. He wouldn't know anything.'

Except that our marriage was a mess, a mistake, thought Helen dourly. Was that the reason he'd been driving less carefully?

'Some chap on the wrong side of the road,' said Marian. 'There wasn't a thing Alex could have done to avoid him.'

Helen called Neil into the office and pulled him against her, holding him to her heart and covering his face and head with kisses.

'I'll have to tell Harold,' she said presently. 'I can't stop here. There'll be things want seeing to. The police . . .'

'They went back to the station, but they'll come out to the house again.'

'Where did it happen?'

'Eh, I can't remember.'

'They'll tell me.' And will tell me more perhaps than I want to know. Because of when this happened, how bad things were between us. And now there'll never be a chance to put anything right.

In the taxi, driving up to The Stone House, Helen began weeping bitterly, as though the heart which had already felt brittle was finally disintegrating.

'I think you'd better go and lie down,' Marian suggested after settling with the taxi driver and helping her sister into the hall. Neil was running up and down, enjoying the sounds echoing from the floor yet darting puzzled looks towards his mother.

'If I lie down I might never get up again. No, we'll

give Neil his dinner, it must be about time. Then I'd better start sorting out what has to be done.'

'The police will tell you that, I daresay, help you find an undertaker.'

'There's the one we had for his father – there'll be details somewhere in Alexander's desk . . . Does Mrs Hartley know? Where is she?'

'Not yet, she's out shopping. I'd told her first thing that I could cope this dinnertime if she wanted to be out a bit longer.'

By the time the police returned Helen was nearly composed. She had made her mind up. All she had to do was get through this next few days without permitting herself to think. There'd be a lot to arrange, people to inform . . . Alexander had so many business contacts. Harold had said something about helping, being willing to do whatever he could. She wasn't going to let him. If she did everything herself, that might keep her mind busy. And it might begin to offset the harm she'd done to her marriage.

The Coroner's Officer came to the house. He had known Joseph Stone and couldn't do enough for his son's family now. The sergeant who was with him had more information about the accident, which had happened near Bakewell in Derbyshire. Helen remembered Marian driving through there on that visit to Stratford upon Avon all those years ago.

'The other driver was badly injured. As soon as he recovers consciousness, he'll be charged,' the sergeant added.

That seemed quite irrelevant to Helen. All she could wonder was what charge a Higher Authority would level at her – like sending her own husband to his death.

* * *

'You're pulling this on top of you, making yourself feel guilty, aren't you?'

That was Marian late that afternoon. She had been home, but only long enough to collect Linda and Mark from school and take them to her parents. During the evening, as soon as she'd made tea and cleared away, Kathleen was coming to stay at The Stone House.

'How dreadful!' she'd exclaimed on being told. 'I must get to our Helen as quick as I can. I know you're doing what you can, Marian love, but she is my daughter. I can't not go to her.'

In some ways, Helen was dreading her mother's arrival, was afraid she would sense the trouble there had been here. Kathleen Clegg had taken to Alexander from the start. She might have had reservations about their differences of class, but that had never stopped her trying to mother him. Marian's, though, was a soothing presence to have around. All day she had simply been here, neither fussing nor uttering all the trite things that people say, and which don't do a scrap of good when you're too upset to heed anything.

Marian had taken Neil out of the room when Helen needed quiet for telephoning or just for thinking. And she had brought him back in when even a few minutes' separation from the boy seemed intolerable. She had known better than to persist when Helen couldn't eat anything, and had had the sense to produce a stiff drink as an antidote for weeping.

'You'll have to get it out of your system,' she had said sympathetically. 'But you don't have to cry it all out in one day.'

Tomorrow the death would have to be registered and her father had insisted that he would take time off work to accompany her. He had telephoned Helen as soon as he arrived home and was told.

'We shall do everything we can from now on to help

you and the little lad, Helen, love. So just think on – there's to be none of the independence that you've allus shown.'

Although grateful, and relieved that she wouldn't have to set off on her own to see to things, Helen remained determined that she would be the one who did all the actual arranging that was necessary. Having her father there must not allow her to weaken and evade things.

Just seeing her mother brought another rush of tears, but familiar arms coming round her as well, and they began to help ease the pain.

'He'll be with his father at least,' said Kathleen, her own eyes awash. 'And with his mother an' all. You must try to think that, love. He won't be miserable.'

As he was with me, thought Helen, and wept more bitterly. Somehow, though, they got through the rest of the evening, and the night. Mrs Hartley had aired the room next to the master bedroom for Kathleen Clegg, before retiring early to her own bed, devastated by the accident killing the young man whom she had served so devotedly since he was a child.

The three women were dry-eyed the following morning, and although naturally sombre-faced seemed prepared to throw themselves into their tasks as an antidote to distress.

'Since I'm here I might as well look after Neil today,' Kathleen offered. 'I told our Marian that was what I'd do.' She had arranged to stay at The Stone House for two nights at least, and didn't intend sitting around idle.

Mrs Hartley was suggesting to Helen that some of the rooms should have a thorough turning out. 'There'll be folk coming for the funeral, won't there, Mrs Stone?'

Helen agreed. Everything felt so unreal that she

found it difficult to care what anybody else did. All she wanted was this week over and the funeral behind her. She had hardly slept last night for wondering how many people would detect that she was grieving for a marriage that had gone wrong as much as for the death of her husband?

Picking up her father at her old home, and watching him settle awkwardly into the taxi that she had hired, Helen recognised afresh how much effort he was putting into supporting her. He was even less accustomed to meeting the kind of officials they would see today than he was to riding round like this.

'Bless you, Dad,' she said, managing a smile. 'I'd have hated doing this on my own.'

She watched him swallow before he nodded. 'Where is it to be first then, Helen love?'

'The Registrar's, then the undertaker's.' The police had brought her the death certificate, and advised her on procedures.

A couple who were there to marry arrived at the register office just as Helen, with Daniel holding her elbow, approached the steps. The evident happiness of the pair seemed discordant, contrasting as it did with her own distress. She straightened her shoulders, though, hardening her resolve to get this matter attended to.

The registrar was younger than she had expected, and appeared nervous as he questioned her and completed documents. She caught herself wondering how such a fresh-faced man coped with confronting so much gloom, and hoped he got his share of wedding ceremonies to perform.

'You handled that right well,' her father said, grasping her arm as they emerged. 'I'm proud of you.'

Helen gave him a smile and hoped he wouldn't say

too much along those lines or she'd go all weepy on him.

The undertaker's was even worse than she'd been anticipating. When it came to choosing the coffin she realised how final and how real this was, and could contain her tears no longer. By the time they went out into the open air, her father was gazing at her in concern.

'Eh, lass – this is a bad do! I wish there was summat I could say that would make even a bit of difference.'

Helen nodded. 'I know, Dad, I know. But just being here for me is all I need.'

When all arrangements were made, however, and she left her father in Halifax and returned to The Stone House, Helen experienced no feeling of relief over what had been accomplished. I just wish there was something I could do, anything, she thought – anything that could change the state of mind in which Alexander had set out yesterday morning.

That night seemed even more intolerable than the one that had gone before. Helen grew so disturbed that she could no longer remain in the room that she and her husband had shared.

Neil was sleeping soundly in the nursery just across the landing, a small hand tucked beneath the cheek on which long pale lashes rested, his glorious hair already thick and golden, painfully like Alexander's. Quietly, she stood gazing down at his tiny bed, until she eventually calmed enough to find herself a chair. She sat there through the rest of the night, too full of emotion to even frame words in her head but silently promising him she would devote her life to compensating him for the loss of his father.

The funeral reminded Helen of Joseph's, only this

time the loss seemed a hundred times harder to bear. Even though they had appeared to get on so badly together during those last months of his life, Alexander had grown to be a part of her over such a long period. There had been the years before the war while their friendship was changing, developing; and then the war itself which had kept them apart such a lot; and afterwards the ups and downs between them. What was it all for? she wondered bleakly, and could only be thankful that their marriage had produced Neil.

They had advised her not to see Alexander. The Coroner's Officer had explained, very carefully, that many of his injuries had been to his face and head. She would not have recognised him, she was told, and the fact that identification had been made through his personal documents and dental records bore that out. All the same, this was one more thing that troubled her. If only she had seen his body she might have been able to accept that he was not going to walk into the office or through the front door of The Stone House again.

Marian and Denis were here this time and, of course, Helen's parents. Denis was being particularly kind, assuring her that neither he nor Marian had been put off by Alexander's cooling towards them.

'We know he only resented anybody making it easier for you to return to work. There's lots of men like that. It just looks as if, despite some of his modern ideas, he was a bit old-fashioned.'

If Helen hadn't witnessed the huge gathering for Joseph Stone's funeral, she would have been staggered by the numbers paying their final respects to his son. As it was, she could only feel heartened that so many people wished to attend, and be glad that they compelled her to keep going. In the church and at the graveside, she willed herself not to break down in front of such a crowd. Afterwards in the house she was thankful that she must give her attention to so many individuals.

At twilight, alone at last, Helen was standing near the windows of the large reception room where she'd first been welcomed to this house. Sounds carried on the still, summer evening. Distantly in the kitchen Mrs Hartley could be heard, giving the place a final tidying after the departure of the caterers. Across the valley the far hillside, darkening now, looked forbidding. Way below her on the road, cars and buses passed along the main thoroughfare between Halifax and Hebden Bridge, and made her ache to escape with them. Her parents had left an hour ago, on her insistence. Her pain wouldn't heal for many a month, if ever. Their remaining another night would only delay the need to confront the prospect of her life as it would be.

More than once today, Helen had been asked if she would keep on The Stone House. How she had yearned to explain that no, she had decided to move to somewhere smaller and more suitable. Instead, she had inclined her head, telling them that it was up to her now to ensure that this place stayed in the family.

Partly, the decision was for Neil. He deserved the home that would have been his had his father lived the expected life-span; and if her own unease here never altered, that was something she must endure. A sort of pledge towards her son's future. But it wasn't for Neil alone that she was so resolved. In this room especially, she felt them about her, Joseph and Alexander – not ghosts, but presences. When she could bear to let memories resurrect, the two would seem clearer still, their voices, faces, that glorious Stone family hair. She'd not abandon them to strangers.

How many years was it now since she had first entered this room – eleven, twelve? How many since Joseph asked her to work with him? And here it had been, not long ago, that she and Alexander had ended their initial estrangement. She wished to God that he could have lived to end their second.

Wearily, she turned from the room, crossed the echoing hall to thank Mrs Hartley and say goodnight. The day had passed as smoothly as anyone could expect.

When she eventually went upstairs Helen paused on the landing, glancing in both directions at the rows of closed doors. What a lot of empty rooms, and only herself, Neil and the housekeeper.

Neil's door was slightly ajar, the way she always left it at night so that the lightest cry would alert her. He wasn't crying but he was awake, his grey eyes large in the pallor of his face.

'Where's Daddy?' he asked. 'Why did you send him away?'

'Oh, Neil, love, I didn't. Daddy had to go away on business.'

'But he isn't coming back.' It wasn't a question. 'You were cross with him. I heard you shouting at him.'

Their son was not quite two years old, and they had been so proud of his early command of language.

Chapter 14

Returning to the office two days after the funeral was even harder than Helen had feared. Neil had clung to her, tearful and refusing to believe that she was coming home at lunchtime, until she had been obliged to hand him over forcibly to Marian.

'I'm sorry, Neil love, I truly am. But you loved being with Auntie Marian before, you'll have to get used to being with her again. I'm only going to work.'

He hadn't been appeased. And she herself was anything but calmed by opening up their offices. Alexander was all around her here as well, just as much as in the house. Steeling herself to endure, she entered the office he'd inherited from his father, now to be hers.

Once she'd rather envied him that partner's desk with its tooled leather top. Longer ago, in that other lifetime, he had held her close on this spot, had taken her with him on to that splendid chair. In those days they had wanted each other so much, their yearning so strong that it had coloured the whole of life, made it exciting.

It's no good, thought Helen firmly, I came here to work, and work I must. In no other way shall I survive, either to make Stone's succeed as it has in the past or to make any sense of my own life.

She would begin on tackling Alexander's desk.

Harold Tilsley had handed her the keys after the funeral. Evidently, Alexander had left them with him before setting out for London. She was too drained now by experiencing so many emotions to care that she hadn't been the recipient.

The windows faced west, making this office cool so early in the day. Even on a June morning the leather of the chair chilled her, making her shudder. Stilling a sigh, Helen fitted the key into the upper of the three drawers.

Wendy came into the outer office then appeared in the adjoining doorway, her attractive face revealing uncertainty as to whether a smile was appropriate. 'Good morning, Mrs Stone. It's – good to have you back.'

Helen smiled at her. 'Good morning, Wendy. Thank you. And thank you very much for being there at the funeral.' Bringing the word into the open ought to ease things and might help her to overcome her own feeling of unreality.

Wendy offered to make a cup of tea which Helen declined, smiling again.

'Not yet, thanks. Better get on.' And she mustn't shorten the day by too many interludes.

The papers in the first drawer appeared quite orderly. Helen began feeling thankful that her husband had possessed a flair for business, and had understood that efficiency meant economy. He had one specification partially completed on which she would need to consult Harold. The other documents were self-explanatory: items of correspondence clipped together and awaiting replies from council officers, builders or contractors. Each set bore the reference number of the relevant plans which would be on file.

The contents of the second drawer would require

more than this quick glance. Folders contained early sketches and notes of schemes proposed by clients. One out of the three related to a project on which she and Alexander had conferred. On the others she would again have to check with Harold.

Helen was unlocking the lowest drawer when he strode in. She heard his brief greeting tossed in Wendy's direction as he made his way through and then he was in the office with her, depositing on the stand the trilby hat he wore even in summer.

'Helen!'

He hadn't expected her, that was evident, as was his shock to find her in Alexander's place. He permitted himself no comment, but Helen read displeasure ill concealed in his eyes.

'How are you?' he inquired.

He might have been a client who had been told of her bereavement but wasn't sufficiently close to Stone's to attend the funeral. Nothing in his demeanour suggested he was an old friend of theirs, a fellow student, and now involved in their work.

'I'm all right, Harold, coping. There's plenty here to keep me occupied. I shall need to discuss some of these with you. Shall we say around ten?'

He had shared the third office with her, though half the time since her return to work he'd been closeted with her husband. She began to understand why he was feeling resentment, and compelled herself not to watch while he retrieved his hat and headed for the door. It was closed behind him but didn't seal off the sound of his footsteps as he went through and into the other office.

So that was it. Amid all the shock, grief and disorientation, it literally hadn't occurred to her that Harold might expect to become the senior partner. But he wasn't a Stone. *She* was, and equally well qualified.

Harold must not be allowed to forget that.

The rest of the morning was no worse, so long as she didn't let herself be swayed by this sudden awareness of Harold's expectations. He came in and sat at her side behind the desk, updating her on matters which Alexander had had in hand. Their conference over for the present, Helen thanked him warmly.

'I'll have to rely on you a lot.'

'Okay, then.' He rose swiftly and stalked out of her office. There had been no smile with the response. She would have to accept that Harold's smiles would now be rationed.

It was a relief to get out of the office and head for home at lunchtime. The insurers had supplied a vehicle on loan, replacing the one written-off in the crash. Helen was thankful this eased getting around, and more thankful still that since she'd requested a more modest car, it provided no gruelling memories.

Neil was much happier and appeared better adjusted. He came running from the doorway of his playroom, yelling for his aunt to follow.

'Mummy's here. Let's show her what we've been doing.'

They went out into the garden to the rear where the old man who came twice weekly grew vegetables to satisfy Mrs Hartley's demands for fresh produce.

'I've got my own little garden,' Neil declared, and demonstrated the couple of square yards marked out with string. 'I planted seeds.'

'That's lovely, darling. We'll enjoy watching them grow.'

'Auntie Marian showed me how.'

Helen turned to her sister. 'I hope she also chose something that'll spring up very quickly.'

Marian grinned. 'So do I! They were just a few ends of packets that your gardener had left over.'

Helen smoothed Neil's golden curls affectionately. 'We'll have to see this young man remembers to water them. I'll get him his own watering-can on Saturday.'

'*Now*, Mummy – today. I couldn't lift the other can.'

It was just like him to have tried. 'Saturday, I'm afraid. Unless Auntie Marian will take you to buy one.'

The interlude at home helped in two ways, reassuring her that Neil had settled again to being cared for by Marian, and giving her a break from the tension with Harold Tilsley. Helen was exhausted, nevertheless, by the end of the day, although she couldn't regret feeling so tired that eating her solitary meal became an effort. She would have an early night, and pray that being so weary might produce the first good sleep since losing Alexander.

During the ensuing few days Helen went out several times, visiting building sites or those where groundwork was in progress, consulting with builders and with clients. Away from the office, she felt more normal. Being compelled to concentrate was a boon and resulted in something resembling her old enthusiasm for her work. Her only regret was her awareness that she was seeking ways to stay out of the office.

It's just for a while, she told herself inwardly. Just until Harold has been given long enough to adjust to the new situation. And that shouldn't be too far into the future. He'd always seemed easy-going and adaptable. But would he be with her?

Neil's birthday was the next real hurdle, but Helen was up to planning carefully now, had schooled herself to shelve problems and anxieties in order to put him first. She had taken both parents as well as Marian and Denis into her confidence. Using two cars, they were organising a seaside picnic. St Anne's was their destination, chosen by Helen purely because it was the only resort within easy reach which they hadn't visited with Alexander.

The day began promisingly, with lots of laughter as Linda and Mark spilled out of the car where they had been crammed into the rear seats with their grandparents.

'These two lumps of trouble insist they want to travel with you and Neil,' said Denis, raising his eyes to the sky. 'Do you think you could bear it?'

'Sure, that's fine,' Helen replied swiftly. With three children in the back, she'd be permitted no time for brooding. Turning to her niece and nephew, she smiled. 'I need you both to look after Neil, you know. You must sit him between you.'

She was glad the car was only a two-door, and once in the rear they would effectively be imprisoned.

'Of course, Auntie Helen,' the pair chorused, for the present in accord.

'And try to restrain his jack-in-the-box tendencies, will you? I'm relying on you to cope.'

All the way along the road out through Hebden Bridge and Todmorden the children chatted behind her, leaving Helen free to concentrate on driving and keeping Denis's car in sight in her rear-view mirror. They skirted Burnley and stopped briefly in Padiham. When Marian checked that her two were behaving, Helen was able to reassure her.

'I've got them playing I-spy. Of course, Neil's hopeless, not knowing his alphabet, but he will keep trying to play. Linda and Mark think his efforts are hilarious.'

'So long as they're no worse than that,' said Denis. 'And if you stay in the lead you can always pull in to transfer them if they get too much for you.'

The children continued behaving remarkably well. It wasn't Linda's fault that she was so pedantic. The trouble began when Neil tired of playing games which he couldn't comprehend and resented losing the attention of the other two.

'My daddy's gone away,' he announced, conscious by now of the way in which this normally won some kind of warm assurance.

Swallowing, Helen listened for a reaction, not wishing to intervene if the youngsters could satisfy him.

'No,' said Linda carefully. 'That's not quite true.'

'He'll be coming home soon,' Neil continued, and Helen heard in his young voice the tiny tremor that invited confirmation. Lord, she thought, how many times have I had to contradict that particular statement already, and it doesn't penetrate? If only he were old enough to understand explanations about death. There is no way until then that he will even begin to accept what has happened.

'Neil love,' she began.

Linda spoke at the same moment, and had none of Helen's reservations about the blunt revelation of a fact. 'He won't, you know. Your daddy's dead, Neil. You're not stupid, you must know that.'

'What's dead?' he queried, awed.

'Not now, Linda,' Helen inserted hastily.

Mark, however, had concluded that such cautioning didn't apply to him.

'It's like our guinea pig was. It went all stiff and cold. Smelly, as well. We buried him under the tree.'

'And Sweetie the budgie,' Linda added. 'That was the year before the guinea pig.'

'My daddy's not smelly.'

'He will be now,' said Linda solemnly. 'Dead things are like that. That's why you put them in a box.'

Helen drew up at the side of the road, and turned in her seat.

'That's enough for now, Linda, Mark. Neil's too little to know all this. It's something I have to explain when he's more grown-up like you two.'

Denis had pulled in behind them, and Marian came round to the window beside Helen. 'Trouble?'

'They're not being naughty – don't whatever you do reprimand them. They just can't fathom that Neil's too young to know where Alexander is.'

'Right, you two – out. Into our car, sharp!'

'Can you get Mum or Dad to sit with Neil? He's a bit upset.'

'Sure, Helen love.'

The rest of the journey was all right, and the bracing wind at St Anne's seemed to drive away some of Helen's disturbance. Everyone gathered for a boisterous picnic, and it all seemed so homely and natural for them to be together that she felt quite guilty about not really missing Alexander.

During the homeward journey Neil slept, a smile on his face as he clutched a toy rabbit, one of the presents he'd been given.

That night, though, putting him to bed, Helen was appalled by another question.

'Did Daddy die because you didn't want him any more? If you're cross with me, will I die and be shut in a box?'

She hugged him close, weeping and cursing herself for having no real answer. What use was it to the child that she could only gasp out: 'No, my love, of course that wasn't the reason. And you won't die until you're very, very old. No matter how many times you're naughty.'

The declaration might have been a prediction. From that day he did seem to grow increasingly difficult.

Initially, however, the problems with him seemed to be overshadowed by the troubles at Stone's. One morning three months after Alexander had been killed, Helen found Harold Tilsley hovering in the outer office when she arrived. He was looking uncomfortable. She soon learned the reason when he asked for a private word.

'It's about my future here,' he began, even before they were seated. 'When I joined the firm Alex indicated that there was a good chance I would become a partner.'

'And?' Helen prompted when he paused.

'Well, unless that's still on offer . . .'

Nay, give me a chance, she thought. 'It may be, in time. As you should appreciate, I haven't yet sorted everything out after my husband's death.' The way she said 'my husband' sounded as though she was speaking to a stranger. And maybe that wasn't far out – Harold had been behaving as though that was what they were, and hurting her into the bargain.

'But you're not prepared, at this stage, to offer a partnership?'

'I'm afraid not, not just yet. Now that we're less hedged in with building restrictions business should pick up. Perhaps soon . . .'

'Forget it,' Harold interrupted. 'I've had a better offer, from another firm. I trust you'll agree to my leaving at the month end?'

There would have been no point in arguing had Helen wished to. As things were, she would only regret the loss of another pair of hands. She would look out for somebody younger, maybe a person returning to complete their architectural studies after war service. Meanwhile, for a time she would cope on her own. Wendy was a damned good secretary who hadn't been used to the full. And, if necessary, she herself could do some of the work at home. With Mrs Hartley in charge of organising the household, and Neil's bedtime so early in the evening, time hung very heavily in that great near-empty house. It wasn't as if she had any social life.

Even before Harold Tilsley left the firm, Helen began taking work home with her and found she rather enjoyed her evenings. As much as she enjoyed anything, these days. Having put Neil to bed, she was glad to have something to study while she ate in the dining room which felt so enormous and, because of the panelling, on dark days quite gloomy. Mrs Hartley had shaken her head at her in motherly fashion.

'Eh, dear, is that what you're forced to do now, Mrs Stone?'

Helen had smiled. 'Don't let it worry you, Mrs Hartley. I'm better when I'm busy.' And, she added silently, since you insist that I shouldn't just have a tray in front of the fire, this is one way of accepting circumstances.

There had been times since Alexander's death when Helen had felt like closing The Stone House and putting it on the market. Strangely, it was memories of Joseph Stone rather than his son which always prevented her. She was beginning to realise now that she would do her utmost to keep the house going. Although she knew already that it wouldn't necessarily prove easy.

One of the early shocks in sorting out Alexander's affairs had been learning that the business was doing little more than ticking over. And if she now understood that her husband's concern about its profitability had had a cause, this was outweighed by annoyance that he'd kept her in the dark.

I was his wife after all, she asserted frequently to

herself, he should have confided in me. For months Helen regulated the amount of thinking back she allowed herself; there was so much pain in gradually being compelled to recognise that in the office as well as in the home theirs had been anything but a true partnership.

She missed Alexander deeply, nevertheless, longing for the optimism which had graced their early friendship, most of all yearning for somebody to share her responsibilities.

Neil was missing him even more: there had been no reservations about his fondness for his father, just as there had been none in Alexander's behaviour towards his son. And since Helen had been the one always to correct or chastise, the boy's memories of his daddy were of an indulgent parent.

Even though Helen adhered strictly to keeping weekends free for him, Neil seemed to sense her preoccupation with Stone's and, not unnaturally, resented any attention it took away from him. Battles began when he learned that his father's former study had been taken over now for accommodating work which his mother brought home.

On the first occasion that she emerged from there for breakfast when Neil came downstairs, his little face glowered.

'That's Daddy's study,' he declared, accusingly.

'It was, I know,' she said gently. 'But I have to use it now.'

''Cos Daddy's dead.'

It was the first time since his birthday that Neil had referred to the fact. Helen had suspected she was being a coward in not explaining his father's death, but he was such a little boy still. And she had no one to advise her on *how* to explain and how soon he would be able to understand. 'There's time enough,' both her parents had said when she had confided her worry to them.

Gravely, she nodded, went down on one knee and drew Neil towards her. 'That's right, love. I'm afraid Daddy was hurt very badly and he couldn't be made better to come home to us.'

'Where did he go then?' he asked in a tiny voice that made him seem even younger than his two years.

'We think of the place as heaven. It's where good people go when they die, and we try to believe it's a happy place.'

Neil nodded seriously. He also appeared to understand when she explained that she was busier now because of doing his father's work.

How incomplete that assumption had been Helen learned on the following Friday. Tired out, she dumped all her papers in the study instead of taking some through to the dining room. As usual, she played with Neil for a while then got him ready for bed. He seemed fractious, though, refusing her offer of the customary bedtime story.

'Daddy knew better stories than you. He was more fun.'

That Helen could believe. There was no real fun in her life these days, not even any relaxation. The only time off that she could justify was time with Neil. And now it seemed what she did for him could never be good enough.

'Go to sleep then,' she said firmly. 'It's Saturday tomorrow, we'll go somewhere nice.'

'I'm not sleepy, not even a tiny bit.'

'Then you'll just have to do as you're told and lie there quietly.'

Because you're too busy to be with me, thought Neil, picturing her going downstairs to the room which had been special. His father's.

He waited, lying curled in bed. After a while, though, bored and wide awake, he decided to find his mother. Not having any story had been worse than not having his father's. And if he could see the work she was doing in that room downstairs and have Mummy explain it, he might feel nearer to Daddy again.

The door of the study was closed, but Neil had grown tall enough to reach the handle, and strong enough to turn it. When he entered the room he was smiling, ready to win his mother round and coax her to leave her work and amuse him. But she wasn't there.

Neil walked towards the desk, scrambled up on to the big chair, and began investigating.

The pile of documents was where Helen had left it, with two sets of plans uppermost. Seeing them, Neil frowned, puzzled. This wasn't work, this was drawing, like he did with Auntie Marian. And it was all in pencil. Mummy hadn't even done it properly, colouring between the lines like he did.

Neil glanced about on the top of the desk for crayons, and found only pens – they looked like the new Biro Daddy had given him. One was red, the other blue. If he coloured this for Mummy she wouldn't have to be so busy all the time.

Helen found him there when, her solitary meal over, she began crossing the hall and noticed the open study door.

'Neil, how could you!' she exclaimed, seeing all the scribbles covering the recently completed plans even before she glimpsed the smile dying on his face.

'I was doing colouring,' he said miserably. 'Helping . . .'

She swallowed down her anger, inwardly warning herself not to vent her distress on Neil. 'All right,' she said, more calmly. 'All right. But in future you're not to come in here when nobody's about. And you must never touch these papers.'

After she had returned Neil to his room, Helen came back to the study. Dejectedly, she sank on to the chair, gazed down at the ruined plans. Not satisfied with 'colouring' the top one, he had begun on the second. Both would have to be re-drawn and, tired or not, she must begin on that tonight.

It couldn't have been simply the copying of those two plans which threw her so far behind, but somehow after that evening Helen seemed to be coping less well. Often exhausted from working far into the night at home, she rarely felt well equipped for the day when she arrived in the office.

With no one else qualified to assist with routine, she was often obliged to rush meetings with prospective clients and with builders. She became aware that while the increasing availability of materials was making more business within the trade, less was coming to Stone's.

The day that her accountant issued the warning against further spending, Helen rushed home and ran to her room in tears. For weeks now she had been taking out only enough to cover food, Mrs Hartley's wages and the weekly sum which she paid Marian. She couldn't manage without someone to look after Neil. It seemed as though she would have to lose Mrs Hartley.

Helen couldn't sleep that night. There was no point in wondering where she had gone wrong. That was plain enough. In letting Harold Tilsley go she'd removed the back-up needed in the office, to say nothing of a second person's ideas which might have generated more business. But with nobody here to look after the house, how could she cope with the sheer physical work of caring for a place the size of this, to say nothing of providing meals for herself and

Neil? Then there would be washing, ironing . . .

Still wakeful at three in the morning, she left her room and walked slowly away along the landing. Pensively, step by step, she descended the exquisitely curved staircase. There, she turned towards the large reception room which seemed bigger still in the faint light from a distant half moon.

Joseph would never forgive me for selling this place, she thought, and then felt guiltier still for considering what he might have wished instead of his son. And thinking of Alexander reminded her of how *he* would have managed well enough without her. Indeed, had done so while she was absent from the firm after having Neil. But she wasn't stupid – wasn't even stupid enough to fail to acknowledge that trying to do everything on her own was what had resulted in loss of business.

There must be some way out, she thought, some way of economising even further, just to keep going.

We don't need this room, she recognised, nor that dining room in which I feel so ridiculously isolated. More than half of the upstairs rooms could be shut off. If that was done, she could manage somehow without a housekeeper. Lots of wives worked and still had no help in the home. It need only be for a short period, until she found a better way of coping at Stone's and started bringing in more business.

Her mind made up, Helen went to Mrs Hartley as soon as she heard her moving around in the kitchen that morning.

'Why, Mrs Stone, you do look poorly,' the housekeeper exclaimed. 'You'd better have a sit down, hadn't you?'

'I'm all right, thanks, Mrs Hartley. Fact is, I've got an unpleasant task and I'm wondering how best to tackle it.'

'Summat to do with me?'

'I'm afraid so. I'm dreadfully sorry, Mrs Hartley, but the business isn't picking up as it should be after the war. I really don't see how I can continue paying your wages.'

'Oh, is that all? Thank goodness it's nothing worse. You mustn't go moithering on about that, Mrs Stone. I know you'll pay me as soon as you can.'

'I don't think you quite understand,' said Helen, and forced down the lump developing in her throat. 'I can't see a way of keeping you on. I'm having to shut up part of the house. It's a case of that or selling it.'

'Eh, dear.' The housekeeper paused for a while, thinking. 'Well, happen this'll be just the opportunity I've been waiting for. I could take a holiday. That's summat I haven't done since afore the war. My cousin in Jersey keeps asking me to stay with her for a while.'

'Good idea,' said Helen, feeling relieved that Mrs Hartley wouldn't be entirely without a home.

'And then after I could maybe get in touch with you, see if things were any better. I've right taken to you, you know. I'd be ever so sorry if you couldn't manage to set me on again.'

Helen felt her eyes filling. 'Bless you, Mrs Hartley, you're being very understanding. I'll do my level best to get the firm on its feet again.'

'I hope you won't go overworking, mind. You look that peaky now, never mind when you'll be seeing to this place an' all.'

'I am exhausted,' Helen admitted, and suddenly tears were flowing again as she thought of how drastically things had changed since Joseph's death.

Before Mrs Hartley set out for Jersey she helped Helen decide which rooms must be closed, and went through them, covering furniture with dustsheets and ensuring that all items of any value were stored correctly. Once she had left, however, Helen immediately began wishing the housekeeper was back at The Stone House. The solitary evenings after Neil was put to bed seemed unbearable. Should I have sold up? she wondered. Living in a smaller house, perhaps nearer to her own family, would have been much more agreeable. In a street like theirs everybody was always so helpful.

'But I couldn't have let them down,' she said aloud one night, thinking yet again of Alexander and his father; and of her son who she'd always been determined would eventually inherit the house.

Until Mrs Hartley had gone Helen hadn't realised how fond of her Neil had become, although on reflection that was no great surprise. The housekeeper who had mothered Alexander would doubtless have gone on to make a fuss of the boy, especially while his mother was absent.

'She used to help me and Auntie Marian to cook cakes,' he said one Saturday morning. 'And I used to dry the dishes for her, ever so carefully.'

'And so you shall for me,' promised Helen. 'We could bake something today.'

The first problem was finding sufficient items for any of her favourite recipes. She was discovering that shopping, even just for the two of them, required more forethought than she seemed able to give it. Today, all she had in was the ingredients for making jam tarts.

'But I'm best at doing *cakes*,' Neil protested, sighing weightily.

'Never mind, you'll be learning something new if we tackle these.'

Rubbing fat into flour was more than a child not yet three years old could manage, but Helen allowed him to weigh everything into the bowl and eventually to pour in the water a few drops at a time until the dough was ready.

'I'll show you how to roll this out, then you can try,' she promised, demonstrating.

Neil took over eagerly, but his enthusiasm was far greater than his skill and the pastry soon was stretching and tearing beneath the rolling pin.

'Start again,' said Helen, gathering the dough into a ball and kneading it. 'And don't press quite so heavily this time.'

When at last the rolled-out pastry was fairly presentable, Helen began cutting it out.

'Me, me!' Neil insisted. 'I'll do that.'

'But the cutter's sharp.' Helen showed him the metal edge.

'Me, me!' he repeated, snatching the cutter from her.

There was a yell, followed by a sustained wailing. She grabbed the small hand and inspected the damage where the cutter had sliced into three of his fingers.

'Well, it was your own fault, Neil,' she reproved. 'It's rude to snatch. Happen you'll remember that now. Come on – we'll find dressings for those fingers. First, though, we must wash them.'

After patching him up and giving him a hug, Helen led the way back to the kitchen table.

'This time, you'll have to watch. Once we get them into the baking tins, though, you can spoon the jam into them.'

Again, however, Neil was not prepared to listen to advice. Because he loved jam he would insist on filling each tart to the rim.

'That'll all boil over and make a dreadful sticky mess when they get hot in the oven, love,' Helen told him. 'Don't put quite so much in them, please.'

'I like them this way,' he announced firmly, giving her a withering look.

Naturally, when the tarts were cooked all the divisions of the tin were covered with a hard mass of jam which was beginning to solidify, riveting the tarts into the tin, and welding them together. Helen concealed an exasperated smile.

'You get them out, Mummy,' said Neil urgently.

If he'd been a bit older she'd have told him to get on with that himself. As it was, she began trying with a knife to prise the tarts out. The first two crumbled, but the third emerged intact and she handed it to Neil.

'Careful, it's still warm,' she cautioned.

He inspected the tart, frowning at the grubby misshapen pastry, and its sticky covering. He sniffed at it, took a small bite which he spat out on to the floor. 'Ugh! That's nasty!' He hurled the rest of the tart across the kitchen.

'And so's your behaviour,' retorted Helen. Her patience, worn down by the laborious process of cooking at a child's pace, finally snapping. 'You're a rude, ungrateful boy. I'm ashamed of you.'

Neil began screaming.

Helen willed herself not to spank him, even though she wasn't at all certain that a smacked bottom was not what he needed.

'You're going to your room,' she said, and began marching him across the echoing hall.

The punishment appeared to be working. Neil quietened as they walked silently up the stairs and along to his bedroom.

'You needn't get undressed,' she told him, eager to get away from him for a break. 'Just take off those shoes and lie on top of the covers.'

On her way to the door, she looked back at him. 'I'll

tell you when you may get up again, so think on and stay there.'

'That's all right, Mummy,' responded Neil sweetly. 'I like bed.'

Returning downstairs, Helen was compelled to smile. Trust him to enjoy the punishment she devised. And she was the one who would now be obliged to do what she could with those wretched tarts and clean up the one that Neil had thrown.

Glancing at the clock, she decided that she would leave him where he was for a little while, giving her a chance to prepare lunch. They would go shopping this afternoon. Maybe that would enable her to keep him occupied whilst catching up on one job that needed doing.

Helen decided that the covered market in Halifax was one place where Neil might be interested in his surroundings. She, meanwhile, would have access to most of the items they required without dragging him in and out of a whole range of shops.

After the first ten minutes inside the market building, Helen was congratulating herself on choosing well. Neil seemed to love the brightly coloured stalls and the cheerful people who manned them. Remembering the ingredients that they had been lacking, Helen went around stocking up her store cupboard. She also selected enough fresh vegetables to see them through the next few days, and began looking for cakes as a treat for the boy.

He had been very good this afternoon, remaining close to her side while she was concentrating on choosing her purchases.

It was near at hand, just a little behind her, that the commotion began. First there was an alarming thud, followed by a sharp shriek, and then an agitated shouting.

'You little devil, you! Now look what you've done! How do you think I'm going to get up again?'

Turning, Helen was appalled to see an elderly lady on the ground, struggling to get to her feet, one of them encased in a surgical boot.

'Is he yours?' the woman snapped. 'Time you kept an eye on him. Pulled my stick away, that's what he did!'

'I'm most terribly sorry,' Helen began, bending to assist the old lady to her feet.

Faded brown eyes were regarding her keenly from behind thick-lensed spectacles. 'Well, I'll go to heck! It's Helen Clegg as was!'

'I'm afraid so,' she admitted wryly, recognising one of her mother's neighbours. 'Are you hurt?' she inquired in concern. 'Shall I get somebody to find you a chair?'

'Nay, lass, don't bother. I'm all right now I'm t'right way up again – it were nobbut my dignity as was hurt. As I reckon yours will be, many a time, afore this lad of yours is much older. I'm surprised at you, you know. Thought you'd have had more about you than letting him get away with daft tricks like that!'

'He hasn't got away with it, I can assure you,' said Helen, grasping Neil firmly by the arm. Unfortunately, though, she suspected that *she* was the one, rather than Neil, who would long remember the incident with mortifying regret.

Chapter 15

As Helen had feared, reprimanding Neil had been less than simple. Aware as she was by now that sending him to bed was no punishment, she resorted to a stern lecture, administered as soon as she had him in the car ready for going home.

'Why on earth did you do that to the poor lady?' she demanded.

'I wanted her to look at me,' he said plaintively.

Which she certainly did, thought Helen grimly. 'But why?' she persisted, determined to get to the bottom of her son's stupid action.

'She was looking at the ground, didn't even see I was there.'

'So – not everybody wants to make a fuss of you. And she probably needed to watch where she was putting her feet. That lady is lame, Neil, she has a poorly foot. And that's why she has to use a stick.'

'I didn't know, I only wanted her to smile at me.'

'If you keep on behaving like that, nobody'll ever smile at you again – and that includes me!'

He had studied her seriously for a minute after that. 'You don't smile much now, do you, Mummy?'

That, more than anything, had hurt, going deeper even than the mortification she had felt when being reproached for Neil's behaviour. And it convinced her that the time had come for reassessing her approach to the boy.

'What am I doing wrong, Marian?' she asked on the following Monday when she and her sister managed a private word before Neil came downstairs.

Marian was still stifling her amusement over the incident, but she attempted to be reassuring. 'You're happen trying to do too much, love, that's all. You're up to your eyes in problems, at Stone's and with the house, it's not surprising Neil gets you down.'

'But your two are so well brought up. How have you managed it?'

Her sister grinned. 'More luck than management, if you must know. And except for during the war they have had both of us around. Even then Mum and Dad gave them a lot of attention – I daresay more than they'd have got at home. Neil, now – well, he lost his dad and, in a way, lost a part of you at the same time, didn't he? Nowt's been the same since, has it? It's not your fault that you can't give him more attention, and it's not his either.'

'I think he was trying to get that poor woman to look at him. That's what he said, any road.'

'There you are then – happen he'll improve when he starts to feel more secure.'

But how will that come about, wondered Helen, now that Mrs Hartley has had to go out of our lives? And Neil is bound to sense how insecure I feel now that the business is doing so badly that we could even be forced into selling the house.

During the spring of 1949 Helen occasionally took Neil with her when she visited sites or even when she had brief meetings with clients. He seemed to respond to having this share in her working life and, if well supplied with books or crayons, could be left to amuse himself for short periods.

Helen wasn't certain the idea went down very well with clients whom she suspected might be seeing her as a part-time architect, more interested in her child. She could only hope the fact that she could leave him unsupervised for several minutes at a stretch indicated that she had trained him properly.

There came a day when she was obliged to leave Neil in the car. This seemed quite safe; from the temporary site office the car was in view, and she was only staying long enough to explain to the builder certain amendments in the plans she was delivering.

They couldn't have been talking more than a couple of minutes when the man interrupted their conversation.

'I say, Mrs Stone, isn't that your car?'

Looking up, Helen was horrified. The car was moving steadily downhill towards the centre of the site.

'Oh, God!' she exclaimed and ran outside.

'Didn't you set the handbrake?' he asked, running alongside her.

'Yes. I'm positive I did.' And then she saw that Neil had scrambled through from the back and on to the driver's seat. 'When it crashes he'll go through the windscreen,' she yelled.

Fortunately, a dumper truck had recently dropped a load of hardcore in a place right in line with the car's direction. In a welter of tiny stones and chippings the front of the car embedded itself in the heap.

Terrified, Neil began screaming.

'It's all right, my love,' Helen reassured him, opening the door and pulling him out to be hugged. 'You're quite safe now.'

'I only touched it a little bit, Mummy,' cried Neil, pointing to the handbrake.

'All right, all right,' she soothed, well aware that she had been at fault in leaving him alone in the car. This was something which would never be repeated.

Neil still wished to accompany her on some of her business outings and by taking Marian along Helen succeeded in finding a compromise, enabling her son to continue having more of a share in her world.

Having drained herself with the effort to increase Stone's business, Helen was pleased by that spring of 1949 to see more work coming her way. Much of the upturn was due to the enthusiasm of her secretary Wendy who had been offered the opportunity to extend her role. Instead of just attending to the routine of typing and keeping records she was learning more about architecture. This meant that she was capable of acting as Helen's personal assistant, coping with the office side of jobs and arranging meetings.

'I don't know what I'd do without you,' Helen often told her, deeply conscious that for the foreseeable future, until she could again take on another architect, she needed strong back-up.

Creating more business, however, had been achieved at considerable physical cost to Helen herself. She had thought in the past that she was tired. These days she was exhausted. And even now she wasn't really happy with the work in which she was engaged. The country as a whole hadn't recovered as everyone had hoped following the war. New building projects were often limited by shortages. Half the time Helen wondered why she still felt compelled to pour all this effort into Stone's.

Easter was approaching, and Marian had been pressing Helen to bring Neil away with them for a short break at Morecambe. It was one of those rare weeks when Denis hadn't a part in the current repertory production. They were going to give Linda and Mark a treat, and tried to insist that Helen should join them.

Although grateful, she didn't really wish to do so. She was longing for a few days at home, simply letting go of everything and catching up on a few jobs. Working full-time ensured that household chores were repeatedly crowded out. She was also determined to make time to look at a prospective site for flats in the outskirts of Leeds. Initially the project hadn't sounded particularly interesting, but she had learned the developers were insisting they must be less like a fortress than the Quarry Hill flats completed before the war.

Helen thought she might go over there on Good Friday. Many West Riding firms took the Monday and Tuesday off instead, but she could manipulate any appointments to allow her to get away on that one day.

'Then why don't you let Neil come with us to Morecambe?' Marian suggested when Helen declined their offer. 'It's only for that few days. He's used to us, isn't he? And happen you'd manage a bit of a rest as well as getting on with jobs if you were on your own.'

Reluctantly, Helen agreed, and was glad when Neil seemed to be elated by the prospect of going away with his aunt, uncle and cousins. On the Friday morning he was awake early, demanding to know when he was going to Morecambe.

'Not till tomorrow night, love.' Denis had two shows on Saturdays, so they were setting off quite late. That was another excitement, although Helen hoped for everyone's sake that Neil would sleep during the journey.

Since Marian was busy with preparations, it had been agreed that Helen would leave Neil in their home on the Friday morning, rather than having Marian come out to The Stone House.

When she drew up outside, however, Helen was surprised to see Denis up and about already, and unlocking their car.

'Where are you off to?' she asked. 'It's not like you to be around at this time – you did have a performance last night?'

Her brother-in-law's grin was rueful. 'I did that! And I'm not going anywhere, and nor will any of us be, unless I get this thing fixed. It was playing up yesterday. Only just about got me home last night.'

'Oh, dear. Anything I can do?' she enquired.

'Not unless you can get me to the Ford dealer in Huddersfield. The local garage hasn't got the spares I need.'

'Oh.' Helen paused, thinking. If Denis didn't get the car put right today, they might all be stranded somewhere late at night tomorrow. 'Tell you what, you take mine for today. I can get a bus over to Leeds. You can't go carting spares around on buses.'

'I can't let you do that. Too much of a cheek.'

Helen grinned. 'When you've both offered to take Neil away for a few days? Don't talk daft, Denis. I'll still be in your debt after.'

'Well, then, if you're sure . . .'

'I'll just take him inside to Marian, and I'll be on my way.'

'Then you must at least let me run you to the bus stop.'

'Okay, fine.'

Helen didn't dislike the journey to Leeds. Sitting in the bus was in many ways more relaxing than driving. Especially when, these days, she found concentrating on anything quite an effort. Heading towards Leeds she discovered she was forgetting her purpose in coming here, lapsing into a sort of daydream that resurrected her student days. She had been so happy then and, despite the intensity of her studies, relatively carefree. Maybe if she had time after inspecting that prospective site, she would go into the city centre. It seemed years since she had been free to walk up and down the Headrow, to wander about, just looking.

The site was larger than she had anticipated from the details she had received. It wasn't difficult to believe that the flats to be constructed here might prove quite prestigious. Helen's resolve to submit designs to the developers grew stronger as she paced out the boundary and set her trained eye to making calculations.

The past few years had provided her with contacts among building contractors within a large area of this part of Yorkshire, and from them she had learned how the minds of most developers worked.

I could do it, she thought, already visualising the exterior of the flats. Suddenly, she smiled wryly to herself. This was just the kind of scheme Alexander would have favoured – modern design had been specified. Well, she too could cope with such requirements, if she had to.

When she had completed her examination of the site and made all the notes which might be of assistance later, Helen remembered her idea of taking a look around the city centre. She was tired now, but nevertheless jumped on a bus which would take her there.

Somehow, though, the prospect of going from store to store had palled. The absence of Neil, instead of leaving her free of anxiety as she had expected, was making her feel isolated. She stood for a while admiring the Town Hall, always her second favourite after the one in Bradford which had such an elegant tower and looked altogether more beautiful. I can't be like this, she silently asserted, I mustn't become possessive of Neil, just because I no longer trust myself alone with my thoughts. Ever since Alexander had died she had worked and worked, and worried about Neil, but wasn't that only in order to exclude facts even more difficult to face?

If Alexander had lived to come home from that trip to London, they might have been able to put their marriage to rights. But could she have contributed her share of tolerance and understanding towards making it work in the future? Had Alexander been all that far wrong in accusing her of never doing anything she didn't wish to?

Trying to obliterate her doubts, Helen headed towards Kirkgate covered market, but even its agreeable Edwardian styling didn't distract her. Weary beyond belief, she trudged along to queue for the bus. She would have to go and pick up the car, and Neil too of course. And now, from wishing he was with her, she had turned to dreading coping with him while she felt so exhausted. Before tomorrow evening she would also have to wash and iron all the clothes he would need with him in Morecambe.

Heavens, I'm becoming a proper Moaning Minnie, she thought, sinking on to the nearest seat as soon as the bus arrived. I'm never satisfied.

But what's it all for? she wondered dejectedly. Why do I have to work myself to a standstill? Every scrap of her earlier enthusiasm about producing plans for those flats had been eroded, all she felt now was the familiar dread of . . . yes, of *everything*.

Nothing makes sense, she thought miserably. Why does there seem no direction to my life? Where can I rediscover some purpose?

The bus was slowing in a line of cars. Presently it halted completely as the rest of the traffic turned left at an intersection. I'll never get home at this rate, she thought wretchedly, forgetting her previous reluctance to cope with the evening, and the next day.

Eventually the cause of their delay became evident, reminding her sharply of what today was.

A procession headed by a young man in cassock and surplice and carrying a simple wooden cross came into sight to the right of them. Flanked by a couple of boys of around twelve or so, he was walking gravely yet with a serenity that Helen envied. Behind him came a robed choir and following them a priest, looking rather austere in his long black cassock. Behind him came representatives of his congregation, but it was on the priest himself that Helen's gaze was riveted. *It was Christopher Maitland.* Regardless of the years that had intervened and despite the brief nature of their acquaintance, there could be no mistaking him.

All but hypnotised, she stared after him until he had passed out of sight along a road at right angles to the one where her bus was halted. As the congregation processed in front of her, Helen felt emotions surging through her, singing in her head. Not getting up and jumping off to catch up with Chris was requiring all her will-power.

When the bus slowly moved on again and began gathering speed, she experienced a curious conflict inside her. A part of her, reassured by seeing Chris again, was pleased that he had fulfilled his ambitions, and from the size of this procession of witness evidently had a good congregation. She was thankful as well to have this reminder that the values he upheld still carried some weight in these confusing times. For herself, though, she was saddened by the thought of how different her life might have been if she had been able to spend it with him.

All these years and the changes wrought by war and bereavement had left one thing unaltered. Those few seconds had proved that she would have gone to Chris today, if there'd been any hope that they might have a future together.

Approaching Halifax, Helen came out of her reverie with a feeling of shock. She was almost home. In another few minutes she'd be picking up Neil, and the car. She would have to pull herself together or their Marian would want to know whatever was wrong.

Her efforts mustn't have been nearly enough. As soon as her sister opened the door to her, she knew something was wrong.

'You look as if you've seen a ghost. Are you all right?'

'A bit tired, that's all. It's seemed a long day.'

'You shouldn't have let Denis have your car. He's ever so grateful, though, we both are.'

'Did he get your car fixed?'

'Yes, thanks.'

'Where's Neil?'

'In the garden, out the back. He's right enjoyed himself today. That's what I wanted to ask you – would it be all right if he stopped here tonight? Both Linda and Mark want him to, and he seems keen as well. It'd give you more time to yourself, and let him get used to being without you before we set off to a strange place.'

Helen hesitated, trying to focus the whole of her attention on to the question of Neil. 'Well, I suppose it'd be okay. But then, he hasn't got his pyjamas and things . . .'

'I can find him a pair that Mark's outgrown for tonight. And we can easily pick up his holiday things from you on our way tomorrow.'

'Thanks for the offer, love. We'll just see how he

reacts when he finds out I might be going home without him.'

Helen followed her sister through to the kitchen and while Marian was putting on the kettle she watched Neil through the window. He was sitting on the swing and Linda was pushing him with a degree of care that brought a lump to Helen's throat. Neil had some smashing cousins, bless them, and they seemed to compensate for the loneliness he must experience in his own home.

'I'll just go out and have a word,' she told her sister.

'Hello, Auntie Helen,' said Linda, steadying the swing to a gradual stop.

'Mummy!' Neil exclaimed, and sprang down to run to her.

While she was hugging him, however, Helen felt his small body tensing. 'You've come to take me home, haven't you?'

'Not if you'd rather stay here for tonight. Auntie Marian says you can . . .'

'Yes, please,' he said very swiftly.

Mark had caught the ball he was bouncing against the wall and ran towards them.

'Is Neil staying with us then? He's going to share my room.'

It will be very good for him, thought Helen as she got into the car and drove away. He'll experience living in somebody else's home as well as staying in that boarding house at Morecambe. And whilst the short holiday would be a real treat, tonight would provide a glimpse of ordinary family life.

Arriving back at The Stone House, Helen recognised that any reluctance to be parted from her son was diminishing. She wasn't even thinking about him. Seeing Christopher Maitland like that had generated such a mass of feelings. There was regret, of course, because of there being no opportunity to talk to him, just as there would always be this deeper regret that he wasn't free to share any aspect of his life with her. But there was much more besides.

Chris had been a part of all the wonder and the awe which she had experienced in the Abbey church at Einsiedeln. Seeing him again had brought her once more to the periphery of the beliefs on which his life was founded. During their first meeting she had quickly realised that he wasn't an unintelligent man, there must be some substance in his having faith in this God whom she could barely comprehend.

I wish I could understand, she thought, longing for stability and the strength to make her endure while her life seemed nothing but hard work and difficulties. If only she could recapture a fraction of the feeling induced by Einsiedeln, even just resurrect the once-vivid mind pictures that had faded with time. But she didn't remember taking even one photograph there.

After making and eating a meal, Helen admitted to herself that she had thought of nothing but the Abbey and Christopher since coming back home. She felt better, though, somehow strengthened, perhaps simply by taking a rest from dwelling on her problems.

I wish there was a church round here that could have that sort of effect on my attitude, she thought, yet knew in her heart that she wouldn't seek one out. Her father's non-conformist faith appeared to have seen him through, never wavering even during two world wars. Yet that had never seemed right for her, and she couldn't think she would find it any different now.

Throughout the evening Helen remained preoccupied. She washed their clothes and draped them over a clothes horse before the fire she had lit in the kitchen and on the overhead creel, but working automatically. She felt unable to think about anything else, even the ideas for those flats which had been so clear in her mind until beginning the journey home. Restless still, despite her resolve to have a much-needed early night, she began roaming through the silent house. The dust-covered furniture like so many strangely shaped ghosts seemed to inhabit the empty rooms, as if to warn her that she would be unwise to dwell on her isolation here.

Searching through Joseph Stone's library, Helen came upon the book; filed in the meticulous order on which he'd prided himself before ill health ravaged his intelligence. An illustrated volume on Swiss Architecture, it fell open on a group of photographs of Einsiedeln.

Memories came chasing back, of her father-in-law talking about the Abbey and, longer ago, of old Mr March, insisting that she must ensure she visited the place. How she yearned for the old days, most of all for her own original enthusiasm. Since the war, so much had altered, crushing her dreams and with them all her energy. There seemed so little inspiration, these days, with nothing but humdrum schemes for housing instead of the magnificent buildings she'd been longing for aeons to create. What could she do, what on earth could she do to renew the driving force that had urged her through all that training?

Still clutching that book as she went upstairs, the thought came to her. Whatever she did, be it mundane or exhilarating, contemporary or classical, she must display that same enthusiasm showed by good architects through the ages. The fact that a project was ordinary need not mean that her approach should be of a lower calibre.

Studying the pictures of Einsiedeln, reading some of the text, Helen fell asleep. In the night she wakened, smiling, recollecting that glimpse of the life Christopher had found for himself, beginning to wonder if her own life could somehow gain a measure of that same stability.

Helen always vowed that the changes in her attitude that day were responsible for her being contracted to design those flats in Leeds. Certainly the will and the energy to complete her initial designs appeared as if from nowhere, generating over that weekend ideas which previously might have taken weeks.

'I'm going to be busier than ever,' she announced to Wendy as she walked into the office on the Wednesday after Easter.

Her secretary smiled. 'You look better, any road. As if you've somehow shifted the load that was holding you back before.'

'Happen I have, Wendy, happen I have.' She went on to outline the information which they must gather. 'You'll enjoy helping, I hope. There'll be lots of regulations to be studied, things to be learned from the authorities in Leeds. I've begun making a list. I mean to have everything at my fingertips when I submit my first drawings.'

The speed with which Helen's early sketches brought a response from the developers provided just the boost that she needed.

'I don't care how hard I work now,' she confided to Wendy. 'It might not look like the kind of scheme I'd set my heart on, but this is the chance I've been waiting for.'

Without really knowing how, Helen completed further drawings, adding refinements, enlarging certain areas to show more detail, producing elevations. The good thing was that internally the flats were to be of only four basic designs. Fitting them together in an attractive arrangement within the overall dimensions taxed her skill, but proved fascinating.

When she took work home, she involved her son, although she knew well enough that he could understand only a fraction of what she was doing. But this seemed to suit Neil, he became more amenable, and so long as he was supplied with paper and pencils was relatively quiet.

The only serious problem was the eternal one of finance. Helen was ploughing back into Stone's amounts received in settlement for other smaller jobs, and taking hardly anything out beyond living expenses. For this large project, however, a model of the design was requested, something for which she lacked both the time and aptitude. Paying an outsider went against the grain, and reinforced her knowledge that to develop Stone's she needed more capital.

The day that the foundation stone was being laid, Helen permitted herself a rare site visit that wasn't for practical reasons. 'I'll be back in the office this afternoon,' she promised Wendy.

Unaccustomed as she was to social gatherings, even those connected with her work, Helen drove to Leeds feeling rather uneasy, wondering why she wasn't tackling something more worthwhile. Arriving at the site, however, she began to feel that the morning could be fun. And fun was rare in her life, these days. By this time she was well acquainted with their client, a developer who was beginning to make a name for himself throughout the West Riding. She could believe that in a few years' time, when restrictions eased further, and supplies permitted him to have his head, he would be showing the way to others.

One or two people concerned in Town and Country Planning she knew, and several local officials whom she had met on several occasions. And then there was a party of dignitaries and their friends: among them one woman, tall and dark-haired, appeared to be especially interested in Helen.

She came over and introduced herself after the brief stone-laying ceremony. 'I understand you're the architect, Mrs Stone. I'm Ophelia Hadgraft – and I'm delighted that a woman is responsible for such an ambitious project. The developers tell me that it's some time since you were involved in such a large scheme.'

'That's right. Not from choice, I assure you. If you're connected with the construction industry or the building trade, you'll know how bad things have been since the war. Still are, in fact.'

Ophelia Hadgraft was smiling. 'Actually, I'm not personally involved in either. I'm just interested in people who show a bit of enterprise.'

'I know what you mean. And I'm afraid this looks like being the last task of any size that I shall be tackling for a while. Again, that's not the way I want things. But I have to be realistic. A project this size takes a lot of time and considerable outlay. Unfortunately, being a one-woman outfit at present, I lack the resources to be choosy. Most of my work has to be bread-and-butter jobs.'

'Ah. Now that's what I was coming to. Mrs Stone, forgive my asking, but would you be interested in an injection of capital?'

'Would I!' Helen couldn't believe this was happening.

'Since my brother died and I sold the family business I've been looking for firms in which to invest. You seem to have all the qualities I visualise in someone who will be expected to make best use of my outlay.'

'Are you serious?' asked Helen, hardly daring to credit that her difficulties might shortly be solved.

'Try me. Show me your premises, outline your future plans, give me some indication of the number of shares you have available.'

Helen wished Alexander was still alive, that he was here to assess this woman's offer. He would have known if her suggestion was viable, and how to conduct all the arrangements. She could only use her common sense, and hope that by being cautious she wouldn't ruin all chance of receiving this assistance.

'I'm certainly willing to do all that. You would expect me, of course, to consult my accountant if you should wish to make this a firm offer.'

'Naturally, and your solicitor. You can't be too careful. And nor can I, although I feel that I already know enough about your capabilities. I've seen your plans, had them explained to me. When do you think would be convenient for my paying you a visit?'

'That's up to you. As soon as you like. With only myself and my secretary, there's not much to put in order at the office. We can't afford to be unmethodical.'

'But today would be too soon, I suppose?'

Helen smiled at the woman's eagerness. 'Not really, no. Having taken the morning off, I kept the afternoon free for catching up on paperwork. This sounds as though it could be more important.'

Important it was. Ophelia Hadgraft brought a certain dynamism along with her offer; Helen could feel herself being infected with new optimism. Having dismissed her chauffeur with instructions to call for her at Stone's offices at four that afternoon, Ophelia accepted the offer of a ride there with Helen.

'We need to talk, to get to know one another. This will start us off very nicely.'

Helen was wondering whatever she would find to say to the woman which might extend to fill the journey and beyond. Before they had driven for a couple of miles, however, she was beginning to believe that she had found a friend.

'I gather you are widowed,' Ophelia began, 'and that you have a son demanding your attention, as well as the practice?'

Helen smiled. 'Neil's a bit of a handful at times. He misses his father. And maybe he needs a firmer hand, though I don't think I'm soft with him.'

'And who cares for him now while you're working?'

'My sister, Marian. She's very good with children, has two of her own.' Helen paused, considering whether personal questions were in order, and decided that she could only follow the lead she'd been given. 'Did someone say that you're not married?'

'That's right. Lost my fiancé in the war. I was already older than most women who're seeking a husband. And there was my brother still at home. His wife was an invalid for years. When she died he came to live with me.'

She asked how old Helen's son was, and seemed surprised that he was only three. 'So it's not all that long since your husband died then?'

'Almost a year. Neil was nearly two.'

'Then you've done splendidly to get yourself together enough to take on a scheme like those flats.'

'Architecture's all I know, and next to Neil it's what I love best. I just wish there was more scope around here at present.'

'I can understand that. I know the south was more severely hit by the blitz, and therefore needs more development, but it seems sad to me that the West Riding isn't looking at these New Towns and the like.'

When Helen didn't immediately reply, her

companion gave her a sideways glance. 'Or aren't you enthusiastic about them?'

'I could be. I certainly applaud attempts at achieving some sort of cohesion in their planning. Just as I yearn to tackle projects that give rein to my imagination. I'm just a bit conservative about styling, prefer traditional to ultra-modern. Although, these days, I'll have a crack at anything that gets Stone's out of the rut.'

By the time they arrived at the office they had exchanged views on twentieth-century architecture and on a mass of other topics until Helen was feeling that she had known Ophelia Hadgraft for some time. This made her realise that she had been lacking a woman friend for many a year. In lots of ways, Marian had filled the gap, but there was also the need for a close association with somebody not influenced by family ties.

Wendy looked up in surprise on finding Helen with a companion, then after being introduced went to make tea for them.

'This is very good,' their visitor approved when she was led through to Helen's office. 'I'm glad you haven't skimped over providing somewhere to impress clients.'

'My father-in-law's doing, actually. Neither Alexander nor I had time to make substantial alterations.'

'And none were needed, if this is the way it's always looked. Did you manage to keep going through the war?'

Helen shook her head as she offered Ophelia a chair. 'Not really. For a time Alexander's father kept the office open, but there wasn't any business coming our way. I went into the Land Army – enjoyed it more than I expected. Then when the end of the war was nearing Father-in-law took away the mothballs, as it were.'

'And you've been fighting ever since to get back to normal? Well, here's hoping we may find a means of ensuring that is achieved even quicker.'

'Let's hope so, indeed,' said Helen, still wondering when she would waken up and find this was all a dream, too good to be true.

Chapter 16

The hopes generated on that day soon appeared to be coming to fruition. Before leaving in her chauffeur-driven car, Ophelia Hadgraft had indicated how much she was willing to invest in Stone's and it seemed to Helen a staggering amount of capital.

Mr Thorpe, her accountant, was equally impressed and suggested that, subject to his discreet inquiries proving satisfactory, Helen should agree to shares being made available.

When he came back with the information that Ophelia Hadgraft was entitled to be addressed as The Honourable, and the family money seemed to be well secured, he was as delighted as Helen that the deal should be completed.

'You will have more scope now, Mrs Stone, and I trust that will set your firm on the upward trend merited by all your hard work.'

Her solicitor also appeared well pleased that the arrangement held no hidden snags, and the transaction was arranged swiftly.

Although glad to be relieved of financial worries, Helen continued to be bound by the eternal regulations and shortages of materials which ensured that most of the work in which she was involved was no more exciting than local authority houses.

'I still need another really big project,' she confided

later during one of Ophelia's occasional visits to Stone's.

'Your opportunity will come,' she was assured. 'I'm certain of that. It's only a matter of waiting now for the right one.'

If only I could take on another architect, thought Helen. That would allow one of us to travel, to go down south and try our chances of getting involved in some of these plans for new towns. Despite the fact that Stone's was more secure, these days, she couldn't help being aware that Alexander would have been better able to generate the right kind of business.

I never expected to want a man to lean on as I practised architecture, Helen reflected, but she was compelled to admit how much she missed having one around. This wasn't only true of her working life. And nor was it true only of herself.

Neil was going through a phase of resenting female company. Even his beloved Auntie Marian was sometimes rejected by him with a cutting 'Don't be so soft!' It seemed that only when he was with Denis or Helen's own father did he blossom into the lovable lad who was too frequently concealed behind moody behaviour.

Unfortunately, Denis worked such long and erratic hours at the theatre that he was never a frequent visitor at The Stone House, and Daniel Clegg had aged so much since the war that he found his young grandson's antics rather wearing – welcome, but in small doses.

'You could always marry again, it's not impossible,' Marian remarked one day when Helen was expressing her anxiety about the absence of male influence in Neil's life.

'That is likely, I don't think!' she exclaimed with a wry grin. 'When do I ever go anywhere to meet a decent bloke?'

'Every day, or so I'd have thought,' Marian responded. 'Don't tell me you don't know anybody when you're always off meeting builders and council officials, and what about wealthy clients?'

Helen laughed. 'But they're different, just blokes I meet through my work.'

'What sort would you go for, if you did have another shot at marriage?' her sister persisted, certain that it was time Helen had an easier time, and someone special in her life.

'Eh, I don't know. I've no time to be bothered with such fanciful notions.'

'That's not like the old Helen. You were allus full of dreams. And there must have been somebody caught your eye once, as well as Alex.'

'Must there?' said Helen enigmatically. And refused to be drawn. Where was the sense in reviving memories, especially when they concerned longings that could never be satisfied? Ever since seeing Christopher Maitland earlier this year, she had willed herself not to wonder repeatedly how things might have been. She was thankful for the reminder that there might be some pattern to life, some higher scheme than any she herself could devise. Beyond that, she would not think – if she let her mind run on uncontrolled, she'd only make herself discontented. And, these days, things weren't all that bad. She had finally decided she could reopen some of the other rooms in the house; best of all, Mrs Hartley was coming back.

'What about them that you met in the war?' Marian persisted.

Although she smiled inwardly, recalling Vittore Fabri, Helen again revealed nothing. That night, though, long after Neil had gone to bed and as she herself was preparing for sleep, she thought about him once more. A smile on her lips, she got out of bed and went to the cupboard where the model of Florence Cathedral lay carefully packed in its box.

Dear Vittore, she thought affectionately, gazing at the tiny model of the cathedral, you were as good at dreaming as I was! Had his dreams materialised? she wondered, aching after all this time to know how he was. Had he patched things up with his wife? And how well had he set about restoring his firm? Were the Italians also restricted to designing mundane housing, or was he indulging his flair for the splendid places he had drawn whilst on a farm here in Yorkshire?

Although being reminded of Vittore like that made Helen think of him quite frequently, it certainly hadn't prepared her for seeing him again just a few months later in the autumn of 1949.

The first news of his arrival in England was a telephone call to the office. All Wendy told her was that a gentleman was ringing from London. Hearing his voice was an amazing shock. There was no mistaking his accent, even when all he said was, 'Helen?'

'Vittore! I can't believe it – are you really in London?'

'Why, yes, indeed. And hoping that we may arrange to meet.'

'We better had!' she exclaimed. 'I'll never forgive you if you go back to Italy without seeing me.'

'I certainly shall not do that. In fact, I am considering remaining over here, if that can be made possible.'

'Really? Whereabouts? In the south, I suppose. There's a lot more interesting work going on down there. Only wish I could get a share in it. And there's the Festival of Britain coming up . . .'

'But you're doing well, I hear? Something about a block of flats.'

'Fancy you hearing about that! Yes, I did enjoy that job, but it seems a long time ago already since my part in it was completed. Never mind, though, when can you come and see me?'

'Later this week, perhaps? Do you know a good hotel?'

'You don't have to stay in any hotel, don't be silly. Come to The Stone House.'

Vittore didn't hesitate. 'I would love that, if you are sure it would cause no inconvenience?'

'None at all, I insist. I've got my housekeeper back and she's itching to do a bit of entertaining. Stay as long as you like . . .'

Vittore arrived the following afternoon, coming to the office where he strode in looking so tanned and healthy that Helen only really recognised him by his voice. She was thankful she'd made time to rush to the shops and was feeling quite dashing in her bottle-green dress. Despite the sensible revers and long sleeves, it had the longer, flared skirt introduced by the New Look, and was very feminine.

Instinctively, they embraced, though his kiss was on her cheek – or both cheeks, which made her laugh. Briefly, he touched her glossy hair, which she wore to her shoulders and curled under.

Helen tried to contain the ripples of sheer excitement created by his touch. 'How fit you're looking now!' she exclaimed.

Vittore laughed back to her. 'All the Italian pasta, *cara*, and the glorious sunshine.'

'Yet you talk of maybe stopping over here. You can't mean that, surely?'

'If I could get the necessary permits, who knows?'

'Tell me all your news then – how well have you

done since going back there?'

His news was mixed. Business-wise, he appeared to have fared very well, accomplishing a lot more than Helen felt that she herself had. His home life, however, had deteriorated, even from what she had understood of his pre-war difficulties.

'My wife had taken a lover whilst I was interned. You will understand how this did not greatly surprise me. I told to you the way things had been. The lover was a Yank who insisted that she must marry him. Because of our Italian laws divorce had to be in the States. When that went through, my family as well as hers condemned me for letting her go. *Me*! I ask you, Helen, was that fair? And I the innocent person.'

'And you haven't married again?'

'Naturally, I have not. I told you, didn't I? I do not believe in divorce.'

'So you're on your own as well now?'

Nodding, his dark eyes solemn, he sighed. 'I was sorry to learn that you are alone, Helen.'

Briefly, she wondered who could have told him about Alexander. But there was so much to catch up on, and it was good to have an old friend here sympathising.

'Not entirely alone. I have my son, you know – Neil. He's old for his years, an' all. He'll soon be good company.'

'But not yet?'

'You'll see. Not very consistent, our Neil. One day he's very cooperative, interested in what's going on; the next he can be just as different. A thorough pest!'

'All little boys are naughty at times.'

She found herself telling Vittore of the episode when Neil had pulled away the woman's stick, and was surprised when he didn't laugh.

'You must have been horribly embarrassed.'

'You can say that again!' Helen smiled. 'Eh, Vittore, it is good to talk to you after all this time.'

They talked a great deal, in the office while she showed him some of her recent drawings and photographs of the present stage of construction on the flats in Leeds, and later at home, while Neil sat at the table entranced, as riveted by Vittore's gleaming dark eyes as he was thrilled to be allowed to sit up late for dinner.

Several hours afterwards, when Neil had finally gone to his room, Helen and Vittore were still talking. Reminiscing about the farm and the comradeship among the workers there, he instilled in her a strong desire to see the place again.

'Let's visit Miss Templer,' she suggested eagerly. 'This weekend, why not? We could take Neil, tell him what life was like there.' This was something Helen had never done. She realised now that not even mentioning the farm since she'd left had been because of Alexander's disapproval of her working there.

They were late setting out on that Saturday afternoon. Neil, who had grown possessive of their exciting visitor, had insisted that they inspect his tiny patch of garden. Somehow, out there a game had developed, kicking a ball around, and Helen hadn't had the heart to interrupt them. When the pair eventually came in for lunch, Neil was so grubby that a second bath had proved necessary.

Here they were now though, noting familiar landmarks as they drove out beyond Huddersfield. Neil, tired maybe after the morning's exertion, was quiet for once, staring out obligingly each time a once familiar spot was mentioned but clearly not comprehending. His lack of interest seemed to isolate the other two with the past, and with each other.

Briefly, Helen felt Vittore's hand on her arm, smiled as she gave him a sideways glance.

'I never thought I would come back,' he said seriously.

'Good thing you did, though,' she asserted. 'This has right taken me out of myself.'

'Mmm?'

He sounded puzzled. Helen smiled again, enlightened him. 'Sorry, what I mean is you've made mc feel so different, much better, not nearly so entrenched in the humdrum life I lead.'

'That is good. Then I also am very pleased.'

They reached the farm and parked in the familiar yard, looking around them for some sign of Miss Templer. An oldish man was just visible beyond the drystone wall of the next field but one.

'I wonder if that's her brother?' said Helen as they got out of the car.

Knocking on the front door felt strange when they had both spent so many years wandering freely in and out of the farmhouse. And an answer was so long in coming that Helen was considering knocking again when the door opened.

'Well, I'll go to heck! It's Helen, isn't it?'

'That's right, Miss Templer, and this is my son, Neil. And you remember Vittore . . .'

'Well, I don't know! I wouldn't have owned you, you have bucked up,' she told Vittore. 'But I'm right glad to see you both, and the little lad – Neil, you say? Come in, come in.'

The big kitchen looked bare without farm workers on every available chair, but otherwise it seemed hardly to have changed.

'Did you really live here?' Neil asked, tugging on his mother's hand.

Helen grinned, turned to Vittore. 'Certainly brings

it all back, doesn't it, love?'

Miss Templer was standing, hands on hips, scrutinising them both. 'They were good days, weren't they?' she remarked, then seemed to recall the internment which had brought Vittore to Yorkshire.

But he smiled widely in response to her questioning grey eyebrow. 'For me also, yes – those times were very good.'

'And now?' Miss Templer enquired. 'Are you two, well . . .?'

Helen shook her head. 'It's just that we're still friends. Vittore's come back to England on a visit.'

'Not only a visit perhaps. If I can obtain the necessary permission,' he repeated, 'I would like to remain here. But tell us about yourself, Miss Templer, are you working as hard as ever?'

'When I'm able. I've got rheumatics, you see, 'specially in my knees. But we manage very well. My brother came back, shortly after t'end of the war.'

'We thought we saw somebody out there.'

'Some of t'others has been to call on me an' all, you know,' Miss Templer revealed, looking delighted. 'Kenneth, was it – the one with the bad chest? Him and one of the other fellows dropped in with their wives, must be two or three years ago now. And Iris comes to stay regular, of course.'

They chatted over tea while Neil played with the farm cat. And then they were given a tour of the fields, meeting Miss Templer's brother who appeared to be a man of few words.

'Miserable beggar!' their hostess muttered before they were quite out of earshot of him. 'I reckon he were far happier on munitions than ever he's been since. Pity they didn't keep him, I say!'

'Can we go home now?' Neil asked suddenly out of the blue.

Helen felt her colour rising. 'I'm sorry, Miss Templer, I'm afraid social graces were rationed when Neil was born. Although he does know better really than asking questions like that.'

'But I want to play football again, Vittore's super at it.'

'I'm afraid that'll have to wait till another day, my lad – by the time we get home it will be dark.'

'That's not fair,' the boy protested. 'It's boring here.'

'If you want summat to occupy you,' Miss Templer began, bending to speak to Neil, 'you can go and help my brother. He'll find you a job.'

That prospect didn't suit either. Neil stubbornly shook his head.

'I would like to walk,' Vittore suggested, then checked if that was all right with Miss Templer, and if she would join them.

'I'm afraid my old legs aren't up to it,' she told them. 'But you take a stroll round, enjoy yourselves. Not that there's much to see these days, except the view. We got rid of most of the sheep, and a lot of the fields where we grew crops have been turned over to cattle.'

The well-remembered vista of high, green hills spreading out towards the skyline was just as beautiful as ever. With the russet tones of autumn and the mauve of heather-capped moors it all seemed particularly lovely. Rain drops glistening on the leaves of an oak witnessed to an earlier shower which had bestowed its special clarity and brought the distant scene into sharper focus. At this altitude the expanse of hills seemed limitless and Helen relished the sense of freedom soaring through her. Today, she could believe that her future might be just as unrestricted.

They walked uphill to where the sheep used to graze,

and Neil began running about happily, exploring the entrances of rabbit burrows, and jumping off the low rocks that protruded from scrubby turf.

As they paused to gaze about them yet again, Helen heard the familiar sound of the wind in telegraph wires. All at once it returned her to the past, to the evening when Vittore had held her close, reassuring her.

Glancing his way, she caught him looking at her, some deep emotion turning his eyes almost to black and his smile to one of tender affection.

Neil had tired himself out. As soon as they said goodbye to Miss Templer and got into the car he yawned and started to drowse.

'It was good to go back to the farm,' said Vittore. 'I was reminded of so much that I experienced there.'

'A lot of hard work!' exclaimed Helen, though she had never considered the work alone out here.

Neil was asleep when they arrived at The Stone House. Before Helen could rouse him, Vittore caught her arm.

'Do not disturb him, there is no need. I will carry him upstairs for you.'

'He's not a tiny boy any longer.'

Vittore laughed. 'And I am not a tiny man.'

She hadn't needed any reminder of his presence which seemed so forceful that she ignored – as she always had – his height which was just about equal to her own. Now Vittore was here, Helen wondered how ever it was that he hadn't remained constantly in her thoughts since their very first meeting.

Following up the long curving staircase, she learned that he still had breath for speaking.

'Which room is Neil's, did you say?'

'Along to the left, here . . .'

She caught up with Vittore and opened the door. 'If

you don't mind putting him on the bed, I'll just slip his outdoor clothes off, and his shoes.'

Vittore was smiling again when he straightened up and faced her. 'Oh, to have the capacity of a child for sleeping well.'

'Don't you, then?' she asked, concerned.

He shrugged. 'Rarely. Especially since I went back to Italy.'

'Is it that bad?'

'Later, I will tell you. When you have attended to the boy.'

Mrs Hartley was waiting below in the hall, and showed Vittore into the large reception room which had just been reopened.

'If you'd like to wait in here, sir. Happen you'd like to help yourself to a drink while Mrs Stone is busy. She always expects her male guests to serve themselves.'

When Helen came downstairs after settling Neil she was surprised that Vittore asked if she did much entertaining.

'Because of the size of this room, you mean?' She shook her head. 'The house was built by my father-in-law. We took it over when he died. I hardly think I'd have gone for anything quite so big myself.'

'But it is indeed a beautiful house.'

'I agree with you. It's just a bit of a waste with only the two of us here now and Mrs Hartley.'

'You are young enough to marry again though, Helen.'

She laughed. 'You're as bad as our Marian! My sister. She was on at me not long since. As if I hadn't enough on my plate as it is.'

'But the right husband would share your responsibilities, would he not?'

'For the house, maybe. And for Neil an' all, I'd hope. But it's not only that, is it?'

'You mean the practice. Does that weigh heavily still?'

'Aye, I'm afraid so. Although a recent injection of capital has helped relieve the anxiety. I ought to be able to get away more, there's that little being built round here, and I don't have chance to go and look at what they're doing elsewhere. Alexander would have done all that.'

'You will miss him in so many ways.'

'Well, naturally. I'd known him so long, even before we were married, hadn't I?' Even to Vittore, she had no intention of revealing how drastically their relationship had deteriorated.

'And young Neil will miss him also.'

'He goes through phases, he's not so bad at present. Sometimes, he's really wilful and moody, and I can see he needs his daddy.'

After Mrs Hartley had announced that dinner was ready and they had gone through to the dining room they both became rather quiet. Helen was overcome by a sudden tiredness, and she suspected that Vittore was growing bored by her failure to provide more in the way of conversation.

The meal and the coffee which followed seemed to restore a little of her spirits, and she was content to return to sit near the fire.

'You were saying earlier, about the firm?' Vittore began carefully, glancing into the blaze rather than towards her. 'How the responsibility, to say nothing of the work, may be a little too much. Have you contemplated taking on another architect?'

'I have, but I've got to be realistic. I can only just survive paying Wendy, my secretary. If I had to fork out for anybody else, I'd be back to where I was before. Too hard up to run this place properly.'

'No, no – you have not understood. I mean as a

partner, someone who would invest in Stone's as well as working for – for you.'

'It'd have to be somebody who thought very much as I do about architecture. I had enough of opinions that clashed while Alexander was alive. So you see, Vittore, it'd have to be somebody pretty remarkable. He, or she, would have to have an eye for any up-to-date developments without wanting everything to be in ultra-modern style. It's a tall order. I'm reaching the conclusion that I'm damned difficult to please!'

'Not necessarily.' He was facing her now, the warmth in his fine dark eyes reminding her how good he was at beseeching with them. 'If I could be granted a permit to work over here, and I would even apply for naturalisation if that would help, I should like you to consider my joining you.'

'You? Eh, Vittore, if only you could. Didn't we used to get on well! I'm ever so glad we went to the farm today, aren't you?'

'But, yes, of course. We seem to have grown so close once more.'

And what good's that, thought Helen, when you still think of yourself as married? You haven't really come back to me. Where's the use in growing attached to you all over again, when it can lead nowhere? Except, possibly, with regard to work.

At around ten o'clock she rose and smiled across at him. 'Time I looked in on Neil to make sure he's sleeping all right. And then I'm going to bed. If you want to sit up, by all means do so. Make yourself at home. You know where the drinks are, and there's some of my father-in-law's books over there if you feel like a good read.'

Vittore chose instead to go up to his room. Tired but at ease, they hardly spoke as they walked side by side up the exquisite staircase.

At the door of her room, he took her wrist and drew her to him. His fingers were warm, powerful, and made her yearn to have him hold her and go on holding . . .

His kiss was firm on her lips. She felt his lips part.

'I need you so much, Helen,' he said huskily against her cheek. 'I've never stopped needing you.'

She made her voice light, rueful. 'And what I need is a good night's sleep, love.'

'There is one way of ensuring that,' Vittore persisted.

Helen shook her head at him. 'That's an old line – and I'm no bit of a lass that's going to fall for it. Sorry and all that, but you'll have to put that idea out of your head.'

'One more kiss then?'

One kiss, two, three – three hundred, she could no longer be sure. All she did know was the blood racing in her veins. Vittore was back, forcing her to acknowledge the acute awareness of him that was strong enough to cause her such fierce agony.

Vittore stayed for a further week in the house at Brearley, filling it with his good humour, often with his strong tenor voice. His fondness for opera seemed irrepressible, and clearly was encouraged when so many of the rooms proved to have good accoustics. Neil was entranced, and far better behaved than Helen remembered him. She herself delighted in having Vittore's companionship, and had to force into her subconscious the longing to have him share their life here permanently.

On the last Saturday of his stay he asked her to find somewhere for a special meal. Mrs Hartley was content to baby-sit for Neil. The restaurant was in Manchester, an elegant place which provided a small group of musicians to play for dancing.

'Remember the way we danced at the farm?' asked Vittore, holding her close as a foxtrot began.

Helen was willing herself not to. Her relationship with Alexander had been an almighty let-down. She wasn't going to be so vulnerable ever again. And besides, there was still everything that Vittore had said about his not being free. A proper fool she would be if she became involved with him now.

No amount of resolve could prevent her from enjoying this evening, however. Vittore's love of music made him an excellent partner. He couldn't know of her barely acknowledged yearning to be held by a loving man.

Helen could not protest when he repeatedly took her on to the floor, she could only revel in their well-matched steps and his mind-shattering nearness.

In the car going home he sat very close, his dark gaze going to her repeatedly so that driving required a serious effort of concentration. And when they went indoors he drew her to him at once, leaning with her into the massive oak door while his taut body spoke even more urgently than his kisses.

'Come to my room, Helen, please. Or allow me in yours. You are so completely desirable.'

'Not yet, Vittore, not so readily,' she said huskily, yet hating the good sense which compelled her to refuse. 'You've only just come back into my life. We've got to be reasonable about this. Sensible.'

'In here with me to the sofa then, just so I may hold you?'

Helen could no more deny herself than deny Vittore. But she would have to be extremely careful. She'd heard about Latin men and the heat of their passion. She mustn't forget how powerful desire could be.

Vittore drew her against him as they stood in the

light from the dying fire. His kisses became searching as they sank on to the sofa and held each other.

He was hard and he was stirring, driving Helen to acknowledge the rhythm of the blood which surged through her own veins. And she was moving with him. The hungry years had brought her to this day with every one of her senses sharpened. For how long they lay there, she could not reckon; only when forcing her own desire into submission grew almost impossible did she finally ease away from him.

'No more, Vittore, no more,' she stated firmly.

She liked him all the better for not attempting to argue. Instead, he assisted her to her feet and with one last kiss and a brief little hug, escorted her to the stairs.

'Sleep well, Helen.'

They were brisk and matter-of-fact with each other in the morning. Only their eyes, seeking and locking in long glances, revealed the yearning which had not diminished.

'May I return?' Vittore asked before they parted.

'There'll be trouble if you don't.'

The house felt emptier than ever in the past. Helen was thankful when work took her away to the office. And there, at least, thoughts of Vittore were permissible, taking on a different aspect. If he should find a way of working over here, nothing would stop her having him in the firm. Stone's would benefit from his expertise, to say nothing of his intended investment. And she would have a very good reason for welcoming him into this part of her life.

Neil began playing up during the week after Vittore's departure. Even Marian complained about his bad manners and spiteful little ways.

'It's not anything really wicked that he does,' she explained to Helen one evening. 'It's just that he really gets my goat by being downright awkward.'

Helen tried talking to her son, and got nowhere at all.

'It's no fun here any more,' he asserted, sounding nearer ten years old than three. 'Did you send Uncle Vittore away as well, like you sent Daddy?'

'I didn't send either of them away. And it's time you grew up a bit and got used to the idea that life can be disappointing. When Uncle Vittore came here it was only for a short stay. But he might come back again, especially if you try to become a likable person,' she added, and hated herself for attempting blackmail.

At the end of that week, Helen decided to confide in her mother. She wouldn't enjoy admitting how difficult Neil could be, but she was beginning to feel out of her depth with him again. And what were mothers for but to pass on advice down the generations?

Helen left Mrs Hartley keeping an eye on Neil while she drove over to Halifax during Saturday afternoon. Her father generally went off to the football match. She and her mother would be able to have a private heart-to-heart.

Kathleen seemed surprised that Helen was alone. She knew her daughter normally reserved weekends for Neil.

'Nothing's wrong, love, is it?' she asked from the kitchen doorway after putting on the kettle.

Helen sighed, staring across the street at the row of gaunt houses. 'Eh, I don't know, Mum. I've certainly come seeking your advice.'

Her mother grinned. 'Mine? Nay, I allus thought you were the clever one of this family.'

'I don't feel it. And definitely not where Neil's upbringing's concerned. I sometimes think I'm making a right hash of it.'

'Never! Not you. He's a grand little lad, a credit to you.'

'You only see him when he's on his best behaviour. He can be a proper little devil when things aren't to his liking.'

'I hope he wasn't naughty while you had that Italian chap staying? Our Marian told me you had a visitor.'

'Vittore, aye. No, Neil was very good, for him, while Vittore was there. It's since he's left that Neil's been playing up. He's so moody at times. Were we like that?'

'Not really, love. Marian was allus on the go, into everything, and you – well, you were quieter, of course, always reading or doing jigsaws if you weren't drawing. You were as good as gold.'

'I don't know if it's with me working and our Marian taking over from me, or what. He seems that changeable somehow. Just when I think he's learning to behave, he starts acting like a spoilt brat again.'

'I don't suppose it's with you going to work so much as him missing his dad. It's bound to have made him feel insecure, you know.'

'Aye, I daresay. He blames me for that an' all.'

'Nay, Helen, how can he? It were an accident killed Alexander.'

Helen swallowed, deciding the time had come for being honest about her great burden – the circumstances surrounding her husband's departure for London on that dreadful day.

'Aye, but we hadn't been getting on before he set off. Evidently, Neil had heard us arguing.'

'Lots of folk argue, love. You can't go punishing yourself for that.'

'We'd talked about splitting up.'

Kathleen's grey eyes narrowed. 'As bad as that, eh? Was – was there another woman again?'

'Not so far as I know. No, I'm pretty sure there wasn't. It was just me. Oh, Mum – he said I wasn't anything like the wife he wanted!'

'Did he now? And what did he expect? You gave him the son he was after, *and* worked in the family firm as well.'

'It was going back there after Neil was born that put Alexander's back up.'

'Yes, well, working wives do creatc a different home life, but that doesn't mean it has to be an unhappy one. And he had known you all the years you were studying – he couldn't seriously have expected you to give up your work.'

'Bless you, you're very understanding. But about Neil – what do you think I ought to do?'

'I don't rightly know, love. You'll have to be patient for a while maybe – till he grows up a bit. The best thing all round would be if you met somebody else, someone that'd be a father to him.'

Leaving her mother that afternoon, Helen felt a different kind of disturbance. Ever since Vittore had returned she had been fighting her own instincts. Perhaps that had been the wrong thing entirely?

Chapter 17

Helen was positive now that she was going to pull Stone's through – she would build up the business again until it regained the kind of reputation it had had while Joseph Stone was in charge. She began her campaign with visits to Sheffield, one of the places nearer to home that had suffered wartime bombardment.

There certainly was scope for redevelopment, and much of it where traditional styling would be more appropriate than anything modern. While she still had no one qualified in the office, she couldn't spend too long over each trip to Sheffield. She could find out what new building was required, though, and also widened her understanding of the area in long conversations with her sister.

Marian, despite the hazards from enemy bombing, had enjoyed her stay driving ambulances there. 'I'd love to see parts of it rebuilt by you, Helen,' she said, surprising her. 'You'd not choose stuff that would clash with what's there already.'

Helen smiled. She'd needed someone to understand her aims. 'Thanks. Eh, Marian – there's that much I long to get involved with. If I'd somebody experienced to leave in charge I'd be off all over the north, sniffing out where reconstruction should be done. Liverpool suffered very badly in the war, then there's Hull an' all.'

Since Ophelia Hadgraft had put money into Stone's Helen had been hoping she'd be justified in taking another architect into the firm, but here she was, still waiting and hoping, and being confronted by warnings from her accountant whenever she tried to expand further. Meanwhile, most of her work was confined to plans for housing. All she could do was remind herself how vital this was, and that when completed to her designs the homes produced were pleasing.

Autumn turned to winter, bringing biting winds that scoured hilltops and moors and tore through steep streets, until everyone felt that going out at all was a battle. Despite her resolve, Helen began to believe that a battle was the nearest description of the whole of her life. When she wasn't wearing herself out at work she was struggling to keep that massive house warm, and to survive Neil's moods.

It was mostly to try and make him feel happier that she became determined to provide a Christmas that was as good as possible. Last year, being the first after Alexander's death, she'd arranged hardly anything. Somehow, she would make up for that.

One Saturday early in December she and Neil arrived home from shopping feeling quite happy. He had been interested in plans for Christmas and in the items they were buying, and had behaved extremely well, reassuring Helen. Mrs Hartley greeted them in the hall with the news that there had been a telephone call.

'From that Italian – Mr Fabri,' she said. 'I told him you would be at home this evening, I hope that's all right?'

Helen spent the intervening hours trying to quell her excitement. Surely the fact that Vittore had phoned meant that he'd either remained in England or had returned here? He wouldn't be telephoning all the way from Italy.

I might be proper daft, she thought, but I do want to see him again. And I'd love more than anything to have him working with me.

When the call came, Vittore made no such promises, but he did say he had a lot to discuss with her. 'I was wondering if it might be convenient for you if I visited Yorkshire next weekend?'

Helen wouldn't have believed that a week could drag so heavily even though she was so busy in the office. Finally awakening on the Saturday morning, she felt drained by days of enduring her own impatience. She had never been like this before. But then, of course, she'd never had to wait to see somebody she'd grown found of.

Vittore arrived a few hours later, stepping from his taxi and gazing up at The Stone House affectionately and with an expert's approval in his dark eyes. Watching from an upstairs window, Helen smiled to herself. It might have been confirmation, had she needed any, of how their tastes converged.

She only hoped his taste in fashion would appreciate her New Look style. She was feeling self-conscious in a dress that she'd originally bought for Christmas but couldn't resist wearing today. In a soft wool that hung in unpressed pleats from a nipped-in waistline, its bodice fitted beautifully but seemed to emphasise her breasts, a factor enhanced by the curving V neckline. The long sleeves felt good, though, after years of Utility skimpiness, as did the mid-calf skirt. And she loved the material, a wedgwood shade that reflected a tinge of blue into her grey eyes.

Running down the elegant staircase, she was in the hall by the time Mrs Hartley had opened the door to him. Neil, however, had beaten her to it. Hurling himself at Vittore, he was lifted clear of the ground in an energetic hug.

Helen felt her throat tighten, and tears stung her eyes. But then Vittore was transferring the boy to one arm and extending the other for her. Holding her against him, he kissed her full on the lips, then kissed Neil also before setting him down.

'I feel as if I have returned home,' Vittore declared, beaming at the three of them as he turned slightly and greeted Mrs Hartley, 'Did I say hallo when you opened the door to me? You must forgive if my excitement took away my courtesy.'

Vittore appeared even fitter than on his previous visit, and was wearing a beautifully tailored suit in a creamy-coloured cloth that no one in the West Riding would have considered practical.

I can't stop myself wanting him here, thought Helen, regardless of all my resolutions. And I've only to look at Neil to know how much he likes his Uncle Vittore.

The rest of the day passed in a sort of daze. Helen was so elated that she'd lost all her customary steadiness. And Neil, bless him, was angelic, remaining surprisingly quiet while she and Vittore were talking, but cooperating with spirit when invited to show what he'd been doing during the past few weeks.

By Sunday evening Helen was growing accustomed to having Vittore around again, and was relishing his company. Early that morning they had walked uphill from the house and strolled along the ridge, glancing occasionally across the valley where frost had rimed bare branches and coated the dark stone walls like fine sugar.

'I love your Yorkshire,' he had told her, his breath frosting too in air that stung their faces.

That evening she wasn't surprised when he announced his firm plans to settle here. 'I've managed to secure permission,' he confided. 'Do not ask me how. I had to persuade someone to pull a few strings. I have also got most of my capital liquidised – and away from Italy. I am serious, Helen, about wishing to join Stone's, if you would consider having me.'

She beamed at him. 'I think you know already that I'd love that. But you'll have to understand that I can't just leap into such an important decision instantly. I'll speak to my accountant, soon as I can, then you and me can talk again, sort out details.'

In the meantime, she asked him to extend his stay. 'If you want to, you could stop with us till after Christmas. That would certainly suit Neil.'

'And you?' he asked quietly.

'And me an' all.'

'I should like to make up to you, Helen, for all the loneliness you have endured since your husband's accident.'

She could well believe that Vittore was capable of doing just that. He had been important to her for such a long time now. Having him back in her life felt as good as recovering after an extended bout of sickness.

On Christmas Eve Vittore startled her by suggesting that they should attend mass at midnight.

'I wouldn't mind,' she said, 'but I'm not Catholic, you know. I couldn't even tell you about the services in their church.'

'No matter. We would attend an English service. I should like that very much.'

The tiny church was almost full. They sat in a pew near the back and Helen felt the calm seeping into her. Decorated for Christmas and full of such a different atmosphere, she could hardly believe that it was the place where the funerals of both Alexander and his father had begun. Despite the large number of people present she was deeply conscious of a strange quiet that had nothing to do with silence. Indeed, the music was glorious, from the full-throated singing of Christmas hymns to the fervent intoning of the rector, all perfectly tuneful.

I wish I'd come to services here before, she thought, aching to belong. I wonder why I've always felt I was merely on the edge of worship, not quite participating?

Glancing sideways at Vittore, she sensed that although the doctrine was different from his own, he was quite at home here.

When they went out into the crisp night air to walk the short distance to the house he took her hand.

'Happy Christmas,' he said, and added, 'thank you.'

They drank hot coffee and ate mince pies left out for them by Mrs Hartley before going to their rooms. During this visit Vittore had avoided any hint that he wished to make love to her. But Helen often read in his glance a longing which echoed her own. Sitting like this in her home, she could believe that the time would come when her restraint would give way.

She was awakened on Christmas morning by Neil rushing into her room with some of his toys.

'Look, Mummy, look what Father Christmas has brought. And this one's special,' he declared, showing her a magnificent model aeroplane. 'This is what Uncle Vittore asked him to bring.'

'He's very kind. You must be sure and thank him.'

'I said thank you already.'

Helen glanced at the clock. It was a quarter to seven. 'You didn't go into his room? Do you know that your uncle and I went to church last night – and didn't get home until after one o'clock!'

Vittore, however, was showing no signs of lacking

sleep. He was dressed in dark slacks and an elegant sweater, and talking with Mrs Hartley when Helen went down to the dining room. And maybe their rising early was for the best, she thought wryly. She had invited all her family over for Christmas dinner.

Asking them all to her was taking a chance. She couldn't be sure how they would get on with Vittore, and was also afraid that Marian, at least, would begin making five out of two and two.

Helen soon discovered, anyway, that her parents appreciated her sparing her mother the work of entertaining the whole family. And Denis, who had visited Italy with ENSA during the war, soon began talking animatedly with Vittore.

Having Mrs Hartley to attend to the actual meal was a great boon, freeing Helen to relax and chat with her guests.

Neil and his cousins were allowed to wrap up warm and romp in the garden just before dinner, an idea that paid dividends when they came in healthily hungry and with enough energy expended to give everyone a trouble-free meal.

During the late afternoon while the children were absorbed in a jigsaw puzzle, leaving the adults free to talk, Helen glanced towards Vittore.

Sitting on one of the sofas drawn up to the hearth in her large reception room, his smile was enhanced by the glow from the fire. His eyes, darker than ever in here, seemed to smile as much as his lips, and every line of his body looked perfectly at ease.

He appears to fit in so well here, Helen thought, smiling also to herself. There had been no awkwardness with any of her family – and his generosity to Neil was evidence of his affection for her son.

There had been a gift for Helen herself – one that

had taken her back to another Christmas. This time, the model he had given her was of St Peter's in Rome. She had been delighted to display them both on a side table in the dining room.

Marian had teased, as Helen had expected, while they were helping Mrs Hartley to clear the dirty dishes into the kitchen. But if she hadn't accepted Helen's explanation that Vittore was simply to become involved as a business partner, she had certainly ceased her questions about the relationship. Helen realised now that although she wouldn't wish to hurry through any part of this Christmas she would be glad to see her accountant afterwards and begin drawing up the deal to finalise their plans.

'You can't mean that!' Helen exclaimed, terribly disappointed. She had spent half the morning with Mr Thorpe, explaining how much Vittore was willing to invest in Stone's and how his expertise as an architect was just what she had been seeking. And here her accountant was, cautioning her against permitting another person to take a financial interest in the firm!

'I'm sorry, but I cannot think such a deal would be to your long-term advantage, Mrs Stone.'

'But whyever not?' Helen persisted. 'Haven't you been telling me for ages that we can't expand as things are? That we need more money behind us?'

'Ah, but there is a difference, you see,' Mr Thorpe persisted. 'I was thinking in terms of funds which were by way of being a ploughing back of your profits. If you let someone else in now you're leaving yourself wide open to difficulties in the future.'

'I don't see how.'

'Oh come, Mrs Stone, you're not that naive. You're already in a position where the Honourable Ophelia Hadgraft has a considerable say if it comes to boardroom wrangles. An additional shareholder would . . .'

'Oh, is that all?' said Helen thankfully, realising that he was visualising Vittore as a potential source of trouble. Nothing could be further from the truth. All Vittore wanted was to make things easier for her, to relieve her of some of the anxiety and increase the possibility of Stone's going after bigger and better projects.

'It's all right,' she went on to assure him. 'I've known Vittore Fabri for years. He's a lovely man who thinks as I do about architecture. About lots of things, if it comes to that. I'm grateful for your considering every aspect on my behalf, Mr Thorpe, but you really needn't have any qualms about this deal, none at all.'

When, a few days later, she saw Ophelia Hadgraft and told her that Vittore was coming into the firm, Helen was thankful that she didn't even express surprise.

'That will do wonders for Stone's, I'm sure. I'm delighted for you, Helen. His investment will indeed put the firm on a very sound footing, and his expertise will enable you to widen your scope.'

'I knew you'd be pleased. It just shows how right I was to trust my own instincts.'

Her instincts seemed to be working overtime since Christmas. Having seen how well integrated into her family Vittore was, she was beginning to lose all misgivings about his staying in her home. They frequently ended the day in each other's arms. And she was fully aware now that if he was to suggest their making love, she wouldn't refuse.

It was a total shock when Vittore himself decided he must move out of the house. On the day that he finally began working at Stone's he told her of his intention.

'Do not look so perturbed, Helen, there is nothing

wrong. You know how happy I am, how much I want to work alongside you. But you know also that I have experienced trouble in the past when involving business with my private life. And so the time has come to find myself accommodation. I have heard of a place that will be convenient for reaching the office, and I trust that you and I will continue to spend some of our leisure hours together, especially with young Neil.'

His decision was a blow, she couldn't find sufficient composure to pretend otherwise. It had come so suddenly, almost as though somebody had put the idea into his head. But if she was perturbed about their personal life she wouldn't let that spoil her happiness concerning their business relationship.

Within days Vittore seemed to have settled as readily into the office as she had once believed he'd been settled in her home. Seeing him each day compensated for missing him at The Stone House, and having Neil to herself again she noticed how he had blossomed under Vittore's influence. He had become a much more cheerful little boy, and much more cooperative.

During the second week that Vittore was in the office Helen realised that she was feeling infinitely better. Not only was she free to go out on business trips, she had regained the energy to enjoy doing so. Even this early in the new year she felt undaunted by the extreme cold and up to facing any falls of snow.

Hull was one of the first places Helen visited, and she learned of several schemes which she hoped might provide work for Stone's. Feeling some of the elation that she'd experienced when first qualified, she was driving back through Halifax when she recognised the car ahead of her as Ophelia Hadgraft's.

They arrived simultaneously at Stone's office and Ophelia, who evidently had recognised Helen's car in her rear-view mirror as they slowed to negotiate the bends of the approach road, waited for Helen by the steps.

'I thought you'd said you were going over to Hull today?' she said, and Helen noticed that although Ophelia was smiling her eyes hadn't warmed.

'That's it. I've had a right good day over there, there's plenty of scope for work. But I wanted to get back and make sure that Vittore was coping.'

As they entered the outer office Helen saw through the doorway of her own office that Vittore was sitting at her desk. He was speaking down the phone to someone and, seeing she had arrived, beckoned her.

'It is the construction company for those flats of yours nearing completion in Leeds.'

The query was minor and quickly answered, Helen's disturbance owed more to finding Vittore occupying her desk. It seemed all too reminiscent of Harold Tilsley. But I'm being paranoid, she reminded herself swiftly, and began introducing him to Ophelia Hadgraft.

Helen had wondered once or twice how the two would react to each other, and would have been horrified if they hadn't got on. It seemed, however, that she need not have worried.

Ophelia instantly extended a hand which Vittore grasped firmly and then raised to his lips. Amid effusive exclamations of 'How do you do?' 'I am so delighted to meet you' and 'I'm so glad that you have joined Stone's', the pair were beaming enthusiastically.

Privately, Helen smiled. It looked as if Ophelia was responding with an older woman's eagerness to flattery from a personable man. And Vittore, she supposed, had the typical Latin flair for impressing any female.

The three of them sat in Helen's office for an informal discussion of future plans. The other two seemed to think her visit to Hull had indeed provided lots of potential. And they readily applauded her idea of following this up with an exploratory trip to Liverpool.

When Ophelia glanced at her watch and announced that she had an engagement that evening and must be leaving, she added to Vittore: 'Can I offer you a lift perhaps? I shall be going through Halifax.'

He accepted readily, thanking her profusely, and tossing Helen a brief: 'Goodnight, see you in the morning.'

Driving home, Helen reflected that if Ophelia Hadgraft had been in less than her evident middle years, she herself might have been perturbed by the fuss Vittore was making of her. I seem to be in danger of becoming neurotic about his behaviour, she thought ruefully. Could this perhaps be a result of the mistrust which her own husband had once generated in her? Would she always doubt every man?

After playing with Neil and seeing him into bed that evening, Helen willed herself to concentrate on the notes that she had made over in Hull. But she seemed unable to forget her impression that there'd been more than the casual acceptance of a lift in the way the others had gone off together. She would just have to school herself to accept that whilst working so closely with anyone there were bound to be occasions when their behaviour appeared inexplicable.

Now that Vittore's presence made her feel easier about leaving the office, Helen found the next few months passing agreeably as well as swiftly. He didn't seem the sort of man who must have a hand in all the big schemes. He appeared happy enough to work on drawing plans, even for relatively mundane houses, while she set off farther afield, viewing potential development sites and eventually organising surveys for one or two projects which she succeeded in securing.

Vittore's evident rapport with Ophelia, which initially had caused Helen such surprise, was proving useful when the three of them met for formal business discussions. Helen was learning that Ophelia possessed a certain amount of understanding of what architecture involved, therefore they rarely wasted much time when discussing this side of running Stone's. For the first time since her father-in-law's death Helen began feeling happier about the way things were heading.

In her private life, too, she was reasonably content. She would have enjoyed seeing more of Vittore, but he did spend several weekends at The Stone House, and his relationship with Neil definitely seemed to be bringing out the best in the boy.

When the chilly West Riding spring developed into full summer and she could relish wearing lighter clothes and feeling the sun on her head while she was visiting sites, Helen believed that this, at last, might be the beginning of better times. She had struggled for so many years simply to do the work that she had wanted ever since she was a girl of fifteen. Now she was going to enjoy every minute of it.

She had been over to Sheffield on the day that she got home rather later than usual and found Marian sitting in the entrance hall, holding her throat and very clearly anxious to go home.

'Are you all right?' Helen asked straight away.

'I do feel a bit off colour,' her sister told her. 'I've had a sore throat for days. All of a sudden it's a lot worse and my neck's very stiff.'

'Eh, dear – I am sorry, love. And I'll bet Neil's led you a dance an' all. He generally does.' Even on a good day he possessed lots of surplus energy. Helen felt Marian's forehead which seemed to burn beneath her fingers.

'He's not been too bad. He's played out a lot. I've just left him having his tea now.'

'Good, thanks. Well, I hope you're soon feeling better, love. If you're not all right tomorrow you must stop at home. Mrs Hartley will keep an eye on Neil while I'm in the office. And I could always pop home at dinnertime.'

Although Helen was naturally concerned because Marian was unwell, she wasn't particularly alarmed. Yorkshire folk, however tough in constitution, were often plagued by the colds which flourished among the smoke of their chilly and frequently damp hills and valleys.

Hearing their mother's voice on the telephone the following morning, Helen immediately expected a message confirming that Marian was no better.

But Kathleen Clegg sounded as if she had been crying. 'It's our Marian, she's ever so poorly. Denis asked me to go and sit with her last night so he could get to the theatre.'

'She certainly wasn't so good when she left here,' said Helen. 'Is it 'flu she's got?'

'Eh, I wish to goodness that were all! I had to call the doctor to her late last night and whatever do you think? It's infantile paralysis . . .'

'Polio? No! Oh, heavens! I am sorry . . . How bad is she?'

'Well, the doctor was afraid for her breathing, evidently that can be affected. But he thought it was just her sore throat making that difficult. No, it's her legs – before I got her to bed she'd nearly lost the use in them. Oh, Helen, I do hope she's not going to end up crippled!'

'So do I. But it's early days yet – we'll just have to hope the doctors can do summat for her. What about Linda and Mark, are they okay?'

'Up to now. The doctor's told us to keep them at home from school, of course, in case they might pass it on.'

God, thought Helen, that means Neil might have caught it already. But she mustn't think only of him just now. 'Are you there now, Mum, at Marian's?'

'Aye, I stopped here last night while Denis got home after the performance, then came straight round again this morning.'

'Are you coping all right? Do you want me to come over?'

'No, love, you mustn't bother. You have your work, and Neil to look after. I was wondering how you'd manage . . . if I ought to come on there?'

'No, Mum. I'll cope, thanks. You've enough on without that. Mrs Hartley will keep an eye on him. But shouldn't I . . .?'

'Marian's asleep now, the doctor gave her summat. And Denis is here an' all. You go to your work, love, we'll see you later on.'

Helen went straight to Neil's room where he was struggling to dress. He had his little underpants on back to front, and his vest was hanging outside them.

'Come here, love,' she said, and hugged him to her before even thinking of sorting out his clothes.

'You're squeezing too tight, Mummy, you're hurting!'

'Sorry, Neil, sorry . . .'

'What's happened, Mummy – don't cry.' He couldn't understand the distress in her eyes, nor the tears appearing in their corners. Mummies didn't cry, did they? That was babyish.

'It's your Auntie Marian, she's very poorly. She won't be able to look after you today.' And, she realised appalled, might never do so again.

When Helen had made the necessary arrangements with Mrs Hartley and finally set out for the office, she felt utterly shattered. On top of all the worry about her sister and anxiety in case Neil had picked up polio from her, was this deep concern about who would look after Neil in the future. For the time being, however, she would have to shelve that particular problem and work out how soon she could get over to see Marian.

The minute she walked into the office Wendy gave her a searching look. 'Whatever is wrong, Mrs Stone?'

'It's my sister, I'm afraid.'

'The one that looks after Neil?'

'Marian, aye. She's been taken ill. The doctor says it's polio.'

Wendy was commiserating with her when Vittore came out of his office. He too asked what was wrong, and crossed swiftly to put an arm about her shoulders. When he heard what the trouble was he sympathised at once.

'You must be wishing to be with her,' he added. 'Why do you not go there now? I can attend to everything here.'

'Thanks,' she said. 'But Denis is at home during the day, and my mother's there an' all. It'll be more use if I can go this evening while Denis is at the theatre.'

'Would it help if I sit with Neil then tonight?'

'Would you, Vittore? I'd be ever so grateful. Mrs Hartley will be tired out after having him all day.'

'I can arrange to stay the night, if you wish. That would mean you need not rush back from your sister's home.'

* * *

Marian was flushed still with her illness and didn't look as bad as Helen had expected. In fact, in her best lace-edged nightdress and negligee, she appeared delicate and rather beautiful. And because the doctor had prescribed something to ease her throat, she wasn't in as much discomfort as the previous day.

'Is Neil all right?' she asked almost as soon as Helen walked into the bedroom. 'I'll never forgive myself if he catches this as well.'

'He's fine so far, love, don't go worrying. And it's nothing you can help. It's not the sort of thing you go looking for.'

'You can say that again! It's a right bugger, Helen!' Marian's blue eyes were awash with tears. 'I can't move my left leg at all, you know. And the other one's not much better. I've tried not to show how upset I am in front of Mum, but I'm scared stiff I'll never be any different. Whatever am I going to do, Helen?'

She forced a smile on to her lips. 'You're going to stop worriting like this, that's what. They've only just started treating you, haven't they, love? And they can do a lot more these days than they could a few years ago,' she added, hoping with all her heart that this was true.

'Denis will go off me if I have to spend the rest of my life in a wheelchair, I know he will.'

'That's nonsense, Marian, and you know it is. You've got a champion husband who'll always cherish you, through thick and thin.'

'Cherish? Denis?'

'Isn't that what you've done for each other, all these years? You've made a right good home together and you've got two smashing kids.'

'That's another thing – I want to be with Linda and Mark while they're growing up. I couldn't bear to be stuck here in bed, or even only able to get about in the house.'

'You won't have to be like that. We'll see something's done. We're not going to let you end up in a bad way.'

Later, though, driving home, Helen was forced to admit that there didn't seem any kind of certainty that Marian would be cured. From what the doctor had told Kathleen Clegg, there was very little in the way of an acceptable treatment for poliomyelitis. And being told that the medical profession insisted that prevention was the answer did nothing to help them.

In her concern for Marian, Helen had virtually forgotten that Vittore was taking charge of things at The Stone House. Finding him walking towards her as she almost stumbled with exhaustion through the front door was a massive relief.

'Helen!' he exclaimed, rushing the last few paces to support her. 'Do not tell me you also are ill?'

She managed a weary grin as she shook her head. 'No, I'm just dead beat. Remember how we used to be after a hard day on the farm? But Neil – is he still all right?'

'If insisting on a game of Indians and Cowboys throughout your garden is "all right", that is what he is!'

'Thank goodness for that. Let's hope he stays that way. I meant to ask what the incubation period was, but I was so upset about our Marian, I didn't think.'

'Come and sit down. I sent Mrs Hartley off to her bed. The poor lady was quite exhausted.'

'I'm not surprised, coping with his lordship all day.'

'You certainly have one very active son.'

'Our Marian used to be the active one of us two,' Helen remarked sadly, and suddenly she was weeping. 'She was that *still* tonight. Propped up on the pillows, and hardly able to move except just her arms when she wanted something off the bedside table. I don't think I'll be able to bear it either if she doesn't get better.'

'Do not distress yourself, Helen, not yet. We can only hope and pray that she will improve in time.'

Pray? she thought, unable to believe that would do any good, unable to believe in anything.

'What's she ever done to deserve this, that's what I want to know?' she demanded fiercely, tears pouring down her cheeks. 'Look how she's helped with Neil. She'd do anything for me and him. This is so unfair.'

Vittore led her to the sofa and held her to him while she wept out a lot of the strain and distress. Eventually, he gave her brandy to drink then took her protectively by the arm and encouraged her to go upstairs to her room.

'I am here, do not forget,' he told her.

'Thank goodness you are, Vittore. I'd never have got through this day without you.'

'Sleep well, *cara*, try not to worry. You must give priority to your sister now. I shall take over more responsibility from you in the office.'

Chapter 18

As their days continued to be darkened by Marian's illness, Helen found she was thankful to be able to lean on Vittore for assistance. And he wasn't the only person concerned for her. When Ophelia Hadgraft next visited Stone's she was full of compassion.

'I didn't know she'd heard about Marian,' Helen remarked to Vittore afterwards.

'I suppose you must have mentioned it while you were so distressed. You probably don't remember,' he said.

Helen didn't reply. Although as disturbed as he'd supposed, she remained certain that she had said nothing about Marian to Ophelia. None of this really mattered, though it did increase an uneasy feeling that was developing at the back of her mind. Ridiculous though it seemed when Vittore couldn't have been more helpful, she often felt that there was some undercurrent which she ought to mistrust.

Life was too complex for delving into mere suspicions, however. Just getting through each week was requiring considerable planning. Between them, Kathleen Clegg and Mrs Hartley were minding Neil, enabling Helen to work. She herself wasn't happy about her mother taking on this additional responsibility while still assisting where she could in Marian's home, but for the present there seemed no alternative.

It was Marian who had insisted that Helen shouldn't make more permanent arrangements over caring for the boy, and none of them wanted to shatter her belief that she would eventually recover sufficiently to resume her original role.

Medical opinion was less specific about her future. The rest which had been prescribed appeared to have eased some of her debility, but only to a degree where she was able, with the aid of crutches, to get to and from the bathroom. The leg most gravely affected seemed to have regained only a fraction of its previous mobility.

The only good thing was that Marian herself got over her depression.

Nevertheless Helen could hardly face her frequent visits to her sister. Seeing Marian like that brought back so many memories of how energetic she'd always been. And Denis had confessed to his father-in-law that he was hard put to avoid breaking down in front of her sometimes. He wasn't sorry that an actor was trained to analyse emotions instead of giving in to them.

'I know, I know,' Daniel Clegg had said while he and Denis sat downstairs, leaving Helen and her mother with Marian. 'I feel the same.'

'I feel quite guilty being glad when it's time to set off to the theatre. Don't get me wrong – I love her just as much as ever . . .'

'I can see that, Denis, we all can. Nobody could be more devoted.'

'It hurts for her sake, you see – noticing all that she's missing with the children. And it isn't enough, just being thankful that my hours mean I can do more for Linda and Mark than if I had a nine-to-five job.'

'Aye, it's a bad do,' said Daniel, shaking his head. 'They've been good though, those two, haven't they? I gather they've started being very helpful.' The fact remained, however, that the whole family was hurt by seeing Marian stricken by such a serious illness.

There were times when Helen felt like letting everything slide simply to spend more time with her sister. The days Marian had passed at The Stone House looking after Neil had drawn them closer than ever in their lives before. Now Helen wanted to give a bit back, yet felt torn in three directions, especially with Neil needing her more because most of his time was spent with a couple of elderly women. And how could she neglect the architectural practice?

Vittore seemed to expect that she would do so. Helen had lost count of the number of occasions that he had urged her to take more time off. She wondered if the Italian devotion to family was responsible for his supposition that she would relinquish some of her duties at Stone's. Certainly, he seemed unable to understand that no matter how torn – or how tired – it wasn't in her nature to slacken her grasp on the reins.

Now that they were into the latter half of 1950 it looked to Helen as if they were at last on the verge of having more scope for exercising imaginative architecture. Indeed, had they been fortunate enough to be sited in the south of England, they could already have been engaged in designing part of one of the new towns. Stevenage had been followed by Harlow and Crawley, and others were on the way. Even though the modernity of some of these schemes wasn't to Helen's taste, she'd have been glad of the opportunity to participate in something so exciting. Secretly, she liked to think that she might have been able to influence the developers with more classical styling.

As it was, she contented herself with designs for reconstruction of buildings in those northern cities which had suffered bomb damage. And the days spent on site there were really as much as she wished to spend out of the office. It was *her* architectural practice, after all, and fond though she was of Vittore she wasn't going to leave him in charge there for extended periods.

She had been perturbed recently when Wendy told her that Vittore always took over her desk whenever she was out for the day.

'Have you told him to occupy your office when you're not in, Mrs Stone? I know it's not really owt to do with me, but I thought you ought to know what's going on.'

Helen had smiled, making light of the issue. If there was a certain amount of antagonism between Wendy and Vittore she didn't want to fuel it. 'I've nothing to hide there, Wendy, so I don't think you need to worry. And he does have all my papers to hand if he gets any queries.'

The day that Helen herself began to wonder if Vittore did cherish unvoiced ambitions she had been over to Liverpool.

She was already feeling rather dejected as she drove back again; the meeting with a potential client had been so unpromising that she was afraid that Stone's wouldn't be invited to submit drawings. He had been a blunt man who didn't trouble to disguise his assumption that a female architect would be below par.

She had also promised to go over and see Marian that evening, a visit which she'd postponed from the weekend when she was suffering from a heavy cold. Risking passing on any infection to Marian must be avoided. And now she was watching the time. Her call in at the office would have to be brief if she was to see much of Neil before a hasty meal and the journey to Halifax.

Helen was astonished when she found Ophelia Hadgraft's car parked outside Stone's. Some additional sense made her enter quietly. When she saw that the door of her own office was closed and then heard the murmur of conversation from beyond its panels, she greeted Wendy with a smile and a nod before crossing swiftly to open the door.

'Don't worry, she doesn't need to know,' Vittore was saying to Ophelia. 'If the worst happens, I can handle it. I'll see she agrees . . .'

The pair of them started simultaneously, and swung round to face the door.

'Hallo,' said Helen evenly, and added that she hadn't expected to see Ophelia.

The older woman's face coloured, an unusual reaction in someone of her sophistication.

'Ophelia was passing and called in, that is all,' Vittore announced, a shade too quickly.

Helen knew he was lying and, whilst she couldn't even guess why he should have cause to do so, that fact together with what she'd overheard made her decide to force the issue.

'It's time the three of us arranged another meeting, anyway,' she announced, pleased that she at least sounded calm. She watched each of the other two control the urge to exchange a glance. 'We're beginning to make a healthier profit,' she continued steadily. 'We've got to ensure that we build on that by not letting opportunities evade us.'

'Naturally,' said Ophelia, forcing a smile. 'And I'm sure that Vittore here is the man to give you all the back-up you require.'

Helen smiled back at her. 'You don't need to tell me that. Don't forget how long I've known him.'

Even if I'm starting to wonder if I don't know him thoroughly enough, she thought, and felt an enormous ache of foreboding and disappointment filling her heart.

The meeting they arranged for a week later passed off very smoothly, yet Helen was left with the feeling that it had all been a shade *too* smooth. Could it be that both Ophelia and Vittore were exerting every effort to maintain a false equilibrium at Stone's for some purpose of their own? It almost felt to her as though they were holding their breath in anticipation of . . . of what, she really could not imagine. And nor could she, for the life of her, see what they might hope to gain by anything covert.

Away from work, Vittore seemed as friendly as ever, when she and Neil saw him – which, these days, was rather less frequently. He appeared to enjoy keeping his personal life to himself; for instance, he'd never told her where exactly he was living, and certainly hadn't invited her there. It seemed odd when she reflected on how he had stayed in her home.

Helen began seriously to doubt his loyalty on the day when she was remaining in the office while he was travelling to Todmorden to survey the site of a house for an influential local businessman.

'Take my car, if you like,' she told him on the previous day. 'You needn't set out before I arrive at the office, and you'll be back before I'm ready for home.'

Vittore declined with a smile. 'I am afraid I cannot do that. I have no licence to drive in England. I thought of ordering a taxi.'

'That'll cost a packet. There's a very good bus service which stops close to the site. There's a timetable somewhere about the office, and I'll give you directions.'

Helen could see that didn't please, but was determined not to relent. Before having her own car, she had found public transport quite adequate. Stone's might be better off financially, these days, but was not yet in a position to throw money around.

Am I being hard? she wondered during the following day while Vittore was out, and then something Wendy said made her steel herself against softening.

'Mrs Stone,' she began while she was taking dictation in Helen's office, 'I hope you don't think I'm turning into a spy, but I can't help noticing that Mr Fabri is spending a lot of time talking on the phone to the Honourable Ophelia Hadgraft. I – well, just thought you ought to know, that's all. Happen there's nothing in it. Did they know each other before?'

'No, of course they didn't,' said Helen hastily. 'I introduced them.' Suddenly, though, her mind resurrected the scene of that introduction, and the prolonged greeting between Ophelia and Vittore which hadn't appeared very natural. 'I'm sure there is some perfectly ordinary explanation of these phone calls,' she added, and reflected that she herself was dissembling now.

Helen was too busy catching up on a backlog of deskwork to pay much heed to Wendy's information. When, during the afternoon, an agitated phone call from Mrs Hartley brought the news that Neil had fallen from a wall in the garden, hitting his head, everything else was driven from her mind.

Telling Wendy that she was popping home to check if Neil needed a visit from the doctor, she dashed out of the office to her car.

Neil seemed chirpy enough now he was over the shock of his fall, but Helen played safe and called the doctor in. After checking the boy thoroughly and reporting he was ninety-nine per cent certain there was no real damage, the doctor suggested a few hours' rest for him.

'You look as if a rest wouldn't come amiss for yourself either, Mrs Stone.'

She laughed. 'I'm fine, Doctor, honestly. I do have to keep going, but that's the way I like my life.'

'Not too many gaps that way, since you were widowed, eh?'

Helen agreed. 'And even before then I was never one for sitting around doing nothing.'

That surely still applied today, and once Neil was settled in his room with Mrs Hartley hovering, her ears alert, Helen decided to return to the office.

Waiting for a gap in the traffic enabling her to drive out on to the main road Helen was staggered to see Ophelia's car again, and even more staggered to recognise Vittore Fabri in the passenger seat.

This can't be coincidence, she thought. It just isn't likely that she would turn up over there by chance and give him a lift.

This time, she resolved, I shall get to the bottom of what's going on. All the way back to the office she was steeling herself to demand an answer to the questions mounting inside her.

Other cars had come along after Ophelia's, preventing Helen following immediately behind them, but they were still in sight when she approached Luddenden Foot. The surprise came when she watched Ophelia continue along the main road rather than turning right for Stone's office.

So he's not even putting in a full day's work! she thought angrily. And grew angrier still as she realised this meant postponing her own questions.

By the next morning she couldn't wait a moment longer, and tackled Vittore as soon as he walked into the office.

'You didn't think it necessary to report back here yesterday after your visit to Todmorden then?'

'It was too late, I'm afraid. Trouble with the buses.'

'It was approximately three-thirty when you were passing through Brearley. And if that was a bus, it was a very splendid affair – and with Ophelia Hadgraft at the wheel.'

Vittore paled before a flush crept upwards from his immaculate shirt collar. 'But I did not see . . . where were you?'

'Just leaving the house. Neil had had a nasty fall.'

'Neil? Oh, I am sorry. How serious?' he began, but his eyes were veiled and the enquiry sounded automatic rather than concerned.

'Not very, fortunately. But I'd been home to call the doctor in to see him. That is why I wasn't where you expected,' she added sharply.

'There is nothing to cause you annoyance. Ophelia merely happened to be returning in the same direction.'

'Very convenient. Or it would be if I believed you. It's time you came clean, Vittore.'

'Came clean?' he enquired, feigning bewilderment.

'Told me the whole story,' she snapped. 'Like what's going on between you and Ophelia Hadgraft.'

Vittore stiffened, alarmed. How much did Helen know of what had happened months ago, while his wish to avoid Alexander Stone was preventing him from contacting her? Had she discovered that he had written from Italy to the man who had been so impressed by his command of English during the war? Colin Hadgraft.

Hoping that Hadgraft might provide useful introductions, he had been shaken at first to learn of his death. But the man's sister had written back in such genial terms that he had asked her for advice on the situation over here, including any information as to how Stone's was progressing. With Ophelia's second reply, Vittore had begun to believe his luck was turning.

The news was that Helen, now alone in the firm, was making a name for herself, to such an extent that Ophelia's investigations had prompted her to invest capital in Stone's. With Ophelia as an ally, and his own influence over Helen already established, he had believed there would be no boundaries to his future here.

He could not relinquish all that; he must bluster this out or risk being finished.

'What do you mean? You cannot be objecting to my being acquainted with her – she is a shareholder in Stone's. You yourself chose her.'

'And you seem to have become very friendly with her in a short space of time. Unless – *did* you know her before you joined the firm, Vittore?'

He was staring at her now, the dark eyes glittering with ill-contained fury. Helen guessed this was because of her having spotted some connivance, but his response gave her no more than a clue that she was correct.

'What right have you to question my friendships?' His voice was rising. 'If I knew Ophelia already, that is my concern, not yours.'

'And you did, didn't you?' Helen said, wondering what else he had been keeping from her since returning to England, and for what motive.

'We were already acquainted yes,' Vittore admitted at last.

'Did she tell you about Stone's?'

'Do not be stupid, Helen. You were the one who told me, years ago at the farm.'

'I don't mean that. Did she inform you that I was on

my own here, badly in need of capital?'

'I wanted to work with you, and I brought in money that you needed, isn't that sufficient?'

'Not when you're concealing things from me. Even though I don't understand your purpose in doing so. I can't work like that, Vittore,' she told him earnestly. 'What made you come back to Yorkshire? What made you choose Stone's?'

'I have told you, yours is the sort of practice where I wish to work. *Mama mia*, I have put capital into the firm, not taken money out! I cannot understand why you are creating such a scene.'

His mentioning the money for a second time in as many minutes distressed her, and made her more determined still to have the truth. 'Can't you? I should have thought that was obvious. You're making me wonder what is happening within my own practice.'

'How like a woman! This is business, Helen, you cannot logically expect to know all the details of everything.'

'When it affects the way that business is run, I can. And you had better believe me.'

'Have I been neglectful of my work? Have I ever? I tell you what is wrong, you are jealous of my private relationships. Have I no right to any life away from you?'

'This has no connection with your private life at all,' Helen stated icily. But she was already beginning to fear that the personal relationship once existing between them, and now displaced, was quite a factor in her distress.

The argument simmered to an uneasy halt, but only so that they might achieve some work that day. Much later, on her way home that evening, Helen began to understand how deeply she was wounded by Vittore's apparent deception of her. And to whom could she turn? She had scorned her accountant's advice when taking Vittore into Stone's, he would hardly sympathise now that she was perturbed.

The only good thing that day was the fact that Neil was his usual self, no worse for the fall, and full of all the things he'd been doing. He often seemed by now to be well able to amuse himself, although Helen was counting the weeks until he would be old enough for school. He would benefit from the stimulation of other children's company as well as the teachers'.

The necessity to put in a full day's work got them through the rest of the week at the office, and by the following Monday the atmosphere appeared to have returned to normal. Nothing in Vittore's attitude conveyed to Helen either resentment or the possibility that he might not be wholly loyal to her. And, these days, they seemed at last to be getting enough of the kind of work which was satisfying as well as made them a profit. Helen was thankful for a sort of truce between herself and Vittore; she couldn't afford to divide her attention when it still ought to be focused entirely on restoring Stone's to its pre-war success.

There was the Fenella March bursary also. For too many years Helen had been obliged to ignore her promise to put back the amount of money which had enabled her to study. Old Mr March was frail, but still hanging on to life. Although his other daughter had survived Nazi internment and had returned to live in Harrogate, he was always glad to see Helen who visited him whenever her commitments allowed. Her dearest wish now was to restore that bursary to its full amount while Mr March was alive to meet the next recipient.

By Christmas 1950 Marian had recovered sufficiently

to be able to get about her own home and, with the aid of a stick, to reach her local shops. Helen had invited her and Denis and the children to The Stone House where her parents would be joining them for Christmas Day. Kathleen Stone had declined the offer of a longer stay there.

'We need a bit of quiet on our own, these days,' she had explained. 'We're not getting any younger.'

Helen had nodded. She had been saddened to notice how the worry concerning Marian, to say nothing of the additional work, had aged their mother. And Daniel Clegg, never an ebullient man, often gave the impression of being weary.

'We love to see the kiddies full of energy, you know,' Kathleen had added. 'But we can only take all that noise and bounding around in small doses.'

When the time came, Helen wondered where her mother had gained the impression that any of the children would be exuberant. Both Linda and Mark had grown up a lot during their mother's illness and still were touchingly attentive to her.

'They really are a couple of loves, aren't they?' Marian exclaimed to her sister when Mark had offered her his arm as they came up the front steps of The Stone House, and Linda insisted on finding for her mother the most comfortable chair in the large reception room. They continued considerate throughout the stay, offering to fetch and carry, and playing quietly with the puzzles and games which they'd been given as presents.

For a four-year-old Neil was quiet also, but was disturbing Helen by reverting to his old uncongenial mood. He had demanded to be told why his Uncle Vittore wasn't there, not a question which she relished answering.

She hadn't expected that her terse reply that Vittore

hadn't been invited would satisfy, and it certainly didn't.

Neil's lip puckered as if he was going to cry, but what emerged was a massive wail of protest. 'You've told *him* now that we don't want him here, haven't you?' he accused her, his expression as well as his tone so reminiscent of his father that Helen itched to slap him.

'I haven't, Neil,' she replied through clenched teeth, the hands at her side equally tense. 'But you will have to accept that he has other friends, and isn't going to spend all his spare time with us.'

'But he likes me, I know he does,' her son insisted. 'It's only you that's nasty to him.'

Helen turned away. She hadn't needed any reminder of Vittore's absence, nor of the reason behind it. Ever since she had first begun to examine his behaviour regarding Stone's she had been compelled to question his motives in everything that had occurred since his return to Yorkshire. What of his apparent affection for her, his kisses, the warm embraces? Had they all been contrived towards the one end – that of having her accept him readily, not only as an architect with her firm but also a shareholder? Had even his attitude towards Neil been calculated as a way of ingratiating himself with her?

At any other time, she'd have found such possibilities cruel. At Christmas, with every corner of her home resurrecting memories of his being here a year ago, they felt unbearable.

For Marian's sake, however, Helen willed herself to set aside this ache that seemed to eat right through her. Her sister, Denis and the family were only just emerging from their own great anxiety. It was up to her now to ensure that they enjoyed the festivities.

Marian wasn't blind, though, and soon saw that Helen was far from happy.

'You've given us a lovely time, bless you,' she said on Boxing Day, 'but I'll be hanged if you look to be enjoying yourself. Is it because of Vittore? He's conspicuous by his absence.'

'Aye, it's him,' Helen admitted now that she was alone with her sister. 'Though not just because he isn't here. I don't mind you knowing that I think he's up to something to do with the firm.'

'To do with Stone's? Nay, he'd never! He's got money tied up in it now, hasn't he?'

'He has that, and I'm almost beginning to wish he hadn't.' She told her sister she felt sure that Vittore wasn't being straight with her. 'There's nowt much that I can put my finger on, a lot of it daft stuff like catching him and Ophelia Hadgraft with their heads together, but I'm sure he's up to something.'

'But what could he do – what would he want to do other than ensure that you continue to do bigger and better business?'

'Eh, I don't know, Marian, I really don't. Happen it's me that's wrong. It is mostly just this uneasy feeling.'

As soon as they were into the new year Helen's suspicions only grew stronger, yet still there was nothing concrete on which to base any further complaint against Vittore. She began arranging more frequent meetings in which the two of them and Ophelia discussed present and future projects. Her idea was that this might tighten their ship, permit fewer loopholes by which either he or Ophelia could manipulate things to her disadvantage.

If these meetings achieved this end Helen couldn't be sure, but what they did reveal was the affinity between the other two. Sometimes in an odd word or so which crept in, more frequently in glances which she intercepted, the evidence of a strong association between the pair grew steadily stronger.

As well as hurt, Helen felt rather foolish. No one enjoyed having advantage taken of them, and she felt positive this was what had been intended all along. She was also once again becoming reluctant to spend too much time out of the office. Wendy still reported anxiously that Vittore often telephoned Ophelia Hadgraft when Helen's back was turned.

She soon learned that although Vittore had lost his direct influence over her, he now had found another tack.

They were discussing the Festival of Britain. Although the style involved in much of the scheme wasn't really to her taste, Helen had once been keen to be one of the vast number of architects involved. The Dome of Discovery might not be to her liking, but from its plans it would seem to be the largest unsupported dome in the world. That, and other constructions on the site, would engage a lot of interest. Neither Vittore nor Ophelia had agreed to Stone's participating. They had given no real reason, and Helen could never see any sense in their refusal to contribute to something which would bring not only work but a considerable amount of prestige.

And then one day Wendy came to Helen with an item of correspondence. 'As you can see, it's on our headed paper, but I swear I didn't type it, Mrs Stone.'

The letter was in Vittore's name and concerned Stone's intention of becoming involved in a construction connected with the Festival of Britain.

'No wonder he didn't want me to look into the possibility of our doing this!' Helen exclaimed. *He* had already done so ages ago, and without so much as consulting her.

The meeting which Helen then called became exceedingly unpleasant. When challenged, Vittore met criticism with attack.

'I was only doing what you should have attempted years ago,' he told Helen, while Ophelia smiled across the table. 'You shouldn't be condemning me for showing enterprise.'

'I wouldn't be, if you'd consulted with me first. That would have been common courtesy as well as diplomacy. The fact that you didn't do so only reinforces my unease about your attitude here.'

'Oh, surely, Helen,' Ophelia interrupted, 'you needn't be put out? Granted, it must be galling for you that Vittore has been so much more perceptive regarding the direction Stone's should be taking, but I do think you should concede that he has our best interests at heart. After all, men are more accustomed to these matters . . .'

Ophelia got no further in this uncharacteristic observation. Springing to her feet, Helen slammed both hands down on the table. She might have been gratified by the way the other two started if she hadn't been too furious to register their reactions.

'That is just the bigoted view that I've been fighting since 1932. I'm surprised at you, Ophelia – even if I'm learning now not to be surprised when you two connive against me. But I'll have you understand, both of you, that this most certainly isn't an attitude that I permit to inhibit me.'

'But, Helen,' Vittore began quite quietly, 'there is no need for you to become angry simply because I have had a good idea. What we must do now is develop it in the best interests of Stone's.'

'Never! I don't care how much we lose by it, this scheme is not going ahead.'

'You *should* care how much we might lose. You

could at least examine it in detail,' Ophelia pointed out. 'Vittore has put in a lot of work . . .'

It was Helen's turn to interrupt again. 'And Vittore knows that he should not have done so in the first place without a word of it to me.' She faced him now. 'You could at the very least have put me in the picture when *I* was talking about the Festival.'

'What are you going to do then?' he demanded, leaning back in his chair and regarding her with all the calm of generations of Italian men who had dictated to their womenfolk. Although his voice was steady, the look in his dark eyes was anything but.

Lord, but I wish I could just sack you, thought Helen. As things stood, she could only offer to buy him out – buy the pair of them out, that's what she wanted to do. And there wasn't a hope in hell of raising the cash to do so.

She breathed in slowly to steady herself. 'All we can do is put our minds, jointly, to keeping Stone's running.' But she was going to need a lot of convincing that she could trust either Vittore or Ophelia again.

Helen couldn't let her mistrust of her fellow shareholders shackle her to the office, preventing her going out to prospective sites. There was one in particular which seemed to hold out possibilities of becoming just her kind of job. A large parish in Leeds had obtained the necessary consent for construction of a new church hall. The original building had been commandeered by the military during the war and had suffered considerable internal damage. Since then a fire had rendered the hall so unsafe that it had been demolished. It had been specified that the external appearance of the new building must harmonise with the adjacent Victorian church.

She might have been dispirited by the behaviour of

Vittore and Ophelia, but she wasn't too demoralised to know that this promised to be a scheme after her own heart. She was going all out to get it.

The site on that Monday morning looked much as Helen had imagined: at the top of a hill but surrounded by densely positioned, mostly terraced, houses. The church was medium-sized with a spire, and built of stone now darkened by a century of smoke. The newly cleared area for the church hall was to its left, at a minor junction along one of the popular routes running eastwards out of the city centre.

Helen spent several minutes standing on the opposite corner, just looking. The proportions of the church itself weren't spectacularly good, but not unpleasing either; she reckoned she'd be able to echo enough of its lines to help coordinate the new structure to be built alongside it. The Gothic windows might be echoed as well, but in a simplified form and on a larger scale. She wanted the hall to have plenty of light.

After crossing to the site itself, she began examining available space, checking with an expert eye the dimensions that had been supplied. Water, electricity, and mains drainage had, of course, been present for the original hall and this lessened the matters needing consideration. She was soon leaning against the church wall while she roughed in her first few sketches.

Ideas were coming swiftly, a sure sign that her heart was in the project. As soon as she'd completed drawings of front and side elevations, Helen turned happily to conceiving the interior. She had been given instructions that there should be one very large room to accommodate a stage and provide space for social functions. Leading off from this should be rooms of varying sizes, suitable for the different grades of Sunday School classes and for meetings of organisations such as Brownies, Guides, Scouts and so on.

The flexibility she was allowed in planning these meant that she could enjoy playing around with her ideas. Before she had spent very long on site, she was beginning to realise that the possible combinations were endless.

I wonder if I ought to ask if they have more detailed requirements? she thought, and turned to hurry towards the church in order to try and find someone. Beside its west door, she saw the noticeboard on which the vicar's name had been painted out. It was then that she remembered being told that the parish was going through an interregnum, something about the new incumbent being unwilling to leave his present curacy until his vicar there recovered after a long convalescence. It seemed there was going to be no quick answer but rather a long wait while she learned if amendments to her proposed design were to be requested by the parish council.

Helen continued forward into the church, however, wishing to get the feel of the place as well as to ascertain whether or not there might be something in its internal styling which again could be echoed in the hall.

The first thing she noticed was incense, still so heavy in the air from the previous day's services that she almost could see its mistiness about the altar. Instantly, Helen recalled Einsiedeln's Abbey church and briefly shut her eyes. Much as she was enjoying today's task, she yearned to return to the spirit of looking forward which had been so much a part of her life in those days. Now she seemed to spend most of her time fighting – if not to survive the eternal struggle at Stone's, then to preserve the house and, perhaps most of all, to rear Neil as a son of whom she could be proud.

'I don't want anything so extraordinary,' she said

aloud into the empty church. 'I only want to do a satisfying job, and find a way of being the right kind of mother to my boy.'

Grimacing ruefully and giving her head a little shake, Helen hauled herself together and began looking about. The church appeared quite spartan, severely furnished, until she neared the altar. There, a reredos carved with saints and painted mainly in red and gold provided the backdrop for a splendid gold crucifix. The altar table was dressed ceremonially in richly embroidered fabric where gold and jewel colours enhanced the thick material of a pale cream shade. The colour combination seemed to be another reminder of that very different church in Einsiedeln.

What would it be like, Helen wondered, to worship here? To spend long enough in this place to at least stand the chance of absorbing . . . *something*.

But work was beckoning again. She'd gathered little in here that would influence her decisions on details of her scheme for the hall next door. Once she arrived home, however, she would begin the serious planning. And then she could find that the very absence of firm guidelines allowed her freedom to let ideas flow. As for this church and the feelings it had aroused here, there would be other times, other visits.

Chapter 19

By the time Helen reached The Stone House that evening, she was itching to begin drawing the initial elevations for the church hall. Even calling in at the office, she had been too impatient to linger over catching up on the day's events. After signing the letters Wendy had prepared and having a brief chat with Vittore about the drawings on which he was engaged, she had been glad to run out to the car.

Neil was going through a more cooperative phase and they often shared supper while he told her about his day. Marian was coming to The Stone House again but, because of her leg, only on alternate days. This had been one of them and Neil was full of all the things they had done together.

After their meal he demanded to be shown the 'pictures' that Helen had brought home with her, so before putting him to bed she took him into the study.

'This is a large building which I am designing,' she told him. 'If the people buy my plans, you can go over to Leeds with me while it is being built. You'll be able to see it growing then.'

Sitting at the desk which Alexander and his father before him had used, Helen glanced sideways at her son. Neil's golden head was bowed in concentration, and his young face wore a half-smile of interest. She was reminded suddenly of an advertisement she had seen long ago of a lad with – was it a Meccano set? She had wished at that time for such a boy, for the opportunity to help shape his future. Would Neil follow his parents' inclinations? she wondered. She'd be happy to think of him continuing the Stone tradition.

The firm, however, seemed to have little prominence in her mind while she began on these church hall plans. Consulting the initial briefing again, she became absorbed in the requirements of that parish in Leeds, and grew so content in her work that she thought not at all of the publicity securing the commission might win for Stone's.

One aspect of the hall's use particularly interested her, and could have helped facilitate the granting of a licence to build. The parish as a whole and, evidently, the prospective new incumbent, were keen to incorporate a youth centre. From what she'd heard, they would cater for people not only of school age but those beyond who were either unemployed or for other reasons had too much time on their hands. In a city the size of Leeds, Helen could believe that would prevent many youngsters falling under bad influences.

All this, together with the ideas forming earlier that day, was running through her head while she completed elevations and began early drawing up of plans. As she continued to spend every spare moment on the project, Helen grew increasingly conscious that this, more than anything attempted in the past, was the work for which she had paid with all those long years of studying. This was *her* scheme above any other, yet she hadn't felt ready even to mention it in the office. And the night they were finished she was so eager to send off her early drawings that she used her private notepaper for the accompanying letter instead of waiting to pick up a few sheets of the firm's.

Vittore was working steadily on plans for council-built homes, and seemed remarkably quiet about his acceptance of this job which gave so little scope for his talents and ideas. Helen couldn't rid herself of the feeling that he was biding his time. The fact that she couldn't for the life of her think what he might be awaiting failed to quash this impression, even if it did leave her feeling she might be guilty now of misjudging him.

The day it all blew up began badly at home. Neil had developed a heavy cold which made him miserable and whiny. Dragging herself away from him was difficult, and certainly not helped by its not being a day for Marian to visit.

Only on the way to the office did Helen recall that she had arranged a meeting with Vittore and Ophelia for ten-thirty. Ever since their first disagreement she had dreaded each meeting as it approached. The number which had passed without altercation had done nothing to reassure her, reinforcing instead her own fear that she was becoming obsessive in her supposition that they would come to an ultimate confrontation.

Today, however, Vittore seemed his old genial self, and when she mentioned that Neil was unwell his sympathy appeared genuine. I'm being silly always looking for trouble, she thought, and was encouraged again when Ophelia came in chatting animatedly about her drive over and the late hour at which she'd left some function the previous evening.

It was that function which turned from a casual topic of conversation to the source of Helen's disquiet. It soon became evident that Vittore had attended with Ophelia, and that it had been hosted by a major local construction company. Helen could feel her eyebrows soaring. Because architects were forbidden to advertise, making themselves known around was a matter of seizing every possible opportunity to publicise their work. If, as it seemed, these two had been representing Stone's, she wanted to know why – and why Vittore had evidently taken it upon himself to do so without her agreement.

'Did the invitation come to you personally?' Helen asked him, deliberately keeping her voice even.

'I know that you don't like to leave Neil of an evening,' he began steadily enough, though his dark eyes were evasive.

'Don't prevaricate with me. I believe in straight answers.'

When he didn't respond Helen rose from her seat, excused herself and went to find Wendy.

'I gather there was some kind of reception last night which Mr Fabri attended. Did the invitation come to this address?'

'Oh, yes, Mrs Stone. But Mr Fabri told me he would be attending, that it was all right because you'd said you didn't want to.'

That was enough. Helen strode through to join the others. 'A pity you chose to air where you'd been, Ophelia. If I'd been kept in the dark altogether, no one would have been any worse off. As it is, I'll remind you what I've said in the past.'

'But I was there for Stone's, we both were,' Vittore protested. 'Keeping our name before that particular construction company, seeing that we remain in line with our competitors.'

'You seem to forget that we're a team, that we should work together and not have one member excluded from *any part* of the life of the firm. Whatever do I have to say to convince you that I am determined to be consulted!'

'But this is such a small matter, Helen,' Ophelia put

in. 'Hardly worth your notice. We know you reserve evenings for family. All we did was go to a bit of a party.'

Helen, who had just seen from the invitation that the function was large enough for a civic hall, grew more furious still. She decided, however, to shelve the matter in favour of something more productive. There was nothing she could do here and now to rid herself of this contention. She needed time to think, and maybe to seek advice.

Over the next few weeks Vittore tested Helen's reaction on a series of occasions by leaving her out of consultations and decisions. After keeping silent for a time while he, and to a lesser degree Ophelia, made plain their desire to oust her, Helen concluded that she must make radical changes. She wasn't going to work like this.

She was bitterly hurt by having her trust in Vittore shattered. It seemed as if ambition had altered him completely, turning him so ruthless that he would go to any lengths to take the firm over. He wasn't a bit like the man who'd returned to England, and didn't resemble the one who had meant such a lot to her during the war.

If she could have, she would have raised sufficient capital to buy out the pair of them. But that would only have been possible by mortgaging The Stone House and that – to Helen – was Neil's heritage, sacrosanct.

The alternative, and one which she doubted would be approved by anyone, much less her solicitor or Mr Thorpe her accountant, was to sell her shares and get out.

Recent months had taught Helen to conceal her intentions. She began speaking in the office of wishing to spend more time with Neil during these formative years. She must, after all, act as father as well as mother to him. There was the difficulty also, since Marian's illness, of often having to leave him with either her mother or Mrs Hartley. Now that they were ageing, this was taxing for them and wasn't especially good for the boy. Helen surprised herself with the extent to which she could emphasise her reluctance to commit her time so completely to Stone's.

Pretending to care less about the firm was one of the hardest things she had ever attempted. Each time that she walked into the office, she steeled herself to give nothing away. Within her own family, she was aware of arousing curiosity by this attitude she seemed to be assuming towards her work. Here, she must exert even greater effort to assure Vittore of these new intentions. To put him off guard.

Meanwhile, working from home and among her many business contacts, she was strengthening her personal prestige. She was determined that as soon as she relinquished the reins here she would have everything ready for the next step in her career.

The day that she offered her shareholding to the other two, they were astonished, but they recovered within the week. And, presumably after putting their heads together, they made a joint bid for Helen's stake in the firm.

By the time they had been persuaded to raise the offer to a sum which she was prepared to accept, Helen was beginning to come round to believing that a life away from Stone's was possible.

But when the transaction had gone through and the day came for her finally to leave the office, she felt devastated and sick. Vittore had let her down so fearfully, changing from the man who had seemed to share so many of her interests and priorities into a schemer who wanted only to take over her business. It seemed a long time now since she had been fond of him, but memories of that affection too were plaguing her as she cleared her desk.

She was taking with her that desk, which had once been Joseph Stone's, and the draftsman's desks that she and Alexander had used.

'I can't leave them here,' she'd told the other two. 'They belong to our family.'

Saying goodbye to Wendy was as hard as anything. She had been an efficient, helpful secretary. Helen just wished she could take her with her.

Wendy was in tears when the parting came. 'I can't see me stopping here much longer, not when you've gone.'

Helen was surprised. There still wasn't full employment after the difficult years that had followed the ending of the war.

'Let me know if you do decide to leave, I might be able to help.'

Wendy gave her a curious look. 'But – do you mean looking after your little boy? I'm afraid I don't know so much about kids . . .'

Helen smiled, gave her a hug. 'Let's just see, eh?'

Passing the small house where she and Alexander had begun their married life, Helen realised even more deeply how a whole era was ending. She had fought a lot, struggled, but had also learned a great deal. And perhaps mostly about herself, and this ability she was acquiring to ensure that she mastered future opposition.

For a month, Helen seemed to devote herself entirely to her family, spending more time than she had for years with her parents. She relished playing with her son, teaching him new skills, and all during hours when normally she would have been at work. She spent more time with Marian, Denis and their children, and availed herself of theatre tickets which he offered. Sitting in the Grand Theatre, she compared her memories of that splendid new theatre in Stratford, where her ambitions had been nurtured, with this out-moded but still popular centre of repertory in Halifax. And somehow the company here seemed more deserving of credit for surmounting obstacles created by inadequate funding.

Underneath all this outward relaxation and time with the family, however, she was putting in the groundwork for her future. Mostly in her head, but also through contact with builders and others within the construction industry, she was asserting that Helen Stone wasn't finished.

And Helen Stone was the name under which all her new designs would be produced. Architects might not advertise, but she was delighted to discover that her name had already begun to mean something. Her greatest satisfaction came on the day she heard that the first project which would prove to everyone she was still very much in business would be the church hall for which she was being contracted.

I might win yet, she thought happily, for once submerging the very real dread that not enough business would come her way. Relying entirely on herself was at once reassuring and something of a weight. She now had behind her the capital raised by selling her shareholding in Stone's, though she had learned during these past few years how a house the size of theirs swallowed up money.

The Stone House, however, was now to play its part in the future she was mapping out for herself and Neil. She already had the study and was turning the sombre dining room into an office. Helen Stone's architectural practice would function from here. She felt certain Joseph would have been glad to see clients meeting her in rooms that he'd designed. She nodded approvingly when she'd installed desks and drawing boards, and placed filing cabinets against the panelled walls.

Working with Neil so close at hand was the proverbial bane as well as blessing. On days when Marian was unable to come out to them, Helen was glad to be there, lessening the responsibility which fell upon either her mother or Mrs Hartley. But both she herself and the boy had to exercise considerable discipline to ensure that some work was accomplished.

The day that building work on the church hall in Leeds began, Helen came home really elated. For the first time in months she felt on top of the world, and the enquiries which she had received since setting up again on her own seemed to indicate that this scheme would soon be followed by others. In the meantime, she had been asked to design a private house just beyond Mytholmroyd, one of the few for which a licence had been granted. Providing that she satisfied the potential owners, her fee would mean that she could face the next six months without dipping into her capital.

'We're going to be all right, love,' she told Neil that night. 'Even though there's only you and me now, we shan't have to do without anything.'

Neil, of course, was too young really to understand, but he did recognise that his mother was happier and therefore the whole atmosphere of the house was improving.

Helen kept her promise to take Neil along with her occasionally when she visited the church hall site. He seemed to enjoy getting thoroughly dirty there, and loved winning the attention of some of the building workers. He had learned some discipline by this time, and knew to obey when told he must keep out of the way.

'I want to make houses,' he confided one evening while they were driving back to The Stone House. 'I want to stick the stones on top of each other like the men do.'

Helen smiled sideways at him. 'You mean you'd rather do that than design the way they must be built, love?'

'Yes, 'cos you have more fun building.'

'Well, we'll have to see, shan't we? You'll soon be starting school, then there'll be all sorts of different things to interest you. You might end up wanting to do something else altogether.'

'No, I won't, Mummy. I'm going to make all the houses that you draw.'

Although she knew this was all just a childish fancy, Helen was nevertheless pleased. She couldn't have done all that badly as a mother if the lad would look forward to working with her.

For the present she was so happy with the way the church hall was taking shape that she could hardly keep away from the site. She had to force herself to ensure that she spent time making certain that new business continued to come in.

The evening that Wendy telephoned her, Helen was quite surprised. She had thought – and indeed had hoped for the girl's sake – that she would settle back into the routine at Stone's once she became accustomed to the new set-up. It soon was plain that this wasn't so.

'I've given in my notice, Mrs Stone. I couldn't stand another week there. That Ophelia Hadgraft is never out of the place now, and it isn't as if she does anything . . .'

'Except help to pay your wages,' Helen reminded her, trying to be fair.

'Oh, that. Any road, it's the way them two carry on that makes me sick. And I'll bet she's nearly old enough to be his mother. Did you know that it was through her that he got to know about you being left on your own an' all that?'

'Well, I can't say I'm surprised. They might have kept quiet about it for a while, but it had become evident that they were well acquainted before Vittore started work there.' Helen paused. 'Have you found another job then, Wendy?'

'Not yet. Haven't really started looking, though. All I wanted was to get out. I finish there on Friday.'

'Well, I can use some help here, although I have to say that I can't employ you full-time as yet.'

'That doesn't matter. I'd love to work with you again, you know that. You're working from home now, aren't you?'

'And loving it. I'd be very happy if you could join me.'

'I certainly will. I'll start on Monday if you like.'

Having Wendy there was good, leaving Helen free to concentrate while telephone calls were answered and letters written. And when she went out on business Helen was glad to know somebody was there, in control. Mrs Hartley was too nervous about business matters to be relied on to take more than the simplest of messages without becoming worried, and was growing too old to be schooled into adapting. Most of all, though, Helen appreciated Wendy's supportive manner.

The long years of training followed by others of being compelled to concentrate on her work had left Helen without any real women friends. Normally, this didn't trouble her unduly, especially since she and Marian had grown close, but she found that having another woman around was very enjoyable.

'I feel years younger suddenly,' she confessed one day when they were sharing a laugh over the strange phrasing of a letter that had come in that morning's post.

Helen could afford to feel light-hearted; the church hall was completed, and the local publicity it was earning her had already produced several enquiries regarding designs for similar buildings.

'I might even go to that,' Helen told Wendy a few days later when an invitation arrived for the opening of the hall.

'Well, of course you must,' Wendy insisted.

'I'll have to see. You know what I'm like – not used to socialising these days.'

'Were you ever?' asked Wendy wryly.

Helen grinned. 'You know me too well!' she admitted, wondering how or why she had accepted having so little social life.

She resolved there and then that she would attend that ceremonial opening.

Driving to Leeds on that afternoon in May, Helen felt strangely excited. And if an element of trepidation was present it seemed to be tempered with anticipation of seeing the hall furnished and joy to have it finally in use.

Entering, Helen paused just inside the front doorway, looking about her. Wide steps led up to the double doors of the main hall, while others to either side of them led down towards the cloakrooms. Before going through into that large main room, she glanced to each side of her, noting the doors that gave on to two of the smaller rooms.

The big hall was what most interested her, however, and she stood just inside the doors, gazing upwards to the windows and then all about her until she glanced towards the stage.

She was beginning to smile. It seemed almost perfect, she was compelled to acknowledge that the design was good, and it had been constructed exactly as she had visualised it. Now she saw it with people filing in to fill the rows of seats she experienced a curious sort of humility, as if she were scarcely able to believe that she was responsible for its planning.

Agreeing to attend, Helen had declined the invitation to sit with the dignitaries who would occupy the seats arranged on the platform. She felt quite conspicuous enough when shown to the place reserved in the front row for her, and she wanted to be free to experience this day without fear that all her emotions would be on show. Creating this hall, especially whilst struggling to overcome all the trouble within Stone's, had been quite a triumph. If she lived to be ninety and worked all the while, she'd never feel that any other place was quite so important.

The group of young musicians filed in first, playing guitars and recorders, violins and brass instruments. As soon as they had mounted the short flight of stairs leading up to the stage, they were joined by a further band of young people, many of them of Caribbean, Indian or Pakistani origin. All were unified by their unqualified joy. Their song, delivered with all the verve they could muster, filled Helen with a pang of sheer pleasure. Somewhere behind her a voice whispered these were the children belonging to the Sunday School. She felt glad to participate in their evident satisfaction that they belonged here.

When the last chords of their song died to silence, a middle-aged man stepped forward.

'As many of you know,' he began, 'I've been in charge of this group of young folk for years while I've been the superintendent of their classes. I've watched their predecessors grow up, and have seen some of them with children of their own. Never before have we had such a fine home for our Sunday classes, and we've certainly never had so splendid a place for concerts and the like. Today being special, we want to thank a lot of people who've made this possible. We also wish to welcome our Lord Bishop who is performing the act of dedication for us. And we are particularly pleased that our new vicar, Christopher Maitland, has at last torn himself away from his old parish!'

It must be a coincidence, thought Helen, so shaken by hearing his name that she couldn't pay any heed to the man who was continuing his speech with a welcome to the Lord Mayor. Christopher was a Catholic, a priest, not an Anglican vicar . . .

And now the city's Mace Bearer was leading in the procession. A fraction after everyone else, Helen rose to her feet. But she couldn't look, couldn't bear the depth of disappointment that she would feel learning he wasn't the Christopher she knew. Fixing her gaze on the hands clasped in front of her, she kept it lowered until she had heard out the movement of feet and the last scrape of a chair as they were all seated on the platform.

Only then did she permit herself to look.

It was Chris. Older, much older than she had expected, bespectacled, but unmistakably the Chris who had seemed to be a part of her life ever since that first short meeting. Her heart gave a distinct jolt. She glanced furtively to those on either side of her, wondering if they could have noticed.

The mayor was speaking. Helen couldn't take in more than the odd phrase. When he mentioned the high standard of the building's design she would have missed his words if it hadn't been for recognising her own name. And then, before she'd begun to recover her ragged composure, it was Christopher's turn to address them.

His voice was almost exactly as she recalled, so familiar that she ached to turn back the years and establish some sort of understanding. The only difference seemed to be that, these days, she could discern more forcefulness in it.

'How fortunate I am,' he began, 'to be commencing my ministry in this parish with such a marvellous crowd of people and in such a grand setting. As some of you are aware, I am particularly concerned for young folk – it's heartening to hear how well they perform together. Indeed, when they combine so well to make such music, I wonder if I'm going to be superfluous!' As laughter died, he continued: 'Seriously, though, I am extremely happy to be here at last. I know that these youngsters performing for us today consider this their "thank you" for these splendid premises. I know how hard they too have worked towards this end, helping to raise funds, warming everyone with their enthusiasm, and challenging others to work to produce just that bit more than anyone thought possible. And so now we have this magnificent hall. I trust that I, along with all of you, will continue their example and good work as we get on with the life of our parish.'

Briefly, Helen closed her eyes. She had designed this for him without knowing it; she had created this building, in which even her astute eyes could detect no fault, for Christopher. It seemed to her that she had worked through every one of the intervening years since they'd met for precisely this purpose.

She opened her eyes as the next speaker began addressing them. Chris was looking straight at her. She would never forget the delight shining in those sherry brown eyes, and bringing a smile to his rather austere face.

He came straight towards her after the bishop's blessing. For what felt like a full minute or more he stood before her, tall and lean, gazing hard into her eyes. And then he took both her hands in his strong yet slender fingers. 'Helen.'

She tried to answer, and couldn't. She simply looked at him, all the emotion contained for so many years gleaming in her grey eyes. Life might have aged them both a bit, nothing else had altered.

'We must talk,' he asserted firmly. 'After all this time, we've got to. And especially because you're responsible for this splendid place. Do you have to rush away? I'm afraid I'm expected to work, help keep things going . . .'

Smiling, Helen nodded. 'I'm sure. And I won't just disappear. There's no rush. My sister's looking after Neil – he's my son.'

Momentarily, the brown eyes clouded. Chris recovered swiftly. 'I'll extricate myself quickly from the others.'

He settled her at a table with the mayor and two or three councillors and their wives before walking away. Helen watched him.

All the time she was struggling to make conversation with the local dignitaries, her glance followed Christopher about the room. Every few paces, he paused to talk with someone. It might be a fur-coated lady who obviously was well connected, or maybe a shabbily dressed woman trailing a bunch of kiddies, but always he had the same ready smile, the same genuine interest in them. He would be the ideal vicar.

When he stopped to speak with the youngsters who had led the singing, she felt emotion choking her. Eagerly, they surrounded him, clearly warming already to the new incumbent to a degree where they weren't in the least awed by his clerical collar. She saw him bend down towards a little girl and give a mischievous pull at her braided hair. And she heard the immediate laughter as the girl and a couple of her friends retaliated by tugging at the short cape of his cassock.

'Ready?' Christopher said to her at last. They made a circuit of the room so that, beginning with the mayor, she could say goodbye to every important visitor.

'I'll see you to your car,' Chris offered then, taking her elbow as they left the room. In the entrance hall he grinned. 'Must preserve some show of decorum. Though actually I'm so thrilled I could toss away all caution and hug you.'

'I wish you could,' she admitted straightforwardly. 'Oh, Chris . . .' And suddenly she blurted: 'You're not Catholic, are you?'

He grinned. 'Catholic, yes – Roman, no. High Anglican's the word. I'll explain if you like?'

'Not just now. I . . . Oh, none of this is making much sense! Aren't you staggered? I mean, with our meeting again like this?'

He spoke as they began descending the steps to street level. 'I have to admit that my surprise isn't quite total. As prospective incumbent here, I was shown all the plans for the church hall. In giving my wholehearted approval, I was happy to know that I was agreeing to a scheme which you'd originated.'

'So you knew it was me?'

'There'd been a photograph in the *Yorkshire Post* at the time you designed that block of flats.'

'You knew then that I'd become Helen Stone?'

He nodded, rather gravely. 'Look – do you have to be home by a certain time?'

'Not so long as I'm not alarmingly late. My sister's not all that brilliant these days. She had polio.'

'I'm sorry.'

'She's come out of it – well, not too badly, but is easily tired.'

Christopher nodded. He was willing his attention away from the rings on her left hand. They ought not to matter to him. He shouldn't have been alerted quite so forcefully to the fact that she hadn't said one word about her husband.

He cleared his throat. 'If you can spare a few minutes, we'll go across to the vicarage. It's just round the corner.'

The house was Victorian, a larger edition of the one which had been her first home with Alexander. Although it was rather drab in itself, Chris had chosen furniture that brightened the high rooms, and pictures which seemed to shout his love of beauty and light.

He took her coat carefully, making her feel that his concern was being expressed in the simple action, and reminding her as well of the moment, aeons ago, when he'd buttoned the collar of that other coat for her. Helen told herself sternly to remember how he'd have shown similar attention to any and everyone back at the hall.

'Your son is how old then?' Chris inquired, his face impassive as he indicated a comfortable chair.

'Neil's four now. A bit of a handful, I'm afraid. Not his fault really,' she added. She was going to explain about losing his father, but Christopher was speaking again, almost as though he did not wish to hear.

'Most youngsters are, or so I believe. I often wonder how I would have coped with my own . . .' And now, suddenly, how it might have been to bring up a family with you, he thought. He forced a grin. 'Just as well I never married!'

'But I thought – I always thought you weren't permitted,' Helen began, before remembering that he wasn't a Roman Catholic priest.

'Yes, that. Bit of a facer really at the time, being told it wasn't likely to work for me. When I was preparing for ordination our Superior cautioned me against vows of celibacy. Strangely, as it turns out, I might just as well have been bound by them. There you go.' He shrugged. 'Enough about me. What's all this about your being on your own as an architect these days? I was sure the firm mentioned at the time of those flats going up was Stone's.'

'It was. I let myself in for a right packet there, and no mistake. You wouldn't believe how gullible I've been.'

'I might believe you'd take people at face value.'

Helen smiled. 'Thanks. First of all it was some woman who wished to invest in the firm, and I certainly needed capital if I was to get Stone's re-established after the war and the difficult years that followed. Then I took on another architect – someone I'd known during the war. He's Italian. He put money into Stone's as well. What I should have guessed was that the pair of them were associates – I didn't grasp that for long enough. By which time they were making life so awkward that the only solution for me was to extricate myself. I can only thank heaven that this job came along at the same time . . .'

'So can I,' Chris interrupted fervently. 'And now we've met up again – what next? Will you meet me some other time, Helen? On a day when you're not heading home and when I'm not tied up with all those people in that hall back there?'

Chapter 20

Helen left without giving a reply. She needed to think. She felt today as if she would need almost as long to get used to seeing him again as it had taken for him to reappear in her life. All the way back to Brearley she passed through smoky towns and stone-built villages without really seeing any of them, only coming to herself as she drove through Luddenden Foot.

Marian met her at the front door. 'By, but you look as though going out has done you the world of good! You've got colour in them pinched cheeks again.'

Helen knew she'd have to tell her, she couldn't keep this to herself. 'Where's Neil? Is he all right if we leave him for a minute? I've got that much to tell you . . .'

'He's fine. Mrs Hartley's giving him his supper. She's keeping yours hot for you.'

'I'm late, aren't I? And you ought to be getting home.'

'Stop fussing, love. Linda and Mark will be okay. I told Denis to get the lady next door to sit with them if I wasn't back when it was time for the theatre. It's only for once, isn't it? And, by the look of you, it's been a once in a lifetime occasion. Were they suited with the hall now it's finished?'

Just for a second, Helen stared at her sister, barely comprehending. 'Oh, yes – yes, thanks. Everybody seemed thrilled with it.'

'But there's more to tell, isn't there.' It wasn't a question.

'Aye, there is. Come and sit down.'

They went through to the sitting room. Marian eased herself down into an armchair, but Helen was so excited and agitated that she couldn't stand still, let alone sit.

'You'll never guess who the new vicar is at that place,' she began, and then checked herself, smiling ruefully. 'Well, of course you won't – nobody would. I've never told any of the family, ever. It was years ago, before the war, when I went on that trip to see Italy and Switzerland. There's an abbey in the Swiss Alps – Einsiedeln . . . I met him there and it was like – well, just like you read about, only believe it doesn't happen in real life. We couldn't stop talking right from the minute we bumped into each other. We thought the same way about so many things.'

'Only?'

Helen swallowed, met Marian's curious gaze. She couldn't imagine what she must sound like, didn't believe she would be making very much sense. 'Only he was training to be a priest. I thought he meant Roman Catholic – calling it "priest" and all that. I didn't understand – not with us being brought up non-conformist – it wasn't till today that I really found out that the Church of England calls them priests an' all. Anyway, it was Chris who said then that we couldn't go on meeting over here. At that time, he did intend taking vows. Only in the end he didn't – take them, I mean. But he hasn't been married, not ever.'

'And you're on your own now.'

'Marian, I mustn't even think that way. I really mustn't. He's got his life, and I've got mine. And there's Neil . . .'

'Needing a father.'

'Don't, love, don't say it. I've no right.'

'No right to happiness? That's the top and bottom of what you're thinking, isn't it? Why, love, why for heaven's sake?'

'I don't know. It's just the way I am. Happen it's still to do with Alexander, the way things were when he set off that day.'

'Whether any of that was your fault or not, and *I* don't think it was, you've paid since. Every day of your life since he died. Are you going to go on paying for the rest of your days?'

'I don't know, Marian, I wish I did. I wish I felt really sure about something. Anything.'

'When are you seeing him again?'

'I don't know that I am.'

'Did he let you come away without suggesting it?'

'No, as a matter of fact, he did want to see me.'

'In another twelve or thirteen years again maybe? Is that what you're saying?'

'Don't talk daft.'

'It's you that's proper daft! Nay, Helen, what do I always keep telling you? We're not practising for summat. This is it – the life we've had given us. You're what – thirty-three? How much longer are you going to wait before you settle for being happy?' When Helen made as though to speak Marian continued forcefully: 'And don't tell me how happy you were while Alex was here – I know he never really understood you. You've earned a bit of pleasure by now if anybody has, and it sounds as if it wouldn't do yon chap any harm.'

Despite her sister's advice Helen remained undecided about seeing Christopher again. Undecided, yet yearning with her entire being to be with him. Knowing every cranny of that church hall and enough about the church to visualise it quite freely, she couldn't avoid picturing him there. Each and every one of her days was coloured with him, filled with the enormous ache to learn more about what the years had done to him.

So many of her questions had not been asked, such a large portion of the time keeping them apart remained a blank to her. Wondering ate into her concentration, making her work suffer, and this time no amount of will-power seemed to overcome this obstacle that rose so consistently between herself and the tasks which she should accomplish.

The letter came one morning while Helen was attempting yet again to put a bit of life into the elevation of a house she was planning. Chris had written at some length, asking her understanding when he explained that he couldn't bring himself to accept that their brief meeting must remain just a tantalising glimpse of each other's lives. Somehow, she could not imagine how, he had unearthed the fact that she was now widowed. His taking the trouble to find this out was enough to convince her of how earnest he was. He was suggesting a meeting on neutral ground, 'where neither of us need pay any heed to anyone's reactions but our own'.

Helen telephoned him that day. She had intended writing back agreeing to see him, but had been overwhelmed by the need to hear his voice. And his voice alone assured her that, no matter how great her own need, it was matched by Christopher's. When he confirmed how urgently he wished to see her, Helen felt emotion rising in her throat.

'Can you make it one evening this week?' he asked her. 'I've got a Confirmation class on Wednesday but the rest are free. I thought we might meet somewhere halfway, but I don't know where to suggest. I'm afraid I'm more familiar with the North Riding after spending so long there.'

'I don't mind where, Chris, so long as it's not too out of the way. I shall be working until after five.'

'Then we'll make it somewhere in your direction. I can get away earlier than you. I'll pick you up if you wish.'

Driving his pre-war Ford through Halifax, Christopher glanced about him as much as traffic conditions permitted. Wasn't this where she'd grown up, the place which had shaped the young Helen? Seeing the drab streets of terraced houses radiating from the main road, and the huge textile mills that towered over almost every street corner, he marvelled that she hadn't become tougher.

Though I suppose I'm just very thankful that she seems as vulnerable as ever, he thought.

That story the other day of how Helen had been conned by the folk who'd infiltrated her architectural firm had resurrected the old yearning to protect her. God knew that he'd be glad to provide some sort of anchor for her.

Leaving Halifax behind as he headed towards the Calder Valley, Chris was glad to see green hills. Some wooded, others with fields and meadows bisected by staunch drystone walls, they were visible between the mills which, even out here, pronounced this industrial Yorkshire. His heart soared with the steep hillsides, reminding him of the ever-present hope which never quite became trampled beneath work or burdens or distress. Enduring was so often the only thing required of anyone. And now he might at last begin to believe that he was being granted the opportunity for which he had longed.

It had seemed such a long wait, while he'd felt bound to remain in his old parish until his colleague was fully recovered. And all the time he'd been tantalised by the sight of Helen's plans for the church hall, by news of her visits to check how building work was progressing. Looking back now, it seemed almost that those months had been longer than the whole of the previous twelve or so years put together.

So preoccupied that he had ceased noticing road signs, Chris was nearly past the turning that Helen had described to him. Changing down with a merciless grating of gears, he drove the little car up the winding lane. Smiling now, he spared a moment to take in the lushness of the fields to either side, and the view over the valley to another slope equally pastoral. This was an appropriately beautiful spot for their reunion.

He rounded the next bend between the rough stone walls, and open wrought-iron gates revealed a curving drive with beyond that The Stone House. If it hadn't been so solitary in this site dominating the hill, he might have thought he was mistaken in believing this her home. He would have been much happier to think he was mistaken.

He had been an utter fool considering these fantasies of his might hold some substance. Helen had it all, hadn't she? The skill and the acumen to succeed in her own architectural practice, the son on whom she centred all her devotion and future hopes, and this. Material evidence that she enjoyed circumstances utterly different from the abstemious life which was his. He'd never before considered the meagre financial rewards of his vocation any great hardship. Suddenly they were overburdening.

If he hadn't felt so exposed to all those massive windows which seemed to scan his every weakness, he would have turned in the narrow lane and fled.

Helen was ready when she saw Christopher's rather battered car nosing up the drive. After dressing carefully in a mauve skirt and new softly draped white blouse, chosen because it was so different from her usual tailored style, she had made certain he wouldn't have to come into the house and wait. She wasn't reluctant to invite him in, but had decided it was too soon for a confrontation between Chris and her son. Neil could be difficult, and this evening mattered too much to run that risk.

She noticed as she ran out to greet him that Chris seemed pensive. She began telling him about her day, and the enquiries coming in now from other folk who wanted buildings that were in accord with older properties surrounding them.

They drove up Cragg Vale where they ate at an unpretentious inn, relishing the good country cooking and the quiet and anonymity in which to talk. Chris held forth for a while, unable to remain subdued for long now that they were together. He enthused about how well he was settling into his new parish, and emphasised how her splendid hall was reawakening a sense of community there.

'I could spend every evening there, if I wanted. So many organisations have resurrected now they've somewhere so perfect for gathering. But, as you might have noticed, it's the youngesters who take priority in my interest.'

'They seem an enthusiastic bunch,' Helen observed, happy just to be there watching how his brown eyes lit, and wondering why no one else she'd ever met seemed to glow with his particular fervour.

'They're that, all right, and when you consider that up to now they've spent too much time on the streets, that's some achievement. Most of the kids have mothers who work, and haven't had sufficient time given to them.'

'I'll bet you're glad to rectify that.'

He grinned. 'Well, I do admit to a firm belief that all most of them need is somebody to show enough concern and interest in them. But I'm sure you don't need me to explain that, especially since you've been trying to be father as well as mother to your son.' When she said nothing Chris continued: 'Why didn't you tell me you were on your own now? Your husband died, didn't he?'

Helen nodded. 'In a car accident over two years ago, yes. And the only reason I didn't mention it the other day was lack of time. It was all a bit of a rush, wasn't it?'

Christopher couldn't argue with that. It had mostly been rather in the public eye as well. The trouble was that since setting out today, knowing that they were finally going to meet away from everyone, he'd grown less able to picture himself expressing his emotions. Seeing that house had made him more inhibited still, acutely aware of how little use he might be to her.

'It was dreadful when Alexander died,' Helen began. 'I know fatal accidents always produce shock, but this was particularly bad. We'd parted on such rotten terms. I'm afraid I didn't love him enough – not to sacrifice my career, which was what Alexander wanted. I've thought since how he couldn't have been unaware of how little I did care for him. It's no wonder he'd cooled towards me.'

'Was it really that bad? Are you certain you aren't remembering only the black side?'

'I'm certain.'

'But you did your best. It wouldn't be you if you'd been guilty of neglect.'

Wanly, she smiled. 'Thanks. I just wish I could put it all behind me. But there's too much that keeps bringing it all back into focus.'

'Your son, you mean?'

'Neil, yes, though he's the one aspect I don't regret. But there's the house as well. You saw what it's like. It's not the kind of place that makes forgetting easy. Joseph Stone – he was Alexander's father – designed the place, and it's got both of them stamped all over every room. I wish sometimes that Neil was grown up, then it'd be his.'

'You can't wish your life away like that, Helen.'

Startled, she gazed at him. What was the alternative? she wondered. Living on this treadmill of designing, raising Neil, everlastingly trying to bring more business her way? Alone.

Gently, Christopher smiled. He was beginning to see where her greatest need lay. He was better at this than at expressing his own longings. 'Come on, let's walk.'

Leaving the car where it was, they strode uphill, side by side, while the head wind buffeted them and drove away anxieties.

At the brow of the hill they paused, gazing beyond the heather and scrubland towards the horizon, hazed now with heat remaining from the summer day.

'It's grand out here,' said Chris. 'Should free you of a few cares, at least.'

'It is doing, or is that your company?'

'I'd like to think . . .' He stopped, sighed, then faced her. 'Helen, I'm no good at this. But it is what I want more than anything – to have some part in making you feel better. Even if it mostly has to be only at the other end of the telephone, being there for you, sharing.'

'You always have.' She sensed how startled he was, and then she was telling him. It all spilled out, in ragged half-sentences: every time when she had remembered, and felt him near. And that Good Friday when she had seen him yet been denied a meeting. 'It did help,' she added fervently. 'I'd reached the end of my tether, but somehow that reminder of the beliefs that anchor you made me keep going.'

'I remember that day. It wasn't my own parish. I'd gone over rather reluctantly to deputise for someone who'd fractured a leg. I'd have preferred to spend Easter in my neck of the woods. But I can see now how it maybe wasn't just chance.'

Helen felt slightly alarmed, perplexed by his steady acceptance of merely being what seemed to her like a pawn in some almighty scheme.

Only Chris had been speaking more directly of how events had conspired to help *her*. And once again all his reservations were overwhelmed by the inner certainty that he must hold on to this contact newly restored between them. No matter about their very different circumstances.

'We can't let life continually keep us apart, can we, Helen? Even if it's to be only as friends?'

'I'd certainly hate to go for years without seeing you again. And though I often feel my life is too full of things that need my attention, I know there's plenty of room for improvement.'

Christopher was nodding. 'Something beyond the everyday, more than all the thousand and one tasks that crowd in on us.' He turned to her. 'Let's make a pact to give each other some time – because it's what we both want.'

They left it at that, agreeing as they walked back to the car that they would keep in touch. Approaching The Stone House, Chris again felt it dominating him, filling him with awareness of an unfamiliar inability to cope.

In a sort of desperation, he suggested that they should next meet on a Saturday. 'I'll let you know when I have one free of weddings. I'd love to meet your son. We'll give him a day out somewhere.'

* * *

Much as she ached to talk about Christopher, Helen kept to herself the spiralling emotions generated by their evening and the prospect of another outing. It all felt so new and insubstantial that she was afraid revealing too much might place a jinx upon their relationship. She had sensed that Chris was holding back which, despite all he'd said, made her determined not to depend too much on having him around in the future.

Regardless of her reservations, though, he had changed her life. I can hope again now, she realised. The wonder of having circumstances bring him back in touch was giving her a whole new outlook. Work flowed more easily, and designs that had been causing her trouble seemed now to cohere. Most of all, though, it was her will that had been restored, simply because future possibilities appeared limitless.

Her father noticed on the Saturday afternoon when she called to see him after Marian had told her that he was unwell.

'It's only a cold, the doctor says,' Daniel assured her quickly. 'There's nowt for you to be worriting about. Although I'm bound to admit it has pulled me down.'

Helen grinned. 'It must have if it's kept you from watching cricket today!'

'Aye, well – there's a keen wind, isn't there, in spite of that nice bit of sunshine. I've got to get myself better for work by Monday, you know. I've had two or three days off as it is.'

It was then that he remarked on how much brighter she was looking. 'You've had me worried, love, many a time. I don't say so much, I know, but that doesn't mean I'm not concerned. You've looked that drawn for many a year, and naturally it's got worse since you lost your Alex.'

Helen smiled reassuringly, and was thankful that she was able to tell him truthfully that she was feeling better now. 'I did have a lot on my plate, especially when the firm was causing so many headaches. I'm finding I'm better working on my own. Happen I'm not so good at getting on with other folk!'

Daniel frowned, taking her remark very seriously. 'Nay, Helen, I won't have that. You've made such a success of your job, and I'm sure you wouldn't have if you couldn't manage to get on with folk. Any road, you do seem to be making a go of it without anybody else, from what I hear.'

'I've certainly as much work as I can handle, Dad. I sometimes think I ought to be widening my scope, but that'd mean going further afield. I can't do so much of that till Neil's a lot older.'

Hearing his name, Neil peered around the door of the kitchen where he was helping his grandmother who was baking.

'I'm a lot older now,' he asserted, his grey eyes sparkling.

Helen and her father exchanged glances and laughed. Neil was joined at the kitchen door by Kathleen Clegg who grasped him firmly by the shoulder.

'But are you old enough to concentrate on what you're supposed to be doing?' she inquired, looking down into his grinning face. 'I'm not wearing myself out beating this cake mixture while you're standing there talking and doing nowt!'

Giggling up at her, Neil slipped a floury hand into her wrinkled palm as they turned away.

'He's a grand little lad, bless him,' Daniel told his daughter.

Helen made a face. 'At times! I just wish I could rely on him to be like this always.'

'Eh, he's all right. You don't want to make a cissy out of him.'

'Have I said I do? No, Dad – it's only that I want him to behave properly, to grow up boyish without turning downright rude like he is sometimes.' And, she added silently, I wish to goodness there was some kind of guarantee that he would respond well to Christopher's suggestion of taking them both out.

The more she thought about that day the more she wished that he hadn't been so eager to meet Neil just yet. She would have liked more time alone with Chris first, time in which to set everything else aside while they became thoroughly reacquainted with each other.

Christopher's feelings were just the opposite to hers. He suspected that Neil could be the bridge which would cross the abyss of what he thought of as his own shortcomings, and bring him closer to Helen. He had seen how complete her world appeared, but believed he could provide something that her son was lacking. And he liked kids, always had done, even while wondering how he'd have coped with any of his own.

Smiling wryly to himself as he sat in his study supposedly working on next Sunday's sermon, Christopher seemed to hear his own parents. Seeing them only very rarely since they had emigrated to farm in Australia, he remembered most of what they had said during his only trip out there.

Concerned by his evident need of a life partner, his mother had asked if he never longed for a family. 'You're not getting any younger, Chris, and with us so far away you're on your own too much already. What's it going to be like later on, when you're not able to get about so readily?'

'I have a very big family wherever I'm working,' he'd assured her. 'Dozens of young folk around me in the parish. I'll never want for company while one generation succeeds another. I feel privileged, do you realise that? They share with me their interests and their dreams. They relish all the activities we arrange for them, but I bet I relish them more – for all the warm-heartedness and fun they generate.'

'That's as may be,' his father had said. 'But it's not a man's world, is it? You'll be missing a lot if you continue denying yourself a man's decisions, the role he plays in taking responsibility for the folk under his roof. All this talk of relating to youngsters is fine and good, as far as it goes. But you're never with them long enough to tackle anything head-on.'

Chris might have disputed that, but had chosen not to. And he could believe there was a lot of truth in his father's observations. He admitted to himself that he hadn't lived the kind of existence that broadened someone's concept of family life. From a boys-only grammar school he had entered university and theological college, and the latter certainly hadn't provided any taste of a mixed-sex adult community. His war service as an army chaplain had seemed male-orientated again, very tough, especially in the desert. Having parents who'd lived abroad after he'd reached his late teens, it was many a year since he'd experienced life as a family member.

It was indeed to a rapport with Helen's young son that he was looking. He forgot himself when he was with children.

On the day that he set out to pick up Helen and Neil at Brearley, Chris was feeling elated. He had in the car an old football abandoned weeks ago by choirboys in the vicarage garden. And there was a kite which he'd purchased yesterday especially for Neil. In reserve, in case the lad grew tired, was a slate, still with its special pencil. Its source long-forgotten, it had survived since before the war and often provided amusement for youngsters who'd never seen anything of the kind. Helen might be thankful if he could coax Neil to be quiet while he and the boy concentrated on drawing or beginning to write.

Even his first sight of The Stone House today appeared less daunting now he was prepared for his meeting with her son.

When Chris drew up outside, Helen was in the hall trying to persuade Neil into fetching a sweater from upstairs rather than ordering him. She hurried to open the front door, burning with the knowledge that Neil was regarding her reproachfully from the sitting-room doorway.

'Come in, Chris,' she said, beaming. 'Lovely to see you again.' Over her shoulder she called to her son, 'Neil – come on now, here's somebody I want you to meet.'

Scowling, the boy remained where he was, half-hidden by the door. She silently blessed Christopher for crossing to him unhesitatingly, his hand outstretched.

'Neil,' she said, 'this is a friend of mine. I think you'd better call him Uncle Chris.'

'But he's not my uncle.'

Helen's hopes plummeted.

'I know I'm not,' Chris was saying, down on one knee to meet Neil at his own level. 'But I was hoping you'd sort of adopt me.'

Stonily, Neil stared back at him. 'I've got two uncles – there's Uncle Denis and Uncle Vittore.' And his clamped lips and stern expression conveyed his reluctance to entertain any idea of acquiring any more.

'Uncle Vittore, eh?' Chris snatched at a possible lead to conversation. 'It doesn't sound as if he's English . . .'

'He used to live here with Mummy.'

Helen held back an appalled gasp. And explaining the ins and outs of Vittore's visits would only make matters worse.

This introduction was failing miserably.

Christopher had succeeded in taking Neil's right hand, but it lay motionless in his large one, as if witnessing that the boy had no desire to cooperate even as far as a greeting.

Helen was itching to scold her son, even to shake some sense into him. These days, he wasn't normally this unsociable.

'This is *our* house,' Neil stated abruptly, grey eyes icy with disdain. 'My daddy won't let you stay.'

Shaken, Christopher turned instinctively to Helen.

'He has been told,' she said. It was some months ago now that she had finally brought herself to try again to explain to the child that what his cousins had said was true, and his daddy couldn't come back here because he had been hurt too badly to go on living. He had seemed to accept the facts at last, to put behind him all need to cling to whatever remained of Alexander in his young memory.

'Uncle Chris is taking us out for the day in his car, and we're all going to have lots of fun together,' Helen reminded him firmly.

'I don't want to go.'

'I've brought a football, and there's a kite for you.'

'Not for Neil, I think, Chris,' said Helen sharply, sickened by her son's behaviour. 'Not if you've any sense. He doesn't deserve them.'

'We'll see.' He smiled encouragingly at the boy.

One small foot darted out but before it contacted his shin Christopher had seized it. 'Now what?' he challenged.

Biting his lip, Neil clung to the door for support.

With his other hand, Chris detained Helen as she

approached, intent on punishing Neil. But she had had enough.

'Get upstairs this minute, Neil. Fetch your sweater off the bed, and then we are going out right away.'

To her relief Neil trudged away, albeit unwillingly.

'We may as well sit down,' she said, leading the way into the large reception room. 'I'm afraid he won't exactly hurry.'

Chris went to a sofa opposite the chair where she was sitting.

Helen noticed his worried look and sighed before speaking. 'It's ages since he reacted this way about his father, pretending he's still alive. I don't know what . . .'

'Don't you? He's being presented with another trauma – in human shape.'

'Good heavens, don't blame yourself.'

'I'd lay money on being proved right. I'm the threat to the status quo, the person who's intruding on his relationship with you.'

'Then he'd better learn to adapt,' said Helen. 'I'll be hanged if I'm going to spend the rest of my life being dictated to by my own son. He'll just have to wait till – well, I suppose till time or something else shows him that I'm not going to disappear.'

Chris smiled slightly, but without meeting her eyes. Not for worlds would he spoil things between mother and son. But it was good to know that the mother, at least, seemed prepared to accept a few changes.

When Neil eventually came stomping back down the stairs, Helen was glad to see Chris stepping forward to help him wriggle into the sweater. And the child actually accepted his assistance.

Going out to the car, though, Neil rather spoiled all that. 'What a funny old car,' he said scornfully. 'My daddy's is newer than that. And very big.'

'Well, I'm not rich,' Chris told him briskly. 'So this is the car that I have. Would you like to sit in the front?'

'No.'

'No, what?' Helen reproved him.

'No, I don't. I don't want to go in his rotten car at all. But you'll make me.'

Wordlessly, Chris folded forward the front passenger seat and indicated that Neil should get into the back. Although he complied, there was a wail of protest when his mother settled into the front.

'Mummy, Mummy, in here! In here with me.'

'No. You're behaving just like a baby. I don't want to sit with somebody like that.'

After several minutes of very audible sniffing while they drove along, Neil quietened and began looking out of the window. The hated car wasn't all bad – being smaller than many it was nearer to the ground and gave him quite a good view of the places and people they were passing. He began pulling faces. Unfortunately, no one seemed to notice.

'I hope you're not going to be terribly sorry that you wished a certain small person on yourself today,' said Helen quietly.

Chris grinned. 'I'll survive. He's bound to resent anyone who claims any of your precious time.' I wonder who that 'Uncle' Vittore was, he thought, and why he didn't last? Assuming that he wasn't still in the picture somewhere. He couldn't be jealous of someone who seemed to have had a relationship with Helen in the days before he himself had come back into her life, but he'd have liked to have known more. If only how far it had gone. Hadn't Neil said this Vittore had lived with her? Strange that. He wouldn't have thought she was the sort.

'Mummy, I've got to wee!'

Again, Helen sighed. 'Chris, I'm sorry – could you stop somewhere along here, please? I'm afraid with all the fuss back there I never checked that he . . .'

Christopher laughed. 'That's all right. I can draw in just here. There's a field with a gate. And at least he warned us.'

After that the day improved. Neil began replying when spoken to and by the time Chris parked at a spot high on the moors, was showing much more interest.

'Did you say you've got a football?'

Chris kicked the ball around with him untiringly while Helen sat among the heather, relishing the fresh air and the hills ranged for miles all about them, but most of all the sight of the two males whom she loved enjoying a game together.

They picnicked from a handy rock and Neil delighted in passing around plates and mugs, and behaving with all the charm of the well-mannered child that Helen had been hoping he might become.

Afterwards Chris demonstrated patiently with the kite and then helped Neil to handle it until shrieks of pure joy rose with the song of neighbouring skylarks.

Leaning back into the slope of the moors, Helen closed eyes that suddenly were pricking with happy tears. Never in her life had she felt more contented. Seeing Neil responding at last to Christopher's interest was such a relief. And as for Chris himself, she could hardly believe the good fortune which had ensured their paths should cross again.

I couldn't let him go, not now, she realised. I couldn't bear never to see him again.

Opening her eyes, she was just in time to see Chris hauling in the kite, and grasping her son's hand as they ran back to join her.

'We're going to rest now,' he announced, plonking

Neil down beside her before hurrying to the car to fetch the slate and pencil.

'What's that for?' asked the boy, frowning at the battered frame of the slate and turning it over to find that the other side was no different.

'It's a slate, to draw on,' Helen told him, and smiled at Chris. 'I used to have one of these, Neil, and your Cousin Linda did a lot of drawing on one. I don't know where Uncle Chris found this, but it's a long time since I saw any.'

'How about showing me how clever you are?' Chris suggested, lowering himself on to the ground beside them. 'Are you going to draw, or can you write your name now you're growing so fast?'

Neil, scowling again, examined the slate pencil then tested it by drawing a long line down one side of the slate.

The half-forgotten screech made both Helen and Chris laugh, but Neil's reaction was anything but amusement.

'That's horrible,' he shouted. 'I hate it!' He flung away both slate and pencil as hard as he could.

The pencil disappeared through low-growing bilberries. The slate struck rock and fell apart, the frame broken and the slate itself split in two.

Helen sprang to her feet. 'You hateful boy! That was very rude and ungrateful. That slate didn't belong to you, it wasn't yours to break. I won't have such awful behaviour.'

But Chris checked her by grasping her hand as she made to hasten past him. Still smiling, although concernedly, he shook his head at her.

'Leave it,' he murmured.

His steady brown gaze seemed to lock on to hers, while his expression told her that they shared too much for it to be destroyed by one small boy's aggression.

God, but I do love you, she thought. And yet she still seemed to feel apprehension gathering about her just as electricity might charge the air, presaging the storm that would ravage these tranquil moors.

Chapter 21

Exhausted by the conflicting emotions of the day, Helen decided on an early night. When Christopher left after having tea with them at the house, she took Neil straight upstairs.

'You were naughty today, and it's only thanks to your Uncle Chris that you didn't get the smacked bottom I was itching to give you,' she told him seriously. 'Now he might be patient with you, but I'm not going to be. You've been taught how to behave and I won't have you showing me up, especially when people are being kind to you.'

'Sorry, Mummy,' he murmured huskily, the eyelashes so like his father's suddenly fringed with tears.

Helen still felt disturbed by the time she went to her own bed, though there was more now to keep her awake. During the day, while they had been with Chris, she had been aware of him throughout the whole of her body. With each accelerating pulse and every tremor deep within her she had been conscious of the growing attraction between them.

Alone in her room, she longed to show him a bit of affection; to have him near, to trace the firm line of his jaw, to feel that crisp dark hair beneath her fingers, to have his arms round her. She longed to kiss those barely remembered lips, to cling as they had just that once in the past, and to have him touch her.

For hours she lay needing sleep, yet torn between surrendering to its calm and remaining with this awareness of being alive again, reawakened by him.

Towards morning she became troubled by misgivings. Wasn't she rushing headlong again, letting emotions overrule good sense? Had she learned nothing from the trauma caused by her poor judgement of Vittore? With him, there had been that long period of working together on the farm – yet she'd still had to discover the hard way how little she had really known him.

There was her disappointing marriage as well, the early years of working alongside Alexander had failed to reveal how ill matched they were. Now Chris had come back into her life after all this time without any contact between them. And here she was like a bit of a girl, preparing to stake all her happiness on their having a future together. She must slow down and *think* before setting the scene for a third disaster.

'I've always loved you though,' she whispered into the darkness where only trees stirring in the breeze interrupted utter silence. More than Vittore who once seemed to matter to me, she reflected, and more by far than I ever loved my husband.

Alongside this needing and this love there was also this great renewal of hope – again, because of Christopher. I'd never ask for another thing, she resolved, if we could make this relationship work.

Screams from Neil's room wakened Helen almost as soon as she began dozing. Struggling out of bed, she stumbled towards the door and, almost staggering with weariness, ran to him.

His eyes were dry, but they seemed the only dry thing about him. The bed and his pyjamas were saturated. She didn't need to ask why he was distressed.

'I'm wet, Mummy,' he announced unnecessarily, sounding indignant.

'And whose fault's that?' she demanded, before reminding herself that reprimanding him would solve nothing. 'Okay, let's have you out of there. Find some clean pyjamas while I change this bed.'

For night after night Neil continued wetting, and although Mrs Hartley calmly accepted all the extra washing, Helen could not concur with her opinion that it didn't really matter. She knew that it did, if only as a symptom of her son's disturbance. Neil had been an easy boy to train. She'd always been proud of how soon he was dry at night as well as during the day. And now this regression. She could only blame her renewed friendship with Chris and the changes it was producing.

Helen tried being particularly loving with Neil, spoiling him far more than she'd ever thought wise. He responded by becoming more demanding, pestering for new toys and trying emotional blackmail as a means of gaining more of her time. And he still wet the bed with distressing regularity.

Chris was keeping in touch with her by telephone, and suggested that she and Neil should come to him for a weekend. 'You've never heard me preach and it's our patronal festival on Sunday. I've got the whole of Saturday free. We could take a trip out, maybe up into the Dales.'

Helen wouldn't stay the night in Leeds, and made the excuse that she had work to do on the Sunday. She wouldn't explain about Neil's bed-wetting, not so much because it reflected on her but rather for her own certainty that it was on Christopher's account that her son had reverted to babyish traits. Chris himself was just as likely to reach that same assumption.

Having agreed just to go over on the Saturday,

Helen soon became convinced that she had made the right decision, if for different reasons. The minute that she'd told him their plans Neil retorted that he was not going to go and see Uncle Christopher.

'He's not my uncle, and I don't want to go anywhere in his rotten car.'

'For heaven's sake, Neil, stop being so silly. You're downright ungrateful. Your Uncle Chris wants to make both of us happy, and if you'd only be agreeable for once you'd begin enjoying yourself.'

On the day itself Neil was silent and withdrawn, making Helen long to shake him. After they had set out from the vicarage – in her car because he had muttered about not liking Christopher's – he lapsed into misery from which no attempts at conversation roused him.

'I'm terribly sorry, Chris,' Helen said fervently, tears filling her grey eyes, when they stopped for a picnic lunch and nothing that Chris had insisted on preparing for them suited the lad. 'I wish I'd left him with our Marian or my mother.'

But leaving Neil with anyone else would be no lasting solution. She couldn't go on for ever like this, being wrenched apart by her love for her son and for Christopher.

They were sitting beside the river at Grassington after driving out via Fewston where they'd stopped to admire the picturesque reservoir. Helen had been thinking that she'd never enjoyed so much lovely scenery, until Neil's sullenness intruded yet again.

During the journey back to Leeds as surrounding limestone rocks gave way to the darker sandstone, Chris said the one thing which Helen had longed for years to hear. Neil was asleep on the back seat. They were running downhill through a sunlit dale, with a river meandering between meadows dotted with grazing cattle and sheep. Woods clothed the steeply sloping hills, with purple moors beyond and craggs on the horizon.

'I love you, Helen, I want you to marry me,' Chris said quietly. 'Lord knows, I've waited long enough. There's only ever been you, and I can't bear the thought that even now we might not end up together.'

'Oh, Chris, I'd love us to marry. If only . . .'

'Neil?' he murmured. 'I do understand, love, that you have to put him first. But I'm not giving up hope that he'll come round. I do know how he must feel – that he can't bear to have me monopolising the bit of free time that you do have. And I think we can win him round, if we put it to him in the right manner.'

They tried that evening after tea at the vicarage, during which Neil had been persuaded into talking to Chris, if only about some of his toys. There had been one difficult moment when he had mentioned the aeroplane that Uncle Vittore had given him. Helen could have done without that particular reminder at this time, but no one else appeared perturbed by it. One day she would explain to Chris that Vittore was the person who'd joined her at Stone's, and how he'd shattered her by trying to take over.

'Would you like to see the room where I think you'd enjoy playing with all your toys?' Chris had suggested as tea was ending.

'I have a playroom, thank you,' Neil responded, rigidly, icily polite.

'Yes, but you see – your mother and I are hoping that some day you might both come to live here.'

'No, never. I want to live in my house, always and always.'

Helen had taken Neil firmly by the hand and after reminding him to say thank you for his tea, led him along in the wake of Chris as he headed towards the rather dark staircase.

The room was large, but had dingy wallpaper and despite a window that overlooked the back of the church seemed drab. Glancing about, Helen noticed that someone had hastily covered the centre of the floor with an ageing carpet. It wasn't quite parallel with the walls, and to one end the polished boards were revealed through a layer of dust in squares and rectangles where boxes had been stored. Picturing Chris trying to put the room to rights for her son, Helen felt her eyes blurring.

Her response this afternoon to his proposal had been instinctive. She would love to marry him. But she mustn't risk making another terrible mistake. While putting Neil forward as the obstacle, she'd known in her heart that she was really protecting them all from the possibility of future disappointment. This room, more than anything, convinced her of the depth of Christopher's feelings for them both. This was reality, down-to-earth evidence of his eagerness to make a place for them with him.

But, although she would never hurt Chris by expressing any fears that he, too, might eventually let her down, she still had to be reassured that none of them would suffer by trying to make a life together. The time needed for persuading Neil would provide a breathing space. Opportunity for them all to become more sure about one another.

'It's lovely and big,' she exclaimed, smiling appreciatively.

'This would be just for you,' Chris told Neil, bending down so that his eyes were level with the boy's defiant grey ones. 'You could do exactly as you liked in here. Nobody would make a fuss about any mess or anything . . .'

'No, thank you,' Neil interrupted coldly. 'I don't like it here. I don't, I don't!'

'But, Neil,' Helen persisted. 'Just think, Uncle Chris wants to look after us both, and especially to look after you. He wants to teach you games, just the way your daddy would have taught you.'

'No. I want to live in my house.'

'But why?' Christopher asked gently. 'You would be surrounded by all your own books and toys, everything that belongs to you. This would be your home. Let me show you the room where we'd put your own little bed.'

Solemnly, Neil continued shaking his head. Helen and Chris exchanged a despairing glance.

'I know,' said Neil after a moment's thought. 'Mummy can live with you, I'll live at Auntie Marian's house. With her and Uncle Denis and Mark and Linda. I like it there.'

Utterly shaken, so wretched that she was on the verge of weeping, Helen gulped. She turned swiftly to stare out of the window.

Chris was trying to catch her attention, but she was in no state for even listening to what he intended as reassurance.

'There's time,' he said calmly. 'I daresay this is too soon.'

It isn't for me, she thought. It feels as if I've waited a lifetime already. And on every occasion that we meet it seems that our ever belonging to each other grows increasingly unlikely.

When she controlled her emotions sufficiently, she faced Neil and spoke sternly. 'There's no chance that you'll ever go and live with your Auntie Marian. You can put that idea right out of your head.'

Helen did decide, though, that if Chris still wanted to see her again she would leave Neil with Marian, perhaps even overnight. Chris was entitled to some private life, if she herself was finding arranging any virtually impossible.

All the way home that evening, Helen grew more and more sickened by what Neil had said. Did she mean so little to him that he could so readily contemplate living with her sister? This reminder brought hurtling back every opinion of Alexander's about Marian caring for Neil. She was thankful that there was no sound from the back seat where her son had fallen asleep again. She hadn't the heart to chatter away as they normally did during car journeys.

For days Helen remained so distressed by Neil's suggestion that she had to force herself to do any work at her drawing board or desk. But if the boy was succeeding in ruining everything else for her, she certainly wasn't going to let him affect her job. While discussing meals or other household matters, Mrs Hartley would frown and ask whatever was wrong. Helen didn't like dismissing the kindly enquiry with a hasty 'nothing', but she had no intention of admitting Neil's hurtful assertion to anyone.

The words had cut so deeply. How could a four-year-old boy be willing to live apart from his mother, especially when he'd already lost his father? Reflecting on how he'd reacted ever since Alexander's death, Helen began believing that Neil must think a lot more of him than ever he had of her. Yet it was over two years now since the accident. She was surprised that Neil had any clear memories of his father. Where was she going wrong?

It was then that she recalled how Alexander had accused her of only ever doing what she wanted. Was that the reason behind this trouble? But that couldn't be true, could it, not of her behaviour towards Neil? Apart from her work, which was after all for both their sakes, she'd spent the whole of the last two years putting Neil before herself. *Until renewing acquaintance with Christopher.*

Helen was compelled to admit that it must seem to the boy that his position as sole claimant on her love and attention was being displaced. Grimly, she began to wonder if the only way of restoring Neil's contentment was by sacrificing her own.

There was still her work. And a great deal that was of interest was going on in architecture now. The contest for designing the new cathedral at Coventry had produced some fascinating ideas. For the first time ever, she herself had fallen for a modern scheme. Perhaps because of its planned use of uncoursed pink sandstone for the exterior or maybe for his decision to incorporate the adjacent ruins of the original, she was very much in favour of the controversial winning design by Basil Spence.

And being delighted by such an up-to-date concept, Helen had felt her own ambitions widening. If only I was free to get around and visit more potential development sites, she thought longingly, I might extend myself. Perhaps in doing so I would discover satisfaction.

It was she herself, after all, who had mapped out her life, selecting this career and working always to achieve her aims. Maybe having some degree of success in that was all she deserved. Wasn't she expecting too much by aching for personal happiness? For love?

The church was empty and, except for birdsong and the thrum of traffic, strangely silent. Chris was accustomed by now to the sound of the congregation behind him; even at early weekday Communion, to the presence of one or two parishioners. Today, though, he had sought this solitude, urged by his own disquiet to pause in his busy life and examine this, his failure.

How long, he wondered, how long have I been deluding myself about my ability to relate to youngsters? This belief in his own affinity with children and teenagers had developed throughout his first curacy and increased ever since. He had thought he understood the way their minds worked, from the blessed simplicity of the very young, right the way through the difficulties of adolescence to the ambitions of late teenage.

Well, if he'd been arrogant in assuming he had some such spark, this certainly was his comeuppance! And the circumstances couldn't have been more distressing. The irony of having Helen restored to him in such a miraculous fashion, only to have their hopes thwarted by her son's attitude, was unbearable. Had he been so very wrong to believe that he might have a real home at last, with the one woman who had awakened him to this yearning for a deeper expression of loving? Why, *how*, had he failed in his determined effort to bring more love into the life of her small son?

God help him, but he was drained now, wrung dry by trying to please the lad, to give him the kind of fun a child should be enjoying, and this additional love. Always love – love which normally is healing.

Heaven knew if there existed any way now in which he might get through to Neil. He literally would do anything, if it were any use, would wear himself out over any means which could reconcile the lad to him. As things stood, it looked as though he would eventually have to resign himself to spending the rest of his life apart from Helen. He had seen the tears in her eyes the other day, couldn't put her through much more of the distress of being torn in two directions.

Proposing to her had been an impulse which he

couldn't have withheld for much longer. She couldn't know how many years ago it was, nor how far away that lifetime now seemed, when he had become convinced that he would marry no other woman.

Thinking back now, the heat of the desert oppressed him, its sand scratched beneath his lowered eyelids. The stink of death filled his nostrils. His hands felt heavy with the spade that too often had been employed to inter his comrades. All too frequently, it had been a solitary business. Forces at war couldn't always spare time from fighting to bury the men dying beside them.

There'll be better times, he had assured himself, just as he had assured his men. He liked to think that some of them, if not all, had believed him. Even when they had been shot to pieces, to lie in the heat, trying to come to terms with severed limbs, nerves completely shattered, or eyes that would remain sightless.

With them and through them, he had suffered his own hell. Had hurt because they were hurting, and he could bring them no real relief. For there were no answers, only the hope which he had tried to hold before them.

His own endurance of that North African campaign had been through moments of escape: when his soul, troubled past bearing by the carnage all around, had sought the only sources of tranquillity which he'd ever discovered. Still fresh in his memory at that time, he'd pictured so often the glorious day of his ordination, and the weeks which had preceded that most solemn occasion.

Being accepted as he was had been the greatest joy of all. In that final term he had laid before their College Superior every one of his doubts about himself. And had found they were understood. That, more than anything, had convinced him that he stood a chance of making a fair job of being a clergyman. Eventually.

Compelled by his innate straightforwardness to lay bare every private misgiving, he'd brought out all the emotions that had troubled him since that day in 1938. He could see now that drab, worn study, and the elderly priest who so often looked no less worn. And he experienced afresh the enormous relief which had followed the old man's opinion.

'Do not try yourself too hard, my son, this isn't an easy life you've selected. Don't make it unnecessarily harder.'

Unnecessarily? But he'd always thought, had believed, that by committing himself to a celibate life he would be making a better offering. Would have become a better priest. More use even . . .

His Superior had smiled, knowingly, knowing him. 'Give all you can – the Lord understands. He won't fail to smile on you, should you feel the need of an earthly partner. Come now, Chris, you're forgetting where your feelings originated.'

War had followed only weeks after that Trinity Ordination in 1939. There had been little time for thinking, scarcely any for private prayer after becoming an army chaplain. And then he had found himself in the desert. The place where he'd confronted the reality that is war, and had been driven by the lives deprived of a future to reconsider his own life.

All those years ago, he'd been bothered still by the readiness with which he'd been relieved of the obligation to commit himself to living a sexless existence. It had seemed to him then to have one purpose only. Freedom to marry had granted him freedom to remember her, his ideal woman.

The impact of that short encounter with Helen had remained as clear in his mind as the Swiss mountain air. Every intonation of her voice had resurrected for him, along with that smile and those exquisite grey eyes. Surrounded by battle, he had turned the eye of his mind inward to find her, and silently to make another vow.

During the intervening years in his first two parishes he'd met no serious challenge to his resolution. There had been attractive young women, of course, the proverbial bevy of them had constituted a part of the congregation. Most had flirted with him, two or three had been intelligent enough to engage more than his male vanity, but there wasn't one among them who'd made him wish to reconsider.

His search for Helen had begun after the war, once he returned to Yorkshire. It had lasted all of an hour. He had remembered she was training to be an architect and, although he had at first been unable to find her under her maiden name in the directory of Architects he'd tracked down, he'd remembered her mentioning Alexander Stone and his architect father. And there he'd found her. Under Helen Stone, her married name.

And now here he was, again brought to his knees, and this time despite their reunion. They had come so near. How could he give up now? He could only set his mind to making more of an effort.

'I want to see you,' he said over the phone, after working his way through extended preliminaries about the weather and other matters of no consequence. 'I'm hoping there might be some way of getting Neil to adjust to the prospect of the three of us having some kind of future together. I thought if perhaps you and I could have a talk, alone . . .'

Even while she was agreeing, Helen felt no more optimistic than she had when they'd last said goodbye. But she was utterly depressed by not seeing Chris and would do almost anything so long as they could meet.

'I've left him with our Marian,' she said as soon as Chris opened the door to her. 'If I'm not back this evening she'll put him to bed, and I've told her I'll pick him up by tomorrow afternoon at the latest. At least Neil's happy about that arrangement.'

'But you're not.' He ached for her. She looked so ill, thinner than ever he'd seen her. Her silky-looking skirt and blouse were navy blue, exquisitely cut, but for the woman she once had been – certainly two sizes larger. All the lustre was gone from the grey eyes which seemed to stare distractedly from her haggard face.

Helen shrugged. 'Would you be happy if your only son had turned round and told you he'd rather live permanently with your sister?'

'It's all my fault.'

'No, Chris, it isn't. You mustn't think that, love, not ever. It's me – something I lack that prevents me providing Neil with the kind of mother he needs.' Her eyes were awash with tears now, bringing a lump to his own throat.

'That's nonsense, Helen.'

'No, it's the truth. Alexander saw it. He was always telling me I ought to be a better mother, that I ought to give all my time to Neil.'

'And make the lad unduly self-centred in the process?'

His words checked her. 'But, Chris, it wouldn't have that effect surely? It's the way I am that's made him so wretchedly insecure he needs all my attention.'

'Rubbish! That's due to losing his father so young.'

It was the sort of thing other people had said. She wished with all her heart that she might begin to believe it. 'But that wouldn't make him want to live at our Marian's.'

'No – and I think that's another, simpler issue. Because being with her family is fun, exciting. Lots of children go through phases of preferring to stay with cousins or friends.'

'Well, it doesn't seem like that to me.'

'Of course not. You're extremely vulnerable to every breath of criticism. And with a son like Neil, I'm afraid there's plenty of that around.'

'There wouldn't be if I always handled him properly.'

'Oh, Helen!' Smiling ruefully, he took her hands and pulled her to him. Locking his arms about her, he kissed her fervently on the mouth. 'I'd do anything, anything – to stop you being hurt.'

She swallowed, looked up at him. 'I wish I knew where to turn. This is all so bloody.'

'I know. That's why I wanted to talk – see if we can sort something.'

'There is no solution. I'm sorry, Chris, but that is the way things stand. Neil won't budge, and I can't see that any of us will be happy while he can't accept the prospect of our being together.' She was weeping now, tears trickling down her cheeks and dripping off her chin.

Chris continued hugging her. 'Leave it for now then, eh? I'll take you out somewhere instead, where we can have a quiet meal, concentrate on each other.'

They drove to Otley where, following their meal, they walked in the evening sunlight beside the River Wharfe. On the water couples rowed tiny boats peacefully back and forth while elderly folk strolled along the path or paused to rest on green-painted seats adjacent to fragrant rosebeds. Near the opposite bank houses, terraced and of stone, stood comfortably with each other and with the tranquil scene. Helen envied quite fiercely all the folk here, visible and unseen, for the absence from their lives of her own massive burden.

'I love you, that's why I want us to marry,' Chris reminded her, taking her hand, smoothing it with his fingers. 'Let me take your anxieties, about Neil, about everything.'

She shook her head. Her smile was sad. 'I wish you could, I wish I could let you. Though you probably carry more than enough weight as it is, through your work.'

'That's different. I'm not so deeply and personally involved.'

'But it can't be easy.'

His short laugh was rueful. 'Nothing is, ever. Remember what you once said, all those years ago? About the "comfort" in believing. I ought to feel that it's there. Somehow I can never even bring myself to preach that it is. What comfort is there among the losses that come in everyone's life, or in wars, in disagreements that arise often simply from expressing one's beliefs, or in circumstances which enforce grave disappointment? Faith doesn't bring an automatic palliative.'

'What then?' Helen asked, more interested now in his thoughts than her own difficulties.

Christopher shrugged. 'Endurance, I suppose. To ensure that one survives long enough to accept whatever's dealt out.'

On the way back to Leeds they both fell quiet, each preoccupied with matters already aired, and to no satisfactory end.

The scenery through which they drove was still lovely, but Helen could hardly bear to look. For most of her life she had been moved by beautiful countryside, perhaps even more so than by the exquisite man-made buildings that had inspired her.

Viewing these splendid hills of her native Yorkshire, she'd often experienced intense yearning simply to share it all with somebody who mattered. And now here they were, so close that their arms were touching in the car, and all she knew was dread that Neil would keep them apart. For ever.

'It's strange, you know,' said Chris, leading the way indoors, 'I could have sworn that it was right for us to end up together, that it was meant.' He ached to tell her of his thoughts during the war. And knew that he couldn't without forcing her hand.

'Me too.' She sounded forlorn. 'I love you so much, Chris. I've realised recently that I've wanted you for so long that nobody else ever stood a chance of measuring up.'

He drew her to him again, kissing her repeatedly, on her hair, her eyelids, and then her lips. 'God, but I don't want to live without you.'

Starved of each other, they clung, bodies feverish with need.

'Lord, but I need you,' Christopher sighed, his yearning somehow increased by reflecting on his miserable failure to win Neil's approval. 'Hold me, Helen, hold me.'

Her arms slid round him, making him groan with delight. Her breasts felt hard against his chest. The force straining from deep within him was moving beyond his will, developing its own impetus.

His hand went between them, caressing her breast, then passing over her flat stomach. A tiny moan of sheer pleasure escaped her lips.

'Yes, Chris, yes . . .'

He drew her down with him on to his old sofa, too eager now even to ensure her comfort. Pushing the material of her skirt aside, he traced her inner thigh, hesitated.

'Don't stop now,' she cried, her lips seeking his mouth.

He felt slender fingers on him, urging him to love her, while her tongue tested his own, willing him to seal their union. His every pulse was awake, beating in echo of this massive lifetime's need. He'd never imagined an impulse so strong, could not think how he had existed without making her belong to him.

And then he thought of Neil, and how the boy would fight to the end to keep them apart. He couldn't do this to Helen. Neil was the centre of her world. Even her work was in aid of the future she would create for him. A future that would be full and interesting without Chris Maitland, the man who only aroused her son's antagonism.

'I'm sorry,' he said quietly. 'I shouldn't have gone this far. The situation's intolerable, isn't it? I'd not forgive myself for letting the worst happen when we know there's precious little hope of marriage.'

'It wouldn't be the worst, Chris. I want to love you.'

Too weak with longing to ignore her words, he closed his eyes, savouring the touch of her hands, surrendering to kisses no less passionate than his own. For this he had waited throughout the whole of his life. Through study, training, the war, and afterwards. To come to this time, this place, to her.

'Let's go up to bed, Chris.'

Her words alerted him to how close they had come, to the hair's breadth that stood between them and . . .

'I'll show you to your room,' he stated carefully, rising as he spoke and willing his light-headedness to disperse. There seemed no chance that the rest of his enormous discomfort would ever be relieved.

He returned downstairs swiftly the moment that he'd seen her to her room. Grimly, recognising that he literally was removing himself from temptation, he went towards his study and closed the door.

It was two in the morning when Chris finally went upstairs, after wrestling for hours to master himself and concentrate on the sermon he must finish.

The door of her room was ajar. Lit by the bedside lamp, her hair gleamed with lights, gilding its brown strands. Her face was as pale as her cream silk nightgown, and looked stricken. A lump rose in his throat to choke him.

'Helen? Are you all right?'

'We neither of us are, are we? I can't bear this.'

He hurried to the bed, sat on its edge and pulled her into his arms. What use was love when he was denied using it for the one person who meant the world to him? For the two people . . .

Chris couldn't avoid kissing her any more than he could curtail this need to hold her. When she leaned back into the pillows he moved with her, pressed his face into the hollow of her throat. Her perfume was delicate, hardly more than a hint, but it filled his nostrils, while her taste beneath his lips seemed sweet, utterly delicious.

He could only draw nearer, sliding one arm beneath her as he edged his body over hers. Helen's sigh was blissful. She raised a hand to his head, then met his mouth with her lips.

Beneath the covers keeping them apart, she began stirring, her hips urging him to move with her. His need tremendous again, Chris could not resist, but only surrender his will. His own hardness alarmed him, renewing awareness of where its force might lead. Not yet, though, he murmured within his head to the cautious half of his nature, while desire drove him to intensify their kisses and to continue this relentless stirring.

There was no solution. They parted after a while,

their glances rueful, admitting that regardless of their needs, they must be realistic, that there were too many obstacles. And remembering that he was a priest.

'But I am also a man,' Christopher added gravely. 'You know how much I want you. Continued self-denial simply isn't practical.'

Helen heard the telephone ringing at five-thirty in the morning, and Chris running downstairs to answer it. I suppose vicars are much like doctors for being called out at all hours, she thought.

Five minutes later he appeared in the doorway of her room. He was tying the cord of the dressing gown he'd grabbed. She'd never seen him looking as anxious.

'I'm terribly sorry, love, that was for you. Your sister. I'm afraid . . .'

'Oh, God – Neil!' Helen interrupted. 'Whatever's happened, is he ill?'

'No, love. There's probably a simple explanation, but – well, he seems to have disappeared.'

'He can't have! He's only little. Children his age don't just go wandering away.' She began scrambling out of bed. 'Is Marian still on the line?'

'No, she rang off.' Marian had said she was phoning the police, but he didn't believe knowing that would help Helen. 'She'd told me all she could. Evidently he seemed to settle all right last night, and she took him to the bathroom around three o'clock. But when her son wakened a couple of hours later Neil wasn't in his bed.'

Helen turned icily cold and was shuddering with dread. 'Have they searched the garden? It's nothing like as big as at The Stone House, but happen he's hiding. I'll have to get there, straight away.'

They took her car, it was speedier and more reliable, but Chris drove. Helen was so shattered that all she could do was sit huddled into her seat, worrying. Even when they began driving into Halifax she could hardly compose herself enough to direct him to her sister's.

Marian was at the door of the terraced house before Helen had hurtled up the short path.

'Denis has gone looking for him with them,' she said. 'Eh, love, I'm that sorry! But I only said it for the best, because I was sure it was what you'd want me to say . . .'

'Said? Want you to say? Whatever's been going on?'

'Come and sit down a minute, both of you.'

'Nay, I'll not,' Helen contradicted. 'I'm off searching as soon as I find out what you've been up to.'

'Well, it was last night, just before he went up to bed. They'd all been having a right good time playing out. And Neil said summat about wanting to come and live here. Well, what could I say? I couldn't let him go on thinking that was likely, could I? So I told him that he belonged with you, that he'd live with you till he grew up and had a home of his own.'

Helen heard Christopher's deep sigh, and then a voice which appeared to be her own saying, 'You were quite right, Marian, love, you mustn't blame yourself.'

Leaving Marian by the telephone, they set out on foot. A thin drizzle was falling, making the terraced houses look greyer than ever, sending Helen's panic racing out of control.

'He'll be wet through in this. He'll get his death of cold, pneumonia even . . . That's if we ever find him.'

'Somebody'll come across him before so long,' Chris began assuring her. 'Now the police are out.'

'Police? *Police*? That means they think he's been kidnapped, doesn't it, or worse?'

'It means nothing of the kind, love. Simply that they're doing their utmost to find him.'

They turned a corner and saw two uniformed officers going from door to door, knocking people up where necessary, and looking into yards and gardens. It all made Neil's disappearance more real and alarming.

'Maybe we can be more use if we investigate some of his haunts. Or has he made any little friends round here?' said Chris.

'Not that I know of. He was usually quite content to play with Mark and Linda. Mostly in their garden. I think sometimes Denis or Marian took them to the park.'

'Is it far?'

'Just across Warley Road – that's the one over there across the top of Hopwood Lane.'

'And the park's not locked at night?'

'I don't know.'

'I don't suppose it's had any gates since they were all taken for salvage. We'll make that our first call, shall we?'

'If you think that's best,' Helen replied, unable to think rationally any longer.

What will I do if something's happened to him? she thought, panicking again. Whatever will I do? I'll never forgive myself.

Chapter 22

The curtains at the lodge were still closed. There wasn't another person visible as far as they could see across the park.

'Do you think we ought to try and find the park keeper?' Helen asked.

Chris shook his head. 'Not for the minute, love. Might as well take a look for ourselves. If he hasn't come on duty yet, he'll not have seen anything either.'

Hurriedly, they followed the curving path, defying the rain driving into their faces as they glanced sideways towards flowerbeds, herbaceous borders, and shrubs.

'We'll investigate those more thoroughly if we don't find him soon,' Chris stated.

'He could be anywhere,' Helen said. 'Even if he is in the park, anywhere at all.'

'Well, we'll have to see.' Chris was thankful there was no evidence of people sleeping rough here.

They came to a terrace balustraded in stone, and stood for a few seconds looking to left and right, and then down to where the ground fell away sharply below them.

In the distance ahead, where the view over the valley should have been, everything was whited out by rain as opaque as cloud.

'Come on,' Chris urged her, taking her elbow and heading towards steps. 'Looks like there's more than one path, we'll have to be systematic. Where does all this lead?'

'Eventually, down to Burnley Road. That's the one that goes out our way.'

'Do you think somebody might have told Neil that, have shown him the direction of The Stone House perhaps?' But surely a lad that age wouldn't have set out to walk there?

'I've no idea.'

They took the first path on the left, began following it downhill. Helen slithered on the surface treacherous with rain and Chris caught her against him. She closed her eyes, yearning just to be held there, to be able to cease thinking.

'What's that?' he exclaimed, suddenly, making her jump.

'Oh, God, let him be all right!' she exclaimed, freeing herself and starting to run across grass that soaked her feet.

In a slight hollow, shielded on one side by a large rock and on another by a collection of shrubs, was a hunched figure. His bright gold hair darkened by the rain, and bare legs tucked beneath him, he was clutching his coat round him. The buttons were fastened wrongly, leaving a gap at the neck and one bottom corner dangling.

'Neil! Oh, my darling!'

'Mummy, Mummy!'

He tried to stand and couldn't. His legs had been cramped too long while he waited there, miserably lost.

'I wanted to go home,' he said. And didn't protest when Chris scooped him up and prepared to carry him back to Marian's. 'Don't forget my things,' he said though, and pointed to a now muddy bundle beside the rock.

Even distressed as she had been, Helen was compelled to smile. The bundle was knotted clumsily to a stick that she recognised from Mark's drumkit.

'I couldn't find a spotted hanky,' Neil explained, quite cheerfully now. 'I took a cover off Linda's doll's pram. It was only big enough for my pyjama bottoms. And some marshmallows – I ate those when the rain started.'

They met Denis with the police after crossing Warley Road again, and were whisked by police car back to the terraced house where Marian hugged first Helen and then young Neil. The next hour was a jumble of thanking the police and relating where the boy had been discovered, while Marian and Denis rushed around in the kitchen cooking breakfast.

Neil was plonked in a hot bath, and emerged to enjoy all the attention, demonstrating to his cousins how he had carried his pack on his shoulder just like the boy in his story book.

Eventually, Chris looked at his watch. 'I'm sorry, but I'll have to be on my way.'

Denis volunteered to drive him back to Leeds as soon as Helen had assured everyone that she was up to taking Neil home.

'I'm all right now, really,' she insisted. But even while she was thanking Chris for everything that he had done she was thinking that this crisis had proved that she couldn't put their life before Neil's wishes. No matter how much heartache she was creating for herself, she couldn't continue upsetting her son.

Helen rushed to answer the telephone. Despite her determination, she couldn't school herself not to hope that Chris might be on the line. He had rung the day after Neil's escapade and had mentioned a concert his church youngsters were giving. Although she'd tried to explain about not seeing him, she'd felt a bald 'no' was unwarranted. This time, anyway, the caller was her father.

'I don't like bothering you on a Saturday, love, not when you've been busy all week. But it's your mum. I'm afraid she's not a bit well.'

'Whatever's wrong, Dad?'

'Eh, I don't know. I'd been at work, you see, this morning. When I came round t'corner of the street, there was quite a crowd gathering in front of our house. I ran t'rest of the way and there she were – your mother. Somebody had fetched a chair out, and she were sat there, her hair all anyhow – you know how she keeps it tidy – and her face the colour of a floorcloth.'

'What had happened then?' asked Helen agitatedly, wishing he didn't take so long to get to the point.

'Seemingly, she'd passed clean out, just as she were coming out of their gate. You know how she will persist in looking after her next-door . . . Any road, as luck would have it, that young woman opposite happened to see. She were t'first to help her up.'

'And Mum – how is she now?'

'She says she's all right, but she never says owt else, does she? Won't have the doctor, of course. I keep telling her that's what this 'ere National Health is for.'

'I'll come on and see what I think, Dad. All right?'

Helen was arranging for Mrs Hartley to keep an eye on Neil for the afternoon when the telephone rang again. Her heart pounding as she imagined her mother having taken a turn for the worse, Helen tore across to lift the receiver.

This time it was Christopher. 'I'm on my way to see you, Helen. I'm going to have another shot at getting Neil on to my side. I love the boy, love both of you. I can't just give up.'

'Eh, Chris – I wish you'd let me know sooner. I've got to go out. My dad's just rung to tell me my mother's had some kind of a blackout. She's refusing to see a doctor, and I'm on my way there to try and sort something out.'

'That's in Halifax, isn't it?'

'Yes, but . . .' Helen jerked around to face the clock. She'd have to get moving.

'Give me the address. I'll meet you there.'

'But, Chris . . .'

'For God's sake – won't you even let me do one thing to help you?'

There wasn't time to argue. Helen sighed and told him the street and house number.

His old Ford was in the familiar street when Helen drew up there. She remembered then that he'd already been on his way over from Leeds. Getting out of her own car and locking it, Helen hurried up the short path to the door.

Chris opened it to her, making her wonder where her father was. Surely nothing had happened to him as well? 'Hallo,' she said. 'Where's Dad?'

'He's only down the steps,' called her mother. 'He won't be a minute.'

'Hallo, Mum,' said Helen, crossing swiftly to the armchair where she was sitting. 'Are you any better now?'

'Aye – I'm as right as rain again, bless you. I were just starting to tell Mr Maitland . . .' Surprising Helen, she laughed. 'I couldn't help seeing the funny side of it all. I said – didn't I, Mr Maitland, when you came through the door? – I thought, "Well, I'll go to heck. Somebody must think I'm not long for this world – they've fetched t'parson." '

Chris gave Helen a rueful smile. 'I'm hoping to convince her that all my work isn't funereal.'

'Aye, well, it looks as though it mightn't be today. We're ever so grateful,' Helen said, trying not to think how good it was to have him around when there was a crisis. 'Have you introduced yourself?' she asked Chris, and he beamed at her.

'As an old friend of yours. And as such I feel I ought to advise calling in the doctor, if only as a precaution.'

'I was going to, anyway. I'll just run to the 'phone box.'

Kathleen Clegg didn't argue against her decision. Hurrying along the street, Helen realised her mother must have been worried. She herself was badly shaken. Learning her parents weren't indestructible had brought her up sharp.

Some while later, Helen and Chris had retreated to the kitchen so that Kathleen, who refused to go up to a bedroom, could be examined by the doctor.

'I'm glad I'm here,' he told her quietly, leaning against the sink.

Helen gave him a look. 'You enjoy picking up the pieces when my family are in trouble, do you?' she asked dryly, sitting on the small table crammed in between the cupboard on one wall and her mother's Baby Belling oven which had stood against the other since replacing the fire range before the war.

'It's what life's about. And I've seen far worse. Blood, severed limbs, mangled corpses – in the desert.'

'So that's where the war took you?' She gazed at him, her grey eyes widening, remembering how she'd wondered at the farm where he might be, had been concerned for his safety. 'You've never told me.'

'One day I will.'

She didn't like there being a part of his life about which she knew nothing. 'Where else did you serve?'

'Various places, though the desert was where I was confronted by any actual fighting. That's how I got involved with wounded men. There's often only chaplains around who aren't combatant.'

Talking of the war brought back all her feelings about its failure to restore them to a really satisfactory peace. Suddenly, she needed to hear his answers. As she did to discuss so many things with him.

'What was it all for, Chris? All the bloodshed, I mean. We're not that much better off, are we? Here we are in the fifties, and we're nowhere near over the legacy of shortages, restrictions, and general dissatisfaction. *What was it for?*'

'Neither you nor I can say that for sure, Helen. Maybe simply to show us that war mustn't occur again. That it needn't.'

'A bit of a costly lesson.'

'Aren't they all?'

'You sound too cynical for somebody wearing their collar that way round!'

Christopher smiled. 'Not cynical, A realist maybe. I hope that I am. There's not much to recommend religion if it's not relevant to real life, is there?'

'Don't ask me – not my subject. Never has been. I'm just as confused as I was in Switzerland.'

'Oh, I don't think so. You're a survivor, Helen, a fighter. They don't struggle on unless they've found some hope.'

Hope, though, was something she found rather elusive during the next few weeks, although her mother had been pronounced by the doctor to be reasonably fit for her age and had felt well enough to discount his advice to take things easier. The blackout was attributed to nothing more alarming than doing too much when she hadn't eaten for hours. After the scare, Helen had realised that her father was nearing retirement age, even though he swore he'd never stop working. And her mother was four years his senior.

This sudden threat made her think. They've had a grand life together, she considered; ordinary, but grand. In their quiet way they had lived out the selflessness in which they believed, and would continue to the end to make this inconspicuous witness.

And what have I done, she often wondered in the night, except go out of my way to prove I could be an architect? No matter what the cost to other people.

There was precious little satisfaction now, even in the way her work was increasing. She had sent Chris away, albeit with her thanks, after that strange interlude in Halifax. Seeing him in her old home, eager to help her folk, had produced emotions in her far stronger than she could ignore. She'd wanted him then, in so many ways, and far more intensely than with mere desire.

If he couldn't continue being a part of her life, then she didn't know how she was going to exist. But there was Neil to consider as well – and he had to come first. He'd always blamed her, hadn't he, for causing his father's loss? She couldn't compel him to live with Chris when he so evidently hated the whole idea. And nor could she continue seeing Christopher, not when they knew that there must be no physical contact between them. She couldn't steel herself for that. Even in front of her mum and dad, she'd hardly known how not to hug him, just for being there. And she knew herself. She couldn't stop at a hug, nor at a kiss, and once she began . . . She'd only ever felt like this with Chris, driven by love as well as all her other senses. She couldn't keep on resisting.

On the day, Helen was wishing with all her heart that she'd been firmer about not going over for the

Sunday School concert. Since that parting on her mother's doorstep she had tussled with the conflict deep inside her.

This had got to stop. After today, it must. She would have to find a way of putting Chris right out of her mind; out of her life. She needed him too much. This had grown obsessive, beyond all proportion. And she needed Neil as well. More importantly, he needed her, would do so for many years to come. And he really would never resign himself to accepting Chris – he'd proved that, hadn't he, by running away? She had felt torn at times in the past, between her work and her son. The pain of that was nothing compared with this massive hurt.

That day over at her mother's had only convinced her more deeply how right she and Chris might have been together. Having come so close to being a part of his world, she couldn't unmake the dreams imagination had fashioned. The only way was to cease everything that brought them back to life.

Schooling herself now to accepting that this would be their final meeting, Helen resolved that she would be stern – with Chris, in permitting no persuasion, but most of all with herself against surrendering to this force compelling her to love him. She would be matter-of-fact, friendly but cool, and firm in her farewell.

The telephone sliced into her thoughts and, relieved to have an interruption, she ran to lift the receiver.

'It's me – Marian. I'm ever so sorry, love, but I can't make it today. I've dropped the frying pan – and before you say owt, no, it wasn't full or anything, it wasn't hot either. But it caught my bad leg, right on the shin bone. Denis would have the doctor, and he's forbidden me to put any weight on it for a day or two.'

After checking that the doctor considered no lasting damage had been done, Helen sympathised, assured Marian that she would cope and promised to ring the following day. Replacing the receiver, she felt further relief wash right through her. She didn't have to go over to Leeds now. She would let Chris know immediately. Not seeing him would enable her to be as firm as she ought to have been already about the future.

'Sorry about your sister,' he said swiftly. 'But what about your housekeeper – Mrs Hartley?'

'She's having a week off, bit of a holiday.'

'Bring Neil with you then.'

'You must be joking!' said Helen. 'Hasn't he been disruptive enough already? And it isn't as if . . .' She stopped speaking, swallowed. She had been going to say '. . . as if it mattered now.' And maybe she should have said it. However far from the real truth it was. She ought to have made him believe that none of this did matter. How otherwise would she – *they* – learn to accept the facts?

'Helen, it's not like you to let me down.'

There had been more, much of it scarcely sounding like Chris, for the words were harsh, almost unforgiving. And she couldn't let it end this way – with sourness between them. She would have to risk going there with Neil.

Chris was backstage when they arrived, but came through from one of the dressing rooms as soon as he learned they were there. Neil was his usual unforthcoming self, barely speaking when Chris said hallo, but he did comply uncomplainingly for once when they were taken through to see the young people preparing for the concert.

'Better not show you in there,' Chris said with a grin, passing the dressing rooms. 'Some are getting changed now. We'll go through to watch folk being made-up. I was sort of supervising. The woman in charge has rather a heavy hand with the Leichner – don't want them looking over-painted, especially the lads.'

'There you are, Father,' said one of the older boys. 'Is this okay? Feels cissy, but I know because of the lights . . .'

'You look great,' said Chris, nodding approvingly. 'And I like the outfit – how's the guitar today?'

'Much better, I think.'

Chris turned to Helen. 'His guitar is second-hand. Unfortunately strings kept snapping, but we believe we've fixed it now.'

'Father,' someone called from across the room, 'Harry's been sick again.'

'Is someone with him?' Chris enquired.

'Aye – Miss Gilbert. And he's all right again now, any road.'

Smiling ruefully, Chris turned to Helen. 'I'm told this happens every time they do anything out of the ordinary. He's rather highly strung, and exceptionally intelligent. Matter of fact, he has ambitions to try something in your line. Sadly, his home circumstances are going to make that virtually impossible.'

'Happen he could try for a scholarship. That was the only way I . . .' Suddenly, she stopped speaking, thought for a minute and smiled. 'Of course – that's it! The Fenella March Bursary. I've finished paying back all that I had from old Mr March, and a bit more besides. Money doesn't go as far, these days. Does this Harry seriously want to study architecture?'

'I'll arrange for you to have a chat with him after the concert, but from what I've heard since coming to the parish, he talks of little else.'

'How old is he?'

'Sixteen or so, I suppose. He's in a bit of a dead-end job at present, that I do know.'

Neil was remarkably well behaved throughout the performance. On the whole the youngsters were very good instrumentalists as well as singers. They had chosen the programme themselves which perhaps accounted for its appealing to Neil. During the interval Helen only saw Chris briefly, from a distance, when he emerged to have a word with the ladies organising refreshments.

She wasn't sorry to have nothing more to distract her than keeping an eye on Neil and watching the concert herself. She needed to think. Her own ready offer regarding the bursary might mean that she wouldn't be making such a clean break with Christopher as she'd intended. She'd pictured herself keeping right away from him, from the folk in his parish. And just seeing him today was resurrecting all the emotions compounded over the years, and especially during these past few months. Her need for him didn't lessen, and she sensed that it never would. How could she live with that if she didn't make the effort she'd decided on, and put him completely out of her life?

Neil was clapping enthusiastically as the concert drew to a close with every young person from five years old to eighteen coming forward to bow to the audience.

'Can we come here again, Mummy?' he asked excitedly, bouncing on his chair.

Why on earth couldn't he have formed some attachment to the place when that was vital? thought Helen. Does everything in my life always have to come too late?

Chris came to them as members of the audience were heading for the exit.

'If you're sure about having a word with Harry Winter,' he said, 'he'd be delighted if you'd come backstage now. Naturally, I've made no promises on your behalf. I simply said you were interested to hear about his ambitions.'

'Okay then, fine,' she said, but glanced down at Neil.

'He'll come with me, won't you, old chap? I'll bet you'd like to have a go at my guitar . . .'

Neil gazed up at him. 'Have you got one, have you really?'

'Yes, indeed. I lent it to Sharon for the concert. Has anyone ever shown you how the guitar is played?'

Harry Winter was waiting in a corner of the room where the other youngsters were having make-up removed. A worried-looking young fellow, whom Helen remembered having played the drums with a gusto which belied his solemn appearance, he invited her to sit as soon as Chris had introduced them.

'I'm afraid it's bedlam in here, Mrs Stone, sorry. But I think all the other rooms are in use.'

'That's all right, Harry. So long as we can hear each other, that's all that matters.'

'Father Christopher says you're the person who designed this building. I think that's super – you must have been so excited when it was opened.'

Helen would rather have avoided thinking about that particular occasion. Subsequent events were proving such a let-down after the soaring hopes awakened by meeting Chris again. With an effort, she smiled.

'It's always great when you see something that has been completed to your designs. I hope, though, that you're not just being carried away by the glamour of that side of things? This job's much more a matter of sheer hard slog.'

'I do realise that,' he said earnestly. 'It's more that I think it must be a very interesting career – planning, and all that. My mum got me to go with her to see about our house when they were being built. Council, of course. I'm the eldest, you see, of five. Since my dad were killed in t'war I've tried to give her a bit of help. Any road, they let us see the plans. I think that were what started me off. Folk were that thankful to be getting somewhere decent to live. I reckoned I'd love to do summat worthwhile like that.'

'And are you any good at art? There's so much drawing involved you'll need to be better than average. And there's figure work an' all – if you can't do calculations, you'll never make an architect.'

When Chris left them to talk, he took Neil's hand and led him up the steps behind the stage. In the wings the electrician was dismantling part of the lighting system, helped by a youth of about fifteen.

'Hallo, Father Christopher,' the lad called, beaming. 'Did all right, didn't we? We never missed one cue, and Mr Jarvis let me work some of the switches.'

Neil was watching and listening, wondering at this strange world and wishing he could join in something that seemed to make everybody all happy and excited. He'd never seen so many children together in one place. It would be even more fun than playing with Linda and Mark. He gazed longingly towards some of the instruments being packed carefully away. He wished he could have a go on them.

'Oh, there you are, Father Christopher,' a teenaged girl exclaimed, smiling as she looked around one end of a section of scenery. 'Here's the guitar – thank you ever so much for lending it to me. I hope you agreed that it sounded infinitely better than that old thing of mine!'

'You certainly made good use of it, Sharon. Well done!'

Pausing while Chris chatted to first one youngster and then another, Neil followed him across to one of the dressing rooms that now was empty.

'Let's see if I can make this sound almost as good as Sharon did, eh?'

For a while, Neil watched, fascinated, while Chris conjured music from the guitar. 'Can I try?' he asked. 'Please . . .'

'You might be disappointed. Your hands are still small for coping with this, but you can certainly have a go,' Christopher offered, drawing Neil towards him and positioning the boy's thumb and fingers near the strings.

Managing a few notes, however tunelessly, delighted Neil and sent him off into high-pitched giggles. 'What else can you play?' he asked, and listened rather wistfully to one of the melodies that he'd heard during the concert.

'I want to do that,' he announced.

'Perhaps when you're a bit bigger. For now, you might find the recorder more your size.'

'Show me,' Neil demanded, grinning.

'I'm afraid I can't play one,' Chris confessed.

A girl who was passing the open doorway smiled cheekily towards them. 'Don't tell me there's something you can't do, Father Christopher!' she exclaimed, then ran off, her plaited hair bouncing.

'Is she your little girl as well?' asked Neil, the forehead beneath his golden curls wrinkling in bewilderment. 'Are all these children yours?'

Chris smiled. 'Not in the way that you mean, Neil. They belong to my church, and because I've come here to help look after them they have become mine. But they don't all live in my house. There'd never be room, would there?'

Thinking of the rather old-fashioned vicarage, Neil shook his head fiercely and continued listening.

'And they're not mine in the same way that you belong to your mummy, or even to your grandma and grandad – they aren't related to me. But I do often think they are like a big family gathered all around me.'

Neil was silent, staring down at the scuffed toes of his shoes. 'But they call you "Father Christopher"?'

'Yes, and I think that's rather nice, don't you?'

Again, Neil nodded. 'Father's like a daddy, isn't it?'

'That's right.'

'My daddy won't come back, Mummy says. He died, and it wasn't because she was cross with him.'

'No, and it wasn't because he didn't wish to come home either. It was simply something very sad which happened. And sometimes when things like that occur, nobody can explain them.'

'Not even you?' The child's eyes looked enormous, their blue-tinged whites emphasising the beautiful grey irises.

'Not even me! We may not see a reason, because it isn't always what someone wants to do – it can be what God plans for them.'

'Who's God? And why did He make my daddy go away?'

Chris was thrown, but did his best to answer in a way that Neil might understand.

'Those are hard questions. And I can't really tell you why He decided to take your daddy. But perhaps if I try to explain what I believe about God you will understand a bit better.'

Neil was nodding, which seemed encouraging.

'Well, love, I think God is like a father, but belonging to everyone, and especially to those who want Him to be their special person. And the best thing about God is that, although we can't see Him, He is there and knows what we are doing.'

'But why did he make my daddy dead?'

Chris swallowed. 'We can't be sure, but we can only think that dying was perhaps the only way to stop your daddy hurting. You know that he was in the car, and there was an accident . . .'

Neil nodded, 'Mummy told me.'

'Well, sometimes when people are hurt so badly, God has to decide that it would be cruel to let them live if they would always be in pain.'

' 'Cos they wouldn't be happy,' Neil asserted.

'That's right, my boy. Now, shall we go and find your mummy?'

'In a minute.'

'You want to hear some more music, do you? See if we can find more instruments?'

Neil shook his head. He seemed to be struggling as if to surface from clinging, tangled reeds. 'No, not today. Another day. I was just – thinking. Why aren't you *my* Father Christopher?'

'I can be, straight away. Because it's what you want.'

From the look Neil was giving him, Chris realised that this was a longing which had been developing during the entire evening.

Walking along backstage in search of her son and Chris, Helen was feeling overwhelmed with emotion again. Young Harry Winter had been full of all the eagerness to design which she so clearly remembered from her own early days. She felt sure she'd be right to recommend that Mr March should offer him the bursary.

It was this place, though – the church hall – which was getting to her. Sounds of sheer enjoyment from the youngsters busy packing up after their concert were filling its rooms, and making her look at the place again. Whatever happened in the future, this would always remain to her the most important of her designs. She had watched it come alive and that, surely, was the real test of any building? Regret because this was the last time she would come here now choked her.

Glimpsing Neil through the open dressing-room door, she saw his interested expression and experienced a moment's relief. At least he wasn't being fractious today.

'Ah, there you are,' she said, trying to quell all her emotions and smile as if she meant it. 'Time we were off, Neil.'

'How did it go?' Chris asked as he looked up and saw her. 'I hope young Harry was duly grateful.'

'Grateful? He was over the moon. As I explained to him, it's really up to Mr March to choose the next recipient for the bursary, but he's old and very frail now, and I don't think I'm being big-headed when I say I'm sure he'll be guided by me. I'm going to have a preliminary word with the old man, then get in touch with Harry if he does agree to see him.'

'That's splendid! Thanks so much, Helen, for thinking of it. Now there's something I've got to discuss with you . . .'

'Sorry, Chris,' she said sharply. 'It's high time we were getting home. Neil should have been in bed long before this.'

'Helen, *please*,' he persisted. 'It's to do with Neil, what he's been saying. We've had a good chat, and now I've got to talk to you.'

'But there's too many folk around here, and you're still busy.'

'I don't have to be. I need only check that the Sunday School Superintendent or somebody will lock up. Come with me to the vicarage, we can talk privately there.'

'Five minutes then. After that we shall have to be on our way.'

'Me as well, Father Christopher, I'm coming with you.' Tugging at Christopher's cassock, Neil was smiling beseechingly up at him.

Helen's gaze had jerked down to scrutinise her son. 'Is that what you meant?' she asked Chris in a shaken whisper.

He nodded. 'I told you we had a bit of a chat,' he explained as they set out. 'About his daddy, and about why everybody here calls me Father Christopher. Neil seems to have taken to the term.'

This made a difference, a vast one, but Helen had grown so used to facing the worst that she couldn't believe it would change things completely.

Once inside his living room, Chris offered to make a pot of tea.

'No, it's all right, thanks,' she said. 'We really do have to be on our way shortly.'

'Can I have a glass of milk please, Father Christopher?'

'Certainly, Neil. Come and help me get it.'

When they returned from the kitchen Helen was still standing. Chris gave her a look. Lord, but she was determined about not hanging on to hear him out.

'You could sit, you know,' he said, anxiety making him sound brusque. 'I shan't chain you to the chair.'

Neil was making himself at home on the sofa. After a couple of sips of milk his fair head began nodding.

'Just look at him,' Helen murmured. 'He's tired out.'

We could find him a bed upstairs, thought Chris, but wouldn't suggest it. If Helen was that determined to get away he wasn't going to interfere. But he would make certain that she didn't go before he'd made her fully aware of her son's apparent change of heart. He couldn't let her decide without a proper understanding of the situation.

Neil dozed, then his head jerked upwards and he regarded Chris through half-closed eyelids. 'Didn't you say that I could have my bed here?'

'I did, and you may. But until then would you like to have a sleep on one of my beds?'

'Can I? Ooh, please.'

Helen couldn't argue. Together they all went upstairs, and after settling Neil on one of the spare beds she and Chris stood looking down at him from the doorway. Eyes closing already, Neil was relaxed, with all dread of the unknown removed.

She was reminded of the times years ago when she and Alexander had gazed at their sleeping son. So like, yet unlike, this occasion that it brought a complex mixture of emotions rushing through her. But it no longer seemed wrong to have Christopher's arm about her shoulders as they went downstairs. She was right to trust him with their future. But she must ensure that Chris understood what marriage to her would be like.

'Before I say another thing,' he said suddenly, 'how is your mother now? I'm sorry. I clean forgot to ask.' He had been so agitated about their meeting and trying to make everything right between them.

Helen grinned as she went to the armchair that he moved towards the fire for her. 'Back to normal, thanks. She says she's not felt the slightest bit dizzy since that day. Nobody'll alter her, though. Dad neither. I daresay they'll both die on the go, just as busy as ever.'

'There are worse ways.'

She gave him a look as he took the chair across the hearth from her own. 'Aye, I suppose so.'

Chris was smiling. 'You've no room to talk. You're their daughter, all right! When did you last let up?'

'Well – you know how it is.'

'Helen, I meant what I said. I do love you, profoundly. I want to make your life easier. Now that Neil's coming round . . .'

'If only that could last!'

'I don't doubt that there'll be times still when he hates my guts – if only for trying to take too much of a share of your time. But it's the load I want you to share with me most of all, Helen, some of the responsibility.'

When she swallowed but said nothing, he continued all the more earnestly: 'It won't be easy, I'm not pretending it will. We've got to face this squarely or not at all. There's the way you'd be uprooting yourself for a start. You must be extremely fond of that beautiful house.'

Helen gave a tiny snort. 'That's one thing you wouldn't have to worry about. I've never wanted to live there. Oh, I thought The Stone House was gorgeous the first time I saw it, when Joseph Stone was living. And I like it now as the place where I do my job – it seems particularly suitable for discussions with clients, and as somewhere to work. I'm glad, an' all, to think of Neil living there one day, when he's grown-up. But I'm much more at home in somewhere less pretentious. Happen you're right, and I am very like my mother.'

'You could have a free hand here, that goes without saying. As you can tell, I've done no more than move in with my possessions. Just about every room needs decorating, but with your ideas and my wholehearted cooperation we could make the place rather nice.'

'Don't rush me, Chris. You're making this sound so tempting.'

'Rush you? How many years is it since we met? If this is rushing, I've never understood the meaning of the word!'

'But you haven't thought this through, love, not properly. You can't have, or you'd never have proposed. I made a real hash of marriage once.'

'Marriage takes two people – to ruin it, just as much as to make it succeed. And I can't see a thing wrong with your decision to stick to your career.'

'Ah, but would you say the same in a year or two – when I can't be content without dashing off up and down the country? Because I know that's what I want. I've missed a lot, being tied to the north while Neil was little. I don't think there's much chance now of my becoming involved in any aspect of the Festival of Britain or anything it's spawning, but I'm determined I'm not going to miss out on anything more. They've had that contest for designing the new cathedral for Coventry. There'll be others, and more new towns.'

'I was coming to that,' he said. 'It's what I've thought all along. Because of my work there's many a time when I could be at home during the week, for Neil.'

I'd be happy to leave him in your care, thought Helen, and realised how much had altered in a few hours. 'It'd be good for him an' all,' she said pensively. 'It's time he had somebody different keeping an eye on him. Me and our Marian indulge him too much, and Mum and Mrs Hartley are worse still. They spoil him something shocking!'

'I hope you're not casting me in the role of

disciplinarian?' Chris said with a grin.

'Only as strict as any father would be.'

'There's nothing I'd rather be – unless it's your husband. That goes without saying. I was badly shaken, you know, when Neil didn't respond to me at all.'

'I am sorry,' said Helen, rising and going to him. 'I wouldn't have brought you trouble for worlds.'

'I know. Stop worrying.'

He was standing as well, gazing into her eyes with such complete affection that she felt the breath catch her throat.

'You're not going home tonight, are you?' he asked, and his dark eyes lit with a brilliant smile when she shook her head.

Strangely, though, Helen sensed that they wouldn't be sleeping together tonight. The attraction had in no way lessened, but had become a promise of happiness in the future – a future that was drawing so close that waiting a little while longer wouldn't hurt.

'Do you want me to go up and see if Neil has settled?' he asked.

'No, I will, thanks.'

She wanted to see her son asleep in Christopher's home, needed assurance that what she believed to be happening was fact.

The boy had hardly stirred, breathing slowly and steadily, quite content on the strange bed and totally oblivious to being almost fully dressed still. Helen hadn't the heart to disturb him by insisting on taking off his clothes. She picked up his scuff-toed shoes and placed them together neatly. They would both have to learn new ways, not to obtrude too forcibly perhaps on Christopher's bachelor existence.

Gazing out of the window, Helen wondered what changes there would be, in her outlook and her way of life. All of them she would face with a smile, sensing already that the hardest going had been tackled. From now on she could look forward to things getting better.

Beyond the vicarage garden was the church. Beside that the hall which had brought her back into Christopher's life. All around were the clustered streets so typical of Yorkshire urban life. They wouldn't seem unfamiliar much longer. Settling here would be like coming home.

Turning from the window, she found Neil's grey eyes wide open.

'Guess what, Mummy? Father Christopher's going to teach me to play his guitar when I'm a bit bigger.'

'You're very lucky,' said Helen. And, she realised, I might at long last be very lucky too.